USS Jefferson

Charge of the Symbios

USS Hamilton Series
Book 4

Mark Wayne McGinnis

Copyright © 2021, by Mark Wayne McGinnis. All rights reserved. No part of this publication may be reproduced, distributed, or transmitted in any form or by any means, including photocopying, recording, or other electronic or mechanical methods, without the prior written permission of the publisher, except in the case of brief quotations embodied in critical reviews and certain other noncommercial uses permitted by copyright law. For permission requests, write to the publisher, addressed "Attention: Permissions Coordinator," to the email address below. This is a work of fiction. Apart from well-known historical figures and actual people, events, and locales that figure in the narrative, all other characters are products of the author's imagination and are not to be construed as real. Any resemblance to persons, living or dead, is entirely coincidental. Where real-life historical persons appear, the situations, incidents, and dialogues concerning those persons are not intended to change the entirely fictional nature of the work.

Published by Avenstar Productions: info@avenstar.net

Paperback ISBN:

- **ISBN-10** : 173724750X

- **ISBN-13** : 978-1737247500

To join Mark's mailing list, jump to: http://eepurl.com/bs7M9r

Visit Mark Wayne McGinnis at: http://www.markwaynemcginnis.com

Created with Vellum

❦ Created with Vellum

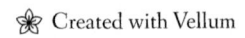

Prologue

Stoiling Build Base
Pleidian Weonan Territory

Captain Galvin Quintos

I awoke with a start. To say I was irritated would be a gross understatement. There was a call coming in on my TAC-Band. Bleary-eyed from lack of sleep, I glanced at the time before answering; it was 0300. At first, I couldn't discern who the hell was yammering at me. As it turns out, the call had originated close to a hundred light-years across the galaxy—had bounced its way from one micro wormhole laser communications hub to another. Clicks and static made the voice on the other end nearly undecipherable.

"Come again... who is this?" I said, sitting up on my bunk.
"Um... maybe you can call back... try for a better connection—"
"No! Fuck, it took me nearly an hour to get this connection! They're sure to take our TAC-Bands away from us."
My head started to clear. "Max? Is that you?"

"Yeah, Cap... listen. I... we need your help."

Sergeant Max was the leader of a small team of highly effective Marines. When a special ops squad was required, let's say for a clandestine mission somewhere within the quadrant, it was usually Max and his four cohorts that I called on for help. Since they were Marines, and I was a US Space-Navy captain, there was no clear command structure between our service branches —with that said, we made things work. How Max and his crew seemed to operate with such a level of autonomy, I had no idea, and didn't actually want to know.

"Where are you, Max?"

"That's the thing, Cap... we're in jail."

"Well, have you talked to a Marine judge advocate? There's not much I can do for you on Earth. I'm still on Stoiling Build Base."

"We're not on Earth, and we're not in any position to call an advocate."

I needed a cup of coffee. "Where are you specifically?"

"Auriga Star System. On Bon-Corfue."

Boy, did that star system bring back memories.

"We'd finished up a simple on-world mission. Everything hush-hush. A quick get-in-and-get-right-back-out job here. Afterward, we stopped in for a celebratory drink at a popular establishment... Hobo-Thom's. Heard of it?"

"Um, yeah, actually I have. So, what happened?"

"Grip is what happened."

"Oh God," I moaned, picturing the gargantuan Marine. The muscular, chiseled, black Marine was not someone you fucked with.

"All I can say is, it wasn't his fault. Drunk or not, you don't whack a Blankie Stick across Grip's back without there being repercussions."

USS Jefferson

I tried to recall what the hell Blankie was and remembered it was a game similar to pool, only the table was octagon shaped and the sticks were energized—you moved the balls around by zapping them in one direction or another.

"Anyway, Wanda, of course, had to come to Grip's rescue... as if he needed any help, and soon a frickin' all-out saloon brawl had broken out."

"You couldn't get out of there? Like before the local constable arrived?"

"That's the thing... the local constable and eight of his pussy-ass underlings were there in a back room, playing cards. Look, I'm not making excuses, but if we hadn't had a little too much to drink, we'd have fled, no problem."

"But instead, you got yourself arrested."

"Tasered and then arrested."

GETTING FROM STOILING BUILD BASE WITHIN Pleidian Weonan Territory out to Bon-Corfue within the Auriga Star System would not be an easy task. For one thing, the journey would require at least three substantial jumps—that meant I'd need to catch a ride on an actual starship capable of manufacturing multiple light-years distance wormholes. *USS Jefferson*, where for several months now I'd been personally involved with her refurbishment, was still in no condition to leave space port. So, currently, I was sitting at the controls of the one and only *Hub Gunther*—a decades-old mining vessel—a kind of space dump truck that had proven over the years to be nearly indestructible.

I'd retrieved the Gunther from the nearly destroyed flight bay of USS *Hamilton*, which was my previous command. The old dreadnought was also parked at Stoiling Build Base—not far

from *Jefferson*. It'd been ransacking *Jefferson's* sister ship for parts for nearly three months now. *Hamilton* was soon destined for the scrapyard, not something I was looking forward to. She and I had a history together. I owed that grand old vessel my life, and each time I ravaged one more part from her nearly destroyed hulk, I felt guilty as hell.

Anyway, *Hub Gunther* had been granted a ride within the overcrowded bay of a Pleidian terraforming cruiser, the *Goss-Platt*, after three wormhole jumps and no less than four stops to replenish the vessel's enormous onboard atmosphere tanks—those used for terraforming a world's atmosphere with gases such as oxygen, nitrogen, and carbon dioxide, which would be conducive for aerobic life to survive and thrive within typical inhabitable carbon and nitrogen cycles.

Reaching the Auriga Star System on the eighth day, I piloted the *Gunther* out of the *Goss-Platt's* flight bay. It took over an hour to get clearance to land on Bon-Corfue, but once I had that, I followed my directed flight plan down to the city of Bon-Fallow, where a small spaceport facility allowed me temporary landing rights. I maneuvered *Hub Gunther* down onto a semicircular landing port, one which was little more than a walled-off, ramshackle erection of stacked block walls and a dirt pad.

The *Gunther's* powerful landing thrusters stirred up so much dirt and debris I could just barely make out the port's overseer, who had come out, making wild hand gestures at me. I didn't recognize any of his gesticulations but could imagine what they conveyed. *Well, screw you, too, buddy; maybe you should invest in a cement landing pad... ever consider that?*

I shut down the *Gunther*, slung a utility pack over one shoulder, and exited through the opened hatch.

I paid the short Bon-Corfue man, who walked with a limp

and had purple scarring around his neck. I gave him a healthy tip, got directions to the local constabulary, and headed off.

Bon-Fallow was not much of a metropolis, more like a once large city that had lost its mojo—a seedy city on a slow and inevitable decline along with a growing older population—the young having moved off to other up-and-coming cities like Creelie and Blint-Onconn or even Priocore.

I typically had a good sense of direction, but each of the narrow, cobbled streets looked identical to one another, and there weren't the typical street signs like you'd find on Earth. I waved down a passing local, an ancient-looking female riding a powered hover-trike. "Excuse me. Can you direct me to the constabulary?"

She didn't even look at me before speeding off. Her departing words were translated for me by my internal auricular implants—something to do with me fucking a crawpoogle... which I knew was the local version of a dairy cow. A space battle here not so long ago between the US Space-Navy's 2nd Fleet and an awaiting Grish armada had ravaged this star system of future, much-needed commerce. The locals knew the humans weren't at fault—we'd been ruthlessly attacked here—but that didn't seem to make any difference; they despised us.

I did find the constabulary twenty minutes later. Entering the facility, my nostrils filled with a kind of briny ocean smell. Dual weapons detector poles standing sentry on either side of the door beeped once—an all-clear indication. I was surprised to find the place was bustling. Lots of elderly males milling about, and there was a long line of locals waiting to talk to what was the equivalent of a desk sergeant.

Heads turned in my direction, and conversations halted. Bon-Corfueions were not all that dissimilar to humans, which made their facial expressions easy to read. Clearly, I, or more precisely, my kind, was not wanted here. I didn't need to read

their collective minds to know they, too, wanted me to go fuck a crawpoogle.

Reaching the counter, the desk sergeant actually took a step backward while grimacing—as if I'd stepped in something foul.

"What do you want?"

"I'm here to pay bail. Five humans... um, involved in a brawl last week?"

"No bail. Next!" He waved me off and looked to the old geezer behind me.

I stayed put. "Hey... I have the money. Just tell me what the bail is... any damages that need reimbursement and—"

"Those five have been convicted... will be transported tomorrow. Come back in a year after their sentences have been completed."

"That's ridiculous! For a bar brawl? Seriously?!"

"I said, move aside! I won't warn you again, human!"

"I demand to talk to your supervisor... the head honcho here."

"I don't know what a honcho is, but I do know you've just earned yourself an overnight stay here at the shithole motel." He raised a hand and gestured to someone.

Two stocky and muscular goons, one on either side of me, took an elbow. I was relieved of my small backpack, which held nothing of use. Then, before I knew it, I was being dragged out of the line. One of them was carrying a large metal bucket—the kind of bucket that one would use to mop floors or maybe wash windows.

Again came the briny ocean smell. The guard on my right plopped his hand down into the bucket's murky liquid. He pulled it back out holding something that was a dark reddish color. Something that was alive and had multiple tentacles. Tentacles that immediately wrapped themselves around the guard's hand and wrist. The thing looked to be a cross between

a small octopus and something else—maybe a bat or a small-headed rodent.

What made me most nervous about the creature was the metallic box adhered to the thing's head. Little blue and yellow lights blinked on and off, and there was an exposed readout of numbers. The guard tapped at the little box and the coiled tentacles went slack, releasing the guy's wrist.

Without missing a beat, he then flung the octopus-bat thing right at me—toward my neck, to be precise. The speed of the transaction took place so quickly, I wasn't able to jerk away in time. The tightening of tentacles around my neck was so abrupt, so startling, I froze. Within seconds my airway was constricted, and breathing was nearly impossible. Added to that, both carotid arteries in my neck were compressed to the point I felt lightheaded and dizzy.

Both guards chuckled. "Don't fight it, human. Stay still for a few moments and the Wrapper will relax... let you breathe again."

I did as told and, in what seemed like minutes but was probably just seconds, the creature did indeed relax. There was a burning sensation where the Wrapper had secreted something—my flesh felt as if it was on fire.

"I know... burns a bit, huh? You'll get used to it."

They kept me moving. I was hustled down a dark hallway where weathered paint was peeling off the walls. The stone floor was wet—and somewhere I could just make out the sounds of water splashing. I imagined a large cauldron of slithering, tentacled Wrappers not far away.

We came to the jail cells, which were at the rear of the facility. Several were occupied, but for the most part, it didn't seem as if crime was a big issue here in Bon-Fallow. Each prisoner wore a Wrapper around his or her respective neck. Eventually,

we came to an abrupt stop in front of the largest of the cells, this one being three times the size of all the others.

Beyond the metal bars and sitting upon the wet floor, five familiar faces stared up at me. Each of the Marines was out of uniform, wearing local civvies' attire. Then again, I, too, was out of uniform—the last thing I wanted to do was bring attention to the fact that I was military. And like me, each of the Marines wore a Wrapper around his or her neck.

Keys jangled, a metal latch clanged, and the gate rolled open. With a not-so-gentle shove, I was propelled inside. Immediately, I was choking and gasping again from a restricted airway. The guard snorted a laugh, and I felt the Wrapper's grip somewhat release. The door rolled shut, and the metal latch clanged home. One of the guards spat into what was now also my jail cell.

"You were supposed to spring us... not get your scrawny ass thrown in here with us," Wanda said.

"Hello to you, too, Wanda," I said with a crooked smile.

Max, getting to his feet, looked happy to see me, as did the twin giants, Ham and Hock.

"Seriously, Cap," Max said, placing a hand on my shoulder, "This isn't good. You don't want to be in here with us. We appreciate you coming for us, but we're in real trouble here. Apparently, there won't be a trial. We're to be transported to an adjacent township. Some kind of mountain labor camp there."

"Yeah, we'll be breaking rocks with hammers or some shit," Wanda said.

"Of course, we won't let that happen," Grip added.

"Look, I downloaded much of that information on my TAC-Band once we arrived here in system. And yeah, I suspected you wouldn't be allowed to leave with a simple bail or by reconciling with the proprietor of Hobo-Thom's. This is a mining world. One that is in dire need of able workers to do the kind of manual

work that the aging and mechanically temperamental bots are no longer well suited for."

"So again, why get yourself thrown in here with us?" Wanda said, making an are you stupid expression and tilting her head to one side. She looked at my neck. "Your Wrapper readout is set for twenty-two hours... that's a full day here on Bon-Corfue." She pointed to the small digital display on her own Wrapper, "One full year, if we stay out of trouble. That's how long we're expected to wear these things."

I nodded, now seeing the numbers counting down. "Have to admit, it's a clever way to keep prisoners in check. Try to escape or even move too rapidly and you're on the ground, out like a light."

She asked the question again, "Why get yourself thrown in here with us?"

I slowly moved over to one wall and stepped up onto the built-in bench, or maybe it was a bunk. I stood up on my tiptoes and looked out through the bars. Good. This was an outfacing wall, one that looked out to an alleyway.

"Don't bother; these walls are two feet thick, Cap," Max said, sounding resigned to our predicament.

Ham said, "I tried to pull one of those bars free. Didn't budge... not a smidge."

Hock glared at his brother. "I told you they were too secure. That you wouldn't be nearly strong enough."

"I'm stronger than you are! At least I tried!" Ham barked.

I raised my hands. "Let's not quibble, boys. I've come prepared." I reached back over one shoulder and felt around within my garment's oversized hood. Finding it, I withdrew an item. The small gizmo fit within the palm of my right hand. I held it up for the others to see; they leaned forward, craning their necks and narrowing their eyes. Tentacles moved but didn't constrict.

"What the hell is that thing?" Wanda asked.

"Looks like a tool of some sort," Grip said in his low baritone.

"Good guess. And yes, it is a tool... called a verislice, it's designed to cut through a starship's tyrillian conduit pipes. Been a handy device while refurbing *Jefferson*."

"Tyrillian... that green metal from the Wo-5 sector? Nah, that shit's like totally impregnable," Max said, eyeing the device. "You're not going to cut through tyrillian pipes with that dinky thing."

I looked out into the corridor and listened for any activity. All was quiet. "No time like the present... you ready to bust out of here, or you want to hang around breaking rocks for the next year?"

The five of them exchanged an unconvinced look.

I had been using this same verislice for weeks now. It always worked well. Was amazing, actually. But I'd never recharged it. I'd never put it back into its little recharging base station back in the ship-wide maintenance area of *Jefferson*.

I tightened my grip on the thing, which constricted a protruding rubberized band that ran around the device's circumference. Immediately, a four-foot-long beam of turquoise-colored plasma radiated out from my raised palm. *Good; the device still has some power left in it.*

"Let's deal with these creatures first," I said. "Who's first?"

Nobody volunteered, their eyes locked on the bright plasma beam. Eventually, Wanda raised a tentative hand. "Don't cut my head off."

"I'll try not to. Just stand still." I took a closer look at the Wrapper creature and thought I saw its head buried within the coils. As I brought the beam closer to Wanda, the Wrapper began constricting its coils.

"Hurry!" she croaked out, looking woozy.

A small beady eye looked back at me. "There you are, you little fucker." I tapped the plasma beam on its small head, and *poof*, in a puff of smoke, the creature slackened its coils and dropped to the floor. Wanda gasped in fresh air, staggered, and then did something unexpected. She hugged me.

"Thank you, Cap... you have no idea how that thing creeped me out."

Over the next few minutes, I repeated the procedure for Max, Grip, Ham, and then Hock. Wanda took the verislice and killed the Wrapper secured around my neck.

After taking a moment to assess the size of the barred window—clearly too small for Ham and Hock's girth, I said, "Stand back. I'm not sure what this beam will do to rock. Cutting through two-and-a-half-foot diameter tyrillian conduit pipes can take up to ten minutes."

The verislice beam cut through the rock wall as if it was made of cheap cardboard. Making four individual cuts, I outlined what looked to be a three-foot-wide and six-foot-tall doorway. Only the interior rock of the doorway had yet to be dislodged. I looked over my shoulder at one of the twins. "You want to do the honors, Ham?"

"Oh yeah." He took several steps backward. Having given himself a running start, he leaped at the wall with an extended size fifteen boot. The wall didn't crumble or come apart. Instead, it fell outward in one big piece—landing in the alleyway outside with a colossal *whump* sound.

We all stared at the door-sized opening.

"Maybe we should go before the shooting starts," Wanda said, already halfway out the opening.

By the time we made it back to Bon-Fallow's small landing port facility, alarms were sounding in the distance.

The attendant gave the six of us a suspicious look. "Best you don't return here... not ever."

"Amen to that, brother," Max said as we all hurried up the ramp into *Hub Gunther*.

Once inside, I provided each of them with a new TAC-Band. "Put these on... you're now officially all back on the clock."

Chapter 1

Stoiling Build Base
Pleidian Weonan Territory

Captain Galvin Quintos

I awoke with a start. To say I was irritated would be a gross understatement. There was a call coming in on my TAC-Band. Bleary-eyed from lack of sleep, I glanced at the time before answering; it was 0300. At first, I couldn't discern who the hell was yammering at me. As it turns out, the call had originated close to a hundred light-years across the galaxy—had bounced its way from one micro wormhole laser communications hub to another. Clicks and static made the voice on the other end nearly undecipherable.

"Come again... who is this?" I said, sitting up on my bunk.
"Um... maybe you can call back... try for a better connection—"
"No! Fuck, it took me nearly an hour to get this connection! They're sure to take our TAC-Bands away from us."

My head started to clear. "Max? Is that you?"

"Yeah, Cap... listen. I... we need your help."

Sergeant Max was the leader of a small team of highly effective Marines. When a special ops squad was required, let's say for a clandestine mission somewhere within the quadrant, it was usually Max and his four cohorts that I called on for help. Since they were Marines, and I was a US Space-Navy captain, there was no clear command structure between our service branches —with that said, we made things work. How Max and his crew seemed to operate with such a level of autonomy, I had no idea, and didn't actually want to know.

"Where are you, Max?"

"That's the thing, Cap... we're in jail."

"Well, have you talked to a Marine judge advocate? There's not much I can do for you on Earth. I'm still on Stoiling Build Base."

"We're not on Earth, and we're not in any position to call an advocate."

I needed a cup of coffee. "Where are you specifically?"

"Auriga Star System. On Bon-Corfue."

Boy, did that star system bring back memories.

"We'd finished up a simple on-world mission. Everything hush-hush. A quick get-in-and-get-right-back-out job here. Afterward, we stopped in for a celebratory drink at a popular establishment... Hobo-Thom's. Heard of it?"

"Um, yeah, actually I have. So, what happened?"

"Grip is what happened."

"Oh God," I moaned, picturing the gargantuan Marine. The muscular, chiseled, black Marine was not someone you fucked with.

"All I can say is, it wasn't his fault. Drunk or not, you don't whack a Blankie Stick across Grip's back without there being repercussions."

I tried to recall what the hell Blankie was and remembered it was a game similar to pool, only the table was octagon shaped and the sticks were energized—you moved the balls around by zapping them in one direction or another.

"Anyway, Wanda, of course, had to come to Grip's rescue... as if he needed any help, and soon a frickin' all-out saloon brawl had broken out."

"You couldn't get out of there? Like before the local constable arrived?"

"That's the thing... the local constable and eight of his pussy-ass underlings were there in a back room, playing cards. Look, I'm not making excuses, but if we hadn't had a little too much to drink, we'd have fled, no problem."

"But instead, you got yourself arrested."

"Tasered and then arrested."

Getting from Stoiling Build Base within Pleidian Weonan Territory out to Bon-Corfue within the Auriga Star System would not be an easy task. For one thing, the journey would require at least three substantial jumps—that meant I'd need to catch a ride on an actual starship capable of manufacturing multiple light-years distance wormholes. *USS Jefferson*, where for several months now I'd been personally involved with her refurbishment, was still in no condition to leave space port. So, currently, I was sitting at the controls of the one and only *Hub Gunther*—a decades-old mining vessel—a kind of space dump truck that had proven over the years to be nearly indestructible.

I'd retrieved the Gunther from the nearly destroyed flight bay of USS *Hamilton*, which was my previous command. The old dreadnought was also parked at Stoiling Build Base—not far

from *Jefferson*. It'd been ransacking *Jefferson's* sister ship for parts for nearly three months now. *Hamilton* was soon destined for the scrapyard, not something I was looking forward to. She and I had a history together. I owed that grand old vessel my life, and each time I ravaged one more part from her nearly destroyed hulk, I felt guilty as hell.

Anyway, *Hub Gunther* had been granted a ride within the overcrowded bay of a Pleidian terraforming cruiser, the *Goss-Platt*, after three wormhole jumps and no less than four stops to replenish the vessel's enormous onboard atmosphere tanks—those used for terraforming a world's atmosphere with gases such as oxygen, nitrogen, and carbon dioxide, which would be conducive for aerobic life to survive and thrive within typical inhabitable carbon and nitrogen cycles.

Reaching the Auriga Star System on the eighth day, I piloted the *Gunther* out of the *Goss-Platt's* flight bay. It took over an hour to get clearance to land on Bon-Corfue, but once I had that, I followed my directed flight plan down to the city of Bon-Fallow, where a small spaceport facility allowed me temporary landing rights. I maneuvered *Hub Gunther* down onto a semicircular landing port, one which was little more than a walled-off, ramshackle erection of stacked block walls and a dirt pad.

The *Gunther's* powerful landing thrusters stirred up so much dirt and debris I could just barely make out the port's overseer, who had come out, making wild hand gestures at me. I didn't recognize any of his gesticulations but could imagine what they conveyed. *Well, screw you, too, buddy; maybe you should invest in a cement landing pad... ever consider that?*

I shut down the *Gunther*, slung a utility pack over one shoulder, and exited through the opened hatch.

I paid the short Bon-Corfue man, who walked with a limp

and had purple scarring around his neck. I gave him a healthy tip, got directions to the local constabulary, and headed off.

Bon-Fallow was not much of a metropolis, more like a once large city that had lost its mojo—a seedy city on a slow and inevitable decline along with a growing older population—the young having moved off to other up-and-coming cities like Creelie and Blint-Onconn or even Priocore.

I typically had a good sense of direction, but each of the narrow, cobbled streets looked identical to one another, and there weren't the typical street signs like you'd find on Earth. I waved down a passing local, an ancient-looking female riding a powered hover-trike. "Excuse me. Can you direct me to the constabulary?"

She didn't even look at me before speeding off. Her departing words were translated for me by my internal auricular implants—something to do with me fucking a crawpoogle... which I knew was the local version of a dairy cow. A space battle here not so long ago between the US Space-Navy's 2nd Fleet and an awaiting Grish armada had ravaged this star system of future, much-needed commerce. The locals knew the humans weren't at fault—we'd been ruthlessly attacked here—but that didn't seem to make any difference; they despised us.

I did find the constabulary twenty minutes later. Entering the facility, my nostrils filled with a kind of briny ocean smell. Dual weapons detector poles standing sentry on either side of the door beeped once—an all-clear indication. I was surprised to find the place was bustling. Lots of elderly males milling about, and there was a long line of locals waiting to talk to what was the equivalent of a desk sergeant.

Heads turned in my direction, and conversations halted. Bon-Corfueions were not all that dissimilar to humans, which made their facial expressions easy to read. Clearly, I, or more precisely, my kind, was not wanted here. I didn't need to read

their collective minds to know they, too, wanted me to go fuck a crawpoogle.

Reaching the counter, the desk sergeant actually took a step backward while grimacing—as if I'd stepped in something foul.

"What do you want?"

"I'm here to pay bail. Five humans... um, involved in a brawl last week?"

"No bail. Next!" He waved me off and looked to the old geezer behind me.

I stayed put. "Hey... I have the money. Just tell me what the bail is... any damages that need reimbursement and—"

"Those five have been convicted... will be transported tomorrow. Come back in a year after their sentences have been completed."

"That's ridiculous! For a bar brawl? Seriously?!"

"I said, move aside! I won't warn you again, human!"

"I demand to talk to your supervisor... the head honcho here."

"I don't know what a honcho is, but I do know you've just earned yourself an overnight stay here at the shithole motel." He raised a hand and gestured to someone.

Two stocky and muscular goons, one on either side of me, took an elbow. I was relieved of my small backpack, which held nothing of use. Then, before I knew it, I was being dragged out of the line. One of them was carrying a large metal bucket—the kind of bucket that one would use to mop floors or maybe wash windows.

Again came the briny ocean smell. The guard on my right plopped his hand down into the bucket's murky liquid. He pulled it back out holding something that was a dark reddish color. Something that was alive and had multiple tentacles. Tentacles that immediately wrapped themselves around the guard's hand and wrist. The thing looked to be a cross between

a small octopus and something else—maybe a bat or a small-headed rodent.

What made me most nervous about the creature was the metallic box adhered to the thing's head. Little blue and yellow lights blinked on and off, and there was an exposed readout of numbers. The guard tapped at the little box and the coiled tentacles went slack, releasing the guy's wrist.

Without missing a beat, he then flung the octopus-bat thing right at me—toward my neck, to be precise. The speed of the transaction took place so quickly, I wasn't able to jerk away in time. The tightening of tentacles around my neck was so abrupt, so startling, I froze. Within seconds my airway was constricted, and breathing was nearly impossible. Added to that, both carotid arteries in my neck were compressed to the point I felt lightheaded and dizzy.

Both guards chuckled. "Don't fight it, human. Stay still for a few moments and the Wrapper will relax... let you breathe again."

I did as told and, in what seemed like minutes but was probably just seconds, the creature did indeed relax. There was a burning sensation where the Wrapper had secreted something—my flesh felt as if it was on fire.

"I know... burns a bit, huh? You'll get used to it."

They kept me moving. I was hustled down a dark hallway where weathered paint was peeling off the walls. The stone floor was wet—and somewhere I could just make out the sounds of water splashing. I imagined a large cauldron of slithering, tentacled Wrappers not far away.

We came to the jail cells, which were at the rear of the facility. Several were occupied, but for the most part, it didn't seem as if crime was a big issue here in Bon-Fallow. Each prisoner wore a Wrapper around his or her respective neck. Eventually,

we came to an abrupt stop in front of the largest of the cells, this one being three times the size of all the others.

Beyond the metal bars and sitting upon the wet floor, five familiar faces stared up at me. Each of the Marines was out of uniform, wearing local civvies' attire. Then again, I, too, was out of uniform—the last thing I wanted to do was bring attention to the fact that I was military. And like me, each of the Marines wore a Wrapper around his or her neck.

Keys jangled, a metal latch clanged, and the gate rolled open. With a not-so-gentle shove, I was propelled inside. Immediately, I was choking and gasping again from a restricted airway. The guard snorted a laugh, and I felt the Wrapper's grip somewhat release. The door rolled shut, and the metal latch clanged home. One of the guards spat into what was now also my jail cell.

"You were supposed to spring us... not get your scrawny ass thrown in here with us," Wanda said.

"Hello to you, too, Wanda," I said with a crooked smile.

Max, getting to his feet, looked happy to see me, as did the twin giants, Ham and Hock.

"Seriously, Cap," Max said, placing a hand on my shoulder, "This isn't good. You don't want to be in here with us. We appreciate you coming for us, but we're in real trouble here. Apparently, there won't be a trial. We're to be transported to an adjacent township. Some kind of mountain labor camp there."

"Yeah, we'll be breaking rocks with hammers or some shit," Wanda said.

"Of course, we won't let that happen," Grip added.

"Look, I downloaded much of that information on my TAC-Band once we arrived here in system. And yeah, I suspected you wouldn't be allowed to leave with a simple bail or by reconciling with the proprietor of Hobo-Thom's. This is a mining world. One that is in dire need of able workers to do the kind of manual

work that the aging and mechanically temperamental bots are no longer well suited for."

"So again, why get yourself thrown in here with us?" Wanda said, making an are you stupid expression and tilting her head to one side. She looked at my neck. "Your Wrapper readout is set for twenty-two hours... that's a full day here on Bon-Corfue." She pointed to the small digital display on her own Wrapper, "One full year, if we stay out of trouble. That's how long we're expected to wear these things."

I nodded, now seeing the numbers counting down. "Have to admit, it's a clever way to keep prisoners in check. Try to escape or even move too rapidly and you're on the ground, out like a light."

She asked the question again, "Why get yourself thrown in here with us?"

I slowly moved over to one wall and stepped up onto the built-in bench, or maybe it was a bunk. I stood up on my tiptoes and looked out through the bars. Good. This was an outfacing wall, one that looked out to an alleyway.

"Don't bother; these walls are two feet thick, Cap," Max said, sounding resigned to our predicament.

Ham said, "I tried to pull one of those bars free. Didn't budge... not a smidge."

Hock glared at his brother. "I told you they were too secure. That you wouldn't be nearly strong enough."

"I'm stronger than you are! At least I tried!" Ham barked.

I raised my hands. "Let's not quibble, boys. I've come prepared." I reached back over one shoulder and felt around within my garment's oversized hood. Finding it, I withdrew an item. The small gizmo fit within the palm of my right hand. I held it up for the others to see; they leaned forward, craning their necks and narrowing their eyes. Tentacles moved but didn't constrict.

"What the hell is that thing?" Wanda asked.

"Looks like a tool of some sort," Grip said in his low baritone.

"Good guess. And yes, it is a tool... called a verislice, it's designed to cut through a starship's tyrillian conduit pipes. Been a handy device while refurbing *Jefferson*."

"Tyrillian... that green metal from the Wo-5 sector? Nah, that shit's like totally impregnable," Max said, eyeing the device. "You're not going to cut through tyrillian pipes with that dinky thing."

I looked out into the corridor and listened for any activity. All was quiet. "No time like the present... you ready to bust out of here, or you want to hang around breaking rocks for the next year?"

The five of them exchanged an unconvinced look.

I had been using this same verislice for weeks now. It always worked well. Was amazing, actually. But I'd never recharged it. I'd never put it back into its little recharging base station back in the ship-wide maintenance area of *Jefferson*.

I tightened my grip on the thing, which constricted a protruding rubberized band that ran around the device's circumference. Immediately, a four-foot-long beam of turquoise-colored plasma radiated out from my raised palm. *Good; the device still has some power left in it.*

"Let's deal with these creatures first," I said. "Who's first?"

Nobody volunteered, their eyes locked on the bright plasma beam. Eventually, Wanda raised a tentative hand. "Don't cut my head off."

"I'll try not to. Just stand still." I took a closer look at the Wrapper creature and thought I saw its head buried within the coils. As I brought the beam closer to Wanda, the Wrapper began constricting its coils.

"Hurry!" she croaked out, looking woozy.

A small beady eye looked back at me. "There you are, you little fucker." I tapped the plasma beam on its small head, and *poof*, in a puff of smoke, the creature slackened its coils and dropped to the floor. Wanda gasped in fresh air, staggered, and then did something unexpected. She hugged me.

"Thank you, Cap... you have no idea how that thing creeped me out."

Over the next few minutes, I repeated the procedure for Max, Grip, Ham, and then Hock. Wanda took the verislice and killed the Wrapper secured around my neck.

After taking a moment to assess the size of the barred window—clearly too small for Ham and Hock's girth, I said, "Stand back. I'm not sure what this beam will do to rock. Cutting through two-and-a-half-foot diameter tyrillian conduit pipes can take up to ten minutes."

The verislice beam cut through the rock wall as if it was made of cheap cardboard. Making four individual cuts, I outlined what looked to be a three-foot-wide and six-foot-tall doorway. Only the interior rock of the doorway had yet to be dislodged. I looked over my shoulder at one of the twins. "You want to do the honors, Ham?"

"Oh yeah." He took several steps backward. Having given himself a running start, he leaped at the wall with an extended size fifteen boot. The wall didn't crumble or come apart. Instead, it fell outward in one big piece—landing in the alleyway outside with a colossal *whump* sound.

We all stared at the door-sized opening.

"Maybe we should go before the shooting starts," Wanda said, already halfway out the opening.

By the time we made it back to Bon-Fallow's small landing port facility, alarms were sounding in the distance.

The attendant gave the six of us a suspicious look. "Best you don't return here... not ever."

"Amen to that, brother," Max said as we all hurried up the ramp into *Hub Gunther*.

Once inside, I provided each of them with a new TAC-Band. "Put these on... you're now officially all back on the clock."

Chapter 2

Stoiling Build Base
Pleidian Weonan Territory

Captain Galvin Quintos

I awoke with a start. To say I was irritated would be a gross understatement. There was a call coming in on my TAC-Band. Bleary eyed from lack of sleep, I glanced at the time before answering; it was 0300. At first, I couldn't discern who the hell was yammering at me. As it turns out, the call had originated close to a hundred light-years across the galaxy—had bounced its way from one micro wormhole laser communications hub to another. Clicks and static made the voice on the other end nearly undecipherable.

"Come again... who is this?" I said, sitting up on my bunk.
"Um... maybe you can call back... try for a better connection—"

"No! Fuck, it took me nearly an hour to get this connection! They're sure to take our TAC-Bands away from us."

My head started to clear. "Max? Is that you?"

"Yeah, Cap... listen. I... we need your help."

Sergeant Max was the leader of a small team of highly effective Marines. When a special ops squad was required, let's say for a clandestine mission somewhere within the quadrant, it was usually Max and his four cohorts that I called on for help. Since they were Marines, and I was a US Space-Navy captain, there was no clear command structure between our service branches —with that said, we made things work. How Max and his crew seemed to operate with such a level of autonomy, I had no idea, and didn't actually want to know.

"Where are you, Max?"

"That's the thing, Cap... we're in jail."

"Well, have you talked to a Marine judge advocate? There's not much I can do for you on Earth. I'm still on Stoiling Build Base."

"We're not on Earth, and we're not in any position to call an advocate."

I needed a cup of coffee. "Where are you specifically?"

"Auriga Star System. On Bon-Corfue."

Boy, did that star system bring back memories.

"We'd finished up a simple on-world mission. Everything hush-hush. A quick get-in-and-get-right-back-out job here. Afterward, we stopped in for a celebratory drink at a popular establishment... Hobo-Thom's. Heard of it?"

"Um, yeah, actually I have. So, what happened?"

"Grip is what happened."

"Oh God," I moaned, picturing the gargantuan Marine. The muscular, chiseled, black Marine was not someone you fucked with.

"All I can say is, it wasn't his fault. Drunk or not, you don't whack a Blankie Stick across Grip's back without there being repercussions."

I tried to recall what the hell Blankie was and remembered it was a game similar to pool, only the table was octagon shaped and the sticks were energized—you moved the balls around by zapping them in one direction or another.

"Anyway, Wanda, of course, had to come to Grip's rescue... as if he needed any help, and soon a frickin' all-out saloon brawl had broken out."

"You couldn't get out of there? Like before the local constable arrived?"

"That's the thing... the local constable and eight of his pussy-ass underlings were there in a back room, playing cards. Look, I'm not making excuses, but if we hadn't had a little too much to drink, we'd have fled, no problem."

"But instead, you got yourself arrested."

"Tasered and then arrested."

GETTING FROM STOILING BUILD BASE WITHIN Pleidian Weonan Territory out to Bon-Corfue within the Auriga Star System would not be an easy task. For one thing, the journey would require at least three substantial jumps—that meant I'd need to catch a ride on an actual starship capable of manufacturing multiple light-years distance wormholes. USS *Jefferson*, where for several months now I'd been personally involved with her refurbishment, was still in no condition to leave space port. So, currently, I was sitting at the controls of the one and only *Hub Gunther*—a decades-old mining vessel—a kind of space dump truck that had proven over the years to be nearly indestructible.

I'd retrieved the Gunther from the nearly destroyed flight bay of USS *Hamilton*, which was my previous command. The old dreadnought was also parked at Stoiling Build Base—not far

from *Jefferson*. It'd been ransacking *Jefferson's* sister ship for parts for nearly three months now. *Hamilton* was soon destined for the scrapyard, not something I was looking forward to. She and I had a history together. I owed that grand old vessel my life, and each time I ravaged one more part from her nearly destroyed hulk, I felt guilty as hell.

Anyway, *Hub Gunther* had been granted a ride within the overcrowded bay of a Pleidian terraforming cruiser, the *Goss-Platt*, after three wormhole jumps and no less than four stops to replenish the vessel's enormous onboard atmosphere tanks—those used for terraforming a world's atmosphere with gases such as oxygen, nitrogen, and carbon dioxide, which would be conducive for aerobic life to survive and thrive within typical inhabitable carbon and nitrogen cycles.

Reaching the Auriga Star System on the eighth day, I piloted the *Gunther* out of the *Goss-Platt's* flight bay. It took over an hour to get clearance to land on Bon-Corfue, but once I had that, I followed my directed flight plan down to the city of Bon-Fallow, where a small spaceport facility allowed me temporary landing rights. I maneuvered *Hub Gunther* down onto a semicircular landing port, one which was little more than a walled-off, ramshackle erection of stacked block walls and a dirt pad.

The *Gunther's* powerful landing thrusters stirred up so much dirt and debris I could just barely make out the port's overseer, who had come out, making wild hand gestures at me. I didn't recognize any of his gesticulations but could imagine what they conveyed. *Well, screw you, too, buddy; maybe you should invest in a cement landing pad... ever consider that?*

I shut down the *Gunther*, slung a utility pack over one shoulder, and exited through the opened hatch.

I paid the short Bon-Corfue man, who walked with a limp

and had purple scarring around his neck. I gave him a healthy tip, got directions to the local constabulary, and headed off.

Bon-Fallow was not much of a metropolis, more like a once large city that had lost its mojo—a seedy city on a slow and inevitable decline along with a growing older population—the young having moved off to other up-and-coming cities like Creelie and Blint-Onconn or even Priocore.

I typically had a good sense of direction, but each of the narrow, cobbled streets looked identical to one another, and there weren't the typical street signs like you'd find on Earth. I waved down a passing local, an ancient-looking female riding a powered hover-trike. "Excuse me. Can you direct me to the constabulary?"

She didn't even look at me before speeding off. Her departing words were translated for me by my internal auricular implants—something to do with me fucking a crawpoogle... which I knew was the local version of a dairy cow. A space battle here not so long ago between the US Space-Navy's 2nd Fleet and an awaiting Grish armada had ravaged this star system of future, much-needed commerce. The locals knew the humans weren't at fault—we'd been ruthlessly attacked here—but that didn't seem to make any difference; they despised us.

I did find the constabulary twenty minutes later. Entering the facility, my nostrils filled with a kind of briny ocean smell. Dual weapons detector poles standing sentry on either side of the door beeped once—an all-clear indication. I was surprised to find the place was bustling. Lots of elderly males milling about, and there was a long line of locals waiting to talk to what was the equivalent of a desk sergeant.

Heads turned in my direction, and conversations halted. Bon-Corfueions were not all that dissimilar to humans, which made their facial expressions easy to read. Clearly, I, or more precisely, my kind, was not wanted here. I didn't need to read

their collective minds to know they, too, wanted me to go fuck a crawpoogle.

Reaching the counter, the desk sergeant actually took a step backward while grimacing—as if I'd stepped in something foul.

"What do you want?"

"I'm here to pay bail. Five humans... um, involved in a brawl last week?"

"No bail. Next!" He waved me off and looked to the old geezer behind me.

I stayed put. "Hey... I have the money. Just tell me what the bail is... any damages that need reimbursement and—"

"Those five have been convicted... will be transported tomorrow. Come back in a year after their sentences have been completed."

"That's ridiculous! For a bar brawl? Seriously?!"

"I said, move aside! I won't warn you again, human!"

"I demand to talk to your supervisor... the head honcho here."

"I don't know what a honcho is, but I do know you've just earned yourself an overnight stay here at the shithole motel." He raised a hand and gestured to someone.

Two stocky and muscular goons, one on either side of me, took an elbow. I was relieved of my small backpack, which held nothing of use. Then, before I knew it, I was being dragged out of the line. One of them was carrying a large metal bucket—the kind of bucket that one would use to mop floors or maybe wash windows.

Again came the briny ocean smell. The guard on my right plopped his hand down into the bucket's murky liquid. He pulled it back out holding something that was a dark reddish color. Something that was alive and had multiple tentacles. Tentacles that immediately wrapped themselves around the guard's hand and wrist. The thing looked to be a cross between

a small octopus and something else—maybe a bat or a small-headed rodent.

What made me most nervous about the creature was the metallic box adhered to the thing's head. Little blue and yellow lights blinked on and off, and there was an exposed readout of numbers. The guard tapped at the little box and the coiled tentacles went slack, releasing the guy's wrist.

Without missing a beat, he then flung the octopus-bat thing right at me—toward my neck, to be precise. The speed of the transaction took place so quickly, I wasn't able to jerk away in time. The tightening of tentacles around my neck was so abrupt, so startling, I froze. Within seconds my airway was constricted, and breathing was nearly impossible. Added to that, both carotid arteries in my neck were compressed to the point I felt lightheaded and dizzy.

Both guards chuckled. "Don't fight it, human. Stay still for a few moments and the Wrapper will relax... let you breathe again."

I did as told and, in what seemed like minutes but was probably just seconds, the creature did indeed relax. There was a burning sensation where the Wrapper had secreted something—my flesh felt as if it was on fire.

"I know... burns a bit, huh? You'll get used to it."

They kept me moving. I was hustled down a dark hallway where weathered paint was peeling off the walls. The stone floor was wet—and somewhere I could just make out the sounds of water splashing. I imagined a large cauldron of slithering, tentacled Wrappers not far away.

We came to the jail cells, which were at the rear of the facility. Several were occupied, but for the most part, it didn't seem as if crime was a big issue here in Bon-Fallow. Each prisoner wore a Wrapper around his or her respective neck. Eventually,

we came to an abrupt stop in front of the largest of the cells, this one being three times the size of all the others.

Beyond the metal bars and sitting upon the wet floor, five familiar faces stared up at me. Each of the Marines was out of uniform, wearing local civvies' attire. Then again, I, too, was out of uniform—the last thing I wanted to do was bring attention to the fact that I was military. And like me, each of the Marines wore a Wrapper around his or her neck.

Keys jangled, a metal latch clanged, and the gate rolled open. With a not-so-gentle shove, I was propelled inside. Immediately, I was choking and gasping again from a restricted airway. The guard snorted a laugh, and I felt the Wrapper's grip somewhat release. The door rolled shut, and the metal latch clanged home. One of the guards spat into what was now also my jail cell.

"You were supposed to spring us... not get your scrawny ass thrown in here with us," Wanda said.

"Hello to you, too, Wanda," I said with a crooked smile.

Max, getting to his feet, looked happy to see me, as did the twin giants, Ham and Hock.

"Seriously, Cap," Max said, placing a hand on my shoulder, "This isn't good. You don't want to be in here with us. We appreciate you coming for us, but we're in real trouble here. Apparently, there won't be a trial. We're to be transported to an adjacent township. Some kind of mountain labor camp there."

"Yeah, we'll be breaking rocks with hammers or some shit," Wanda said.

"Of course, we won't let that happen," Grip added.

"Look, I downloaded much of that information on my TAC-Band once we arrived here in system. And yeah, I suspected you wouldn't be allowed to leave with a simple bail or by reconciling with the proprietor of Hobo-Thom's. This is a mining world. One that is in dire need of able workers to do the kind of manual

work that the aging and mechanically temperamental bots are no longer well suited for."

"So again, why get yourself thrown in here with us?" Wanda said, making an are you stupid expression and tilting her head to one side. She looked at my neck. "Your Wrapper readout is set for twenty-two hours... that's a full day here on Bon-Corfue." She pointed to the small digital display on her own Wrapper, "One full year, if we stay out of trouble. That's how long we're expected to wear these things."

I nodded, now seeing the numbers counting down. "Have to admit, it's a clever way to keep prisoners in check. Try to escape or even move too rapidly and you're on the ground, out like a light."

She asked the question again, "Why get yourself thrown in here with us?"

I slowly moved over to one wall and stepped up onto the built-in bench, or maybe it was a bunk. I stood up on my tiptoes and looked out through the bars. Good. This was an outfacing wall, one that looked out to an alleyway.

"Don't bother; these walls are two feet thick, Cap," Max said, sounding resigned to our predicament.

Ham said, "I tried to pull one of those bars free. Didn't budge... not a smidge."

Hock glared at his brother. "I told you they were too secure. That you wouldn't be nearly strong enough."

"I'm stronger than you are! At least I tried!" Ham barked.

I raised my hands. "Let's not quibble, boys. I've come prepared." I reached back over one shoulder and felt around within my garment's oversized hood. Finding it, I withdrew an item. The small gizmo fit within the palm of my right hand. I held it up for the others to see; they leaned forward, craning their necks and narrowing their eyes. Tentacles moved but didn't constrict.

"What the hell is that thing?" Wanda asked.

"Looks like a tool of some sort," Grip said in his low baritone.

"Good guess. And yes, it is a tool... called a verislice, it's designed to cut through a starship's tyrillian conduit pipes. Been a handy device while refurbing *Jefferson*."

"Tyrillian... that green metal from the Wo-5 sector? Nah, that shit's like totally impregnable," Max said, eyeing the device. "You're not going to cut through tyrillian pipes with that dinky thing."

I looked out into the corridor and listened for any activity. All was quiet. "No time like the present... you ready to bust out of here, or you want to hang around breaking rocks for the next year?"

The five of them exchanged an unconvinced look.

I had been using this same verislice for weeks now. It always worked well. Was amazing, actually. But I'd never recharged it. I'd never put it back into its little recharging base station back in the ship-wide maintenance area of *Jefferson*.

I tightened my grip on the thing, which constricted a protruding rubberized band that ran around the device's circumference. Immediately, a four-foot-long beam of turquoise-colored plasma radiated out from my raised palm. *Good; the device still has some power left in it.*

"Let's deal with these creatures first," I said. "Who's first?"

Nobody volunteered, their eyes locked on the bright plasma beam. Eventually, Wanda raised a tentative hand. "Don't cut my head off."

"I'll try not to. Just stand still." I took a closer look at the Wrapper creature and thought I saw its head buried within the coils. As I brought the beam closer to Wanda, the Wrapper began constricting its coils.

"Hurry!" she croaked out, looking woozy.

A small beady eye looked back at me. "There you are, you little fucker." I tapped the plasma beam on its small head, and *poof*, in a puff of smoke, the creature slackened its coils and dropped to the floor. Wanda gasped in fresh air, staggered, and then did something unexpected. She hugged me.

"Thank you, Cap... you have no idea how that thing creeped me out."

Over the next few minutes, I repeated the procedure for Max, Grip, Ham, and then Hock. Wanda took the verislice and killed the Wrapper secured around my neck.

After taking a moment to assess the size of the barred window—clearly too small for Ham and Hock's girth, I said, "Stand back. I'm not sure what this beam will do to rock. Cutting through two-and-a-half-foot diameter tyrillian conduit pipes can take up to ten minutes."

The verislice beam cut through the rock wall as if it was made of cheap cardboard. Making four individual cuts, I outlined what looked to be a three-foot-wide and six-foot-tall doorway. Only the interior rock of the doorway had yet to be dislodged. I looked over my shoulder at one of the twins. "You want to do the honors, Ham?"

"Oh yeah." He took several steps backward. Having given himself a running start, he leaped at the wall with an extended size fifteen boot. The wall didn't crumble or come apart. Instead, it fell outward in one big piece—landing in the alleyway outside with a colossal whump sound.

We all stared at the door-sized opening.

"Maybe we should go before the shooting starts," Wanda said, already halfway out the opening.

By the time we made it back to Bon-Fallow's small landing port facility, alarms were sounding in the distance.

The attendant gave the six of us a suspicious look. "Best you don't return here... not ever."

"Amen to that, brother," Max said as we all hurried up the ramp into *Hub Gunther*.

Once inside, I provided each of them with a new TAC-Band. "Put these on... you're now officially all back on the clock."

Chapter 3

As things turned out, the Empress was as good as her word. Within hours of our conversation, Pleidian shipbuilders, technicians, even craftsmen arrived at *Jefferson* in droves. One glance out any diamond-glass observation window revealed swarms of spider-like robots scurrying about the outer hull. Bright welding torches flashed like twinkling fireflies, perpetuating their dusk into nighttime rituals.

A small army of workers arrived at the bridge. Eleven hover carts, each stacked high with equipment and supplies, were maneuvered into the compartment. the bridge, CIC, and my ready room would be closed for business for an undetermined amount of time.

Thus far I'd been putting off any visits up to Deck 23's LabTech area. It was here where Derrota and several of his team had set up shop to work on the ChronoBot. Fortunately, this was one area where the dreadnought work crews had yet to initiate any of their renovations.

Much of LabTech was a clean-room genetics type lab, but entering the multi-compartment department with its tall glass walls and stark white floors and ceilings, I was surprised to see at least one area of this old vessel still held a resemblance to the ship's original glory.

I found Derrota in one of the farthest astern compartments, where he was leaning over a long lab bench. A lab bench that was supporting the highly reflective and gleaming metal carcass of an inert ChronoBot. Derrota glanced up as I approached.

"I was wondering when you would find your way here," he said.

"Seems there are few places on board where I'm not in the way. Talk to me. How's your progress with... the robot?"

"I was going to wait until later, but now is as good a time as any."

"Time for what?"

"To power on this ChronoBot. Galvin, there is nothing more I can do. The Bio-AI portion of the robot was severely damaged. Thanks to the Grish, much of it was turned to cinders by repeated energy strikes to his head. What I was able to do is take those few unaffected areas, membranes really, and genetically duplicate them."

"Like cloning?"

"Exactly. In humans, the process is called neurogenesis, where new neurons... brain cells develop within the hippocampus, the brain region responsible for learning new information and storing long-term memories. It even regulates one's emotions."

"So, you've been working on Hardy's hippocampus?" I said, using Hardy's actual name, which had been something I'd tried to avoid until now. It had made things easier. No—less painful than having to deal with the loss of someone who had, somehow, become my best friend over the past two years.

"The robot's AI does not have a hippocampus per se. But it has an area not all that dissimilar. I've done all I can to propagate new cells there. The question is if Hardy's memories, his personality, can emerge again... well, it's far too early to tell. Best we keep our expectations low."

"And LuMan? The base programming for this ChronoBot?"

"Oh, he should be fine. LuMan's base programming is stored within an entirely different area of the AI... one which was unaffected as far as I could tell. He will still remember you, and I suspect, will still be overly protective of you, as before."

"Okay... can we power the robot up? See what we got?"

"Did so while we were talking. Give it a few moments. LuMan is just now reinitializing and going through a series of self-tests."

Suddenly slight vibrations stirred from the side of the lab bench where my legs were making contact. The ChronoBot's face display became active with a series of alien characters and symbols—refreshing over and over again at an astounding rate. The ChronoBot suddenly sat up.

I waited until my patience ran out, which was about ten seconds. "Hardy?"

The robot's large, tear-drop-shaped head turned to face me. The face display was obsidian black. "Captain Quintos... no, I am LuMan."

"Is Hardy in there with you?"

The ChronoBot seemed to consider the question. "No."

Derrota had warned me to keep my expectations low, which I hadn't. I said, "Welcome back, LuMan. Are you ready to come back to work?"

"Affirmative." The seven-foot-tall robot swung his legs over the side of the bench and pushed himself down to the floor. Standing fully upright, LuMan waited for his next command.

Derrota looked almost as dejected as I felt. He said, "LuMan should be fully functional and fully capable of assisting you in any way."

The thing was, I didn't need a personal robot to shadow my

every move. What I needed was a thinking, articulating crewmember that was self-aware and capable of self-determination. What I needed was Hardy.

I directed my question to Derrota, "Does LuMan maintain the same mental acuity as he did before?"

"Absolutely. His capabilities should be comparable to what we're used to."

"Good. I want that PE3 compartment of yours up and running as soon as possible. Can LuMan help with that? Bring that about any quicker?"

Derrota looked at the rigid ChronoBot. "Of course, but I'm not so sure he'll stay here if you're not here. Oh, and I've assigned a compartment off of Whale's Alley, not far from the bridge, for that."

I nodded. "Maybe we should come up with a name other than PE3."

Derrota thought about that. "It'll still use the same quantum entanglement physics as its predecessors had. Maybe something like the Quan-Tangler?"

I shrugged. "Maybe. Let's keep working on a name."

WE PUT LUMAN TO WORK RIGHT AWAY. HE MIGHT not have been Hardy, but that didn't mean he wasn't still the most advanced ChronoBot robot in the sector. Although clearly reluctant not to be shadowing my every movement, LuMan was directed to stay with Derrota to expedite the building of the new PE3 compartment, or whatever we would end up calling the damn thing...

It was on my way to my quarters when I was contacted by MATHR via my TAC-Band. The cryptic message said that my presence was required within Engineering and Propulsion.

Arriving there ten minutes later, I was surprised and

pleased to find Craig Porter, my former chief of engineering and propulsion from *Hamilton*, taking a look at *Jefferson's* antiquated drive engines. He was hunched over a console display, scrolling through hundreds of lines of diagnostic readings. His expression said it all: the propulsions system on this ship was junk.

I said, "What do you think... a little baling wire, maybe a few wrappings of duct tape and all will be as good as new, right?"

He straightened up, still looking at the readout. Hands on hips, he shook his head—like a doctor informing his patient that his illness was terminal.

My old friend smiled. "It's almost better that there's nothing worth saving here." He looked at me now. "It's good to see you, Galvin. Been wondering what you were up to. You've been mostly all alone here all these months, idling away on this old wreck. If you ask me, a waste of the fleet's most accomplished captain."

"Accomplished, maybe, but I do tend to make waves... me getting back into the action will be tied to getting this dreadnought back into service."

Craig gestured to the surrounding compartment with one hand. "All this... it has to go, buddy."

"Okay."

"Really? You're willing to just scrap all this? No worries about allocated budgets and repair versus replacement cost ratios?"

"No. In fact, my orders are to make this ship the best it can be. Better. More advanced than any ship in the fleet."

He looked thoughtful.

"There's one caveat, though," I said.

"You need it done yesterday?"

"Bingo."

"Figured as much. I have just the thing. Thought I'd need to come here prepared. There's a new groundbreaking propulsion system technology I've been involved with from an advisory standpoint. And let me be clear; it's not even in production yet... everything's top secret, all hush-hush. The good news is it's made in the good ol' USA. Made by a company called Silver-Stream Power. Has advanced jump spring technology already integrated. Wormhole manufacturing will be near-instantaneous, and the jump distances will be far greater."

"Sounds terrific, Craig, but we need a propulsion system now, not one that's still in the prototyping stage."

Loud voices disrupted our conversation. We turned to see three large men in white overalls entering the department. I caught sight of the logo patches on their chests: *Silver-Stream Power*.

One of the Silver-Stream Power guys said, "No demo yet? Criminy... all this shit's got to go... like right now. Freighter's got other deliveries to make, you know."

I looked at Craig. "You brought the thing with you? The whole damn propulsion system?"

"Of course. You think you've been the only one working late hours to get this old tub operational again? Admiral Block's been riding my ass for months now... but I think you'll be quite pleased with the results."

"Admiral Block doesn't own this 'old tub,' as you put it. Would have been nice to be in the loop on such things."

"I don't know what to tell you; it's your call. Want to send these guys away and tell the freighter to hit the road?"

"Ah... no, I'm more than grateful for the help and the new propulsion system."

"Thought you'd say that. Oh, and I came on board with someone else you might be happy to see." Craig gestured to a slew of others now entering the department. These crewmen were wearing dark US Space-Navy overalls.

"Lasalle?"

Ship-Wide Maintenance Crewman Lasalle was originally from Louisiana. The muscular, somewhat imposing, albeit soft-spoken Black crewman had served on *Hamilton* with me and was a true historian—he knew more about the history of the three sister dreadnoughts, USS *Hamilton*, USS *Jefferson*, and USS *Adams*, than just about anyone in the fleet.

"Good to see you again, Captain. You know... I was thinking about retiring. But I got a call from Fleet Command... was offered a raise and another promotion if I'd re-up for another stint. Truth is, hearing I'd be serving on another of these fine old dreadnoughts, and under your command, I would have done so anyway."

I looked at the embroidered name and rank on his overalls. "Well, Master Ship-Wide Maintenance Crewman LaSalle, welcome aboard *Jefferson*."

"Thank you, Sir. I'm told you need some help demoing these old drives?"

"Along with the reactors, cooling emitters, feed lines, all of it," the Master SWM crewman interjected.

No less than fifteen SWM crewmen had ambled in by now.

LaSalle said, "Best you let us get at it then, Captain."

Chapter 4

I tossed and turned for several hours that night. Sleep was becoming more and more elusive of late. I sat up and turned on my bedside light. It was then that I saw I had an awaiting TAC-Band message. A missed call from my brother. Strange... the two of us hadn't spoken in several years. Seeing Eric's blinking message indicator both irritated me and, surprisingly, stirred a kind of nostalgic longing.

I'd tried to tell my brother about what had happened within Empress Shawlee's faux *Hamilton* town of Clairmont. Shawlee's kindness at recreating the whole scenario for me, having my Symbio-Poth parents stopping to help and discovering what really happened at the scene of an accident that had destroyed my family, had allowed me to start a healing process—something Eric had subsequently been denied. But when I'd tried to explain the way things had really happened, he'd hung up on me, cursing. Since then, I'd been waiting for Eric to make the first move in repairing our relationship.

Without listening to it, I saved the TAC-Band message. It was 0200. Realizing there was no way I'd be able to get back to sleep, I pulled on an old pair of shorts and tank top and headed off to the gym.

Much of the exercise equipment was broken, and few of the free weights remained on the rack. But the rubber mats were still in place, providing adequate space for me to practice combat scenarios. I engaged the combat training projector that Wanda had given me. I'd configured the three combat avatars for aggressive hand-to-hand battle attack mode.

The three alien-looking avatars sprang to life, all coming at me at the same time. This was nothing new—the combat program was innovative and always full of surprises. The reason for that was Wanda, who was constantly updating the damn program. I was fairly certain she had a sadistic streak. God forbid I ever get complacent with my training. But what I was coming up against here was not anything we'd agreed to.

Each of the virtual killers was armed. That, and the green lizard-looking guy was the only one of the combatants that had not been given a new form. He was brandishing a kind of curved sword or cutlass. New was a rhinoceros-looking guy, walking upright, a kind of rhino warrior, and he was holding an immense Thor-like hammer thing. The third virtual combatant was a black-robed Varapin that not only hovered but held a long metal spear. A spear that crackled as it radiated electrified energy.

I ducked as the lizard's cutlass swiped for my head. As I spun to my right, the rhino warrior's hammer rammed into my solar plexus. Bent over and gasping, I had barely enough time to dive away from the point of the Varapin's spear—which apparently didn't need to actually impale me, since the thing could shoot short, electrified bolts of energy. It was as if a white-hot poker had jabbed me in my left butt cheek. I yelped while just barely skittering away from the lizard's sword where it stabbed the air I'd just vacated.

Finding my feet and catching my breath, I shot a Tang Soo Do back kick into the chest of the rhino warrior, which staggered the beast, but did little more than that. Seeing his hammer come up, I dropped to the mat while evoking a twirling Krav Maga leg sweep. That put the virtual fatty down on his back. The gym literally shook from the impact. I dove, instinctively knowing the Varapin would want to take advantage of my vulnerable predicament. Once more, a white-hot energy bolt shot into my ass.

Dammit! I wanted to scream at Wanda. How unfair this was, arming the combatants as she had. She'd simply tell me war wasn't fair; battle wasn't fair. Light reflected off the lizard's cutlass as it swung for my head once more. In that split second, I wondered if Wanda had programmed in adequate safeguards, or was my head soon to be separated from my neck? But I moved into the strike, avoiding the business edge of the blade by a nanosecond.

Instinctively, I instigated a double-handed Shaolin block to the lizard's incoming forearm, which I followed up with a reverse esophageal throat chop to his neck. There was a satisfying crunch sound as the reptilian avatar dropped his sword and grabbed feebly for his throat—he attempted to suck in a breath but wasn't having much success.

In my peripheral vision, I saw both the rhino warrior and the Varapin were almost upon me. I jumped backward but knew it was too little too late. With their weapons already raised, there would be nothing I could do to save myself.

In a sudden blur of motion, someone or something came between my attackers and me. A broad reflective metal back took the hammer blow in stride, while one articulated arm appendage parried the incoming metal spear. The ChronoBot punched the Varapin in the face, then turned and punched the rhino warrior in his face too—neither blow was fancy, but both were powerful and devastating, causing the rhino and Varapin combatants to puff away into virtual clouds of dark smoke.

The remaining alien lizard avatar, having fallen to the mat, still gasping for breath, encountered a similar fate. A ChronoBot foot stomp to the head, and then there was one more puff and a virtual cloud of dark smoke rising into the air.

Catching my breath, I stared at the seven-foot-tall robot. I made an irritated, bewildered face. "What the hell was that shit, LuMan?"

The robot turned to look at me.

I gestured to the remaining wisps of rising smoke. "Hey! I didn't need you to protect me! Hello... Those were training avatars... not real." Truth was, I wasn't so sure that was actually true.

I continued to stare up at the ChronoBot's face display. A face display that was no longer featureless and black. I pointed, "What's that? What are you doing?"

"Oh crap... hold on," the robot said with a familiar Bostonian accent. He flipped the digitized three-dimensional face a hundred and eighty degrees, so it was now right side up. The somewhat chubby-cheeked, friendly-looking John Hardy face offered up a crooked smile. The face of a man that had lived some six decades earlier but now resided within the consciousness of the ChronoBot.

"Hardy?"

Chapter 5

"The one and only."

"So... you're back. Back to normal?" I asked, sounding unsure.

The ChronoBot attempted a shrug unsuccessfully. "Well... there are, um... gaps."

"Gaps? What kind of gaps?"

"Like gaps in my memory, Thom."

"My name's not Thom."

"I know... kidding. But I do have memory gaps. Like I can't remember where I put my shoes."

I rolled my eyes. "Now you're just being annoying."

"My long-term memories are addled. Like the time period when I was a child."

"So, you're talking about your John Hardy memories, not LuMan's memories?"

"Why would I give two shits about LuMan's memories?"

"I don't know; I'm just trying to get a clear handle on what the issues are here," I said defensively.

"I can't remember my father's face. Or his name."

"It's in the database. MATHR can—"

"That's not the point!" Hardy said, irritated. "I want to remember such things myself... I want to retain some semblance of who and what I am. I'm not just this metal robot."

"Okay, I'm sorry... I get it. We'll talk to Stephan. I'm sure there is a solution."

Hardy didn't respond.

I looked around the gym, ensuring no one was around. "Are you okay to..."

"What? Carry on? No. I think I should go back to my quarters and mope for the rest of the day."

"You don't have your own quarters, Hardy."

"See... I'm useless."

I wasn't sure if Hardy was pulling my chain or not but suspected he was. At least he hadn't forgotten how to be totally aggravating. Seeing Hardy's head droop, I could almost feel his melancholy. "Hey, buddy, it'll be okay. I'll get you the help you need. I promise."

The truth was, I wasn't at all sure I could keep that promise. Hell, my own state of mind was hit or miss at best. "How about you give Stephan a hand with the transporter? I'll let you know what I come up with."

IT WAS LATE, CLOSE TO 0100, WHILE I CAUGHT UP on doing what seemed like endless administrative tasks within my ready room. I'd sent Admiral Block a message four hours earlier in regard to Hardy's mental facilities and the possibility of getting someone here to assess and hopefully help him. Having a fully operational ChronoBot on board *Jefferson* was a strategic and military advantage no other ship in the fleet could match—but having a defective ChronoBot was dangerous.

My desktop MATHR interface pinged. Seeing the incoming hail was from the Admiral, I accepted the prompt.

Block's face appeared on my halo display. He looked far more refreshed and alert than I felt.

"Good morning, Galvin... you look like shit."

"Thank you, Sir. You look bright-eyed and bushy-tailed. What time is it there on the East Coast? 0700?"

"0600. I received your message. I understand you want to help Hardy."

"You know he's proven to be an invaluable resource. Without Hardy, we wouldn't have been able to defcat—"

"You don't need to justify the ChronoBot's worth to Fleet Command to me, son. It's just that..." his words trailed off. Block smiled. "Look, it's beyond a coincidence, but there's already an individual en route to Stoiling Build Base as we speak. A doctor of sorts."

"Doctor?"

"A psychiatrist, to be exact," Block said, fidgeting in his seat.

"Why do I get the feeling that that doctor, as you put it, isn't on his way here to talk to Hardy?"

"Look, Galvin... I haven't hidden the fact that others within Fleet Command are hesitant about giving you another dreadnought command. Sure, your accomplishments have been nothing less than stellar. But your decision-making goes beyond unorthodox. It's cost lives."

"I disagree. I think it's saved lives. I think it's—"

"Hold on, hold on... this is not a recrimination. But you have to acknowledge the fact you've been through a lot. PTSD is nothing to brush off. So, you get thoroughly checked over, spend some time with the good doctor... let him evaluate your, um, mental state, and you're back in business."

"First of all, it's called delayed-onset post-traumatic stress disorder, or DOPTSD. And I don't need another shrink's diagnosis to tell me what I've already been told. I'm managing.

Truth is, I haven't had any kind of mental paralysis in months. I've started a physical training routine."

"Yes, I know about your good work with Max and his crew. With Wanda," Block said in a tone that was far more condescending than I appreciated.

How the hell did he know that? It took all of my mental faculties not to blow my lid, but I did just that and kept my expression neutral.

"It's as simple as this... meet with the psychiatrist and pass his evaluation, or we'll find someone to replace you to captain that ship."

"Fine."

That put a smile back on the Admiral's face. "Good. And as a bonus, I'll tell the doctor he will be working with two individuals. See how nicely that all works out?"

"Oh joy, joy," I said, not hiding my sarcasm. "And when should I expect him?"

The Admiral checked his TAC-Band. "Today. I'm actually surprised he hasn't arrived yet."

Having said our goodbyes and cut the connection, I stood and stretched. It was then I remembered I hadn't caught the psychiatrist's name. No worries; I'd get that when he arrived. For now, I was beat and needed some sack time.

As I was heading out of my ready room, my TAC-Band vibrated. I was tempted to ignore it but glanced at it anyway. It was my chief of engineering and propulsion—not someone I could put off.

"What's up, Craig? If this can wait till morning, I'd really appreciate it."

"No can do, my friend... best you get over here, pronto."

Fuck. "On my way."

Out in Whale's Alley, I saw movement farther down the passageway. More and more crewmembers had been arriving on board today. Where I'd typically roamed the corridors of this dreadnought by myself, not seeing another individual sometimes for hours, that was no longer the case. But as I drew near, I could determine that this was no ordinary crewmember. Reaching him, I said, "Hardy? What are you doing out here? What are you doing?"

"I'm pacing."

"Why?"

"Because your chief science officer kicked me out of the transporter room." He gestured to the closed double-wide hatch door behind him.

I had yet to check out the progress of Derrota's Quan-Tangler compartment and was tempted to take a peek inside.

"Did you do or say something to warrant being booted like that?" I asked.

Hardy's face display changed to a monocled thinking man's icon. "I suppose I was less than present... my concentration may not have been what it once was. But in my own defense, I have important things on my mind. Like my dog."

"You have a dog?"

"No, but I think I did. As a boy. A Rhodesian Ridgeback, or maybe it was a Weimaraner..."

"They don't look anything alike, Hardy."

"Well, if my memory was intact, I'd know that, wouldn't I?" he said, his frustration evident.

"Whatever. You can come with me. There's a problem in Engineering."

He fell into step next to me. I said, "Oh, I have a doctor on his way here to talk to you."

"You mean the same doctor Admiral Block is sending to talk to you?"

Crap. "Dammit, Hardy! How many times have I told you to

respect people's privacy? You can't be listening in on personal calls! Especially those of the Captain!"

"Sorry. I needed something to get my mind off of myself."

Once more, Hardy's head drooped as he fell into another quiet stupor.

We weaved our way through a dozen composite crates, looming tall like haphazardly placed towering skyscrapers. Packing material was strewn all around the deck. Reaching the bank of GravLifts, to my surprise, I saw they had all been replaced, which was indicated by their blazingly bright white SmartCoat finishes.

In contrast to the old, outmoded sliding hatchway doors still prevalent throughout the ship, SmartCoat accessways or apertures kind of spread open organically within the blink of an eye. Hopefully, soon, the rest of the old dreadnought's interior would sport this same remarkable coating.

Several of the new cars seemed to be operational. Multiple apertures were opening and closing alternately. LaSalle stepped out into the corridor through one of them, followed by another SWM crewmember. Both were wearing tool belts and holding handheld testers of some sort.

LaSalle directed his subordinate off to work on one of the other lifts before greeting Hardy and me. "Captain, you've come to admire progress being made?"

"No. Wasn't even aware this was happening today," I said.

"Right now, there are two hundred and seven factory technicians upgrading the ship's zero-friction conveyer routes throughout the ship."

"Excellent... any one of these GravLifts operational yet? I'm needed aft."

"Where exactly?" LaSalle asked, scratching his head while pondering upon the assortment of new lifts.

"Engineering and Propulsion," I said.

"This one here can get you there. Should be operational... has the necessary functioning conveyer routes."

"Should be?" I repeated.

"I'm confident it is fine. Best I come with you though," he said, gesturing toward the third delineated section in the bank of GravLifts. The three of us hurried in through the open aperture, taking in the new car smell permeating the interior space. LaSalle looked pleased with the new technology. He reached out and placed his palm on the lift's bulkhead; a glowing blue ship's legend appeared. He tapped at Engineering and Propulsion.

Immediately we were on the move—the new lift system as quiet as a whisper, with none of the jarring and clanking movements I had gotten used to over the previous weeks. LaSalle eyed Hardy, who at this point had stayed quiet. His faceplate was pitch black. The SWM crewman looked to me questioningly, and I offered back a furtive shake of my head.

LaSalle, looking uncomfortable in the silence, said, "This is a fine ship, Captain. Soon it will be spectacular."

"I hope so," I said.

"Jefferson was my favorite president. An amazing, complicated man."

Hardy's head came up, apparently somewhat interested.

"Yeah, of course. He was the primary writer of the Declaration of Independence, but there are a number of little factoids most people aren't aware of about the third president of the United States."

Hardy said, "I don't remember much about the man."

LaSalle's eyes narrowed, looking unsure why Hardy would have a problem remembering anything. He continued, "Jefferson and Adams hated each other... The two men, once cordial while Jefferson was still Adam's vice president, grew to resent one another. They looked differently at diplomacy and politics in general. While Adams' preference was for a more centralized and meddlesome government, Jefferson felt a small, less intrusive government was imperative."

"They ever, um, reconcile?" Hardy asked.

"No, not really. Interesting though. They died on the same day, within hours of each other, July 4, 1826... which was also the fiftieth anniversary of the Declaration of Independence being adopted."

The GravLift was starting to slow.

LaSalle said, "Thomas Jefferson had a pet bird... did you know that, Hardy?" As if sensing the ChronoBot was in a funk and in need of a little camaraderie.

"What kind of bird?" Hardy asked.

"A mockingbird. Got the bird sometime before the revolution, ended up bringing it to the White House. He pretty much let the thing have the run of the place, upsetting the staff responsible for cleaning up after it. Jefferson, who was known not to be the snazziest dresser, was often seen with the bird perched upon his shoulder. A shoulder splattered with bird shit. Apparently, when Jefferson practiced his violin, the mockingbird would join in with a chorus of beautiful tweets."

I said, "Thank you, LaSalle. You are truly a wealth of information. I look forward to learning more about Jefferson, and this vessel, his namesake, in particular."

The GravLift came to a full stop and the aperture expanded, allowing us to scurry out into Engineering and Propulsion. This area of the ship was farther along than most others. Gleaming white SmartCoat enveloped all of these bulkheads. A virtual army of technicians was at work installing new laser braid cable conduits, inset lighting fixtures, and access panels and consoles and workstations. Many of the deck plates had been opened up for easy access.

We hopscotched our way farther into Engineering, where I

found Chief Craig Porter, a large wrench in hand, speaking to five Propulsion techs in overalls. "Jackson, I already told you... we have power coming into that junction. Caldwell here traced each and every connection point along the route... all are hot."

Behind the huddle of E&P crewmembers stood two massive brand-new drives. They spanned up to eight decks high, so I had to crane my neck to see all the way to the top of them—and how they managed to shoehorn these big engines into the space was a feat of engineering unto itself.

What I also knew, I being the one spending late nights doing the administration for the ship's rebuild scheduling and milestone completions, was that these drives were supposed to be on. We were spending the equivalent of billions of dollars for a ship's new propulsion system, ensuring that, in the future, the meantime between failure calculations could be realized, but the damn things needed to warm up post-installation... to sit here idling for no less than forty-eight hours.

I cleared my throat, getting Craig's attention. He looked over the shoulder of one of his techs and saw me, along with Hardy and LaSalle. Craig dispersed his team with an annoyed wave of a hand.

"Galvin... just the man I wanted to talk to."

"Impressive-looking things, aren't they?" I said.

"Oh yeah... amazing. And you haven't seen the reactors farther aft. And the new jump springs—"

"Talk to me. What do you need from me?"

He turned to look at the massive drive systems, like two god-like sentries standing guard.

"They don't work... simple as that. Tried everything."

"What's the main issue?" LaSalle said.

"The drives refuse to initialize. Stubborn fuckers. Seems they're not getting the necessary raymithlison liquid coolant circulation."

USS Jefferson

I said, "Have you checked—"

"Look, Galvin, I know you're just trying to help, but you're in my realm here. If I tell you we've checked and rechecked every valve, pipe, sensor, and regulator manifold—"

We all jumped at hearing loud metal clanging coming from the opposite side of Drive 1. It was then that I noticed Hardy was no longer standing alongside me. *Shit!*

Craig, hurrying away, looked as if he was ready to kill someone. LaSalle and I exchanged a look and followed.

There, knee-deep within a labyrinth of thick pipes and curling elbow joints, stood Hardy. Hardy and a twenty-pound sledgehammer. The ChronoBot glanced our way before continuing to pound the business end of the hammer down onto a lever mechanism.

"Stop! For God's sake, robot, STOP!" Craig yelled, trying to make his way through the obstacle course of pipes, each wider than a person. "This is delicate, sensitive equipment!"

Ignoring Craig's rantings, Hardy gave the lever one more substantial blow. Making a painful screech, the lever pivoted around a hundred and eighty degrees.

We all stopped. Craig, his brows knit together, placed one palm on the nearest pipe. "Raymithlison liquid is moving through this pipe... what did you do, Hardy?"

"I opened a stuck valve...the same valve that allows coolant to circulate up into those new drives of yours."

As if on cue, both drive engines came to life—a baritone hum emanating and vibrating the pipes, the deck below our boots, the very air around us.

Craig turned to look at Hardy. "How did you know which pipe and valve needed to be flipped?"

"I rechecked the installation guide... I asked MATHR for it. The problem was clearly evident, plain as day."

Craig looked impressed and a little humbled by Hardy's intervention.

I pointed to Hardy's still-blank face display. "Come on, big guy... I know you want to do it."

Hardy hesitated and then did it. A bright red S on a yellow background filled his face display. The three of us, palms out, bowed in mock deference to our onboard Superman.

Chapter 6

Two weeks later...

To say USS *Jefferson* had undergone a transformation over the last couple of weeks would be an understatement of gross proportions... the dreadnought, both inside and out, at this point, was barely recognizable. Just about all of the ship's primary systems had now been replaced.

Every component within the bridge and CIC was new and state of the art. More work had been done on MATHR, her voice altering with each software upgrade. As of now, she had a far more casual lilt to her voice—like that of a trusted friend, that trendy young woman that lived next door to you.

Bulkheads, overhead ceilings and ducting, hatch doors, you name it, now glistened white with SmartCoat. And where *Hamilton* lacked views of space beyond the hull, *Jefferson* was now equipped with many thousands of diamond-glass portholes, some as large as an entire bulkhead.

New weaponry was being installed too—Phazon Pulsar cannons, railgun cannons that fired AI smart spike munitions, and new, one-of-a-kind technology, both fusion-tipped and nuclear-tipped micro-missiles—capable of defeating enemy defenses with a kind of shared swarm consciousness.

And finally, the broadsides had undergone a complete technological overhaul. More than a few times, these ginormous cannons, six per side, had saved *Hamilton* from certain destruction. Like the original, these house-sized cannons fired twelve-hundred-pound bowlers, nicknamed for their visual similarity to massive-looking bowling balls and their strategically placed circular, finger-like holes.

Prior to impact, these holes were the dispersal element for magnesium scatter frags, which effectively weakened enemy hull armor plating a nanosecond prior to impact and allowed the giant explosive cannon balls to decimate anything and everything they came into contact with.

The problem was that the original broadsides were somewhat unstable. And the on-ship hold magazines for the bowlers tended to be dangerous—like storing unstable TNT. All that had been remedied with the advent of new bowler munitions, somewhat smaller, with magnesium scatter frags that not only breached shields and ship hulls but actually moved within a ship's corridors and passageways like streams of white-hot molten lava, zeroing in on an enemy ship's hottest components—the propulsion system.

Everyone was busy; everyone was putting in long days—up at 0500, and sometimes that same hour came around again before heads hit their pillows the next day. Hardy was splitting his time between the Quan-Tangler compartment with Derrota, Chief Potter in Engineering, and sometimes with me, helping to put out one fire or another—it was always something. Hardy's mental state had improved little though. Which was strange, since his memory was steadily improving every day. Something had happened to his psyche with that last near-death experience.

USS Jefferson

I'd always wondered these past years how John Hardy the person, the Bostonian with the big personality, had managed, or should I say coped, with being a robot. Human on the inside, an ultra-sophisticated battle-bot on the outside. Well, it seemed as though grappling with that unique dichotomy was now not so easy. All I could do was be there for him for those times when debilitating depression grabbed hold of him, with hopes that eventually he would find his way back to how he once was.

New crewmembers were showing up on a daily basis. I typically tried to get myself down to Flight Bay to greet the new arrivals and welcome each new crewmember as he or she descended the shuttle's respective gangways. I watched their expressions—seeing them struck by the sheer size of this dreadnought, the voluminous breadth of the flight bay, the abundance of Arrow Fighters all lined up in tidy rows, many so new they were still shrink-wrapped. Many of the crewmembers were young, coming right out of the academy; others were old space dogs, arriving on board with years, sometimes decades, of service on one warship or another.

Typically, the ships I'd commanded over the years, for one reason or another, were dangerously undermanned. I wasn't used to commanding a fully manned warship, and at close to twenty-eight hundred men and women currently on board *Jefferson*, this was nearly a fully manned warship. With crewman John Chen at my side, my reluctant acting XO, we saluted the new arrivals. As they approached, I introduced myself, introduced them to the XO, verified their names were indeed on our ship's roster, and sent them on their way to find their respective department heads.

We were using several dozen hovering maintenance bots as guides for the new crewmembers to chase after. I say chase because we'd configured the bots to move just quickly enough to where one would be required to jog to keep up with them. Hell, we had to find entertainment where we could find it, and watching the young new arrivals nervously scurrying off, double-time... well, it was a nice diversion.

The last of this batch, a few stragglers, were coming down the ramp. Looking at my tablet, I checked the remaining names on the roster. I froze.

"You okay, Cap? You look like you just saw a ghost," Chen said.

I didn't reply; instead I watched as Major Vivian Leigh and Eric Quintos, seemingly deep in conversation, leisurely strolled down the gangway.

I greeted Doc Viv first, forgetting to offer up my standard salute for the new arrivals.

"Viv... you're supposed to be deployed on a star carrier with the 9th."

"Good to see you too, Quintos...I was pulled. Something I'm not happy about. It was a good post, a great post. Do you know how many HealthBay doctors, nurses, and techs reported to me on that star carrier?"

I shook my head.

"Close to one hundred. A HealthBay that rivaled medical facilities in New York or Los Angeles!"

"I didn't request a transfer for you."

"No, you didn't... Block did. Twenty minutes before we were to jump out of system, I got my new orders." She glanced around with a tight, forced smile—she radiated irritation.

"I'm sorry... perhaps I can have you transferred back—"

She waved off my words. "Don't bother. I'm already here. I'll make the best of it; be a good little soldier. Oh, by the way, Pristy wanted me to say hi to you for her."

I remembered Gail Pristy was also with the 9th Fleet, skippering her own small ship. Viv turned to give the man beside her a warm smile and then a quick hug. "We'll catch up later, huh? Time for me to see what HealthBay hellhole I'm supposed to oversee." She walked off at a fast pace, one of the maintenance droids hurrying after her, barely able to keep up.

I turned my attention to the tall, tanned, and ruggedly handsome man—the brother I hadn't set eyes on in close to five years. Then I thought of the boy Symbio-Poth version of my brother from the recreated town of Clairmont on *Hamilton*. "Eric... what are you doing here?" I said.

Before he could answer, someone else was making his way down the ramp. *Shit, today keeps getting better and better,* I thought. Chaplain Thomas Trent, dressed in a navy-blue suit, black button-down shirt, and white clergy collar, steepled his fingers in a prayer-like gesture. He stopped at Eric's side and placed an affectionate hand on his shoulder—as if they were old friends from way back. *Anything to irritate me, huh, Trent?*

"Captain... I had no idea you had such an accomplished, and might I add, affable, older brother. We had quite the discussion on our passage here. Perhaps I now understand some of your, um... sometimes erratic behavior."

My eyes flicked to Eric. Seriously, you're telling tales to this disingenuous old blowhard?

Eric smiled and made a quick shake of his head, a mannerism meant to play down the chaplain's words. Eric said, "My baby brother has accomplished much in his life, but not without his share of trauma—"

I held up a hand, cutting my brother off. "How about we *not* discuss my psyche as if I wasn't standing right here." Leveling my gaze on Trent with a forced smile, I said, "Chaplain, I wasn't informed you'd be joining the crew this deployment. In fact, I was under the impression you had retired."

The older man's face went serious. "With the ill-timed, and some might say the felonious death of Captain Tannock... I felt it was my duty and honor to delve deeper into the circumstances of his death. What better place to do that than right here?"

"Your..." I hesitated, careful with my next words. It was common knowledge Trent and Captain Tannock had been more than just friends, "Your colleague died with honor. His sacrifice was his to make. Implying anything else discredits his actions, his memory."

"Don't you dare lecture me on the heroism of Captain Eli Tannock!" Trent spat. "You may have convinced Fleet Command to minimize your involvement in his death but not me. I am accountable to a higher ideal, and there will be a reckoning... I assure you of that."

The chaplain nodded to Eric with a sanctimonious smile before heading away, his hands returning to their previously steepled state.

"I see you haven't changed one bit," Eric said.

My mind flashed to the latest Korean Taekkyon knife-hand nose chop I'd recently learned. "As nice as it is to see you, Eric... again, what are you doing here? I'm extremely busy readying this vessel and her crew for deployment."

It was then that I noticed he was wearing a US Space-Navy officer's uniform—light gray slacks, matching short jacket, dark gray dress shirt, and light blue necktie. On his jacket lapels were US Space-Navy Medical Corps collar devices. Sure, I knew Eric was a doctor, more specifically a psychiatrist, but when had he joined the service? Hell, it could have been years ago with our minimal communications.

"I'm here at the bequest of Admiral Block, Galvin. From what I understand, my presence here is a condition of your being entrusted with this command."

"You're my brother. How is that not some kind of conflict of interest?"

"Well, I guess desperate times and all that..."

"I'll talk to the Admiral. This is unacceptable."

"He anticipated as much. If you check your TAC-Band, I believe you'll find a personal message from him."

I raised my chin in an unconscious gesture of defiance.

"We will be meeting at least once a day in private. You will be open and communicative. I have had much experience with DOPTSD patients..."

"Listen, Eric, I honestly believe you have good intentions here. But I've dealt with my childhood... with what happened in Clairmont in ways even you haven't."

He offered me a trite smile.

I signaled for the closest maintenance bot to escort my brother to his quarters. Eric looked about the voluminous bay. "What an amazing vessel." With that, he trudged off after the bot. He turned to face me, walking backward. "Oh, I'm here to talk with your ChronoBot as well... Hardy, is it?"

Chapter 7

The ship was ready, or as ready as it was going to be. Compared to the renovations that *Hamilton* had undergone, *Jefferson's* had been far more extensive. The dreadnought was virtually a new ship—an immensely powerful new warship. As of this morning, there was a full crew complement on board—thirty-three hundred men and women who were as anxious as I was to get underway.

For the past week, I'd done my best to skirt my brother's request for therapy sessions, and typically dodged Chaplain Trent at every opportunity. As for Doc Viv, neither of us had made any attempt to reconnect.

Three hundred and seventy miles off the starboard side of *Jefferson* was a decommissioned frigate, a destroyer older than me, and a space carrier with an overall length longer than that of *Jefferson*. Today, I was standing amidship at one of the large, newly installed deck-to-ceiling diamond-glass viewing ports, with Hardy on my right. Derrota was situated in the CIC, responsible for processing tactical command and control information. Crewman Chen was at the controls within the bridge but virtually present on my TAC-Band.

We waited as the Pleidian tug moved away from the distant frigate. The diamond smart glass had zoomed in on the target ship. Today we were testing the dreadnought's newly installed weaponry—rail and Phazon Pulsar cannons, as well as the broadsides.

"On your command," Chen said.

Several more of the crew had joined us, but my attention was on the target. "Give me a ten-second burst of rail spikes, XO. Turrets three, nine, and eleven."

Immediately, bright white tracer rounds illuminated the span between the frigate and *Jefferson*. All but two rail spikes missed—disappearing into the far-off depths of deep black space.

"Adjusting targeting parameters..." Derrota interjected from the CIC.

Another ten-second burst shook the deck plates beneath our feet. I could see hull damage; vented debris was spewing out into space from the distant frigate. Chen came back with, "No misses this time, Captain."

I said, "Ready Pulsars, XO."

My TAC-Band vibrated, and I saw that it was Empress Shawlee Tee. I tapped my ear, directing the call to go to my internal auricular implants. The Empress' face looked back at me from my wrist.

"Yes, Shawlee?"

She smiled and, as she often did, had a mischievous smile. "Galvin... I have a request of you."

"Anything," I said, and meant it.

"You're scheduled for your first run to fire up those new drives and check operational systems, yes?"

"Later today, if everything goes well with our weapons check."

"I was wondering if you would mind giving me a lift. I

haven't been back to Weonan for weeks, and I'm needed there by tomorrow evening. My vessel does not have that kind of jump range..."

"You're more than welcome to catch a ride, of course. It'll be a tad longer maiden voyage for *Jefferson*, but that should be fine."

Someone was talking to the Empress, pulling her attention away for a moment. Turning back to me, she said, "As you know, I have a good many of my own builders and craftsmen there on board."

I did know that, but not how many.

"Have you kept your promise, Galvin?" she said, giving me a sideways glance.

Momentarily panicked, I tried to remember what promise I'd made.

"To stay away from Decks 49 and 72/73..."

I didn't remember making that promise but nodded just the same. These were the crew recreational areas on board the ship. Shawlee took great pleasure designing and implementing amazing, impeccably realistic, interactive venues. On *Hamilton*, it had been the expansive Japanese gardens, hot springs, and officers' cabins on Deck 49, and of course, there was the mock recreation of Clairmont, my childhood town, with walking, talking Symbio-Poth townsfolk. Townsfolk that included my mother, father, and twelve-year-old brother, Eric.

"What are you up to, Shawlee? I can see that glint in your eye... Are you planning something?"

"I'm up to big trouble. And I'm way, way, beyond the planning stage. Just make sure you and your crew stay off those decks, agreed?"

"Agreed."

"Good. My personal vessel is en route to Stoiling Build Base now, but I'm still almost a full day out."

"See you when you arrive." I cut the connection.

"Target the destroyer, XO. Commence firing Phazon Pulsars when ready. All starboard side guns," I said to Chen.

Bright blue energy beams streaked across the spatial divide. The Pleidian destroyer, its shields operational, held back the barrage for several minutes before sections of the hull began to fragment off and drift away like scratched-away scales from a reptilian creature.

"Pulsars are right on the money... no targeting errors, Captain."

"Copy that, XO. How about we give a few of our broadsides a go?"

I was most interested in this test. Supposedly these big guns were far more automated and required fewer hands-on crew teams to operate them.

From too close behind me, I heard a familiar voice. "I know what truly happened to Captain Tannock," Trent seethed—his stale breath could be felt against the back of my neck. "That mission may have been off the books, but word gets around, Quintos. Captain Tannock wasn't in a clear state of mind after his time in that memory buffer. You took advantage of that. You wanted him gone, and you seized the first opportunity you saw! There will be a reckoning... there will be retribution."

I let out a weary breath. There had to be an airlock I could shove the chaplain out of somewhere nearby. I slowly turned to see Trent glowering at me

I said, "Hardy... would you be so kind as to escort the good chaplain here away from this restricted area?"

"No need to bother yourself, Hardy. I was just leaving," Trent said.

I was furious at Trent's accusations but tried not to show it. A small voice in my head wondered, though, could Trent actually be right? How many times had I had this same inward battle? Should I have disallowed Tannock to go up with that ship? I was starting to question how much good I was really doing in life—considering there were so many people pissed at me. I needed to be assigned an operation, and ASAP. At least I knew that was where I could be of some use.

I flexed and unflexed my fists several times to alleviate tension. I needed to vent—no, I needed to hit something. "XO, augment that last command... ready all starboard broadsides. Fire at will."

It took thirty seconds, which had to be a record for readying those big cannons. Unexpectedly, Chen fired all of the broadsides at once—*Boom! Boom! Boom! Boom! Jefferson* shook with each percussive blast. Bowler fireballs set off on their respective trajectories toward the largest of the three targets. In moments, the space carrier was exploding in a thrilling display of brilliant fire—then, just as quickly, was snuffed out in the cold vacuum of space.

Hardy said, "My sensors tell me the remaining particles are not much bigger than an extra-large pizza."

"Damn, that felt good," I said.

My new captain's mount was in the process of being installed, and I, for no good reason, wanted to be there on the bridge as that occurred. Maybe because this was like the proverbial ice-cream sundae's placing of the cherry on top—a final component installation as part of the ship's months-long renovation.

While LaSalle and several of his SWM techs collected the strewn-about shipping materials and stuffed them back into the delivery crate, I took a slow stroll around the impressive glass, brushed metal, and various composite materials chair. Raised slightly higher upon a swiveling pedestal, the elevated captain's mount allowed for optimum viewing of the bridge while also offering a commanding presence for the bridgecrew.

I saw Hardy entering the bridge.

I took a seat and leaned back into the plush faux leather cushions. "What do you think?" I asked, swiveling the mount back and forth.

"I think it's glitzy and snazzy. Was glitzy and snazzy what you were going for?" Hardy said, miming the placing of a hand beneath his chin thoughtfully.

"No, I wasn't going for glitzy and snazzy... what are you saying? That it's a bit over the top? It does a lot of cool things, apparently. None of which I understand and know how to operate yet..."

"Hey, it's a fine captain's mount, Cap; you look good sitting in that thing. I just read the operating instructions. I can give you the lowdown whenever you want."

"Thanks. Uh, where have you been?" I asked.

Hardy raised his mechanical arms a bit awkwardly. An attempt at a casual "nothing much" gesture.

I mimicked his same arm gesture. "What does that mean?"

"It means I was doing a little of this and a little of that."

I continued to stare at the ChronoBot, blank-faced.

"Fine. I was completing my hours for this week."

I made a perplexed expression. "What kind of hours? Did I give you some kind of project—"

"Not you, per se, but the Admiral."

"Since when do you take orders from the Admiral?" I asked. "Why don't you stop pussyfooting around and tell me what's going on?"

"Fine! I was getting a bit of counseling from Dr. Quintos... is that okay?!"

"Wait, you're getting therapy from Eric?"

"Actually, I have been meeting with him several times a week. This was my fourth session."

I had forgotten that was actually a favor I'd requested of Admiral Block—help for Hardy. I just hadn't counted on that help being sessions with my psychiatrist brother. I don't know why that bothered me so much, but it did. The last thing I wanted was for my know-it-all brother to be shoehorning himself into my personal business.

But this was Hardy's business, and Lord knows, he needed help. A clinically depressed ChronoBot would not only infringe on the robot's effectiveness, but who knows, could be dangerous. A highly advanced Bio-AI ChronoBot, one that was also unstable—no, that couldn't be a good combination.

I offered up a consoling smile. "Hey, I'm being an ass. You have every right to seek help. I only wish I could have done more for you myself. So, tell me... is it helping? You talking to my brother?"

"I don't know. He tells me I have anger issues... issues that I hide by being a jokester. He used the word 'deflect.' I deflect my inner turmoil."

"What do you think about that?"

"I don't know... I mostly only half listen to him. Sometimes I spend the hour running alternative code subroutines for the Quan-Tangler or converse with MATHR... you know, she's gained a sense of humor with her most recent upgrades."

"If you're not going to listen to Eric, what's the point of even going?"

"Cap, I have access, through LuMan, to the computational equivalent of a hundred MATHRs. I assure you, the percentage of CPU bandwidth taken up by our exchange would not even be considered multitasking... more like minnow tasking."

I nodded. "But still..."

Hardy continued, "Okay, yeah, I suppose at some level it

helps. He's an all-right listener. Makes me talk about my John Hardy life. We go all the way back to my childhood years."

"That's all coming back to you now? Your memories?"

"Yes, Derrota had said that they would probably return. Even my more recent memories are coming back to me."

"That should make you feel better, no?"

"I suppose... I'm mostly still dealing with not being human. But the doctor says I'm as human as anyone here is. That being human is not just physiological; it's bigger than that. No one can take away my humanity, that thing that makes me, me."

Maybe my brother being here wasn't such a terrible thing, I thought. Hardy might not notice it or want to give credence to it, but he was improving. I should have gone to see Eric myself—I'd make an appointment. At the very least, I should attempt to mend our familial fences.

A soft *ping* brought my attention up to the halo display. There was an incoming hail.

"I've got it," Hardy said, striding over to the nearby comm station. He tapped at the board, and the big 3D display came alive with a familiar face.

"XO Pristy," I said, then corrected myself, "Captain Pristy... good to see you."

Her hair had grown out a bit, and there was something different about her. She looked more composed, but then again, perhaps more worn down, as well.

"It's good to see you too, Captain. And you, Hardy. There you are, looking all buffed out, shiny, and new."

I now could see the worry, almost desperation, behind those pretty eyes of hers.

"As I'm sure you are aware, I'm with the 9th Fleet. I'm skippering an old petite frigate called *Starlight*. I have a crew of sixty-three, and we're mostly responsible for inter-fleet support.

Transferring of foodstuffs, munitions, and crew exchanges... that sort of thing."

"Like a delivery skiff," Hardy said.

Irritation flashed on her face, "Not a delivery skiff, Hardy. We're doing important work."

I shot Hardy a scowl before prompting Gail to continue. "Tell me. What is it you need from me, Gail?" I said.

"As you know, I've been in more than my share of desperate battle situations. And yes, Hardy, I'm being underutilized here, so don't rub it in. The fleet has been engaged by the Varapin for close to a week now. The battle has shifted, Captain... the Varapin are losing far fewer ships than the US Space-Navy. No one wants to admit it yet, but I know things aren't looking good for the 9th Fleet."

"I'm not there. What does your CO say?"

"I'm not high enough here in the senior command loop to ask such questions. But I keep asking myself, what would Captain Galvin Quintos do in this situation?"

"I'm probably the last person you should be using as an example."

She looked about herself, as if checking to see if she was truly alone. "No, on the contrary, nobody here seems to have any balls... God! I'm not used to such ineffectual leadership."

I wanted to warn her about talking like that. Second-guessing one's fleet command, not to mention sharing those views over a non-secured channel, was dangerous. But Gail was a seasoned bridge officer. Cool as a cucumber under fire, the very best at what she did. If she said things were dire there, fighting the Varapin, they were. My ex-XO was in trouble.

I contemplated the battle-readiness of *Jefferson*. Was she ready? Was the crew ready—was I?

"What should I do, Captain? Crap, maybe hailing you was a mistake..."

"What you should do is do your job. Do what you're being paid to do, and do it better than anyone else in the fleet. Your crew is counting on you to be amazing. Just as I did while you were the XO on my bridge."

My words stung, and I could see her face flush with embarrassment. But I wasn't her mommy or daddy. She needed to pull herself up by her bootstraps and be the person I knew she could be.

"You're right. I'm sorry, Captain; this was a bad idea," she said, now sitting taller and straightening her shoulders.

"Look, I'm still waiting on my orders. *Jefferson* is as ready as she'll ever be, but I don't make the decisions as to where we'll be deployed. As you know, the Grish and Varapin are making gains on multiple fronts. What I can tell you is I'll try to persuade Fleet Command we can best serve the Alliance there alongside the 9th Fleet."

"Thank you. I can't ask any more than that. And I'm sorry for the sniveling-into-your-shoulder routine."

A part of me would have loved to have had her here with me now—her sniveling into my shoulder sounded more than a little compelling.

"I'll be in touch, I promise. Chin up... be confident for your crew."

Hardy cut the connection. "Kid may be in over her head," he said.

"Nah... she's just frustrated. Not used to being sequestered off to the sidelines."

Chapter 8

I arrived at Eric's office on Deck 10 early the following morning. I hadn't realized he'd set up shop so close to HealthBay—but I supposed that made sense since medical-affiliated practices should be centralized for the crew. A plaque was affixed to the side of the entrance: **Dr. Eric Quintos, Doctor of Psychology**

I waved open the automatic door and stepped inside. Sure enough, this was an office: a desk, several armchairs, and even a couch with overstuffed cushions. What was missing was the practicing shrink. I said aloud, "MATHR, give me the whereabouts of Dr. Quintos."

Dr. Eric Quintos is next door in HealthBay.

I left Eric's office and proceeded over to HealthBay. What struck me first was how busy the medical department was. Never having had a full crew on *Hamilton*, such as we now had here on *Jefferson*, there were now doctors, nurses, and med techs bustling around doing busywork, although only one of the many available beds seemed to be occupied.

I stopped a young nurse. "Have you seen Eric... Dr. Quintos around here?"

She looked flustered and tucked a loose stand of auburn hair behind one ear. "I think I saw him go into the major's office, Captain." She pointed down the passageway leading toward the surgery center.

I glanced at her embroidered ID badge. "Thank you, Nurse Williams."

I proceeded down the passageway and found Doc Viv's office door partially open. This was a real door on hinges, not the typical automatic hatch doors now prominent throughout most of the ship. I knuckled a soft tap at the door and peered inside.

Standing in front of her desk, Viv had one hand casually placed on Eric's shoulder and the two were laughing. Noticing me, their smiles turned to expressions of surprise, then something else—self-consciousness. Viv pulled her arm back, and Eric crossed his arms over his chest.

"Quintos," Viv said with a new, far less relaxed smile on her pretty lips. "I was just telling your brother—"

Eric placed a finger on Viv's lips, shushing her. "You don't need to justify our private conversation, Vivian," Eric said.

I looked between the two and got the message—you've interrupted an intimate moment; go away!

"Sorry for just barging in here."

"No, it's fine. We were just joking around. What can I help you with, Quintos?" Viv said, having recomposed herself.

"Um... I was actually looking for my brother. But it can wait... nothing remotely important."

Eric's brow came together in puzzlement. "Me? What is it I can do for you, little brother?"

Again, I looked between the two of them and felt awkward. "You had asked me to come talk to you. Actually, I think it was a threat—I come talk to you, or I don't get cleared for command. But it can wait, big brother. I assure you I have much to do today."

Sure, that was a snarky response, but in my own defense, what the fuck was my brother doing in here, all laughing and standing so close to Viv? And how cozy had the two of them gotten!?

Eric made a dramatic point of looking at his TAC-Band and making a concerned face. "I have some time now... if we can keep our session to a half hour." He looked back at me questioningly—as if he was doing me a big favor.

"Okay... um, I'll wait for you in your office."

I left without making eye contact with Viv, but I could feel her stare—her unspoken desire to explain something that needed no explanation.

It was another ten minutes before Eric arrived back at his office. Ten minutes of my allocated thirty. I was seated in one of the armchairs, which apparently was the wrong place to sit. Eric stopped and looked at me, looked at the couch, and then, letting out an exasperated breath, sat down next to me in the other chair.

He smiled and took me in. "You look tired, Galvin. I imagine tremendous stress comes with your command, no?"

"Sometimes... but I haven't been under much stress lately. Readying the ship, I guess has its own kind of—"

He cut me off, making a contrite face. "Can we dispense with the chitchat? Is that okay with you?"

"You asked about stress—"

"The thing is, Galvin... there are so many serious things that need to be dealt with."

I nodded. Fine. The truth was this was Eric's show. He knew how therapy was supposed to work. I didn't have a clue.

"You've never dealt with the terrible, horrible circumstances of our childhood. And let me tell you, it's taken me years of therapy to deal with all that. I get it; you have father issues... maybe mother issues."

I looked at my brother's face and wanted to punch it. He couldn't be any more condescending if he tried.

I held a palm up to him. "I don't have fucking mommy issues, for God's sake. That's not even remotely true, Eric... and I have dealt with my issues. Probably in more depth than you have."

He looked at me, annoyed at being corrected.

I calmed myself and said, "How familiar are you with Clairmont... the faux Clairmont town that was constructed within the top decks of *Hamilton*?" I half expected him to start yelling at me since we'd argued about this before when I'd tried to tell him the truth about our family's tragedy.

To my surprise, his eyes went up and to the left, tapping into the memory part of his brain. "Yes... I heard something about that recently."

From Viv, no doubt, I thought. Well, if she could get through to him, fine by me. I continued on, recounting how Shawlee had constructed a mile-long, remarkably detailed recreation of the town of Clairmont. This time, Eric actually listened. I told him about the Symbio-Poth townsfolk, the Symbio-Poth versions of Mom and Dad, and a twelve-year-old Eric. How, over the span of a week, I'd gone back and visited the recreation, finding myself becoming more and more immersed in a narrative that took place when I was eight or nine years old.

Eric sat facing me, listening to my every word. Periodically, he asked a question or two, but for the most part, he just listened. That in itself was a change.

"And then, finally, that fateful night arrived," I said.

"The Fourth of July..."

"And there I was, sitting in the back seat of Dad's old truck. Mom in the passenger seat, you in the back next to me."

"And Dad driving."

"Yeah, driving like a lunatic. Angry at the other car—"

"The Volvo..."

"Yeah, well, the driver of the Volvo."

Eric said, "And did you see the boy?"

"Uh-huh. Scotty Miller, a year or so younger than me. He was wearing an Indianapolis Coyotes baseball cap. Dammit, I can still see it all so clearly. The Volvo jerked to the right and clipped our truck. Tore off the driver's side mirror. Dad went from angry to furious. Instead of slowing and letting the car have the road, he swerved left."

Eric waved his hands, motioning me to stop. "Galvin, if this is too emotional for you..."

I looked at him like he was crazy. "You honestly don't know, do you?

"I know that this is a highly charged, emotional moment. Something that shouldn't be taken lightly..."

I stared back at him. "Do me a favor... shut the hell up for five minutes. Can you do that for me?"

He shrugged. "Fine. Go on."

"This is what really happened that night all those years ago, Eric. Yes, the Volvo suddenly jerked to the right and clipped our truck."

"I can still hear that loud *clank!*"

I let his interruption go unchallenged. "The truck's driver-side mirror went flying off behind us. I watched as Dad went from angry to furious. Instead of slowing down and letting the other car have the road, Dad pulled the steering wheel hard to the left, knocking the Volvo off the road. You and I turned around, watched as the Volvo practically went airborne. One moment it was there on the road next to us; the next, it was shooting off at an angle out into the open field."

"I remember," Eric sniffed, deep in recollection.

"I screamed. Mom screamed, and you screamed. Dad slowed the truck, and we all watched as the Volvo rocketed nose-down into a ditch or gulch. Seconds later, the car exploded. Yellow light filled the truck's cab. I remember seeing Mom's horrified face—the shock and terror in her eyes."

"She screamed... didn't she?" Eric asked.

"She yelled, 'Carl! We have to turn around!' You began to cry as Mom pounded her fists on Dad's arm and shoulder. 'Stop the truck! Dammit, Carl! Stop the truck!'"

Eric was sitting back in his seat now, awful memories invading his thoughts. "But Dad didn't stop... He drove away, drove us home so we could pack up and leave Clairmont before dawn..." He looked at me, a resigned expression on his face. "Why are you smiling?"

"In my recreation of events, what you would call reenactment trauma therapy, Dad did stop. In fact, he turned the old truck around. Soon, we were bouncing and jostling across the open field, headed for the distant flames. He swerved around the skeletal, rusted remains of an old broken-down tractor, coming around a big mound of dirt. We skidded to a stop; both Dad and Mom already had their doors open and were running toward the gulch on the other side. You were still fumbling with your seat belt, but I was already out my door and chasing after our parents."

Eric looked at me, mesmerized. "Well, what the fuck happened?"

I almost laughed. "I didn't want to see the exploded car—see that young family being burned alive—but my legs kept running anyway. I couldn't stop. I ran, winded, trying to see, but the stupid mound of dirt was obstructing my view. I remember slowing, my face already grimacing in preparation for what I was about to see."

"What did you see, dammit!"

"I saw the raging fire's bright flames reaching high into the night sky—that, and the large, blackened propane tank beneath them."

"What propane tank?"

"The big tank had been pierced by some kind of agricultural tiller rig, like the kind pulled by a tractor when plowing a field. I didn't see the Volvo. At least not at first. I found it some thirty feet farther back within the gulch."

"I don't understand," Eric said.

"Mom and Dad had reached the Volvo and were helping the Millers out of their wrecked car. Mrs. Miller was crying, as was little Scotty. Mr. Miller was limping and holding a palm over his chest. I heard Mrs. Miller say the words 'heart attack on the road,' which explained the Volvo swerving. But more importantly, the wrecked Volvo hadn't actually exploded, Eric. Instead, the Volvo hit the metal tiller thing, which, in turn, was propelled into the propane tank, causing it to explode. Everyone was alive. Everyone was just fine."

Eric was already shaking his head. "No! That's not what happened! They died... they all died in that fucking car. Dad rushed us home, where we packed. I couldn't bring my toys, my chicken... I had to leave my chicken!"

I'd forgotten about Eric's damn chicken. Tears were brimming in my brother's eyes now. Unfocused, he was trying to reconcile what I had told him with what he thought had been reality. He looked at me. "Are you sure? That the Millers—"

"Lived?" I nodded. "Yeah. I checked. Mom and Dad's commitment to not looking back, not even checking the newspapers, was a big mistake. Empress Shawlee Tee played things out for me the way things actually happened. Well, if we had, in fact, turned around and checked on them."

"And you're just now telling me all this?! I've been carrying this shit around with me since... since fucking forever."

"I'm sorry, Eric. I should have. Honestly, I didn't think you'd believe me. Thought you might think I'm making things up."

"No, I know it's true." He let out a breath and let out a chuckle. "And here I thought I'd be counseling you. Big brother coming to the rescue, setting things right." He looked at me. "You've given me a gift, Galvin... I'm both angry and relieved. Angry at our parents and relieved we'd been living a fantasy. A dark and unnecessary fantasy."

"It will take you some time to sort things out... the past, the present," I said.

"You really are doing better, aren't you?" he asked.

"I wasn't dealing with the whole DOPTSD thing prior to Shawlee's help. Now, along with other things I'm doing... yeah... I'm better."

"Now I feel like a fool," Eric said. "I know I can be an ass..."

"An arrogant ass," I added.

"Fine. But we need to talk more. And I see no reason not to sign off on you commanding this ship."

"I appreciate that."

Chapter 9

This was a big day for *Jefferson* and her crew. Chief Porter had given the go-ahead for a test drive around the proverbial block. Engineering and Propulsion had had its share of issues with the install, but according to Craig, he was optimistic that the ship's power plant was ready to be put through a series of stress conventions and evaluated. While *Hamilton* had three reactor cores and four drive engines, *Jefferson* had two far more efficient and powerful drive engines, and just two, albeit colossal, reactors.

I was more than ready; in fact, I was itching to get out there, even if this was just a seven-hour local jaunt here within Pleidian space, culminated by a series of short, manufactured jumps of .5 lightyear's distance each.

Sitting upon the captain's mount, I gave the order for the Stoiling Build Base docking clamps to be retracted and for maneuvering thrusters to be engaged. As the three-mile-long, extensively renovated dreadnought moved out into deep space, I felt as though a weight had been lifted off my shoulders. *Finally.*

Over the course of the next five hours, with a comms channel open to Craig almost the entire time, we put the big ship through her paces. Rapid acceleration evaluations, sub-light maneuverability assessments, cloaked and uncloaked running, and finally engaging the big drives up to full FTL capacity. The jump springs worked flawlessly, allowing us to make a series of rapid rush jumps without the typical long waits required for the manufacturing of a jump wormhole. Even with the accelerated spatial anomaly formation of a manufactured wormhole, it still never ceased to amaze me.

The spectacle both beautiful and awe-inspiring, I watched as the same confluence of brightly colored prismatic spatial distortions formed into a yawning wormhole mouth, but now, it became a virtually instantaneous process. The throat beyond was already there, and I knew another mouth had already formed at the opposite end so many millions of miles away. We pushed things, and seven times we felt the momentary jolt as we shot into one fully formed wormhole after another.

By the sixth hour, I was ready for a break. We were headed back to Stoiling Build Base. Craig needed to do more sub-light evaluations, so we'd be more or less coasting back to the base. Getting up from the captain's mount, I allowed myself a few moments to review any TAC-Band messages I'd missed, or more accurately, had ignored. There was a message from Captain Pristy. Was this becoming a habit with her?

Apparently, the long ongoing fight with the Varapin was heating up again. The 9th Fleet had lost two more battle cruisers, twenty-five hundred souls lost between the two warships. I could feel her growing desperation, even though she hadn't expressed such feelings in so many words. *What the hell is the Admiral waiting for? How many more lives have to be sacrificed?*

Exiting the bridge, I'd pretty much come to a decision; if I didn't have new orders by the end of today, I'd take my own initiative. I was a big proponent of the old "it's easier to ask forgiveness than it is to get permission" philosophy.

I'd been meaning to check on Derrota and Hardy within the new Quan-Tangler compartment. From what I'd heard and surmised, the two hadn't quite gotten all of the bugs out of the transporter system yet. Approaching the new compartment's entrance, my TAC-Band vibrated. It was the Empress. I answered her call.

"Empress Shawlee."

"Ah, so glad I caught you, Galvin," she said, sounding a bit out of breath. "We've just landed."

"Landed? Here?"

"Yes, here... My schooner just set down within *Jefferson's* flight bay."

"Welcome aboard. I haven't forgotten; you're still needing a ride to Weonan, I take it?"

"Yes, most definitely. But that's not the only reason I'm here... Do you have some time, like right now?"

She told me to meet her on Deck 49. I exited the GravLift and found her already there waiting for me. I'd been more than a little curious about her secret construction projects taking place there, as well as on Decks 72/73.

Her face lit up at seeing me, and she hugged me tightly. "I've missed you, Galvin," she said, looking up at me.

"How is Twinwon? Are you two still—"

"Madly in love? Yes. And we're talking marriage... although that's a complicated subject... me being the Empress and all. Not everyone believes Twinwon is the right person or has the necessary social station to marry into Pleidian Weonan's high realm circles."

"Screw the naysayers, Shawlee... you deserve to be happy."

She beamed at my approval. "And what about you, Galvin? You do know that your love life is a constant subject of conversation within your crew and even among many in my circle of friends?"

I shrugged off the question.

"Still keeping two women dangling on a string?"

How did she even know that? I wondered. Ignoring her question, I took in the sprawling landscape of Cherry Park. I was hoping that Shawlee's builders and craftsmen would recreate the amazing park. And from what I could see, it was identical to the one on *Hamilton*.

Before me was a one-hundred-meter-wide by two-hundred-meter-long cherry-tree-lined promenade amidst rolling grasslands. A meandering stream ran down its center. Overhead, a projected azure sky and heat-emitting yellow sun would slowly trek across a celestial sphere each day from east to west. Right now, the setting sun was descending beneath a distant horizon into brilliant hues of crimsons blended with oranges and purples. Each day there would be a different, unique, and breathtaking virtual sunset.

I smiled; this place had been a favorite place for a little R&R for the crew. Beyond, there was a path, softly illuminated by traditional Japanese tōrō lanterns. Made of stone, the path eventually led to another far more intimate garden area called a Korakuen. Korakuen, in Japanese, came from the word *kōraku* and was derived from a poem by Fan Zhongyan. It referred to the phrase later pleasures, which stemmed from *hardship now, pleasure later.* My mind flashed to the secret hot springs where Viv and I made love.

Shawlee said, "The officers' sanctuary is there too. The same two full acres of solitude." She was referring to five individual rustic log cabins situated within a densely wooded landscape.

"Thank you, Shawlee. Your kindness is—"

"This is nothing. This is what you had back on *Hamilton*. Come, let me show you what's on Decks 72 and 73."

"No longer the little town of Clairmont?" I asked.

Her expression turned serious. "Oh no. Did you wish for that to remain? Oh my... have I made a terrible mistake?"

"Hell, no! I'm done with that little town, thank you very much."

She looked relieved, but in truth, I did still have a sentimental attachment to the faux world she had created for me.

Five minutes later we had arrived on the combined decks of 72/73. Before the lift doors could expand open, she placed a hand upon my chest. "Before we go out there, I want you to listen to me, Galvin."

Out there? That was a strange bit of phrasing.

"I've invited a few of your friends to meet us here; I hope you don't mind." The lift doors expanded and there stood six of my crew: Chief Craig Porter, Captain Wallace Ryder, Stephan Derrota, Hardy, Doc Viv, and my brother. *Is Eric a friend?*

They all turned in unison as we stepped out of the lift. None of them looked particularly happy to see me—or was it, none of them looked particularly happy to be here? A brilliant lightning strike lit up the nighttime sky. Rain began to fall, and blowing wind tousled Viv's long hair. Beyond was dense and ominous forest, and off in the distance, I could just make out high, pointed tower panicles and an interconnecting battlement. What came to mind was how... how could a castle of such magnitude proportions, such breadth, be here?

A thunderous screech called out from the high, distant clouds.

Hardy pointed. "Is it my imagination, or is that a dragon quickly descending from above?"

Chapter 10

Standing there in the diffused moonlight, I was transfixed—my senses were being accosted all at once. I could smell and even taste the woodsy, mossy air. A steady breeze swirled about that was chilled and wet and carried the sounds of a distant brook or stream—that and a slew of nocturnal forest animals I imagined were not all friendly. Instinctively, I knew this, whatever *this* was... was a dangerous place. A place someone could get hurt, maybe even killed.

The six of us exchanged furtive glances. At some point, Shawlee had taken my hand, which I only now looked down at and noticed. She pulled me away from the others. The smile on her face never wavered—she had expected this reaction.

Speaking in low tones, so only I could hear her, she said, "You ever wonder why Pleidians such as myself are typically happy, generally optimistic... day in and day out?"

I thought about that and it was true. As a people, the Pleidian Weonan were probably the most well-adjusted, upbeat individuals I'd ever encountered.

"I'll tell you a secret... it's because we know the power of play."

"Play?"

She nodded and then laughed. "We set aside a time each day to play... not just relax or take it easy for a spell as you humans like to do, but actually play. Get out of our heads and be as childlike and silly as you can imagine."

"That sounds like a fine idea, Shawlee, but how practical is that for the crew of a US Space-Navy warship... a warship soon to be deployed into battle?"

"All the more reason to play!" she said with conviction. "Think about it... You yourself are wrestling with a form of PTSD; even your robot has depression issues... right? You all have so much pent-up stress; it's a miracle you don't have more mental and physical ailments."

I had to give her that. Humans in general were a tightly wound species. I looked out to the nighttime scene before us. "Just how safe, or maybe I should say *unsafe*, is this place? I believe that was a dragon... an unbelievably real-looking dragon, I saw circling above us, is that right?"

"Indeed it was, Galvin. Symbio-Poth, of course, but you would not be able to distinguish it from a real one."

"And... let me guess. It's a fire-breathing dragon to boot?"

Her expression said it all, *of course it is...* She waved the others over and said louder, "No one should worry for their life. At least not when using the game's default settings."

"Game?" Eric said, looking quizzical.

Shawlee gestured to the all-too-realistic and foreboding landscape beyond. "Let there be no doubt about it... This place, what you encounter here, is all contrived in accordance with a high-stakes game. There will be winners and there will be losers here."

"So, what's the actual point of this game?" Ryder asked.

I knew Captain Wallace Ryder better than just about anyone; we had endured Space-Flight Academy together. The man was not only competitive; he was downright ruthless—no, cutthroat, when it came to any kind of bouts of gamesmanship.

Viv said, while securing her long wavy locks back into a knot, "This all looks medieval. The dragon, the distant castle..."

"Nothing escapes that nimble mind of yours, huh, Viv?" I said with a crooked smile.

"Bite me, Quintos... you have no idea how much trouble you'll be in here."

I had little doubt that was true.

Shawlee said, "I had help with the design, with Earth's timeline of events and historical references."

I said, "Let me guess... LaSalle?"

Shawlee nodded. "An amazing resource. And now he knows all the secrets of this place."

Hardy, who had been mostly quiet to this point, said, "So what are the rules? All games have rules."

"Good question, Hardy," Shawlee said. "The rules are available on your TAC-Bands, but I'll go through some basic thoughts that will assist you." She held up a feminine left hand and made a fist. She extended one finger. "First, the game is played in three-hour installments. So, make sure you visit the head before you come here. You will be notified via your TAC-Bands at the ten-minute mark, letting you know to start wrapping things up for that episode. No one plays more than one episode per twelve-hour cycle. Basically, you can play twice a day, if you have the will and energy to do so."

Shawlee's smile was anything but genial, and I suspected this game, as she called it, was anything but easy.

She extended a second finger. "Second, you must remain in character while playing the game. This game is called Convoke Wyvern. With the exception of your TAC-Bands, you will only play with the items and weapons acquired here in this world. So, welcome to Anglo-Saxon England. This is medieval

England, the time period around the eleventh and twelfth centuries, for your historical reference. Basically, a period at the end of Roman Britain until the Norman conquest around 1066."

"So no bringing along a tagger or shredder, I take it," Derrota said.

"Correct, Stephan," she said. She extended her third finger. "Third... this is also a quest game. In order to win, you must acquire certain items as a team along your journey. It does not matter which of you acquires them. Interacting with the locals is an essential part of this game. Some locals will be friendly, even helpful; others... not so much. There will be occasions where you must fight to survive. Swordplay may be necessary...so I suggest you practice."

Viv looked concerned. "Wait... you're talking real swords... with sharpened blades and all that?"

Shawlee became a bit more matter-of-fact with her expression. "This is not a game for the timid, Vivian... all participants of Convoke Wyvern will be issued chain mail. The material issued is, of course, not derived from that time period. It cannot be pierced, torn, or sliced. Now, does that mean you cannot be injured? Absolutely not. I assure you, although the point of an opponent's sword cannot penetrate your armor, it can bruise, and even break bones. With the default game settings, no one will be striking at your head or face. No one will die here... but I suspect trips to your HealthBay may occur."

"Terrific," Viv said, rolling her eyes.

"So, everyone will be competing for the same thing?" Ryder asked.

Shawlee extended her fourth finger. "Fourth... the short answer is yes *and* no. Each game, participants will be looking for the items I mentioned earlier; those items are listed on your TAC-Bands. I personally selected those items as part of your quest. Now, when the rest of the crew starts playing, MATHR will assist with that aspect. But you six are the game's first test competitors and will help with getting any bugs out of the contest.

Once all the quest items have been acquired, the one player who has collected, by any means possible, the most items will endeavor for the larger game objective. And his or her teammates, among the six of you, will assist you at this stage of the game. You can examine the name of this game for a hint as to what that endeavor will be."

Viv said, "Convoke Wyvern... what the hell does that even mean?"

Hardy said, "Convoke is to call or summon. Wyvern, well, that's just another word for a dragon."

"We're to summon a dragon?" I asked.

"Summon, capture, and tame a dragon. For you will need to ride that dragon into the Gorge of Destiny to claim your prize."

Derrota looked apprehensive. "So...what, we just go out there... wander around by ourselves?"

"Good question, Stephan," Shawlee said. She extended all her fingers and thumb. "Fifth... you are playing this game to win singularly, but you cannot win alone. You may find yourselves breaking off into smaller teams of two or three. And sometimes all will reunite together when it's advantageous."

Viv said, "Who exactly are we playing against... other than ourselves in this group?"

The young Empress gestured toward the distant stone castle —barely discernible above the tree line. "We are within the province of Dorset, and that is Corfe Castle, which is currently under the reign of one King John, a ruler who was notoriously cruel. John had a tendency to do away with those he didn't like, or worse, trust. And usually by grisly means. He once ordered twenty-two captive knights to be taken to his castle's dungeons and slowly starved to death. He did the same to his wife and son... and later his best friend, William de Briouze.

"Here, the unhinged ruler is both despised and greatly feared by those that do his bidding, his knights of course, but also those within the surrounding countryside—serfs and lords and such. A note of caution: be careful who you put your trust in."

"That it?" I said.

"One more thing... each of you has unique expertise in one area or another. Vivian knows anatomy; Stephan knows physics and the sciences; Craig, you know engineering... how machines operate. Wallace, your particular strength is battle strategy, yes? Hardy, you have all of those capabilities but are also innately in tune with righteousness and honor."

"I am?" the ChronoBot said, his face display momentarily coming alive with colorful animated pinwheels before fading to black again.

"What about him?" Viv said, pointing a finger at me.

"Ah... Captain Galvin Quintos." She appraised me with a thoughtful stare while tapping a finger upon her lips. "No one here should underestimate this player... don't get me wrong; he is a good man, but he can be ruthless and calculating. Just look at his track record in battle."

I wasn't so sure I liked that. Pretty much the same characterization I'd had of Ryder. *Interesting*.

"So, when will this world you've created be ready? Operational?" Ryder asked, already chafing at the bit to start competing.

"From what I understand, we are a good five hours out from reaching Stoiling Build Base," Shawlee said. "If you will allow me, can I make one suggestion?"

"Sure," Hardy said, "It's your game."

Empress Shawlee Tee stepped behind us to the left of the

cleverly disguised GravLift doors, which appeared to be embedded within a massive tree trunk. A ramshackle-looking cabin stood nestled beside a large boulder and several trees. She swung open the double doors and, without looking back at us, said, "Come along... time to dress in your characters' proper attire and choose your weapons."

Chapter 11

We stepped into the old shack, which now seemed to be more like an old barn with a hay-strewn floor, crudely made hand axes and shovels—everything illuminated by flickering wall-mounted candlelit lanterns.

The Empress said, "In this make-believe world of ours, we do not discriminate between any of the sexual orientations." She said to Viv, "Here in the province of Dorset, badass women knights are commonplace. Here we go by a single name, and your name is Cassandra." She gestured to the back wall, which we were all already gawking at. It was a mass collection of various types of weaponry, metal armor, and, with no better word for it, costumes.

Three people appeared; from where, I had no idea. A bent old woman, an equally old man, and a very large younger man with copious amounts of chest hair sprouting from his open shirt. All were dressed for the time period in frayed and filthy peasant attire. Pungent body odor affronted my nostrils. I knew the three were Symbio-Poths on an intellectual level, but hell, they looked and smelled remarkably human.

Shawlee said, "These peasants, Mary and Halcomb, are serfs under the rule of Lord Briggans... they will assist you with getting dressed. Big Gunther here will outfit you with proper weaponry. Please remember the weapon you select today will be the same weapon you take with you over the course of this game.

Choose wisely. Ask yourself, do I really want to carry around a ten-pound chain and ball mace? Contrary to all the old movies, a knight's sword is not heavy. In fact, most are little more than a few pounds. Gunther will explain and even demonstrate the selection of various longswords, maces, poll axes, flails, battle-axes, daggers, and lances. I will leave you now, my good friends. Do not forget the one item you cannot prevail without."

"That chain mail you spoke of earlier?" Ryder said.

"Yes, that, but even more important is your sack."

Viv said, "I'll need a sack?"

Shawlee was already out the door and out of sight. But her departing words could still be heard, "A sack to carry your collected quest items. Enjoy the competition..."

We stood there looking at each other for several beats. I felt awkward and a little guilty. I was a warship's CO—I had responsibilities. Allowing myself playtime, well, it just felt overly self-indulgent. As if reading my thoughts, Viv said, "You've been cloistered here in this big boat for months now, Quintos. When was the last time you had a break? When was the last time you allowed yourself to do something that wasn't connected to US Space-Navy responsibilities?"

Craig said, "I for one need a break. You know what the stress has been like in Engineering and Propulsion these days?" He strode over to big, hairy Gunther. "Okay, man... show me what you've got." Craig pointed to one of the broadswords affixed to the wall. "How about something like that there?"

Gunther tilted his immense head from side to side. "Thou art too slight a lord... no, this one is best for you."

Craig, looking somewhat abashed, took the shorter sword and hefted it, swung it around as if combating an invisible opponent. "Yeah, this one feels pretty good!"

Derrota and I exchanged an amused glance.

Gunter appraised Hardy. "Ah! Now thou, a lord of such grand stature... thou should hast the weapon of a true warrior!" Gunther plucked the largest of the battle-axes from the wall. Gunther tossed the weapon over to the ChronoBot, which Hardy easily caught. Once again, the twirling pinwheel appeared upon his face display.

I decided to take advantage of Halcomb's free time. "What do you think I should wear, good Sir?" I said goodheartedly.

His scowl let me know in no uncertain terms I'd said something stupid.

"I am a simple *villein*... a serf... not a Sir, no, not by any means." He gestured to me with a jutting chin, "Thy name is Merek. Come, thou shall gown thyself accordingly. We will start with thy undergarments and chain mail."

Over the next hour, the six of us were properly outfitted and provided appropriate weapons as suggested by Gunther. Eric complained that nothing fit properly, and he was having second thoughts about playing. Five minutes later, I noticed Eric was no longer among us—he'd opted out of play, apparently.

We were each endowed with our new Convoke Wyvern–given names. We'd already learned that Viv was Cassandra, and I was Merek. Derrota was Sedon; Craig was Asher; Ryder was Favian, which he hated; and Hardy was Gorvenal, which he seemed to like.

Leaving the old barn, none of us had been outfitted with metal suits of armor. We were knights, all of us, but we were travelers too. All I can say is nothing I was wearing was comfortable. The chain-mail shirt, called a byrnie, chafed, and the tough leather overshirt made me sweat. I wore my broadsword's scabbard across my back, as did the others.

"Fare-thee-well," Mary said, waving.

"Godspeed you," Halcomb said, also waving.

Gunther simply grunted and didn't wave.

With our oversized, maroon, Santa-like sacks tied around our belts, we headed off to unknown adventures that awaited us.

Chapter 12

Perseus Arm of the Milky Way
US Space-Navy
***USS Starlight* of the 9th Fleet**

Captain Gail Pristy

Pristy groaned at being awoken in the middle of the night. She checked her TAC-Band. She was needed on the bridge ASAP! She was tempted to bury her head under her pillow as dread weighed down on her shoulders and back—nearly immobilizing her. *What is wrong with me? Get a grip, Gail!*

It had been days since the Varapin fleet had made a move. A kind of battle stalemate, two combating forces so equally matched that trading smart missiles and energy fire seemed almost fruitless. The US Space-Navy had arrived here within a region known as Perseus Transit, having 20 percent more assets than the enemy—but that advantage was now gone as the Varapin had slowly and methodically destroyed some of the more vulnerable 9th Fleet warships—older, less advanced warships like Pristy's own petite frigate, USS Starlight.

How long before one of those Varapin fusion-tipped smart missiles locks onto my ship?

Not having time to shower, Pristy quickly dressed, and five minutes later was hurrying onto the bridge. She took the captain's mount, seeing Admiral Bennings' face up on the forward display. For a moment she thought the Admiral had been waiting for her but then realized Bennings was in the process of addressing the entire fleet. No less than fifteen thumbnail image feeds outlined the display—the other stern-faced ship COs—the latest of which to appear was her own.

Pristy glanced about the bridge in as casual a manner as she could muster. Heads turned away—her bridgecrew unwilling to make eye contact with her. Shit! She wondered if anyone here respected her. *Am I maybe too young or too pretty to be skippering this ship?*

The Admiral looked grim. "No doubt, most of you are already aware of this latest development..."

Latest development? Pristy leaned forward and pursed her lips. What fucking development?

"While the 9th Fleet has been fully engaged by this Varapin fleet—and we've been holding our own, I might add—a new, cloaked Varapin asset has arrived in the system. This is a Rogue-Slaughter Class Battle Cruiser called the..." the Admiral looked down at her tablet, "*Oblivion*. Everyone... she's so new, we have little in the way of up-to-date intel on her. Leave it to say, though, she is big, fast, highly maneuverable, and suspected of having superior firepower to anything we have... maybe with the exception of one newly renovated asset not anywhere close to us."

And that would be USS Jefferson, Pristy surmised.

The Admiral continued, "Currently, she's cloaked, but

we're doing our best to decipher more about her capabilities. I'm not going to lie to you, people... these next few hours, maybe days, if we can hold out that long, will be intense and challenging. I have my orders; the 9th Fleet is to stay and fight... to hold the line until reinforcements arrive."

Captain Illiack from the *Paramount* asked, "Admiral, will it be the 11th Fleet? They're less than eight light-years distance—"

"No, Captain... I'm sorry to inform you the 11th has been completely destroyed by the Grish. Those of you who had family or friends with the 11th Fleet, my deepest condolences. This war continues to take so many of our finest servicemen and women..."

Feeling crestfallen, Pristy knew a good many that had served within the 11th Fleet. She heard her Ensign, Clair Bottoms, mumble something about, "What's the use... we'll all too soon be little more than Varapin bitches."

Pristy shot Bottoms her coldest stare. "Knock it off, Ensign."

Sitting back in her seat, Pristy listened as the Admiral finished with what had to be the least motivating pep talk in history. She thought of Galvin and wondered if there was any chance *Jefferson* could be deployed here. Hadn't the Admiral alluded to that? But would Galvin make it here in time to even make a difference?

Chapter 13

Pleidian Weonan Territory
Stoiling Build Base

Major Vivian Leigh

As they set out, Viv looked at her TAC-Band. Only the first quest item was listed—something called a *dog whelk seashell*.

Ryder, also looking at his TAC-Band, said, "We're near the sea?"

Viv looked about the dense forest. From where they stood, they could only see trees—trees in every direction.

Quintos said, "Apparently, we'll have to acquire the first quest item before we are clued into where we should go."

Derrota said, quickly scrolling through screens of information, "As far as the further rules, we are not allowed to threaten, manipulate, or otherwise bully the locals into giving us information regarding our quest."

Viv saw that Hardy, towering at least a head taller than the rest of them, had stopped and was looking about. "What are you doing?" she asked.

"Attempting to utilize my Galactic Positioning System... pinpoint the direction of the ocean."

Derrota splayed his palms. "Really? Using your GPS? Did you forget we are on Decks 72/73... that none of this is real?"

Hardy just looked at Derrota, blank-faced.

Viv shook her head in frustration. "Just stop, everyone. I know England. Lived there for four years." Surprising everyone with her geographical knowledge, she gestured with a knife hand, "The ocean is that way." She then turned, making the same gesture in quarter turns, "That's north. That's south. That's east, and that's west."

"You can't possibly know that from looking at a hundred tree trunks," Quintos said.

"You're right, but I am capable of looking at the moon and the heavens above Earth."

Hardy was the first to look up. "Now I feel really stupid..."

Quintos gave the ChronoBot a pat on his shoulder. "You're still recovering, buddy. Best we keep on moving. Viv, how about you take the lead since you know where we are?"

The six of them started off, and there was some talk about splitting off into separate groups, like Shawlee had mentioned, but it didn't yet seem like the right time for that. Viv glanced about the motley-looking group and had to stifle a laugh, especially about Hardy, who was wearing a dark red shirt, leather vest, and short, tan-colored trousers appropriate for this time period. The peasant, Mary, had referred to them as *braies*. Sure, Hardy had dressed in regular clothes or uniforms before, which never looked right, but how he was dressed now was beyond ridiculous.

Earlier they'd come across a two-track road. Now, trudging through the mud, all of a sudden, an arrow struck Hardy in the back and bounced off of him. Immediately, a group of eight filthy ruffians was upon them.

Craig asked, "Are they pirates? They look like pirates."

"No, they're not pirates. Does it look like we're out on the open sea here, Craig?" Viv said. "Look at them; they're bandits."

Quintos offered Craig a sympathetic shrug.

One of the bandits, one who might have had fewer missing teeth than the others, said, "Give us thy coins if thou wants to live!"

Quintos took a step forward. "We're new here. We don't have any coins yet. I suggest you move on and bother someone else."

Erupting in laughter, the bandits cajoled and slapped each other on the back. Then they raised their assortment of weapons—several rusty longswords, a couple of knives, and what might have been a few broom handles.

Quintos looked to Hardy. "Sensors not working, huh?"

"I promised the Empress I wouldn't use them in here." The robot's face display was showing what looked to be a smoldering mountain—no, it was a volcano about to erupt. Sounding more than a little perturbed, Hardy said, "I can't just let this go... you all saw it. One of them shot me with an arrow."

"And that would be me."

The voice came from behind them. And there stood the ninth bandit. He was holding a raised bow with a notched arrow.

"I've got this," Hardy said while raising his battle-ax in one hand. The bandit archer loosed his arrow, and once more Hardy was struck, this time in the head. The arrow ricocheted off his chrome dome, disappearing into the nearby trees. Hardy took four long, quick strides, swung his battle-ax, and lopped off the ill-prepared bandit's head. That, too, rolled and disappeared into the trees.

No one spoke or moved, for that matter, for several moments. It took that long for the Symbio-Poth's headless body to teeter over and splash down into a roadway puddle.

"Okay then," Viv said, exasperated. Yes, it was a Symbio-Poth, but a part of her still recoiled at the level of violence she'd just witnessed. But no sooner had she said anything than the other bandits were on the attack. Hadn't they just witnessed what Hardy had just done?

Back at the barn, Viv had opted for a lance instead of a sword. She dodged the knife blade of the nearest bandit, feeling a swoosh of air as it just missed her cheek. *Shit, these guys are playing for real. What was that Shawlee said about the locals here not going for the head or face?*

She jabbed the point of her lance at her opponent, but he easily sidestepped away. Again, he attacked, his face now a vicious snarl revealing gaps where incisors and premolars had gone missing. The point of the knife poked Viv hard in the solar plexus, causing her to screech out in pain. Going down on her knees, she gasped for breath. Sure, the chain mail had kept that knife from skewering her, but the pain still brought tears to her eyes.

Only partially aware of the raging battle going on around her, Viv used her long lance to heave herself back up to her feet. Her assailant had moved on and was now fighting, along with one of his mates, Quintos—or Merek, if she was going to stay within the spirit of the game. Spinning and dodging, she watched as *Jefferson's* Captain moved like a true warrior. All that hand-to-hand combat training shit obviously had had a positive impact. And look at the guy; he was thoroughly enjoying this. Viv couldn't help but smile herself. Her attacker's back was mere feet in front of her. *When in Rome...*

Gripping her weapon in two hands, she thrust the business end into the bandit. Somewhat amazed by her own strength, Viv stepped away, seeing her half-buried staff just sticking out of the bandit's back. He turned to face her, and she saw the other end of the bloody staff protruding out from his gut. She remembered that was called a through and through. The bandit's eyes rolled back into his head, and he toppled over like a felled tree.

Quintos dealt a deathly sword strike to his opponent, who also toppled over. He looked over to Viv, "Having fun yet?"

"This is cruel and vicious. We're acting like a bunch of Neanderthals."

"You didn't answer my question..."

Viv looked away, forcing her mouth into a straight line. "Maybe just a little."

The battle was just about over. Eight of the bandits were on the ground and looked dead—or as dead as Symbio-Poths could look.

Derrota was on the ground, rubbing at a knot on his head and moaning.

Craig, beyond exhausted-looking, was fending off his own bandit. The only bandit smaller than Craig. But he was fighting with more vigor than Craig. *Good. We need at least one to give up any kind of clue or maybe item,* Vivian thought. Then, *Oh no...* Hardy was on the move, his battle-ax already raised high.

"Stop! Hardy! Stop!" she yelled.

The ChronoBot had already commenced his downward strike, but he stopped as directed. Unfortunately, just a tad too late. The ax was partially buried in the little bandit's right shoulder. No more than an inch, maybe two.

Craig took a step back and glowered at Hardy. "What the fuck! You know I had this on my own. What's with big-footing yourself into my fight like that!"

Hardy gave the ax handle a tug and pulled it free.

Bellowing now, trying to grip his injured shoulder, the lone surviving bandit staggered and fell to his knees.

Viv was on the move. "We need to abate the flow of blood! Get me something to make a compress... a rag or—"

"This work?" Hardy said as he took a fistful of one of the dead Symbio-Poth's shirts and yanked upward. He held the torn garment out to her.

"Perfect." She took it and quickly wrapped it under the bandit's armpit and up around his shoulder. She tied it into a double knot.

Quintos glanced around at the surrounding bloodbath. "So, now you want to play Florence Nightingale? Maybe a little late for that, don't you think?"

Viv didn't bother looking at Quintos as she continued to tend to the ailing Symbio-Poth. "You want to get the next clue... or should I just let this one die?"

"Oh yeah... good point." Quintos knelt down next to the incoherent bandit. "Tell me...what's the first clue or item we're looking for?"

The bandit's eyes cleared and became a bit more focused. He raised his uninjured arm and pointed into the forest. "Fairies there... in the nearby woods. They like to collect seashells. Thou... Thou stumbled across their collection once." He made a sorrowful expression. "You know, that was the closest thou ever came to seeing the ocean."

The bandit got to his feet. Hunched over and holding his shoulder, he staggered his way into the woods.

"Should we just let him go like that?" Ryder said.

Quintos shrugged. "He's already gone. Might as well."

Dusting themselves off, the group resumed trudging forward upon the muddy road.

Quintos said, "So, do we continue to the ocean or search for these fairies and their seashells?"

The discussion became heated as the group didn't seem to be able to come to a consensus.

Viv said, "Hold on. Hear that?"

Stopping, everyone listened.

Ryder said, "A river... one of pretty good size, I'd say by the sound of it."

They veered off the road and sure enough, there was a raging river that was paralleling the road. There was a waist-high slack rope running its length, obviously used for a handhold.

"It can't be an accident there's a convenient footbridge here," Derrota said. "I say we cross."

No one disagreed, so, with Hardy bringing up the rear, one by one, they started to cross.

Halfway across, the wooden planks beneath them started to shake and sway.

Derrota, the first in line, pointed. Suddenly, what looked to be some kind of troll appeared at the far side of the bridge.

"Just terrific," Craig said.

The troll was taller than Hardy by at least two feet. He was green, broad-chested, and beyond ugly. Pounding his chest in a cheesy manner, the troll shouted, "Thou shall not pass!"

Almost in unison, the group turned to look back at Hardy. There was no way he'd be able to maneuver himself around them to get to the troll.

"At least he just has a club... things could be worse," Quintos said.

Derrota was not appeased. "Then you go first, Galvin!"

"You're supposed to call me Merek."

Viv shook her head. *This is silly.*

Derrota turned sideways and side-shuffled around Quintos. He said, "There you go, *Merek*... have at 'im."

The troll grunted and began yanking on the rope again. the bridge began swaying uncontrollably back and forth.

Viv, three back from Quintos, said, "I don't know about you, but maybe don't get too close to that... whatever it is. Maybe use my lance?"

Quintos eyed the long spear, looking unsure.

"Let me," Ryder said from behind Viv. "I threw the javelin in high school competitions."

"Did you win?" Craig asked.

"Just let me pass. I'll get the son of a bitch."

Everyone turned sideways as Ryder sidestepped to the front of the line. No easy task with the bridge swaying like a ship on an angry sea. Viv passed her lance forward once he was there. Ryder hefted it a few times and frowned. "It's a lot lighter than the javelins I used on the field."

"Here we go... the excuses," Craig said dismissively.

Ryder gave Craig an annoyed glance before turning his attention back to the giant troll. Ryder widened his stance and raised the lance above his shoulder.

"Well, he looks like he knows what he's doing," Derrota said, offering support.

They waited as Ryder readjusted his stance again.

"Are you going to throw the damn thing or just make goo-goo eyes all day at him?" Quintos taunted.

Chapter 14

Ryder threw the lance hard. It hit the troll dead center in his chest. He bellowed like a wounded moose. With the lance half buried in his chest, the troll tried to pull it free. Unfortunately, he stepped forward instead of backward. The already unstable footbridge became impossible to stay upright on. The first to go into the river was Ryder.

Viv heard the splash and saw the top of Ryder's head being swept downriver. She seemed to remember something about him not ever learning to swim. *Shit!* Without giving it a second thought, she jumped in after him.

Fighting the fast-moving current, she barely made it to the opposite bank. To her surprise, Ryder was already there. He offered her an outstretched hand and she took it. Once back on solid ground, coughing up river water, she said, "I thought you couldn't swim."

"Must have been one of your other suitors... I can swim just fine. Fell in on purpose. All part of the plan." He unsheathed his sword from his back and put a finger to his lips. The two of them hurried back toward the bridge.

How the troll was still alive after taking a spear to his heart was a miracle. *Then again,* Viv thought, *I doubt Symbio-Poths have actual beating hearts like humans do.*

Both Quintos and Derrota were using their swords to fend off the troll's heavy, swinging club. From how things looked, the troll was getting the better of the two.

Viv watched as Ryder, now gripping his broadsword in two hands, slowly crept up to the opening to the bridge. Three more steps and he'd be able to stab or chop or whatever the troll. That's when Derrota looked at Ryder and smiled.

The troll swung around and, just in time, blocked the incoming sword with his raised club. The blade, hacking deep into the wood, was caught there. The troll pulled the sword from Ryder's grip—and was now in possession of both the club and Ryder's sword. Laughing, the green giant raised both arms in the air in triumph.

Viv instinctively took a step back, as did Ryder. Suddenly, the point of a sword thrust out from the troll's belly. Quintos had taken full advantage of the distraction. Pulling the sword free, the troll, bloodied and still with the protruding spear in his chest, wobbled there a moment, then fell ass over tea kettle into the river.

Those still on the bridge now carefully traversed it to join Viv and Ryder.

Viv noticed her TAC-Band was vibrating. Actually, everyone's TAC-Band was vibrating. She said, "Saved by the bell... that's our ten-minute mark." But she saw that Hardy was preoccupied with something else.

"What is it, buddy?" Quintos asked.

Following the direction of the robot's gaze, Viv now saw it too—a shimmery, small flying thing, deep in the woods. "A bird, maybe," she said.

"No, it's a fairy," Derrota corrected.

Without further comment, Hardy set off after the fluttering sprite.

Quintos yelled after him, "We need to go back... that was our ten-minute—"

But Hardy was already on the run.

After a quick exchange of bewildered looks, the group headed off after the ChronoBot. They found Hardy a hundred yards deeper into the forest, his deep-set tracks in the moist soil having been easy to follow.

Viv saw Hardy was bent over, peering into the hollow of a massive tree. Joining him, the group could now see what had so captured Hardy's attention. There was a cluster of hundreds of brightly colored, sparking seashells nestled into the tree's hollow.

Fluttering in the air nearby and having appeared seemingly out of nowhere, the sprite said, "Those are dog whelk seashells."

Hardy abruptly stood up, nearly bonking the small sprite with his head. Now face-to-face with it, Hardy said, "Hello, little friend... my name is Hardy."

"Gorvenal," Craig corrected him.

The fairy's translucent wings suddenly caught the light, reflecting an opalescent rainbow of colors. "And my name is Foxglove."

Viv leaned in. "She's a pretty little thing, isn't she?"

Ignoring her, the fairy pointed a tiny finger. "Follow the road of jewels."

Suddenly, an alarm sounded on everyone's TAC-Band, signaling it was the end of this play period.

Chapter 15

Pleidian Weonan Territory
Stoiling Build Base

Captain Galvin Quintos

Twenty minutes later, I was standing in the shower—letting the hot water run and soothe the many aches and bruises all over my body. *Stupid game. What was I even doing playing?* I had a ship to command. Rolling my shoulders, I had to admit, I did feel better—less stressed. So that's what it was like to have a little fun. It had been a while. *So why do I feel so guilty?* Truth was, I still hadn't been given official deployment orders. Why shouldn't I get in a little R&R?

Reluctantly, I turned off the water, toweled off, and put on a fresh uniform. I checked my messages—a few minor issues to attend to, but fortunately nothing cataclysmic.

I stopped by Eric's office. According to MATHR, he wasn't seeing a patient at the moment, so I chimed his hatch door. Gaining access, I took in his office. There were a few small, empty crates on the deck and strewn-about packing materials.

"Got everything unpacked, I see."

Eric had hung his medical diplomas, as well as a few framed photographs, on a bulkhead. I recognized several from Clairmont—our parents and Eric and I standing in front of the old farmhouse. I had a cast on my arm, so this was just after roughhousing with Eric, where he'd shoved me from the branch of a tall oak tree.

"We look happy. You remember who took this picture?"

Eric looked up from whatever he was working on. He let out a breath. "Um... maybe a neighbor? Or one of Dad's friends? I don't remember. Is there something in particular you wanted?"

"You left the game early. Actually, before things even got started."

"Very observant of you, little brother. Yes. I left early."

I sensed this was not something Eric wanted to talk about. So, I pressed on. "Too violent, maybe? Maybe goes against your moral—"

Looking irritated, he said, "Galvin, I'm a big boy. I can separate the violence of a silly game from reality." He put down the tablet he'd been tapping at and stood up. Coming around his desk, he gestured to another picture on the wall. "You recognize that?

I looked at the photo but had no clue as to the location. Then I noticed the slim, drawn woman standing alone, posing in front of a university. "That's Mom. She looks..."

"Broken?" he said.

It was the University of Pennsylvania, where Eric had gone to medical school. I figured this must have been taken after his med school graduation. I thought of the Symbio-Poth version of my mother—young, pretty. This woman in the photograph was a mere shell of that person.

Eric continued, "This is a while after Dad died."

"I'm sorry I wasn't there much... for your graduation," I said. "I found it hard to—"

"It's far too late for excuses, Galvin. What's done is done. We can't go back and..." He stopped. "Then again, that's exactly what you did... went back and changed things in your make-believe world."

"Not so much changed things. Just saw things for how they actually were in Clairmont," I said. *Is he jealous I had that opportunity?*

Eric turned to look at me, his face expressionless. "I have much work to do. Need to prep for a patient, that sort of thing."

"I'll get out of your hair. Just wanted to check in on you. See if you maybe wanted to join us when we play again."

"Let's see how it goes..." He glanced at his TAC-Band. "I'm pretty busy."

He moved back to his desk and sat down. There was no way he'd be joining us for another round of Convoke Wyvern.

Continuing my rounds of the ship, I stopped by the ship-wide maintenance department. The place was bustling with SWM personnel coming and going. Even maintenance bots, usually all lined up within their charging stations along one bulkhead, were out and about, doing whatever they did throughout the ship. I found Master Ship-Wide Maintenance Crewman LaSalle in his office deep within the department. He was talking to one of his subordinates. Noticing my arrival, he sent the young man away and smiled. With raised brows, he said, "Captain... didn't expect a visit from our CO today. Is there anything—"

"No, no. This is just a casual hello. Making my rounds."

"Uh-huh. I see," the older man said in his Louisiana baritone, letting me know he didn't buy that in the slightest.

I said, "Shawlee conveyed how crucial you were in helping

with the historical world-building for Convoke Wyvern. Accuracy of the game and all that."

"I enjoyed working with her and her creative team." He eyed the purple bruise on my left cheek. "Evidently, you've already started playing."

I rubbed at my cheek. "She says you know all the game's secrets... even helped come up with—"

"Captain. You're not, by any chance, here to get an inside scoop? Say, an advantage over the other participants?"

"No! Absolutely not! Me? Hey, I always say, if you can't win a game fair and square, it's not a game worth playing."

"Hmm, I never actually heard you say that before," LaSalle said, studying my face.

I LEFT THE SWM DEPARTMENT, NOT GAINING ANY further insights into Convoke Wyvern. Hell, I'd had to at least try. I was up against Doc Viv and Ryder; both were going to be ruthless rivals.

My next stop was the midship mess. I usually ate in my ready room, having a bot deliver me a sandwich or bowl of soup, but since I was already there and I was starving, why not crank up a food replicator and eat with the crew? Entering the large compartment with its numerous tables and chairs and replicator panels along one bulkhead, I realized I was all alone.

Checking my TAC-Band, I saw why—it was close to 2300 hours. I selected a pulled pork sandwich with a side of coleslaw and a piece of lemon meringue pie. While the machine manufactured my meal, I poured a tall glass of milk and brought it over to the closest table. The replicator dinged. *Suppertime.*

Halfway through my sandwich and slaw, my TAC-Band vibrated. I quickly chewed and swallowed my oversized bite, wiped my mouth with a napkin, and answered the call. "Captain Pristy!" I said more enthusiastically than I'd intended.

"Can you knock off the captain shit?"

She looked like a woman carrying the weight of the world on her shoulders. I said, "Is that a sweatband you're wearing?"

"I'm in the gym. Couldn't sleep."

I could see now she was swaying back and forth, probably riding a stationary bike. Her forehead glistened with perspiration, and she was breathing hard.

"What's happening with the fleet... the battle—"

"I didn't contact you to talk about the damn battle. Things are not going well. I think my crew regrets being saddled with such a young, inexperienced CO. They hate me, Galvin."

She rarely called me by my first name. We both had tried to maintain a certain level of formality within our working relationship.

"You're coming, right? I talked to Admiral Block. I'm probably going to get reamed for going around Admiral Bennings to get information."

"What did Block say?"

"He basically told me that that information was well above my pay grade. Galvin, I've never been in a battle like this... one that just drags on and on. It's like the enemy is playing with us, taunting us, but not yet ready to finish us off."

It did sound like that. The Varapin were devious and calculating. *What are they waiting for?* I could see Gail was on the verge of tears. I needed to get her mind off her troubles. I said, "Well, I certainly miss having you here as my XO. But someone with your abilities was bound to get scooped up for her own command."

Evidently, that had been the wrong thing to say. Her face blushed and her eyelashes fluttered. Looking away, I saw her eyes well up with moisture. A few moments passed before she spoke again.

"You ever think something was meant to be," Gail said, "only to get it and then realize you might have been totally fucking wrong? That the thing that was meant to be yours turned out to be a missed opportunity?"

I tried to unravel what she was saying. "Sure," I lied. "We all just try to make the best decisions with the information we have at the time."

I looked at her pretty face on my TAC-Band. She did look so young to be skippering her own ship. But I'd never served with a more competent XO. Could it be she just wasn't ready yet for her own command? I saw the emotion in her eyes—the longing to be anywhere but where she was. I did miss her as my XO, but was it more than that?

"Did you know I'm not a real captain?"

I shook my head.

"It's a new position called a soph-captain. As in sophomore. As in not ready for a frickin' real captainship."

Before I could respond, she lamented, "Dammit!" Looking furious, she shook her head. "I have to go; we've got incoming. Missiles... a whole lot of missiles." The connection broke, but I continued to look at the blank screen of my TAC-Band for several more beats.

∽

The next morning, I awoke as Jefferson was just approaching an orbital spaceport above the Empress' home world of Weonan. I had just enough time to shower, dress, and get myself down to Flight Bay to bid Shawlee goodbye. She looked hurried and distracted; she was the Empress of the Pleidian Weonan realm, after all. She hugged me, turned away, and then turned back to me.

"Galvin... do not take the game of Convoke Wyvern to extremes. It is just a game. With that said, be mindful of who your friends are."

"Who my friends are?"

She nodded, "In and out of the game..." With that, she was hurrying up the ramp to her vessel.

I watched as her personal craft rose off the bay's deck, spun a hundred and eighty degrees around on its center axis, and then accelerated out through the bay opening.

I checked my TAC-Band. No new messages from Admiral Block, meaning still no deployment orders. At our current position, we were a good deal closer to where the 9th Fleet was battling the Varapin. Once more, I was tempted to just give the command to head on out to Perseus Transit. If I did that, though, I could kiss my career goodbye. No, I'd wait for official orders.

I stood there within Flight Bay, watching the dozens of men and women going about their jobs. I thought about Convoke Wyvern. *Seems I do have some time on my hands...*

Chapter 16

To my surprise, all of my fellow game participants were open to playing another round. En route to Decks 72/73, I decided to check in with Eric.

"Good morning, Galvin. How can I be of service to you today?"

He certainly sounded chipper this morning. "Good morning to you too. Thought I'd invite you, once again, to the upper decks. See if you wanted to—"

"Vivian's already beaten you to the punch."

"Beaten me to the punch?" I asked.

"First thing this morning. She asked me to rejoin the game."

He saw her first thing this morning? I didn't want to think about what circumstances would have them seeing each other first thing in the morning. "Okay... well, just wanted to ask."

"Oh, I'm in. I was talked into it. Seems, from what Viv tells me, I have a stick so far up my ass; it's amazing I can still swallow."

"Then you're playing? A tad behind the rest of us... just so you know."

"I don't need to win, just to have a good time. I'll see you up there."

Prior to heading up, I dropped by Derrota's Quan-Tangler compartment back within Whale's Alley. I waved the hatch door open and found Derrota and Hardy, as well as Coogong and two other Thine scientists, hard at work within the newly constructed transporter room. I had been informed that the Thine scientist, who had undergone a kind of genetic upgrade months earlier, had arrived the previous night.

Seeing Coogong's smiling face still caused me to do a double take. His lower body was literally a stick figure. His brain's neural junctures had been reassigned connections to his formulated torso's, arms', and legs' Tendril Albicon construct.

He raised one of his stick-figure arms and waved a thin, twig-fingered hand. "So good to see you again, Captain Quintos." His wide smile radiated behind the faceplate of his helmeted head. Ambiogell, the goo-like substance the Thine breathed, distorted his worm-like features.

"Likewise, Coogong. I take it the five of you are making good progress with this contraption?" I glanced about the compartment. There were now six raised and glowing transport pedestals and a main control console to my left. The console was partially taken apart and had a big tangle of multi-strand laser fiber braid dangling from one side.

Derrota answered for him, "Seems for every step forward, it's another three steps backward. No wonder no one's perfected this damn technology yet."

That was actually good news to me. So politically charged was the use of this tech; I wasn't sure I even wanted it on board *Jefferson*. "Take your time and get it right. No rush."

The five of them simply stared at me.

"Um... anyone up for—"

"Convoke Wyvern!" Hardy said, already striding toward the door. "Takes me longer to get outfitted. I'll meet you up there."

Neither Derrota nor I commented on Hardy's new face display, a kind of elaborate coat of arms, a shield with two crossed longswords behind it. Inscribed across the front of the shield was the title: **Gorvenal the Great**.

Derrota turned to Coogong. "Uh, I can stay... help rewire that control interface."

Coogong shook his helmeted head. "No, no. We have this under control. Go have some fun."

I let MATHR contact the others to let them know the game was afoot. To meet us up on the Symbio deck and remind everyone the game would not recommence until we were back at the location we'd left off at.

After dressing, Hardy, Derrota, and I walked down the still muddy road, veered into the trees, and found the precarious plank bridge. There were no bandits and no oversized troll greeting us this time. I still had the seashell in my sack—a prize that was credited to all six of us.

Approaching the tree where we'd found the seashells, I saw the others already waiting for us: Craig, Ryder, Doc Viv, and Eric.

This time, three fairies appeared, fluttering around the group. Giggling, the playful trio made it clear the game had once again begun.

One of them introduced herself as Iris and whizzed around between us, then settled upon the ChronoBot's shoulder.

Looking up to Hardy's face display, which was still exhibiting the same coat of arms, Iris said, "I like how very shiny thou art. Thou art the strongest of the lot here... I have no doubt of that. Oh, a true hero thou art, yea?"

Hardy nodded, "That I am, little bug creature, that I am."

"I am not a bug. I am a fairy! It is not wise to insult the fairies of Shee."

Hardy shook his head. "Oh sorry... I didn't mean to hurt your feelings."

Doc Viv rolled her eyes. "Can we get going here? We're burning daylight and all that."

I noticed the fairy from yesterday, Foxglove. "Can you tell us about the, um, riddle?"

Foxglove fluttered around then came to a stop, face-to-face with me.

"Follow the road of jewels." She repeated her instructions from our previous encounter.

I exchanged uncertain looks with the others.

Craig said, "There appears to be just that one road back there."

Foxglove took flight again and said, "Time to go! Time to go!"

At a loss, we headed back across the bridge and toward the road. While Iris stayed put upon Hardy's shoulder, the other two fairies vanished at some point along the way. Back on the road, we trudged forward. Within a matter of minutes, we came upon a fork in the road.

Craig said, "We should follow the road that heads toward the castle."

Derrota said, "This way parallels the river. We should keep going that same way."

I stayed quiet as an argument broke out about the best way to proceed. I eyed the fairy on Hardy's shoulder, who seemed highly entertained by the verbal exchange.

Derrota was still standing his ground. "Look, we should stay on the road we're on... next to the river."

Viv stood on her tippytoes. "Uh-uh. I say we head for the castle. Seems to make more sense. Likely would have the jewels in it."

In the end, we decided to break up into two teams—I, Hardy, and Derrota on one team, Viv, Ryder, Eric, and Craig on the other. Derrota was happy since we would be taking the road along the river.

We strode off, heading away from the other group. I looked over to the other team and caught Viv lagging behind the others. She was looking back at me. She waved and hurried after her teammates.

It wasn't long before we heard a familiar, dreadful screech coming from overhead.

"It's the dragon!" Derrota said unnecessarily.

Looking up, I said, "Yeah, and I think it's pissed off."

Sure enough, the creature was circling above us. Great plumes of fire erupted from its snout periodically.

"How is that possible?" I said. "Even with the combined height of these decks, that dragon is way higher—"

Derrota, ever the scientist, said, "I've been thinking about that too. Must be a combination of virtual 3D halo projections afar, then, when closer, the real Symbio-Poth dragon takes its place."

Hardy was less interested in the dragon than with his conversation with Iris sitting upon his shoulder.

"Crap!" Derrota said, "Two more of them!"

"And they're diving toward us!" I said. "There! Toward that cliffside. A cave... hurry!"

Running, I noticed a large boulder adjacent to the opening. Over my shoulder, I said, "Hardy, can you maneuver that rock enough to keep out those dragons?"

Derrota and I waited inside the opening of the cave while

Hardy jockeyed the big boulder into place. He left a gap just wide enough for him to turn sideways and squeeze through. Immediately, as if day had turned to night, the dragons' shadows darkened the entrance. Then blazing fire erupted, causing me and Derrota to scramble backward. While Hardy was impervious to the flames, Iris fluttered from her perch upon his shoulder while spewing high-pitched insults back toward the opening of the cave and the three angry, screeching dragons.

"Now what?" Derrota said, gesturing to our closed-off, only way out.

Hardy made his face display go bright white, creating enough light for us to see our surroundings.

Looking deeper into the cave, I said, "What's that?"

"Not sure... but maybe we shouldn't go any deeper. Who knows what terrible creatures lurk in this place?" Derrota said, his eyes shifting left and right.

Hardy said, "I know what that is."

"Me too," Iris said with a mischievous smile, coming to rest upon the ChronoBot's shoulder again.

I walked toward what seemed to be an assortment of small lights. Derrota, two steps behind me, opted not to be left behind in the dark. I slowed when realization hit. "Oh no."

They did indeed sparkle like jewels. Iris giggled some more.

Derrota said, "Dragon eggs? Seriously? Follow the road of jewels means dragon eggs?"

Hardy dimmed the light from his face display, which allowed the eggs to sparkle and glow on their own. Each was a little larger than a football, and there were close to a dozen, each one unique and emanating its own colorful hues.

But the eggs weren't the only items left here deep within the cave. Propped up along the surrounding rock walls were all manner of metal and wooden weaponry. A collection of shields and armor too. That, and skeletons.

"Why do I get the feeling taking an egg or two might not be the best idea?" Derrota said.

Derrota said, "It appears others have tried to enter this dragons' lair and failed. I'm sure the eggs are a prized possession. Or maybe the locals are attempting to stop the dangerous dragons from reproducing?"

I shrugged. What I did know was that we were supposed to take one of these things. I closed my eyes and let out a breath. What I also knew was that doing so was a really bad idea. "Hardy, how about you toss me one of those eggs?"

Both Derrota and Hardy stared back at me.

Hardy said, "Okay... but it's your funeral."

Derrota said, "Probably all our funerals."

Jumping and reaching for the egg, which was tossed a tad too high, I was just able to get a hand on it. I fumbled it, reached for it again, bobbled the thing, then dropped it.

"Oh my..." Iris said, putting tiny hands to her mouth. "Thou have done it now. Thou art an idiot of epic proportions."

I stared down at the ground and the fragmented pieces of colorful eggshell. Splattered blue yolk goop spread into an expanding puddle.

Outside the entrance to the cave, all three dragons shrieked —fire billowed in through the opening. I felt the heat rise and perspiration form on my brow.

"You know this is becoming an oven, right?" Hardy said.

We all stared at the now congealing, soon-to-be-frying egg on the ground.

This time I grabbed another egg myself and gently put it into my sack.

"Why do you get to carry the item? You're getting all the items," Derrota said.

"You want to carry it?" I reached into my sack and pulled the egg back out, offering it to him.

Derrota looked back toward the flames and shook his head. "No, you keep it."

The big problem was getting out of this increasingly hot cave. I scanned what items we had to work with. This was a game, after all; surely there would be something here that could help us.

While Hardy seemed perfectly content to chat with Iris, Derrota and I began rummaging around the weapons and other items strewn about the back of the cave.

"What is this?" Derrota said, his form barely visible in the cave's gloom. I joined him and took in the wooden contraption on wheels.

"Some kind of cart, maybe?" I asked.

The thing was about fifteen feet long and easily thirty feet high. There were ropes and metal fittings, but the true tell-tale indication of its purpose was the long timber arm connected to a kind of bucket, which I had to crane my neck to see high above us.

Derrota said, "Ingenious!" He walked around what was now obviously a medieval catapult, touching the various mechanical constructs.

"Do you think it's operational?" I asked.

He climbed up on the catapult's frame and tried to pull down the throwing arm/bucket assembly. Then, seeing the winch handle on the side, he tried to turn it. As if it wasn't connected to anything, it spun around freely. "Winch is broken. No way to lower that throwing arm."

The heat in the cave had risen another twenty degrees, and I could feel sweat streaming down my back. I used my sleeve to wipe sweat from my eyes. "We're not going to last much longer in here." For the second time, it occurred to me the game's safeguards seemed to be turned off.

I said, "Hardy... can you at least try to stay interested in what we're doing here?"

Hardy, Iris perched upon his shoulder like a pirate's parrot, lumbered over to us. Taking in the medieval contraption, he tried turning the winch as Derrota had done. "Thing's broken."

"We already know that," I said, shaking my head. *When is the old Hardy I know and miss going to return? Or is this it?*

Chapter 17

The ChronoBot climbed up on one of the wooden wheels, then onto the main framework of the weapon.

"What are you doing?" Derrota asked.

Hardy didn't answer, but then again, he didn't need to. The answer had become self-evident. The ChronoBot, reaching high with both mechanical arms, took hold of the timber-throwing arm and, using his substantial weight, pulled it downward. The catapult creaked as ropes became taut. Within a minute, Hardy had the throwing arm and empty bucket parallel to the ground.

Derrota was already on the move. "Hold it there! Let me secure it into place..."

I hadn't noticed the hinged metal fixture at the back of the weapon. Derrota flipped the securing latch to the bucket, which allowed Hardy to let go. He shook out his arms overdramatically, like a weightlifter releasing oversized barbells.

"Thou art the biggest and strongest, that thou art," Iris said.

I rolled my eyes. "Okay, now for the hard part."

Both Derrota and Hardy glanced my way and then followed my gaze forward—the large boulder blocking the entrance.

Derrota scratched at his chin. "We'll need to turn this thing so it's pointed in the right direction."

"You and I can do that. Hardy, be ready to move that rock out of the way," I said, already getting into position to turn the catapult. A new blast of flames poured through the front of the cave.

Squeaky wheels complained as Derrota helped me turn the catapult to face forward. Hardy stood at the entrance, fire billowing around him. Iris had fluttered off to a location unknown.

"Do you mind hurrying things up?" Hardy complained. His face display showed an animated melting ice-cream cone.

"Few more seconds," I said as we gathered pretty much anything we could find to toss into the oversized bucket—rocks, knives, femurs, and skulls. We took up our positions behind the catapult while Derrota readied to pull the release fixture.

Hardy, his metallic, once-shiny chrome now blackened with soot, said, "You know, I could just shoot the big lizards and be done with it."

From high above, Iris said, "Cheat and thou wilt be disqualified!"

"We're playing by the rules, big guy," I said. "Now heave that big rock out of the way and stand clear!"

As if realizing what was about to happen, the dragon fire increased. Several leather armament vests closer to the front were smoldering—which I was sure my skin was about to do if we didn't move things along. *How can this supposedly fun game become so dangerous?*

Hardy set his legs and heaved. The boulder toppled away, exposing the three dragons, looking momentarily dumbfounded by their good fortune.

I yelled, "Get out of the way!"

Hardy disappeared out of sight around the corner. Derrota pulled the release fixture.

Nothing happened. He pulled it again. Nothing happened, and we looked at each other.

First one, and then the other two dragons took tentative steps, entering the cave. Now close enough to see their bodies, I could make out the oily, glistening scales that covered their entire forms. Each had a long snout with oversized, snorting nostrils. Their parietal green eyes locked onto us and then onto the broken egg on the ground, which was looking pretty much cooked and scrambled by now. Jaws gaped open, displaying massive white and all too sharp-looking teeth.

"Why don't they spew fire at us... just get it over with?" Derrota said with a trembling voice.

"Their remaining eggs... they don't want to cook their young."

The dragons were on the move again, getting closer. Not knowing what else to try, I kicked at the catapult's bucket. *Clang!* That did the trick. The release fixture let go, and the long timber-throwing arm swooped upward in a blur of motion. The collection of rocks, odd bones, and metal knives shot forth in a hail of shrapnel that hit the first two dragons square in the face and torso. Agonized screeches filled the rock cavern to the point we had to put hands over our ears.

I watched as both dragons staggard about as if drunk. First one dropped, and then the other. Their heads were a mass of shredded scaly flesh and exposed bone. Long, serpent-like forked tongues drooped limply from gaping mouths—both were deader than dead. The third dragon, injured but still standing, stood mesmerized, staring at his two fallen comrades.

"I think we're fucked," Derrota said. "What kind of game is this anyway?"

"One that plays for keeps. Stay still."

"You think?" Derrota snapped back, his eyes as wide as dinner plates.

Realizing I had little to nothing to lose, I took a step forward and then another. Slowly, I bent down and picked up what I guessed was a humerus bone. I hefted it—felt its weight in my hand. *Not a bad club.* Three more steps and I was standing over the remaining dragon eggs. Dragon number three began to screech while pacing side to side in a kind of feral fit. Small puffs of fire spewed out with each overexcited exhalation. I knelt down next to the closest egg while raising my makeshift club over my head.

Looking into the dragon's eyes, I said, "Your move, but know I'll take out a few of these eggs before you can fry my ass to cinders. Or you can fly away and let us leave. Up to you, dragon breath."

I had no idea if the dragon, the Symbio-Poth, could understand my words. We waited as the dragon looked at me, then down to the eggs, then back to me again. A low, rumbling growl emanated from deep within the dragon's core, but he, or maybe it was a she, slowly began to back out of the cave. Once outside, its wings spread wide, and the beast took flight while screeching and billowing breaths of fire.

Doc Viv, leading her band of three other players, Chief of Engineering and Propulsion Craig Porter, Captain Wallace Ryder, and psychiatrist Eric Quintos, was starting to have doubts about her sense of direction. The road, if you could even call it a road—more like a meandering path—was deep within the wooded forest. Any sign of the distant castle's tall spires had disappeared behind tall treetops hours earlier.

"I don't know... seems like we're off course, Viv," Ryder said.

"I second that. We're walking in circles," Craig said.

"I think we should give the major the benefit of the doubt," Eric said, catching up to her and placing a protective hand on her shoulder.

Viv appreciated Eric's vote of confidence but never much liked suck-ups. She wasn't sure what she felt for Eric. He'd made no attempt to hide his intentions—his interest in pursuing a relationship with her. Things thus far had not progressed into either of their quarters, but it seemed to be headed that way. But she had to wonder how much of this flirtation and several stolen kisses was about her interest in him, or was it a means to get under Galvin's skin? Was it Eric's younger brother who still had her heart?

As casually as she could manage, she stepped sideways and away from Eric's reach. "How about we give this path a few more minutes? And I'm fine with someone else taking the lead."

Ryder shrugged while Craig said, "Sure, whatever..."

Eric gestured to something up ahead. "Seems we've come across our first clue. Looks like a mule-drawn wagon."

"That and our bandit friends," Viv added. As they approached, she could see the same bandits that had accosted them earlier and had had their asses handed to them. They were in the process of harassing three disheveled, nervous-looking peasants still seated upon the wagon's seat. Evidently, several Symbios had been repaired or somehow regenerated overnight.

Ryder was already unsheathing his sword. "Seems these guys haven't learned their lesson yet."

"Seems not," Craig said, pulling his own weapon free.

"Maybe the lesson here is not to react with violence. I'm willing to talk to them."

It was Viv who spoke up first. "Eric, I mean, Ulric... this is not real life. People didn't so much talk their way out of trouble in the twelfth century." She stopped and looked at him with a sideways glance. "Where's your weapon?"

Eric feigned indifference. "I had one... one of those big swords like Wallace has there. I tossed it aside earlier. Seemed silly. I'm not a violent man. I feel disputes should be handled with diplomacy."

"Discarded it?" Ryder said, indignant. "So anyone, like one of those bandits up ahead, could get hold of it... maybe use it against us?"

"I hid it under pine needles and leaves."

"Can we deal with the problem at hand here?" Viv said, looking down the path to the distant cart and bandits, who had subsequently extricated the peasants from their wagon.

"Enough talk," Ryder said, striding forward, sword raised and ready for battle.

Viv and the others followed. Annoyed by Eric again, she wondered what he thought this game was about. *I'm willing to talk to them...* she shook her head. *Is he daft?*

By the time the bandits noticed them, two were in the process of rummaging through the wagon's contents, while a third was going through one of the peasant's pockets. Seeing the various musical instruments lying on the path, it was evident these were not simply peasants but musicians on their way somewhere.

The leader of the pack stood to face them. The others stopped what they were doing and joined him at his side. The bandits assessed them while looking about the tree line.

"They're looking for Hardy, no doubt," Ryder said.

"Wouldn't you be?" Viv added.

The tall middle bandit said, "Your numbers have dwindled, strangers to this land."

Ryder said, "Our numbers are plenty enough to deal with your kind."

Viv actually wasn't so sure. These filthy heathens were big and had proven to be far more practiced with hand weapons than they were. Without Hardy, and Quintos with his slick moves, they very well might be in trouble. *Then again... it's just a game, right? We're four against three. We do have our chain mail. And there are safety restraints built into this game, right?*

All three of the bandits were bearded and wore thick leather vests. As they raised their own swords, clearly not intending to back down, a waft of sour body odor accosted Viv's nostrils. In a momentary lapse of concentration, she wondered if these advanced Symbio-Poths knew if they were not human, but a kind of biological machine construct. Contemplating this, she wasn't ready for the attack. The bandits came at them with a ferocity that scared her.

She ducked the sword blade of one bandit, lost her balance, rolled, and then crab-walked backward. It might not have been pretty, but she still had her head. *Was I really in that kind of danger?* she wondered.

Ryder was doing better, now defending himself against Viv's attacker as well as another. Meanwhile, Eric had stepped back and become little more than an onlooker.

That pissed Viv off. She got to her feet, unslung her bow, and notched an arrow. Taking aim, she now wished she'd practiced with this thing more. Ryder was bleeding; his cheek had a vertical slice down it. Viv saw Craig being chased into the trees and loosed her arrow. She'd been aiming for the bandit's middle back, but it struck him in the ass instead. He bellowed in pain and staggered while clutching at the protruding wooden shaft.

"Thanks!" Ryder yelled, now only having to fight one combatant instead of two.

Viv notched another arrow and swung around to find another target. She knew Craig was in the trees, somewhere, but where was Eric?

Catching movement to her right, she turned and let her

arrow fly. It missed Craig's head by mere inches. He stood there, wide-eyed, mouth agape. "You could have killed me!"

"Sorry... guess I was a little overexcited," she said. "Good thing I'm a shitty aim, right?" she added, trying to make light of a serious situation. She saw that Craig's sword was slick with blood. He'd obviously been able to fend off her attacker. Looking around, she saw all three of the bandits had fled.

Ryder was helping the musicians to their feet while Craig helped toss their previously strewn-around belongings back into their wagon.

Teary-eyed, one of the musicians bowed his head before Viv. "How can we repay thy brave deeds, chivalrous knights? Thou have saved our worthless lives at great risk."

"Don't mention it," Ryder said. "All in a day's work."

Viv didn't hide the roll of her eyes, which only made Ryder's grin grow even wider.

Up in the wagon, another of the traveling musicians was clutching a stringed guitar-looking instrument. Viv remembered it was called a lute.

"Just point us in the right direction of the castle," Viv said.

"Thou're on the right track. Keep on the path and thou'll reach the castle soon."

The one standing in the back of the cart was strumming his instrument now. "We will accompany thee... come sit within our cart."

"That's all right. We're good," Craig said, looking more than ready to move on.

"No! We travel all together. I insist!" the musician said.

Viv's TAC-Band vibrated. She stared at it, shocked by the message.

"What is it, Viv?" Ryder said, catching her expression.

"It's from one of my med-techs down in HealthBay."

"Someone hurt? You need to go?" Craig asked.

She looked up, first to Craig and then to Ryder. "It's Eric who was hurt." She looked into the dark surrounding forest. "His hand. It... got lopped off by one of the bandits. He contacted HealthBay. Two emergency MediBots were deployed. He's being treated. His hand will be reattached within the hour."

"I feel terrible," she said. "I totally forgot about him. He didn't want to fight. Had stepped back."

"It's not your fault. Nothing to feel guilty about," Ryder said.

"Yeah, but isn't this game supposed to be relatively safe?" Craig asked. "Losing a hand is no small thing. And any one of us could have lost our heads!"

"I wilt sing thou a song of appreciation then," a musician said from atop the wagon.

Viv felt sick to her stomach. *What are we doing here?*

A second musician, a young man who had retrieved his instrument, said, "My name is Harold. We can take thou to the castle. I am a scop... a professional poet, if thou wilt. Now, this fine woodwind instrument is called a shawm."

Viv was hardly listening to him.

"What do you want to do, Viv?" Ryder asked. "Call it a day? Let you check on your, um... friend?"

She looked at Ryder and then to the awaiting wagon. "There's nothing I can do for Eric that's not already being done for him. He's in capable hands."

"Then we... keep playing? For a little while?" Craig said, pulling himself up into the back of the wagon.

Both Ryder and Craig were smiling. And, strangely, Viv found that she was too. God, she hadn't realized how addicting this game was. Did she really want to let Quintos and his team gain even more of an advantage on them? *No way. No fucking way.* "Let's keep playing," she said, taking Ryder's outstretched hand and pulling herself into the wagon.

The three musicians sat shoulder to shoulder upon the seat. One held the reins to the mule; the other two played their instruments. It wasn't long before the cart made a left turn onto what Harold told them was a shortcut through the woods. He began to sing, clearly composing the song on the fly. Viv found the man somewhat annoying, especially the song about "traveling higher, higher... to the grand spire." Over and over again, the same damn lyrics.

Finally, it was Craig who spoke up, "How about you take a little break with the music, man?"

Unflappable, Harrold started doing light magic. Viv and the others watched, bedazzled, as several beams of sunlight filtering through the trees started to sparkle and swirl in the air. Then, with a dramatic display of his hands, Harold made his shawm instrument vanish into a puff of smoke. Immediately, the shawm popped into view before them, floating near a tree. Just as suddenly, it vanished and reappeared upon the mule's stout back, then, in another puff of smoke, was back in Harold's hands once more.

"Nice trick," Craig said, looking more than a little impressed.

But Viv wasn't in the mood for magic tricks and only offered a weak smile. "Look!" she said, pointing. Finally, the castle had come into view. Remembering Harold's annoying song, she wondered if the "jewel" was there—somewhere up in one of those tall towers.

All at the same moment, their TAC-Bands began to vibrate. The ten-minute warning; this game period was ending. Viv looked off toward the approaching castle. She said, "We'll have to pick things up here later. Real life awaits..."

Chapter 18

Pleidian Weonan Territory
Deep Space

Captain Galvin Quintos

After showering and changing, I left my quarters, intending to head for HealthBay, but I saw Hardy was there waiting for me.

"Hardy? You okay?"

"I am better than okay. I am pretty good."

I wasn't so sure there was much difference between the two but let that go. "What are you doing here?"

"I'm doing what I am tasked to do inwardly by LuMan, and also by my own conscience. I apologize, Captain... I have been selfish these last few weeks."

"You have been recovering. No one's to blame for that. And I don't need a bodyguard. I never did."

"Perhaps not as an unassigned asset."

"Unassigned asset... what are you talking about? This is an unassigned asset. That's why we're playing taxicab for the

Empress... why we've been freed to play silly games up on the Symbio decks."

Hardy reached out a mechanical arm and took my wrist in his hand. "These TAC-Band thingies can't read themselves."

I looked and saw that I had missed a high-priority message. Scanning it, I saw that it was from the EUNF and US Space-Navy's Five-Star Fleet Commander, Admiral Cyprian Block.

> **Admiral Bock:** You have your damn orders, Galvin. We have no other assets to send. Go. Do what you can to help out the 9th Fleet. It may already be a lost cause. If so, do not sacrifice that dreadnought and her crew. Have I made myself clear?

I looked up to Hardy. "We have a mission... we finally have a damn mission!" An animation of colorful fireworks erupted on Hardy's face display. "I need to get to the bridge—"

"Hold on there, Mr. Excited. You think maybe you're forgetting something?"

I looked about the corridor. "Forgetting what? We've got our orders. Time to get underway."

"You think just maybe you should drop by HealthBay first?"

"HealthBay?" Then I got it. "Oh yeah... my brother. The whole hand being chopped off thing."

WE ARRIVED AT HEALTHBAY, WHERE I FOUND ERIC sitting up in bed, looking over a tablet. Doc Viv was sitting at his side, a little cozier than I liked.

The two looked up as I approached. Viv, looking like the cat that ate the canary, fussed about and abruptly stood up—while Eric simply smiled. *Cocky bastard.*

She said, "We were just going over his physical therapy schedule for the next week."

Eric raised his arm. Secured to his forearm was a CIB, a cellular infusion bracelet, used to promote faster organic cohesion of mended bone, muscle, nerves, and epidermis.

I said, "Too bad they put that hand on backward."

Both Eric and Viv, wide-eyed, looked at his perfectly normal hand.

"Gotcha!" I said.

"Screw you, Quintos," Viv said, unsuccessfully hiding her smile.

I said, "Does it hurt? The arm?"

"What do you think?"

"Maybe less now than when it happened... but yeah, I suppose it hurts."

"CIB distributes anesthetic directly to damaged nerves," Viv said. "The bigger question... is how the hell does something like that happen? It's supposed to be a game, not a life-and-death encounter every time one plays!"

I held up my palms in mock surrender, "I'd love to tell you I have that figured out. I was on my way to talk to LaSalle but got diverted."

"Sorry if I'm that unwanted diversion," Eric said, looking somewhat hurt.

"No, I didn't mean that. Our order came in. We're being deployed to the

Perseus Arm of the Milky Way—"

"To assist the 9th?" Viv said almost accusingly.

"Yeah... what's wrong with that? We have a warship that's been given clearance for battle, a crew chafing at the bit to do their jobs—"

"And a captain all too eager to rescue his first mate," Viv spat.

Eric observed, as if watching a ping-pong match. "I don't think we call it that anymore. First mate is old vernacular—"

Both Viv and I simultaneously said, "Quiet, Eric!"

I wasn't sure what Viv was so angry about. Clearly, she and Eric were becoming an item, and I was at least trying to be good with that. But she couldn't have it both ways.

I smiled, and in as calm and forthright a tone as I could muster, I said, "Eric, I'm glad you are okay and on the mend." I looked to Viv, "I promise I will find out what is wrong with the Symbio decks. Best you avoid further gameplay. It's clearly way too dangerous—"

Her brows came together. "Wait! Are you going to stop playing? The others... Stephan, Ryder, Craig?"

"Um... well... I think we're still up for playing, but we haven't talked about it."

"But you are!?"

I nodded. "Well, yeah... But rest assured, I'm talking to LaSalle first thing; it's not safe."

"Well then I'm playing too," Viv said indignantly.

"That's fine. No reason to get upset about it," I said, knowing full well pointing out she was upset would only make her more so.

"Don't you have a ship to skipper?" she said.

I HAD MATHR MAKE A GENERAL ANNOUNCEMENT to the crew, letting them know playtime was over, that USS *Jefferson* was now on a mission, and that we would be underway and manufacturing a jump wormhole within the hour.

All smiles and nervous energy, Ensign Plorinne, the young Pleidian, greeted me outside of the bridge. We entered the ship's command center together, and I was instantly taken aback at seeing the full bridgecrew. At every station, every post, there was an able-bodied crewmember dressed in full dress uniform. Currently, each was standing with back ramrod straight, eyes forward. And to my surprise, each was holding a proper salute—right hand raised with fingers and thumb joined and extended.

Their palms faced downward with the tips of their right forefingers poised at the rim of their caps' visor and just slightly to the right of the eye. I, too, was dressed in my formal US Space-Navy officer's uniform—captain's cap, light gray slacks, matching short jacket, dark gray dress shirt, and light blue necktie. I'd even shined my shoes prior to leaving my quarters after changing. Reaching the captain's mount, I stood upon the slightly raised platform and assessed the eager-looking team around me.

This voyage would be different from any of my preceding ones aboard *USS Hamilton*—although this was a similarly outfitted heavy dreadnought. But there was nothing like having a full complement of able-bodied spacers on board when going into battle. Previously, my limited bridgecrews had to juggle two and often three job posts at once. Moving forward, all that would change.

I eyed Thom Grimes standing at the helm station. He had been with me from the start and was low-key and unflappable under pressure. He'd recently been promoted to petty officer, second class, a promotion well-deserved. And there was John Chen, also with me back on *Hamilton* and also promoted to petty officer, second class. He was standing at the comms station. Both men were looking proud and more than a little excited to be back on mission.

At the tactical station, directly in front of the captain's mount, was a short, mousy-looking man in his early thirties with thinning brown hair. A senior chief petty officer, his name was Stanley Handly. Acknowledging him with a nod, I briefly wondered if he'd paid a high price for that name back in grade school.

Looking at the empty seat, I couldn't help think of Gail Pristy and how I'd have to deal with her no longer being a part of this crew.

I turned to face the junior officer of the deck—the JOOD. His name was Awaale Samatar, and I knew from reviewing his file he was from an area in Somalia, the southern Ethiopian region of Ogaden. I didn't know the man well, but he'd come highly recommended, and he seemed eager to make a good impression. As the JOOD, he'd be supervising much of the enlisted personnel here on the bridge.

Turning to the console behind me, I saw an actual boatswain's mate of the watch, BMOW, more commonly referred to as a bosun. Her name was Johanna Polk, and she was the most serious, humorless-looking individual on the bridge, perhaps the entire ship. But like Crewman Samatar, she came highly recommended, and I intended to make her feel both welcome and appreciated.

The bosun was considered the backbone of every ship's crew—she was the enlisted assistant to the OOD. She would basically be in charge of such things as ensuring crewmembers of the watch were correctly posted—monitoring the comings and goings of crew, and keeping an eye out for personnel who were not alert or not wearing the proper watch-standing uniforms. *That just might be a problem.*

I'd never been a stickler for rules. In fact, I had a tendency to break rules just for the sake of doing so. I gave Bosun Polk a curt nod of my head and turned to another newly filled post, the ship's quartermaster of the watch (QMOW). The quartermaster in today's US Space-Navy was the de facto interface between the ship's CIC, which was the adjacent compartment to my executive bridge team.

Our new quartermaster was a bright-eyed and bushy-tailed young woman named Harper Vargos, whom everyone simply called Ty, for reasons still unknown to me. She'd be reporting directly to both the ship's CIC chief science officer, Stephan Derrota, as well as whoever was the current ship's bridge officer, currently, me. There were others here on the bridge as well, most holding minor support positions.

Two more officers, and a very tall ChronoBot, were now headed my way. Derrota was wearing a uniform that looked a tad rumpled, even though I knew he'd just taken it fresh from his closet. I'd never figured out how the man could so quickly attract wrinkles and mustard stains—in that respect, he was a lot like a four-year-old.

Head of security was Alistair Mattis. Tall, bald, and with a bird-like quality, the man was a good friend, but often rubbed people wrong. He always seemed to be having some kind of feud or heated discussion with someone or other. The man was like the ship's chief of police—and he often had to lay down the law, something that was not high within my skill set.

Both Derrota and Mattis took up their customary positions, standing to my left with Hardy, now looking polished and wearing an oversized officer's uniform. I scrutinized his attire; the uniform looked uncharacteristically similar to that of a US Space-Navy Admiral.

About to address my still-saluting bridgecrew, I noticed an almost imperceptible golden glow emanating from the top of Hardy's breast pocket. As compelling as that was, it was nothing compared to what I saw next.

Peeking out, her head and shoulders just barely visible, I saw the tiny fairy from the Symbio deck—*Iris!* Giggling and looking duly contrite, she put a feminine finger to her lips in an overdramatic, conspiratorial manner. She took one last look around and disappeared back within Hardy's breast pocket.

USS Jefferson

Looking up at Hardy's face display and expecting some kind of jokester animation going on, I saw there was nothing but black. I took that to mean that his fairy friend was his secret, and he meant to keep it that way.

I offered Hardy a smile and a wink—if having a pet fairy helped the big goofball with his recovery, who was I to protest? Then, looking past Hardy, I saw Bosun Polk, her eyes narrowed, had observed our quick interchange. The phrase *angry schoolmarm* came to mind.

Standing tall, I returned a smart salute—holding it for five seconds. "At ease, everyone," I said. I noticed more of the crew was still coming into the bridge and taking up standing positions along the rear bulkhead. I saw SWM Chief LaSalle, my favorite Marine squad of Sergeant Max Dryer, Wanda, Grip, Ham, Hock, and Captain Ryder, along with Lieutenant Akari James. Perhaps the biggest surprise was seeing Flight Bay chief Frank Mintz—who I was certain had already retired.

All in attendance were outfitted in their dress uniforms. Besides Wanda's latest fluorescent green hair color, I had never observed a more proper and dignified-looking assemblage of crewmembers. The last to arrive was my brother Eric, still wearing his cellular infusion bracelet, along with Doc Viv, who was wearing her major's dress grays.

Bosun Polk had turned around and was making an expression similar to that of someone who'd just taken a bite of a sour pickle. She looked back at me. "This is highly irregular, Captain... unauthorized crew on the deck—"

"Bosun, what do you say we bend the rules just this once? A lot of people have contributed, in one way or another, to today's maiden voyage. I for one could not imagine not having these people here to witness *USS Jefferson's* return to active service."

She spoke just loud enough for only those in close proximity to hear. "Very well. You are the captain. But the rules are there for a reason, Sir."

I caught Derrota's eye and he made a *WTF* expression.

I cleared my throat. "Thank you, everyone. Many of you have spent months helping to get this old girl ready for this moment. And, as she stands now, USS *Jefferson* is the most powerful, most advanced warship of any EUNF US Space-Navy asset. As you know, the war has turned for the worse these last few months. The Grish, with the aid of the Varapin, have started to retake hard-fought territories. Resources have become limited. At the moment, the 9th Fleet is in grave peril. The Varapin have our ships surrounded, cordoned off from escape using a kind of dampening field we haven't encountered before. So, slowly and methodically, our ships are being taken out."

"So, what are we going to do about that, Cap?" Wanda yelled from the back bulkhead.

Chuckles erupted from around the bridge.

I avoided the bosun's glare. "What do you think we should do about it?" I retorted, looking at the faces around me.

"I think a little whoop-ass is in order... show those floating ghouls who's the real boss," Grip said.

Doc Viv, looking less amused, said, "Advanced and powerful, *Jefferson's* still just one ship. Will we be arriving a day late and a dollar short, so to speak?"

Sobered by her question, the compartment went quiet.

"That may, unfortunately, be the case. What's needed is an entire fleet... what the 9th is getting is one ship. Let me be perfectly honest: the odds of success with this mission are not good. In fact, they suck."

From behind, my usually reticent helmsman, Grimes, said, "But aren't our odds of success always crappy? Isn't that why the Admiral's sending you?"

I shook my head. "No, it's why he's sending *us*... and this great ship. There needs to be a turning point for this war, or it won't be long before the enemy is bringing the war to the home worlds of the Thine, Pleidians, and humans."

All eyes were on me. The nervous anticipation was evident on everyone's face.

"Who here is ready to bring the fight to the Varapin... as Grip says, bring some whoop-ass to the enemy?"

Without hesitation and in unison, the responding voices yelled, "I AM!!"

"Helm... has MATHR provided endpoint coordinates for our first jump?"

"Affirmative, Sir. Jump springs are fully energized and primed for wormhole manufacture."

I looked about the bridge. The nervous anticipation could be cut with a knife. Searching, I set my eyes on one person. "Lieutenant Akari James... would you do the honors?"

The small firecracker of an Arrow pilot lit up with an ear-to-ear grin. "Be my honor, Sir." She stood taller while setting her gaze on the forward halo display. "Helm! Jump this ship!"

Chapter 19

Perseus Arm of the Milky Way
US Space-Navy
***USS Starlight* of the 9th Fleet**

Captain Gail Pristy

It wasn't the first time that Pristy contemplated what Galvin would do in a situation like this. It was evident what was happening here—the Varapin had set a very enticing trap. Sure, Admiral Bennings hadn't come right out and said as much, but it was obvious to Pristy and the other Cos within the fleet. Bennings had been manipulated, duped, outplayed into doing exactly what Varapin command had ingeniously wanted him to do.

The enemy had orchestrated tactical perfection, and now Pristy and everyone else knew the reason the Varapin had not simply destroyed the 9th Fleet. Instead, over the course of several weeks, they had corralled the larger US Space-Navy vessels into a very specific configuration. It hadn't seemed premeditated at the time, but each 9th Fleet warship had been coaxed, baited, or even rammed into a predefined spot on a kind of spatial gameboard.

Pristy regarded the forward display. *Ingenious.* The distance between each ship was three hundred miles, measured almost down to the foot. The Varapin assets were interspersed just as precisely. What the Admiral had not foreseen was that allowing this intricate puzzle to take shape would allow the Varapin to initialize a powerful, interconnecting, dampening field. Each Varapin asset was a receiver/transmitter point within this ingenious kind of spider's web.

So now here we all sit, Pristy thought. Missiles couldn't leave their firing tubes, and even comms between ships were spotty. And making any attempt to send an encrypted micro-wormhole laser-link transmission out of system had proven impossible. Subsequently, informing Fleet Command of their current situation, that this was a trap, was now out of the question.

She studied the unmoving gameboard—unmoving with the exception of *Oblivion,* that Rogue-Slaughter Class Battle Cruiser slowly moving about the outer perimeter of the two joined fleets. *God, that ship is big—has to be five miles long.* Perhaps this really was the Varapin technological equivalent to USS *Jefferson*. And like *Jefferson,* and *Hamilton* before her, few, if any, warships would be her match.

"Why isn't she running cloaked?" Pristy said aloud, not expecting anyone to answer her. It was late, and the second shift had yet to arrive on the bridge. Had she become too complacent? Sure, there was absolutely nothing for anyone to do, but that would eventually change. She needed to stay vigilant—her crew needed to stay vigilant.

Pristy was surprised to hear a response to her previous question. Clair Bottoms said, "Because she wants to be seen, obviously."

Pristy turned in her seat and looked at her Ensign. "We can see her just fine via sensors... the Varapin tech isn't that good. So why make a show of it? Why parade around like that?"

The Ensign shrugged, then said, "Clearly it's for someone else then. *Oblivion* is sending a message... don't fuck with me. Don't fuck with my game."

Pristy smiled and slowly nodded. She turned to the display. "So, there's someone else out there... someone who's damn good at evading long-range sensors."

She stood, rolled her shoulders, and stretched her neck from side to side. Pristy was exhausted, having had little sleep these past few weeks. It wasn't uncommon for her to stay on duty for two full shifts—to stare at the damn display hoping something, anything, would change. And now, thanks to her bitchy Ensign's observation, maybe something *had* changed.

"Friend or foe?" Pristy asked.

"I don't know," Bottoms said, getting to her feet. "Isn't that your job to figure out?"

Before Pristy could answer, Bottoms turned to leave. "My shift ended twenty minutes ago. I need some bunk time. Suggest you do the same."

The next shift, looking bleary-eyed, was arriving on the bridge in twos and threes.

"Still here, Cap?" Don Holder, Pristy's chief petty officer, said at the helm station, with only a modicum of surprise in his voice. Holder was as close to an XO as she had, and she'd come to appreciate his frank, no-bullshit attitude. Young like herself, Holder was smart, but a little too cynical for his own good.

Several more of her bridgecrew strolled in and sat at their stations. A few contagious yawns had Pristy reconsidering her bunk. "Holder... I want you on Tactical today."

He looked to the empty station seat, annoyed. "Why? What on earth would—"

"No arguments, Chief Petty Officer... just do it and I'll explain."

The man, not unlike a petulant child, huffed, got up, and moved over to the tactical station.

Pristy watched his performance with growing irritation. How had things come to this? Was it like this on every ship in the fleet? She suspected to some degree, yes. The 9th had a reputation for being, well, lax. The word *slipshod* came to mind. Strange. Galvin was the least authoritative CO Pristy had known, and yet, his crew exhibited such respect and an excellent work ethic. He wasn't even aware that young recruits out of the academy, as well as seasoned warship crewmen, jumped through hoops to get a post under his command. *Why?* Her thoughts were interrupted by Holder.

"So, what am I doing here?" he said, making an exasperated expression.

"It's what am I doing here, *Sir*. And knock off the attitude, Mr. Holder. Or you'll find yourself slopping a mop in one of the more disgusting areas of this ship... like the Deck 3 forward head." She knew Holder was a bit of a germaphobe. His overly pale skin tone, slicked-back black hair, and uncommon pointy widow's peak had been a mild curiosity to young female crewmembers on board *Starlight*—but eventually, his all-around weirdness and obnoxious arrogance always proved too much to overlook.

Holder said, "Apologies, Sir," and he continued to stare at her for several long beats.

Ignoring him, Pristy said, "Our long-range sensors aren't picking up what the Varapin are picking up on... alien drones, another ship, a fleet of ships. I want you to figure out what's out there."

"Me? With the outdated technology on board this petite frigate... a frigate that is older than the Admiral?"

Pristy returned his pointed stare. "I didn't say you had to use *Starlight's* tech, Mr. Holder. Bend the rules. Think out of the box. Go bananas with your imagination."

"But we're supposed to just wait. The Admiral—"

"Screw the Admiral, Holder!" Pristy exclaimed, only now realizing that the bridge had pretty much filled, and everyone was looking at her, both aghast and maybe just a little impressed.

"Well, I'm not limited to *Starlight* sensor tech. Maybe the tech off-ship... maybe the *Lexington*. She's new, or newer, but still..." Holder's words trailed off as he looked upward. A new thought had occurred to him.

"What?"

"It's stupid. Wouldn't work."

"Spill it anyway," Pristy said, practically seeing the gears turning in the young helmsman's head.

"Remember when we first got here in system?"

Pristy nodded.

"Like always, we were on scud duty, transferring rations between the larger vessels."

Pristy made a rolling gesture with a finger, prompting him to get to the point.

"We literally plowed into that Lorg-Mav reconnaissance drone. You had the thing dragged on board and put into the aft hold. Didn't want any other ships crashing into the thing."

Intrigued, Pristy said, "Yeah, I thought it was strange the Lorg-Mav would have positioned a spy drone twenty-five light-years out from their home world."

Looking more excited, Holder said, "The Lorg-Mav have stayed neutral during this war... a people with higher tech than humans but in their own odd way. Utilize active sensors that compare surrounding molecular structures instead of how we, and just about everyone else, just ping specific spatial areas while measuring for any returning radiation anomalies."

She saw where Holder was going with this. "You think that drone could pick up on what's out there?"

He shrugged and rubbed at his widow's peak. A habit that had always annoyed her.

"Thing was still working when we scooped it up, so... maybe."

To Holder's left, the newly arrived Molly Brown, sitting at Comms, said, "How do you know so much about it? How do you even know what kind of active sensors the drone utilizes? How do you know it's still functioning, for that matter? I was there, and I couldn't tell. Are you like a drone psychic?"

For a moment, Holder looked stymied, then contrite. "Fine. Had a bot bring it up to the lab. It's on the bench right now, hooked up to a power supply. Been tinkering with it. I've always been interested in alien tech... so why don't you just shoot me, Molly?"

Feeling her heart skip a beat, Pristy was up and out of her seat and heading for Holder. Eyes wide, he recoiled in his seat, but not fast enough to avoid the big kiss she planted right below that dreadful-looking widow's peak. "You're a genius, Holder!" she said with an ear-to-ear grin. "Get up! Take me to that lab and that pet drone of yours."

∾

Three hours later , Pristy, Holder, and six other handpicked engineers sat shoulder to shoulder at a workbench within *Starlight's* Deck 7 Aft Lab. Like the rest of the ship, the compartment was poorly lit, with exposed vertical bulkhead support girders and a patch-job of power and communications conduits. But at the moment, all of Pristy's attention was on the three-foot-by-three-foot puke-green cube situated on the benchtop. Spewing out from seven different access panels on the drone, the engineers had affixed multi-strand laser-fibers, which connected to various test apparatuses alongside the bench.

A good 90 percent of what the tech heads were saying was over Pristy's head, but, unfazed, she had them translate their geek talk into understandable English. What she'd learned over the course of the last few hours was that the Lorg-Mav reconnaissance drone was even more than that. It was an advanced communications hub as well, utilizing a variation of microwormhole laser-link tech. Holder and the others hadn't quite figured out how to interface that aspect with *Starlight* but were encouraged they'd be able to figure it out. As for its active and passive deep space sensors? That aspect seemed to be working, although the six engineers, along with Holder, didn't know how to read the data.

Pristy stared at the Multiflux Scope display on the bench before her, the colorful, dancing waveform signals. One of the engineers used a touchpad to adjust signal amplitudes.

Holder reprimanded him, "Hey... put that back the way it was! I was just starting to make sense of the fucking thing!" He looked at Pristy. "Sorry."

Ignoring him, she said, "Can't MATHR figure it out? Isn't that why we have an onboard AI?"

The engineer named Derrick chuckled, "Our MATHR is nothing like that fancy AI you had on *Hamilton*, Captain. This one couldn't chew gum and tie her shoes at the same time."

"That's not the right expression," another of the engineers said.

Keeping this lot on point was testing Pristy's patience. "Can we just try it? Do we have to make some kind of other connection... maybe more multi-strand laser fibers?"

"Ah... no. Drone's all hooked up to the ship's central database now."

That gave her pause. An advanced alien drone was connected to *Starlight's* database? *That can't be safe.* She shook it off. At this point, she couldn't chance distracting the eggheads. "How do we ask her to analyze the data?" Pristy said, exasperated. The lack of sleep and having to deal with these seven was taking its toll.

"You just ask her," Holder said mockingly. He looked up and said, "MATHR, do you have any idea what these data readings are telling us?" He and the others rolled their eyes collectively, followed by patronizing glances toward Pristy—the intellectually challenged, way-too-young female captain.

When MATHR's voice blared forth from a staticky speaker overhead, Pristy shushed them. "Listen up. I want to hear this."

Lorg-Mav sensor disseminations are present within my data code lexicon.

"What does that mean?" Pristy said, thinking it sounded hopeful.

Holder, far more serious now, said, "MATHR, can you prompt this drone to passively scan surrounding space? Space beyond that of the Varapin and our own fleet?"

Optimally, the Lorg-Mav drone would operate better outside of *Starlight's* hull. Although, it has detected twenty-five cloaked vessels within relative proximity.

Pristy leaned back on her stool. "I need to talk to the Admiral. Keep working, boys. If that box can also allow us deep space comms, we may just have a chance to survive."

But MATHR wasn't finished.

In addition, the Lorg-Mav drone is capable of dynamic cloaking technology currently unavailable to known science within the Alliance.

Pristy slowly nodded. "Explains why nobody's ever gotten a good look at a Lorg-Mav starship."

Chapter 20

USS Jefferson
Perseus Arm of the Milky Way
US Space-Navy

Captain Galvin Quintos

We didn't want to stress the propulsion system. New drives, new reactors, new jump springs, new everything. So, we made a series of smaller jumps, five instead of the three we could have initiated. We chose an endpoint wormhole exit seven hundred light-minutes from the last known coordinates of the 9th Fleet, which came out to around eleven million, one hundred eighty-four thousand, six hundred eighty miles. Well out of long-sensor range of the Varapin, as well as any US Space-Navy asset.

At the tactical station, I saw Senior Chief Petty Officer Stanley Handly—*God, I'll never get used to that name*—suddenly tense. "I've got something, Captain."

I looked to the halo display and saw nothing. But considering that, these days, virtually all interstellar capable starships had some sort of cloaking capabilities, that wasn't all that surprising.

"Radiation trail. Change that—multiple radiation trails."

"The Varapin?" I said, feeling a sense of dread.

"No, Sir... these craft are spilling ridiculous radiation levels. Older vessels, that's for sure."

Bosun Johanna Polk said, "Regulations specify we immediately go to battle stations, Captain. We are in hostile territory; there are known enemy forces in this system, and—"

Hardy swung around to face the prim-and-proper-looking woman, "Look, dearie... back when I lived in lower Boston, my wife used to comment on my driving. You know, give me little helpful hints like how to maneuver our family hovercar on the road. I didn't like it then, and listening to you here, I don't like it now. Best you learn right off the bat. Cap's going to do what he's going to do... with or without your meddling."

The woman blanched; her lips pursed into a puckering kiss. "My job is to ensure proper protocol is adhered to. I might add, the Admiral himself has asked me to... assist the Captain with maintaining standardized fleet practices."

I couldn't help but smile. I didn't give two squats about Polk's meddling; she'd learn in time, my command style was unorthodox but seemed to work. What caught my interest, though, was that Hardy had been married. It struck me just how little I knew about my friend prior to him being this towering metal robot.

"It's okay, Hardy. I'm quite capable of fighting my own battles, even against such a formidable opponent as Bosun Polk." I gave Polk a quick wink and turned back to the halo display. "Tactical, how many vessels are you detecting? And yes, go to battle stations."

Before Handly could reply, Chen on Comms said, "We're

being hailed, Captain." He turned to look at me—his expression spoke volumes; it was as if he'd seen a ghost.

"What is it?"

"It's... it's Thunderballs."

Behind me and slightly to the right came an unsuccessfully restrained feminine giggle. Without turning around, I said, "Quartermaster Harper Vargos, I would appreciate a little decorum on my bridge."

"Sorry, Sir, but is that a real name? Thunderballs?"

Bemused, I shook my head. Ah, to be young and rambunctious again.

Before answering the hail, I contemplated a moment on good ol' Captain Cardinal Thunderballs. For lack of a better word, the man was a pirate. He'd been the leader of a ragtag fleet of miscreants and had been the self-imposed landlord of a once-Pleidian space structure called Ironhold Station. The man was charming in his own way, but it would be a grave mistake to turn your back on him.

He was quick of mind and a shrewd tactician. What I hadn't expected, while evicting him and his villainous tribe from Ironhold, was that he'd been keeping hostages, the most important of which was none other than Empress Shawlee herself, along with others of her royal covey. Enough to say, Thunderballs was a dark soul and was not someone to be idly trifled with.

"On screen," I said. "Let's see what the man has to say."

And there he was, bigger than life with a broad, mischievous smile. In his mid-thirties, he was an interesting-looking character. Long dark locks fell over one shoulder, while his goatee was neatly trimmed. From his splayed-open, white button-down shirt collar came his characteristic billowing thatch of dark brown chest hair. His shirt sleeves were rolled up, exposing muscular forearms that were equally hairy—like two unpruned garden hedges. I remembered this aspect; the guy was proud of his hairiness—his machismo.

He spread his arms wide. "My good friend Galvin... at last, we meet again. You are looking good... perhaps working out in that gymnasium on board *Hamilton?*"

"Different ship, Thunderballs. What are you doing here?" If I knew one thing for certain about the Pylor pirate, it was that he always had ulterior motives. He was not one to drop by for a cup of tea and idle talk about old times—he wanted something.

"Now, now. Is that any way to greet a comrade? Yes, I'll give you, we have a certain history together. And granted, Galvin, we haven't always seen things the same way—"

"You stormed and plundered Ironhold Station; you took hostages, killed innocents, and to top it all off, you abducted and abused the Pleidian Empress and her court."

"Much of that I dispute. But this is not the time to quarrel. I am here to offer a friend assistance, because dear Galvin... you do need my help."

"No, thank you. I suggest you move on, Thunderballs. Next time we cross paths, I won't be so amicable." It was then my internal auricular implants gently pinged. I heard Derrota's voice.

"Galvin, this is Stephan."

I was tempted to roll my eyes. His Mumbai-accented voice was like no one else on the ship.

"I wanted to tell you, sensors have yet to pick up on any nearby vessels. But the pirate's comms' signal strength is strong, indicating he is, in fact, quite close. I don't have proof of the matter, but I have a gut feeling he is not alone either."

That *was* concerning. A pirate ship or multiple pirate ships that were cloaked with a technology that even this upgraded high-tech dreadnought wasn't able to detect.

Thunderballs continued. "You're here as a shining knight...

here to rescue another one of your damsels in distress, no? Do not deny it, Galvin; I know all about young Captain Pristy, not to mention the ill-fated 9th Fleet." He placed a hand over his heart and made a sorrowful face. "I, too, am a lover, a romantic... so I will help you."

I felt my face go hot. Furtive glances from my bridgecrew darted in my directions. "You're mistaken. Now, what can you tell me about the disposition of the 9th Fleet?"

"You were smart to arrive at a distance... your arrival has yet to be detected by the Varapin."

It was the first time he'd referenced the Varapin by name, I noted. Perhaps he did know something about the situation after all.

"The hooded ghouls have laid the perfect trap, you know. Although, I would have thought your Admiral Billings would not have been snared so easily. I know you certainly would not have been... not the now infamous Captain Galvin Quintos who has bested the Grish on multiple occasions, the Varapin, even my own small contingent of independent freedom fighters."

A snort came from my left. It was my new Somalian JOOD, Awaale Samatar. He said under his breath, "So is that what marauders call themselves these days?"

I let the remark go, staying focused on Thunderballs. "Tell me what you came here to say, Thunderballs. No more games, no more idle conversation."

He feigned indignant surprise, then dropped the pretense. "Fine... I suppose I owe you that much. The two of us have a common goal in the matter."

"And that is?"

"I thought that was obvious... the destruction of that Varapin fleet. And perhaps, saving a few US Space-Navy warships in the process. But let me be perfectly frank, Galvin; you will not be able to destroy the enemy on your own."

I'd had enough of this. "We'll see—"

Thunderballs spoke over me. "The Varapin... they have a new toy. She's called *Oblivion*; it's what they refer to as a Rogue-Slaughter Class Battle Cruiser. Eight kilometers, five miles long. A beast of a ship." Thunderballs steepled his fingers. "Your *Jefferson*, I am sorry to say, will be no match for her."

For the first time, I was starting to believe at least some of what the arrogant pirate was saying. "The fighting—what is happening right now? What are the battle conditions?"

Cardinal Thunderballs laughed out loud at that. "The battle conditions? There are no battle conditions. The 9th Fleet no longer has the capability to defend itself. All of the warships have been ensnarled within a powerful dampening field. Their weaponry is dysfunctional; their communications capabilities are greatly hindered. What makes things worse is this could all have been avoided. Like little lambs to the slaughter, your fleet commander was all too culpable—"

"Enough with the blame game. What do you want? Look, I know you don't give a rat's ass about the Varapin or the well-being of US Space-Navy assets and crews."

"Galvin, you will need a fleet of warships to mount an attack on this enemy. An enemy that has set a trap specifically for you and that grand dreadnought of yours. And the bait, like flies stuck upon so many sticky fly strips, is the 9th Fleet."

"You've said as much."

Before I could continue, Stanley Handly at Tactical said, "Captain..." gesturing to the halo display. One by one, starships were disengaging their cloaking systems. As more and more of them came into view, I realized just how busy Thunderballs had been since I'd last seen him.

There were indeed twenty-five formidable-looking warships. Not a one of them, from my perspective, looked new, but they did look capable. Derrota passed me his tablet with meta-tag information attached to each vessel. There was an interstellar mix of three Pleidian, five Rolmp, two Zacairy, three Blork, two Thine, and three US Space-Navy warships. For the latter, they were all midsized battle cruisers that had seen better days. I reminded myself if I wasn't careful, a refurbished US Space-Navy dreadnought might just get added to this fleet.

"What do you want in return for your help?" I couldn't believe I was even asking the question. This pirate would just as soon stab me in the back if it suited him.

"We have visited the Pleidian Stoiling Build Base. We were cloaked, of course. We have spent many days, weeks actually, close by. All your communications back and forth to Fleet Command on Earth... to your dear Empress. Even inter-ship TAC-Band comms... all were being monitored."

I had a really, really bad feeling about what Thunderballs was going to say next.

"Simply put, I want the technology residing within your Quan-Tangler compartment."

He'd gone so far as to use the ridiculous interim name we'd given our transporter room. There'd have been no other means for him to know that stupid name unless he indeed had been eavesdropping on our internal comms.

"Look, Thunderballs... Cardinal... I'm not even supposed to have that tech. And it doesn't even work half the time. It's dangerous."

Thunderballs waved away the comment with a hand. "I know all this. Any new technology is rife with idiosyncrasies. I have my engineers, my scientists. They will work closely with your Thine... with Coogong."

Shit! He knows about Coogong too? This wasn't good. Still, I pondered the proposition.

As if on cue, Bosun Polk approached where Derrota, Hardy, and I were standing.

"You cannot be considering this, Captain. You would be violating interstellar agreements with the Alliance... not to mention disobeying direct orders from Admiral Block."

I smiled at the halo display and the patiently waiting pirate there. "One moment, Thunderballs." I sent a glance to Chen on Comms, and he got the message to mute our audio.

I turned my back to Thunderballs and addressed Derrota, Hardy, and the uninvited bosun Polk. "Options, people?"

Polk eyed Hardy, making a face, obviously not considering the ChronoBot a person.

Derrota looked to be thinking. He said, "Do we have a choice in the matter, Galvin? We can easily verify what the pirate leader has said... maybe transport a cloaked drone into that area of space."

"Good." I looked to Hardy. "You?"

"After that's verified, and I do believe Thunderballs is telling the truth, we should contact Admiral Block... see if he can send us additional ships."

"Totally unnecessary," Polk said. "I've been in contact with Fleet Command."

"Hold on. You contacted Fleet Command on your own?" I said, my ire rising.

Polk looked defiant. "It was part of the arrangement, Captain. You would not have been given this command without, um, certain assurances. The Admiral may very well be one of your biggest cheerleaders, but Block does not work within a vacuum. Everyone answers to the EUNF, including US Space-Navy Fleet Command."

"So, you're a what? A spy for Earth's United Nations Forces? Your loyalties should be to Space-Navy—"

Polk cut Derrota off, "My loyalties are to Space-Navy. But without the EUNF, funding gets cut off... ship-build contracts are terminated; military academy appropriations are diverted to other organizations. And I'm not a spy; I'm a referee. You may not like that I'm here, but without me making sure your Captain plays by the rules, we're all out of a job."

I said, "That's ridiculous. We're in the middle of a war; the last thing the EUNC wants to do is curtail Earth's ability to defend itself."

"With all due respect, Captain, you're not the only fish in the pond. There are multiple contracts already in the works; other dreadnought builds nearly completed. Alternate command crews soon to be assigned. And those individuals will be hand-picked by EUNC executives. The simple fact that you own this vessel, as you did *Hamilton*, is a burr under everyone's saddle... frankly, the EUNC has had enough."

She wasn't telling me anything I didn't already suspect. Of course there were new dreadnought builds. I didn't know how far along in the build process they were, but it made no difference. Here and now, this ship was what they had to work with.

"So, Bosun Polk, let me ask you... what do *you* suggest?" I counted off on one hand.

"One, we can turn around and let the 9th Fleet fend for itself. Two, we can attack, even though *Jefferson* would make little difference to the battle's outcome. It would be little more than a suicide mission. Three, we can accept Thunderballs' offer to fight the Varapin together, in trade for our transporter technology. Or four, we can attempt to negotiate with the Varapin directly. Because if what Thunderballs is telling us is true, it makes sense the Varapin are seeking the same damn thing... the transporter technology. And that's the reason for their baited trap. Apparently our closely guarded secret is not so secret."

The older woman raised her chin and narrowed her eyes. "It's not my job to make that sort of determination."

Derrota, Hardy, and I continued to stare at her.

"Well, you can't negotiate handing over military technology to the Varapin... to our enemy, that's obvious," she said. "And simply turning away from helping the 9th Fleet— well, that's an even more inconceivable suggestion. We could make a surprise attack. This is a remarkable warship... it's possible..." her words trailed off. She wasn't buying her own bullshit.

Hardy did one of his ridiculous-looking shrugs. "That leaves us working with the pirates, dear lady... unless you have another option up your sleeve."

Polk shot Hardy an icy glance. "There has to be another option. A fifth option."

"I'd love to hear it if you've got it," I said, looking contrite. The truth was, I actually did have another option but wasn't ready to talk about it yet. For now, we'd need to work with this despicable pirate, and I could tell Polk was coming around to that unsavory determination on her own.

I said, "Bosun Polk, you can return to your station." I looked to Hardy and then to Derrota. First one, then the other nodded. I faced the halo display. "Crewman Chen, unmute the channel, please."

Thunderballs raised his brows. "I see you have come to a decision, yes, Captain?"

"I have."

"And do we have a deal?"

I stared at the man, hating what I was about to say next. "Yes... but with nonnegotiable conditions."

"And what conditions would those be?" he said, his smile faltering.

"We'll give you a copy of the materials list and build schematics up-front, but not the operating software. That's delivered only after we've defeated the Varapin together."

Thunderballs looked to someone off-camera. Turning back, he let out a breath and nodded.

"And you agree to never, ever use this technology against *USS Jefferson* or the US Space-Navy or any of our allies, namely the Thine or the Pleiadeans. In effect, you will be choosing sides here, Thunderballs."

"I can agree to those conditions."

"One more thing. You will never acknowledge where you got this technology from. Is that understood?"

"Of course! It will be our little secret." The pirate winked and smiled broadly.

I felt sick to my stomach. It occurred to me I'd have to talk Coogong into working with Thunderballs—I didn't relish having that conversation.

"One more thing, Thunderballs. I want all your intel on the enemy and the current situation with the 9th Fleet. I suspect you have some kind of game plan in mind to defeat the enemy?"

"Oh, Captain, the strategy I have in mind is nothing short of breathtaking."

Terrific...

Chapter 21

The cloaked drone we sent into the battle area provided excellent information. That was before it was destroyed. Clearly, the US Space-Navy's cloaking capability was no longer state of the art. What we had learned, though, was that pretty much everything Thunderballs stated turned out to be true. What was left of the 9th Fleet was indeed trapped in some kind of powerful dampening field.

Now, only eighteen US Space-Navy warships remained from the original thirty-three. And what made things worse was, any attempt to make contact with any of our ships came back fruitless. That was a problem—a big problem. For Thunderballs' breathtaking—*his words, not mine*—plan to work, communication with Admiral Bennings was going to be imperative. Still, we'd have to move forward anyway and hope something broke our way in the process.

The plan, as it was, was for *USS Jefferson* to arrive in the system alone. Thunderballs assured me the Varapin had no clue his pirate fleet was present. Their cloaking technology was beyond even what the Varapin could detect. From there, we were to make contact with the CO of *Oblivion*, that Rogue-

Slaughter Class Battle Cruiser. I would feign ignorance as to what they wanted from me—our transporter tech. After heated debate, and nearly going to battle stations, I would agree to a deal similar to the one made with Thunderballs. And once the Varapin deactivated their dampening field as a sign of good faith, the pirate fleet would initiate its attack.

There were countless ways in which this plan could, and probably would, fail. I knew much of what was about to happen would require thinking on my toes. But I'd done that before—more times than I could count.

"Helm, are we prepared to jump?"

"Propulsion is ready... jump springs are charged; we have our manufactured wormhole endpoint locked in."

I made one last glance about the bridge. "Jump us into that system, Helm."

Arriving in a flash, along with the associated jump nausea hitting my stomach, we appeared within two hundred miles of the two warship fleets. On the halo display, I saw the US Space-Navy locked into place—unmoving and looking sadly vulnerable—caught within that invisible web. And, like a protective mother spider, there was *Oblivion*—like the sweep of a second hand around a clock face, the Varapin Rogue-Slaughter Class Battle Cruiser was slowly circling her quarry.

I looked to Chen at the comms station. He was to initiate communications with the 9th Fleet first thing. He turned to me and shook his head. "Nothing, Sir."

I gave it a few more moments, then said, "Okay, Comms... hail *Oblivion*."

Looking surprised, Chen said, "The vessel is already hailing us, Captain."

I stood and said, "Open the channel... on display."

I didn't think I would ever get used to any initial appearance of a Varapin. And this was not the first time I had made the correlation between the ghoulish-looking beings and the common characterization of a grim reaper. In this case, the Varapin commander was wearing a dark maroon robe. Deep within his oversized hood was an obsidian skeletal head. In stark contrast, his exposed jaws and pointed teeth were bone white. A glint of light reflected off two black, pea-sized eyes. He was hovering, never quite stationary. When he spoke, the rasp had the tone of two metal files scraping against each other.

"Ah, Captain Quintos... welcome to the party."

Terrific, a ghoul with a sense of humor. "Thank you. And please... who is it I am addressing?"

"I am First Warrior—what you would call an Admiral—Veesh Slat. But please, you can address me simply as Veesh... we are all friends here, no?"

"So, our arrival here was expected, I take it."

"Of course; you are the belle of the ball, as your human idiom would put it. Shall we get down to business? I so want to be done with all this drama."

"I already hate this guy," Hardy said under his breath.

"He's a real fucker," Derrota said just as quietly.

"You can start by releasing the hold you have on the 9th Fleet. Then... you go your way, we go ours... perhaps meet again to fight another day."

"If only it was as easy as that, Captain. You are outmatched... and then some. *Oblivion* was built with the intention and capability to destroy Earth's heavy dreadnought class warships such as USS *Jefferson*. You are outgunned by a factor of three. *Oblivion* can maneuver better, and our resilient shields can deflect virtually anything you fire upon her... yes, even those big broadsides of yours will have little impact."

"Well, talk is cheap. I've defeated every Varapin vessel I've ever come up against, and today will be no different. You do not want to go to war with me, First Warrior Veesh Slat. Maybe you should ask Conductor Sprin-Rop Kyber, or Haite Caheil, how well they've performed against me in the past... oh wait, I'm sorry... they're both dead, aren't they? I killed them."

It was no secret I had a unique way of getting under people's skin. I could be super irritating when I put my mind to it. In this case, since the Varapin didn't actually have skin, I'd gotten under his bony surfaces. And by the way Veesh was now looking back at me, I'd already accomplished a high degree of annoyance. *Good. Fuck him.*

In a calm, albeit still grating voice, he said, "Do you want to choose, or shall I?"

"Choose what?" But as soon as I asked the question, I already knew what he was referring to.

"How about I choose this one?" he said, sounding bemused.

The halo display split into two feeds, Veesh on the left and a view of the two fleets on the right.

"We've got three smart missiles leaving *Oblivion*," said Stanley Handly at tactical. "They're big... high-yield, fusion-tipped."

"Can you take them out?" I asked.

"No way, not with that dampening field in place. Be like shooting a beebee into Grandma's green pea soup."

I watched the trajectory of the three missiles. Fiery tongues of bright blue propelled them forward ever closer to their target. Together they moved as one, swerving in and out around other vessels—both US Space-Navy as well as Varapin warships. The sudden fireball explosion lit up all surrounding space but was short-lived as the vacuum of space deprived the flames of necessary oxygen.

"Tactical?" I said.

"A petite frigate, Sir."

Oh God, please no... I waited to hear if it had been *Starlight*, which I knew was Gail's ship—a petite frigate.

"It was the *Everest*, Sir."

Hardy said, "All lives lost, according to my sensors."

I looked at Veesh. "You'll regret that, Veesh. I promise you... you'll lament the day you ever laid your beady little eyes on me. Cut the feed," I spat, tasting bile in my mouth. I sat down and took in several measured breaths.

Derrota looked down at me, looking deflated. "Now that the enemy has shown they have the capacity to penetrate their own dampening field..." He shook his head. "I don't see how we could possibly bring an effective offensive against that kind of technology."

Hardy spoke before I could. "Don't give too much stock to that so-called technology. I imagine it took quite some time to build that house of cards."

I added to that, "And what does it take to bring down a house of cards?"

Derrota thought about that. "The removal of just one card... But this isn't a house of cards."

"Captain! Incoming hail, Sir."

"Tell First Warrior Veesh Slat we're still—"

"I'm sorry, Sir, but it's not him. Transmission's coming in via a Lorg-Mav RCHD."

Huh... that's weird, I thought. What was a Lorg-Mav reconnaissance and communications hubs drone doing way the hell out here? I looked to Hardy. "Anything you can determine from that signal?"

"A Lorg-Mav's RCHD is ridiculously advanced... I hadn't picked up on its presence here in system. And I suspect, nor did the Varapin or your Pylor pirate friends."

The thought occurred to me that though the Lorg-Mav were always neutral when it came to interstellar conflicts, they were so reclusive that few knew what they looked like. Any ship that ventured into their spatial territory, even by accident, would

USS Jefferson

find itself atomized into space dust—no discussion, no apologies accepted.

Stanley Handly at Tactical was looking back at me. "What is it, Senior Chief Petty Officer?"

"If you were wondering... this is not their territory, not even close."

Actually, I knew that. We were light-years from their remote little enclave of space.

"Open the channel, Mr. Chen," I said and pointed to the halo display.

Hardy was the first one to speak. "That's definitely not a Lorg-Mav... they supposedly have five ears."

Hardy had said the obvious since I was looking at the concerned face of one Captain Gail Pristy.

"Captain! Oh God... I can't believe we've gotten through to you."

I saw that she was sitting alongside others of her crew in a dark compartment, one that was not *Starlight's* bridge. "How..."

"Shut up and listen!" Her features softened a bit. "Sorry, but time is of the essence. We picked up this Lorg-Mav drone a while ago and it's allowing us, and apparently only us, the ability to get word out to you."

Looking overly excited, the young tech sitting to Gail's left said, "Thing's flipping amazing. It's an advanced comms hub, a spy drone; it has cloaking capabilities up the wazoo, and get this: it can project complete faux ship signatures that even your bad boy of a ship's sensors wouldn't be able to decipher as fake."

Gail, looking annoyed, cut in, "Listen, Captain, we're able to pick up everyone's comms channels with this thing—the Varapin and the Pylor pirates'. Captain... you're being played. Thunderballs has no intention of allying with you."

I stared back at her. "You're sure of this?"

"Yes, I'm sure! We just listened to Thunderballs and Veesh

Slat. As of twenty minutes ago, you won't just be going up against the Varapin; you'll be going up against Thunderballs' degenerates as well."

I thought about what she was telling me. "Have you told Admiral Billings yet?"

"No. Was just about to do just that." She waited and then gave me a sideways look. "I do need to tell the fleet commander about this, Captain."

"Of course you do."

"But?" she said, her thin brows knitting together.

Bosun Polk was already out of her seat and approaching the captain's mount—heading right toward me like a runaway train.

"Sit back down, Bosun!" I ordered.

We held each other's gaze for several long moments before she relented, turned on her heel, strode back the way she'd come, and dropped back into her seat. She crossed her arms over her ample breasts and glared.

I turned and held up a palm to Gail. My mind was racing to catch up with the situation at hand. Yes, Gail should be talking to her superior officer. An officer that, now that *Jefferson* had entered the system, was also my superior officer. But... this was a different kind of situation. There were all kinds of deceptions and misdirections afoot. Simply put, playing by the rules was out of the question. Could get everyone dead. This was my kind of game; nobody could deceive and misdirect like I could. Nobody could break the rules like I could.

I turned to Derrota and Hardy. "If you had that hub here... could you analyze it?"

"Sure," they both said at the same time.

Gail, looking concerned, continued to stare.

I said, "As of this minute... the PE3, the Quan-Tangler, is it operational?"

Hardy's face display turned to a cluster of animated spinning gears. "Maybe."

Derrota was already shaking his head. "I'm already a step ahead of you. No way, Galvin. Transporting that RCHD from *Starlight* to *Jefferson* would be no problem if the Quan-Tangler is in fact operational at this moment, but the signal would not go unnoticed by the Varapin. They'd see that something had been transported. Maybe not right away, but their Varapin AI tech would decipher that quantum entanglement anomaly at a molecular level... and it just might get *Starlight*, well... obliterated."

I hadn't thought of that. Veesh Slat had already demonstrated his total lack of compassion. I said, "How long?"

Derrota's confusion at my question turned to clarity. "Before the Varapin deciphered what had happened?"

I nodded.

"That's an abstract question. No way of knowing."

"How long would it take you, Hardy?" I asked.

"My inner LuMan is more advanced than that AI piece of—"

"Just throw out a number, a time frame!"

"It would take me eight minutes on a good day. Thirteen on a not-so-good day. It would take the ghouls fifteen, at least, probably twenty minutes."

I looked to Derrota, who shrugged. "But I still don't get the advantage of doing this."

"It's because you're not as devious as he is," Gail said, looking annoyed.

I said, "Captain Pristy, what is your crew complement at present?"

She leaned back as if smelling something stale. "*Starlight's* a small ship." She said it defensively. "And we've lost crew in the battle."

"How many, Gail?"

She closed her eyes then opened them again. "Down to eighty-three. No, eighty-four."

I looked at Derrota.

"NO! No way. Not within fifteen to twenty minutes."

"Why? You have four PE2 pedestals that can operate simultaneously. That's twenty-one transports. Let's say it takes twenty—no, we'll give it thirty seconds to move each batch over here into our Quan-Tangler compartment. That's..."

Hardy said, "Ten minutes and thirty seconds."

"So, we'd have five to ten minutes to spare," I said.

Gail was already shaking her head. "Absolutely not! I am the Captain of this vessel, and I am not going to abandon my ship on the whim of another captain's clearly reckless plan! And don't forget, I don't report to you anymore! Admiral Billings is the damn fleet commander here, Galvin!"

She was clearly mad. Which was understandable. But I was ready for her objections. "Bosun Polk, would you please approach the captain's mount?"

Reaching us, she looked tentative and a little unsure. "Captain?"

"You are well versed with the current US Space-Navy rules and regulations manual?"

"I am," she said, her interest perking up.

"Can you tell me... who is the commanding officer during an active battle situation?"

"Without getting bogged down in a lot of rules and regulations techno-talk, it would ultimately be the ranking US Space-Navy officer, such as a fleet commander, in this case, Billings, of course."

Gail responded with an *I told you so* smirk.

"And what if communications lines to, um, say that fleet commander, were disrupted for an indefinite period of time?"

"I don't like this, Captain," the bosun said. "There could be mitigating factors to take into account. But it's called a shift immediate superior in command, or an ISIC. And it would depend on any orders given prior to the comms going down."

"Let's say that no specific order was given addressing a captain's necessity to abandon her ship. And that doing so would actually be for the greater good of the entire fleet."

Bosun Polk looked like she'd eaten a bug. "Well... unless otherwise previously stipulated by a fleet commander, such as Admiral Billings, authority would have to go to the next highest-ranking officer who was within direct communication to the subordinate service personnel."

"In other words, as of right now, as far as Captain Pristy is concerned, I am the commanding officer?"

Gail was already speaking up. "No. I could just as easily have contacted Admiral Billings. So, this is all moot. And I'm not abandoning my ship! And remember, I know just how quirky that transporter thing can be."

"Captain Pristy... Gail... do you trust me? Would I do anything to endanger you and your crew if it wasn't absolutely essential?"

She looked back at me with a measured stare. "Well, you don't always have the best judgment. But no, I suppose you wouldn't."

"I honestly don't see how we're going to come out on top here. Not unless I'm allowed to—"

"Cheat, swindle, and bamboozle your way to a win?" Gail said mockingly.

"Well?" I prompted.

"This better not slap back at me. And I'll be following your orders with objections... I have witnesses."

"Noted."

"Just know, I'll be the last of the crew to leave *Starlight*."

Chapter 22

The *Jefferson* was now being hailed by both Thunderballs and First Warrior Veesh Slat. I had instructed Chen to relay that I was in conference and would get back to them within two hours. Even that amount of time would be cutting things close.

I stood at the front of the Quan-Tangler compartment as the first of *Starlight's* crew began transporting over. Hardy was at the controls with instructions to closely monitor the system for any anomalies—initial outgoing transport readings and incoming readings, a checksum kind of analysis, exact down to a molecular level. Thus far, the Quan-Tangler was performing flawlessly.

Four *Starlight* crewmembers were now taking shape in front of me in a rapid, block-by-block segment transition that took mere seconds to complete. Having successfully transported, the three young men and one woman looked at each other, clearly relieved to have survived the process. After some nervous laughter and exhalations of breaths, I greeted them by individual names and ranks. I returned their salutes and, realizing the thirty-second clock was ticking, gestured for them to hurry and step off of their respective pedestals. I introduced them to Awaale Samatar, my JOOD. He would be in charge of new crew orientations, assigning of quarters or barracks, and specific job assignments here on *Jefferson*.

Already the next set of *Starlight* crew was transporting in. I looked to Hardy. "You got this?"

"Absolutely."

I turned to Samatar. "And you? You'll greet each arrival by name and rank... welcome them aboard."

"Yes, Sir. Have no worries; this is what I do..."

I hurried from the Quan-Tangler compartment and headed for the GravLifts. I had a lot to do and little time to do it. When I entered the Deck 23 LabTech area, still ungodly cold, I found Coogong and several other scientists working on the Lorg-Mav's RCHD, which had been transported over prior to any of *Starlight's* crew.

"Talk to me, Coogong."

From within his Ambiogell-filled helmet, Coogong's warm smile greeted me. "Captain, we have indeed made progress." He gestured with a twig-like Tendril Albicon construct finger toward the RCHD¬, which was spread open, exposing all of its inner technology. Tiny lights blinked on and off while hundreds of clear connecting tubes throbbed with multicolored light pulses.

"Looks complicated," I said.

"Complicated, and at the same time, all so elegantly simple."

"So... you have it figured out?"

Coogong shook his head. "I'm afraid it would take far longer than the half hour you've given me for that. But I do have many of the fundamental principles—"

"Coogong, sorry to be abrupt here, but pretty much everything depends on you being able to duplicate this tech... and fast."

"I'm afraid I would need days, perhaps weeks, to do as you have asked. I am sorry, Captain."

I stared at the complex blinking lights within the open cube. There had to be something, some way to duplicate this technology without having to reinvent the wheel. *Wait... could it work?* "The Quan-Tangler makes an exact molecular copy of original matter that is to be transported, and nearly simultaneously, it destroys the original matter."

Coogong said, "I see where you are going with this. You want to use the transporter as a basic copy machine. Unfortunately, the Quan-Tangler has many new safeguards in place that would make doing so impossible."

I rubbed at my forehead. I could feel the minutes, the seconds ticking by.

"Although..." Coogong said. "We do have the original Sir Louis de Broglie prototype on board. That thing has little in the way of safeguards... a deathtrap if you ask me." He looked over my shoulder, past me. "It's in the lab area next door. I do believe it is operational to some degree."

I could have kissed the Thine alien right then and there. I smiled. "Okay... button this RCHD¬ up and make sure it's fully operational. I'll need as many copies as you can make. Whatever it takes, do it. If you need more bodies in here, I'll assign them. Please get to work."

I contacted Hardy. "Status?"

"Eighty-three of *Starlight* crew have successfully transported over."

"Eighty-three, not eighty-four?"

"Captain Pristy has yet to arrive. I've contacted her, and she promises she'll be ready soon."

USS Jefferson

Dammit! "Tell me the Varapin have yet to detect the transporter signals."

Hardy hesitated. "We're well beyond the time frame I would have been able to do just that. Let's just hope *Oblivion's* AI's not on its game today."

That wasn't likely. "With or without her go-ahead, I want you to transport her over to *Jefferson* in two minutes."

"Copy that."

I cut the connection. Derrota was hailing me. "Go ahead, Stephan."

"Are you sitting down?"

"No, I'm not sitting down; I'm on the GravLift."

"I know what happened on the Symbio deck."

"Wait, with everything going on, you're calling me about—"

"Just listen, Galvin..."

Bewildered, I did just that—and then I proceeded to get angrier with every word he spoke. Afterward, I cut the connection with Derrota and contacted Samatar. "I need you to assemble my senior officers—Captain Ryder, Science Officer Derrota, Captain Pristy when she arrives on ship, Hardy, Chief Mattis, Bay Chief Mintz, Doc Viv, Chief Porter, and Chaplain Trent. Get Colonel Drake Bonell, as well as Sergeant Max Dryer and his crew there. And have my brother Eric attend as well."

Samatar said, "Yes, Sir. And Senior Chief Petty Officer Stanley Handly? He is your acting XO, no?"

"Fine, Stanley Handly too. Have everyone get to the captain's conference room at once... chop chop, Samatar."

By the time I got to the captain's conference room, it was already filling up. At not seeing Gail there, a feeling of dread caught me by surprise. I took a seat at the head of the table, closed my eyes, and tried to assemble my thoughts. Two minutes later, when I opened them again, most of the seats were taken.

All eyes were upon me. Both Hardy and Gail Pristy were not in attendance.

"Okay, everyone, thank you for coming on such short notice."

The hatch door slid open, and Captain Gail Pristy stormed through like a hurricane. Hardy entered moments behind and took up a position at the back of the room, next to Sergeant Max Dryer and his Marines. Gail looked for an open seat, making no effort to hide her inner rage, and plopped down directly to my right. She had yet to make eye contact with me. I could hear her barely contained heavy breathing.

Stanley Handly gasped. Pointing to the room's halo display, we all took in the feed. Two missiles had emerged from *Oblivion*. Tracking their trajectory, there was no doubt as to their intended target. The explosion flash made everyone tense in their seat. *Starlight* was no more.

"No lives lost," Hardy said.

I looked to my right and caught Gail's eye.

Under her breath, she said, "I sure fucking hope you know what you're doing."

"Me too..."

I took in the room and saw the anticipation in the eyes of my senior officers. "To say we are at a disadvantage here is a gross understatement. We have very little time to get a hell of a lot done." I looked to Handly. "Why don't you give us all a current state of affairs, Mr. Handly?"

"Currently, the 9th Fleet is immobile, held within a Varapin dampening field. Of the original thirty-three US Space-Navy warship assets, only eighteen, sorry, seventeen, now remain viable."

All eyes went to Gail, who kept her expression impassive.

Handly continued, "The Varapin have a total of thirty-five warships, including that Rogue-Slaughter Class Battle Cruiser,

Oblivion. The only good news regarding the current affairs with the Varapin is that as long as that dampening field is in place, their ships are also being kept stationary... although they do still have communications and access to their weaponry, where the 9th Fleet does not."

"And the Pylor pirates?" I asked.

"On their own, their twenty-five mismatched warships would not be a problem for *Jefferson*. Although they do have excellent cloaking capabilities. Add them to the already overwhelming advantage of the Varapin... well, suffice to say, we are at a colossal disadvantage here."

"Thank you, Mr. Handly." Once more I took in the faces around me. And then I smiled. "We're already screwed, folks... come on, we can admit it. Right?"

Nods were unanimous around the table. Nobody else saw the humor though.

"So, who here would like to mix things up a little? Come on. If we're already screwed, why not really screw with the enemy... both enemies?"

Now there were a few reluctant smiles. Gail was not one of them though.

My TAC-Band was practically vibrating off my wrist. Glancing down, I saw it was the bridge: persistent incoming hails from both First Warrior Veesh Slat and Thunderballs. *They can both wait.*

"First, we have an internal issue that must be dealt with. Later, you'll see how it relates. Stephan, you have the floor."

Derrota stood. Not comfortable speaking to a crowd, he fidgeted with his tablet. When he looked up, he said, "As most of you know, thanks to the generosity of Empress Shawlee, we have a new crew recreation area up on Decks 72/73."

"Really?" Wanda said.

Derrota said, "Um, it's still being tested." He looked down at his tablet then back up again. "Taking place on what we're calling the Symbio deck; it's a kind of medieval quest game. There are knights and bandits, peasants and fairies. And a castle we haven't gotten to yet."

"Really, and what... we peons aren't allowed up there to play?" Grip said, looking genuinely hurt.

It was then that I noticed Hardy, still wearing his uniform, was covering his breast pocket with one hand as if he was saying the Pledge of Allegiance. But I knew what the robot was really doing—he was keeping that damn fairy from peeking its head out from the top of his pocket. I made a mental note to talk to Hardy about bringing pets to work with him.

Derrota continued, "What we came to notice quickly was that this supposedly fun and safe interactive game was anything but safe."

"Now I really want to play," Wanda said.

"I just couldn't let it go," Derrota said. "I know enough about AI programming to discern proper code algorithm context. I kept thinking, how could Eric have lost his hand like that in battle?"

Wanda said, "I think I need a cigarette."

Ignoring her, Derrota said, "Any of us could have just as easily been hurt or killed. The game was too dangerous—hell, it was downright murderous!"

Derrota's eyes moved from Eric over to Chaplain Trent.

"Go on," I said.

"With Chief Mattis' help, I went back and reviewed all the security tapes. It took a while, but we saw that certain files had been deleted. But MATHR is very efficient. She keeps backups of backups, which most people aren't even—"

"Stephan, we're on a tight schedule here," I coaxed.

"Anyway, we have him dead to rights, sitting at the Deck 72/73 Symbio-Poth administrator's console." Derrota tapped at his tablet, and the halo display showed what was obviously a security feed with a running time-code stamp. And there Chaplain Trent sat with Ensign Plorinne beside him at a workstation. I already knew the young Pleidian certainly knew his way around Pleidian computer code, but I had to admit I was shocked to see the young Ensign sitting there.

Heads turned in the direction of Chaplain Trent.

His face darkened into a deep shade of red. But the chaplain glowered back at those now scrutinizing him. "This is obviously a setup. Can't you see? You all know it. Quintos hates me. That feed has been doctored; can't you see what is happening here?"

Derrota spoke over him, "The two of them altered the game's security measures. Basically, all safeguards were removed."

"Cockypock!" Trent bellowed.

"Add to that, Captain Quintos and his brother Eric's biosignatures were set to be specifically targeted. Targeted for kill-level aggression on the part of the game's various Symbio-Poth opponents. Including the dragons."

"Oh, no way! There are dragons!?" Wanda exclaimed.

I had already heard all this from Derrota while back in the GravLift; my mind was still on Ensign Plorinne. It saddened me the young crewmember was involved with this. I'd be speaking with him as soon as time permitted.

Chaplain Trent was up on his feet now and wagging a finger in my direction. "Fine! Yes, I did it!" he stammered. "It was time you got what was coming to you, Quintos. If it wasn't for you, the fleet's most dedicated, finest captain, and my dear, dear friend, would still be alive." Tears were now running down the man's lined face. "You killed my Eli... you!" He looked up as if talking to God himself, "Judge me not, Father, for my actions have been long overdue and are holy and righteous!"

I nodded to Chief of Security Mattis, who stood and made

his way over to the now-babbling incoherently Chaplain Trent. Once he was escorted from the room, I said, "Thank you, Stephan."

While Derrota took his seat, Doc Viv and Eric both got to their feet. She said, "I think we should attend to the man. Obviously, he's not well."

Captain Wallace Ryder offered a crooked smile from the opposite side of the table. "As entertaining as that was, do we really have time for all this?"

I said, "I think it's all about kismet."

That even got Gail to look at me.

"If this craziness with the good chaplain had not taken place, then what I'm going to propose next wouldn't have popped into my mind."

"And what's that?" Ryder said.

"We're going to even the odds, or, at the very least, attempt to even the odds."

Up on the halo display was a full-screen view of *Oblivion*. "That there is one hell of a warship, people. Close to five miles in length and packed with an assortment of weaponry, I can't imagine any US Space-Navy warship having the capability to match it... including *USS Jefferson*." I looked about the room. "And we're going to board that ship and make it our own."

"Really... just like that?" Gail said, not looking amused. "And with what warship assets... what army?"

I splayed my palms out to the room. "*Jefferson* and... those dragons of ours."

I waited for the laughter to die down. "Look, we have the one thing that everyone wants. Transporter technology. Sure, it has its quirks, but it will be a total game-changer for modern warfare. The Varapin know it, and the Pylor pirates know it. The secret's out—has been since *Hamilton* used it to help defeat that Varapin fleet months ago."

USS Jefferson

Chief Porter raised a hand, not unlike a third grader. "So, now that the transporter thing is working, why don't we just deliver a number of fusion or nuclear bombs into each of the enemy bridges? Set a timer and kaboom!"

Derrota answered that one, "The simple answer, Craig, is that it doesn't work. We tested that option back on *Hamilton* a number of times. Something about the quantum entanglement process... it deactivates the nuclear chain reaction. Self-sustaining critical mass cannot be achieved. No steady rate of spontaneous fission, which causes the necessary proportionally steady level of neutron activity."

I added, "What we'd be doing, in effect, is delivering perfectly fine munitions right into our enemies' laps. There may be a solution, but we haven't figured it out yet."

"Fine. Can we get back to the dragon reference?" Porter asked.

"Craig, you saw them. Those Symbio-Poth dragons. What havoc they are capable of. I've done some research. We have six of them left up on Decks 72/73. We're going to unleash those beasts on the Varapin... we're going to make those floating ghouls rue the day they ever entered this war."

Sergeant Max laughed, "So... we're going to use the transporter to what? Send the dragons over onto that ship?"

Few others saw the humor. And even fewer seemed to be acknowledging the genius of my plan.

"Perhaps you should go over your complete strategy, Captain," Stanley Handly suggested. "Because while we're sending dragons over to *Oblivion*, we still have two enemy fleets to contend with."

A lot of cross talk murmuring had erupted, and it took me standing up and shushing them to get their attention. "Look, there *is* a plan. And yes, it's unconventional, to say the least. Thanks to Captain Pristy here, we now have in our possession a

Lorg-Mav's RCHD. As we speak, hundreds of these drones are being duplicated."

"Why? What do they do?" Ryder asked.

"Glad you asked," I said. "In addition to having advanced comms and variable cloaking capabilities, they can project faux, highly deceptive warship signatures."

"Meaning what?" Ryder pressed.

"Meaning we're going to specially equip your Arrow Fighter squadrons. Each will have an RCHD on board. Each will have a semi-cloaked signature of a US Space-Navy battle cruiser or a heavy destroyer or a gunship... perhaps even another dreadnought such as *Jefferson*."

"A fleet of fake ships."

"*Jefferson* will have its hands full taking out Thunderballs' pirate ships. So, we'll need our fleet of fake ships, as you call them, to buy us time until we take *Oblivion*. More importantly, I'm hoping the Varapin will be forced to confront this new fleet."

"Which will force them to abandon their hold on the 9th Fleet!" Ryder said. "And we shouldn't forget, Arrow Fighters can do a good bit of damage; they won't just be decoys."

Colonel Drake Bonell said, "And I take it that's why I'm here, Captain?"

I said, "Yes, you and your military units will be infiltrating *Oblivion*. How many boots will you be able to deploy for the siege?"

"That's the problem, Captain; we don't have a full complement of Marines for this deployment. We have four hundred and thirty men and women ready for combat, though."

That was significantly less than what I had been counting on—but it would have to do. "If it is acceptable to you, I'd like to have Max's team assigned to take *Oblivion's* bridge."

"I figured as much, you having them here attending this

meeting," the colonel said, not looking thrilled at having his authority in the matter somewhat circumvented.

Once again, the cross talk had started, only this time it was constructive—teams would need to work together; implementation of the various attacks had to be synchronized.

"This meeting is adjourned. I'll expect tactical plans submitted back to me within one hour."

"Seriously? One hour?" Bonell said, looking dumbfounded. "You want a four-hundred-plus ship-to-ship tactical siege plan constructed in an hour?" He'd raised his voice, which put a stop to the cross talk within the conference room.

I looked at the colonel, who easily had twenty years on me. "Do you want me to ask First Warrior Veesh Slat and Cardinal Thunderballs for a little more time, Colonel? I'm sure they'd like you to have all the time you need before they start taking out the rest of the 9th Fleet."

The colonel regarded me with a sobering stare.

"I'm sorry. I know what I'm asking you; all of it is beyond acceptable. But we were given a crappy hand, people. We have to play the cards we have... and do our best to save the lives of our fellow US Space-Navy personnel. Now, let's get to work... right now, I need to buy us some time."

Chapter 23

As the meeting started to break up, Captain Pristy stood and placed a hand on my forearm. "Captain, can I steal a moment of your time?"

"Of course. But first, I'd like to say, again, I'm sorry. Yanking you and your crew off of your ship like that was, frankly, brutish and bullying. Seeing it destroyed must have been a hard pill to swallow."

"You're right; it was. And it made me look bad in front of my crew."

I nodded; she was right.

Hardy had stayed behind with his back against a bulkhead—observing, listening. He nodded, his face display making his swirling flushing toilet animation with accompanying gurgling noises. I ignored him.

"With that said, I'm glad you did it." She eyed Stanley Handly, who was also hanging back while others filed out, waiting to talk to me.

"I have no right to ask this of you, and I'm sure you'll say no... but I want my old job back. I want to be your XO again. I wasn't ready... I wasn't ready to command a warship."

"Bullshit. Gail, you were ready months ago. But you were handed an obsolete frigate that should have been mothballed years ago and a crew that, well... needed discipline. You want your job back; you've got it. I'd be honored to have you as my second again... but only until your next command becomes available."

She looked unsure about that but smiled. "Thank you." Her eyes went to Stanley Handly. "Um, what about him? Isn't he your acting XO?"

"Yeah, well, life's not a bed of roses; best he finds that out now. I'll talk to him. He's competent. Perhaps he can work the tactical board with you? I'd like you to take a more active role with the battle plans we're implementing."

"Of course."

"Stay here," I said and waved Handly over.

"Sir?"

"Captain Pristy will be resuming her position as my XO. I don't want any hard feelings, and I don't want any drama. You'll be working alongside each other at Tactical."

The man swiped at his thinning hair, not doing a very good job at hiding his indignation. "Fine, Sir. Welcome, Cap—I mean, XO Pristy."

Gail said, "There's still the issue of Admiral Billings... Fleet Commander Admiral Billings. You have the RCHD here on board. There's no justifiable reason for not contacting him, is there?"

There wasn't. And this wouldn't be the first time I'd breached military conventions. Bypassed proper lines of command hierarchy. Do the right thing and get my superior officer involved, or do the thing that would most likely work to get us all out of this mess? But I had to ask myself, would Billings be willing to do what had to be done? Would he be willing to send fucking dragons onto an enemy ship to lure away scores of Varapin warriors?

I didn't see it. I knew it wasn't my job to second-guess my superior officer—that wasn't how the military worked. And I knew all this. But knowing what I was supposed to do wasn't enough to convince me to toe the US Space-Navy line. Someday I would have to pay the price for my arrogance. But that day wouldn't be today.

Gail must have seen my inner struggle—my dilemma. She said, "I suppose the damn thing is unreliable at best. Especially the RCHD's comms aspect. I know I tried reaching out to the Admiral... a number of times."

Of course, that was total BS, but I wasn't going to dispute her personal account of what happened.

My TAC-Band was vibrating again and looking at it, I saw I was needed on the bridge right now.

THE FOUR OF US ENTERED THE BRIDGE—Handly, Gail, Hardy, and me. Up on the halo display were two feeds; one was that of First Warrior Veesh Slat, the other, Cardinal Thunderballs.

Chen said, "They can't see or hear us; both are adamant they be put through to you, Sir."

While I took my seat at the captain's mount, Hardy made himself comfortable standing to my right. Both Handly and Gail took seats at the tactical station in front of me. I considered my two opponents. Both wanted to make a deal, but only one was being two-faced about it—Thunderballs. I found it hard to even look at the man, knowing what he had done to Shawlee and her sister back on Ironhold Station. *I may just have to kill you, asshole.*

"Go ahead. Put the Pylor pirate through."

USS Jefferson

"Finally! Captain Quintos, you certainly know how to play hard to get. Are you having second thoughts about our... arrangement?"

"Not at all. I do have a ship to command. And there was that matter of two 9th Fleet vessels being blown to space dust."

The marauder feigned a look of sympathy. "I am sorry... although my science officer tells me there were, how do I say, suspicious molecular distortions in the area of that ship just prior to her demise. Would those have been the result of, say, quantum entanglement anomalies at a molecular level? Such as those created by a transportation device?" His eyes lowered, taking in the very much alive Gail Pristy sitting not two paces in front of me.

I caught Chen's eye and made a subtle gesture. Chen now had both feeds open, and while Veesh Slat would now have an open feed into *Jefferson's* bridge, he could also see the feed from Thunderballs. Something the pirate was unaware of.

"And your previous offer still stands, Thunderballs? That you'll assist us in our fight against the Varapin... trick them into thinking you'll be fighting on their side?"

His smile faltered. Looking confused and taken aback, Thunderballs slowly shook his head. "I don't know what..."

"So, I see the real truth. Thunderballs... your deceit will cost you. Evidently, humans will side with one another even when there is no chance of victory. So be it!"

I held up a hand. "Now hold on, First Warrior. I have no deal, no agreement with this man. And you're right; he's a scoundrel. You can see he can't be trusted. As you may well know, he and I have history. We are not friends. So, if you still want the transporter technology... in trade for letting the 9th Fleet leave this system unaccosted, I'm ready to move forward with that."

"I protest! First Warrior, can you not see Quintos is playing us against each other?"

As the Varapin commander and Pylor pirate continued to exchange angry words, I caught Chen's eye. He and I had not strategized any of this beforehand. And that was the beauty of working with an amazing bridgecrew, one that could read a situation and could anticipate what one another were thinking. Chen was not the most animated of fellows, but I did see the corners of his lips turn up. And while this apple cart was thrown into disarray, I was buying valuable seconds for my officers to strategize battle plans. Would the Varapin and Pylors come together in the end? Of course. But for now, I was readying for battle.

I knew I had to bring Admiral Billings into the mix now. I was less worried about my own career than I was for my subordinate officers. I'd come to terms a long time ago with my tendency for insubordination and maybe even dereliction of duty. I played by my own rules, and the day was rapidly approaching where my time as a US Space-Navy Captain would be coming to an end. I was also keenly aware my freewheeling actions were not so different than that of a Pylor pirate—although I certainly did have a high moral compass. My actions were always for the good of the country and Earth. But if there was to be blowback, I wanted it to rest solely on my shoulders, not on Gail or Derrota or anyone else's.

Hardy and I entered the Quan-Tangler compartment where Coogong stood alone, awaiting our arrival. I'd contacted him twenty minutes earlier, giving him a head's-up on my plan.

"Ah, Captain Quintos, Hardy..."

"Coogong," I said. "I trust the transporter is still operational."

The Thine scientist eyed Hardy, who was now out of uniform—his highly polished metal construct glistening under the overhead lighting. He did still wear a black leather vest though—something I was sure was from that costume shack at the entrance to the Symbio deck. A vest that conveniently had a small breast pocket just large enough to accommodate a small Symbio-Poth fairy named Iris. We all had our idiosyncrasies. I let it go for now.

"Yes, Captain... the device is working surprisingly well. I might go as far as to say we have gotten the kinks out of the design."

"Good to hear since the two of us will be making use of it."

I took up a position on one of the four lightly glowing pedestals as Hardy took up a position on the one next to me. I looked to Coogong at the controls. "Please put us right outside of the bridge, within his heavy battle destroyer."

Gail entered the Quan-Tangler compartment. "You should know, Veesh Slat and Thunderballs have been making nice with one another. You'll have less time than we'd guesstimated."

"Understood. Take care of my ship while I'm gone."

"If Billings decides to keep you—"

"That's not going to happen," I said. I looked to Coogong. "You just be ready to bring me back. Absolutely no tinkering with this damn thing while you're waiting. Is that understood?"

"Of course, Captain," said Coogong, offering a slight bow of his head. "Quansporting now..." he said.

Really? Quansporting... that's what he's calling it? But no sooner had the question reached my frontal lobes than we were being de-segmented and then re-segmented onto the main corridor of *USS Goliath*.

We'd quansported, *ugh*, in front of five astonished-looking crewmembers. Mouths agape, they stood momentarily paralyzed at our sudden appearance. As recognition set in, both

Hardy and I were easily recognized within the US Space-Navy.

"Captain?" a young first Lieutenant said, remembering to salute a senior officer.

"At ease," I said. I gestured to the bridge. "The Admiral's on the bridge?"

The crewman next to her, still looking awestruck by the seven-foot-tall ChronoBot, said, "Uhh, yeah... I mean, yes, Sir."

Hardy and I entered the *Goliath's* bridge, a much smaller version than that of *Jefferson*. Here, there were two captain's mounts situated forward within the compartment. As with my own bridge, there was a CIC department off to the left and a hatch door to the right that led to the captain's, or maybe the Admiral's ready room.

As more and more of the bridgecrew stirred, turning in their seats, eventually the ship's skipper, Captain Lugano, and Admiral Billings spun in their seats to see what all the commotion was about.

Hardy said, "Be weird having an Admiral sitting next to you all day like that."

Hardy was certainly right about that, but the ChronoBot had said it a little too loud.

Billings was the first to stand. "Captain Quintos!"

I wasn't sure at this point if that was a loud recrimination or a welcome. I said under my breath, "Be good, Hardy. No antics, okay?"

His face display was now a portrait of his younger self. *Good, some normalcy.*

"Good day, Admiral. I apologize for dropping in uninvited."

"Apologize? I am ecstatic!" He gestured to the forward halo display, which was emanating little more than gray static. "We've been in a total communications blackout for days now! The fleet's immobilized... crippled."

"Yes, Sir."

"So... you transported over to the *Goliath,* Captain? I didn't think the thing was fully operational."

"Quansported," Hardy said, correcting the older man.

"Sir," I said, giving Hardy a warning glance, "I felt it imperative we make direct contact. That the risk was warranted."

"Excellent. What can you tell us? Give me a sit-rep."

I shot a glance about the bridge.

"Yes... let's head on into the ready room. I'm sure you have much to tell me." He half-turned to Captain Lugano, "You have the conn, Captain."

Lugano looked momentarily crestfallen by what I took as being a contemptuous brush-off. Billings really was an ass. Following behind the Admiral, I shot Hardy another warning scowl as he cut short his flushing toilet animation.

The Admiral took up a stooped stance behind his desk. The man's uniform looked oversized on his thin, frail-looking frame. It occurred to me the fleet commander was possibly ill. With that said, his eyes were bright and alive. "Talk to me, Quintos... no bullshit; there's no time for any of that."

I noticed the Admiral's eyes had locked onto Hardy's vest pocket.

"Sir, I've been in direct contact with both the Varapin commander, as well as the Pylor Captain... Thunderballs. Although I have made attempts to stall things, they are working together—"

"Hold on. The Pylor pirates are here in system?"

I'd forgotten there would have been no way for the Admiral to know this. Not with the pirates' late arrival and excellent cloaking. "Yes, Sir. Twenty-five warships... a mismatch of older, yet still effective assets."

"And they're working in cahoots with the Varapin? That

doesn't sound like the most strategic long-term move on their part."

"I agree, Admiral. Then again, to my knowledge, the Varapin have stayed loyal to the Grish."

He shrugged his thin shoulders. "So far..."

"I need to get back to my ship, Sir. I knew it was imperative I bring you up to speed—"

"I will be returning to *Jefferson* with you. Of course, you do realize that. I cannot very well command the fleet from here."

I nodded while offering as sympathetic a face as I could muster. "If only US Space-Navy regs allowed for such a thing."

"What are you talking about? Of course I will be taking command of *Jefferson*."

"Sir, the Quan-Tangler is an experimental device. Not ready for prime time, as they say. We checked in section five, subsection 3180 A. Regulations clearly state that in times of battle, lives of Space-Navy officers of the rank of rear Admiral and above are not to be placed in jeopardy with the use of experimental means of transportation."

I could see the Admiral, clearly not convinced, was trying to recall such a strange regulation. Hardy turned his big head in my direction—his face display revealed a cartoonish profile of young Pinocchio, his nose steadily growing longer and longer.

Ignoring Hardy, I said, "I believe we will be able to reestablish communications within the hour. If not with the entire fleet, between the *Goliath* and *Jefferson* for sure."

He looked at me through narrowed eyes. "I don't believe a goddamn word you've said, Quintos. You've played the lone maverick far too many times, and this is no different. Fuck the regulations—if that's not something you've simply made up on the spot. I'm taking *Jefferson*, and I don't want to hear another word about it."

USS Jefferson

"Aye, Sir... very good, Sir." I looked to Hardy, "Can you make contact with the RCHD on *Jefferson?*"

"I am."

Billing's brow furrowed into multiple deep furrows. "That's 'I am, Sir.' You will address your superior officers with proper decorum, robot!"

I saw that Hardy's face display had gone completely black, which was not a good sign. I let out a breath. *Why, for the love of God, did I come here?* About to apologize for my impertinent ChronoBot, I saw Billings was looking a tad off-kilter. Eyes wide and lower jaw hanging agape, the man was struggling to speak.

"Admiral? Are you..." Not finishing my sentence, I saw what had put Billings in such an apoplectic state. Iris. The little fairy was now standing upon Hardy's left shoulder, hands on hips and little translucent wings fluttering. She raised a pointing finger.

"I don't know who you think you are, but I have a right mind to turn you into a bog frog, or maybe a waggle worm... yes, most definitely a waggle worm." With that, the little sprite leaped into the air and began circling the Admiral's head.

I shot Hardy the angriest glare I could before placing a comforting hand on Billing's shoulder. "Sir... are you all right? Did you say... fairy?"

Hardy finally said, "I'll get us some help." He left, and moments later returned with Captain Lugano and a female crewmember. Both rushed in, looking concerned.

"What is it? What has happened?" Lugano said, now standing beside the Admiral.

The Admiral continued to look up and all around, as if scouting the location of an invisible insect. "She was right here, you idiot! Look for her... find her!"

"Find who, Sir?" Lugano said, now looking about the ready room too.

"The fairy, the little flying fairy. She's wearing a tiny little dress with sparkles... and she's got a mouth on her. Rude is what she is."

Both Captain Lugano and the young female crewmember looked to me with *what the hell do we do* uncertainty.

I said, "I think it best you contact your chief medical officer... the man's obviously been under a great amount of stress."

Lugano was already speaking in low, hurried tones into his TAC-Band.

The woman, whose name tag read B. Miller, gave the air above Billings one last glance. She now looked at the Admiral with pity.

Within minutes, two HealthBay techs arrived along with a medical doctor. Looking concerned, they began coaxing the Admiral out from around his desk. Billings, no longer looking for Iris, was now getting physically agitated.

"I'm fine, dammit! Let go of me! I said get your hands off of me!" Billings looked to me, "Tell them, Quintos. Tell them what you saw... that I'm not crazy. I'm as sane as anyone on this ship!"

Hardy raised a mechanical hand and touched the closest of the passing techs' shoulders and said in a quiet, conspiratorial voice, "I think the poor man may have soiled himself... he'll need a good rinsing off. And bed rest. And surely powerful sedatives."

The four of us, B. Miller, Captain Lugano, Hardy, and I, stood by as Admiral Billings was ushered from the ready room.

I said, "Captain Lugano, you will be taking command of the *Goliath*." It was not a question.

He nodded, still staring at the compartment's entrance. "Um, uh... yes. I suppose I will."

Hardy said, "I have already filled out the necessary forms and sent them to Goliath's MATHR. With four witnesses, there shouldn't be any question of the Admiral no longer being fit for duty."

"No, I suppose not," Lugano said. "It's just a shame. As infuriating and caustic as the man could be, he was still a brilliant officer."

I, too, wasn't thrilled with how the situation evolved. It was never a good idea to mess with a ChronoBot, and add the Hardy aspect... well, obviously things had spiraled. I just hoped Billing's career wouldn't take too much of a hit for this, whatever this was. Who was I kidding? The man was seeing fairies.

Chapter 24

By the time we quansported back onto *Jefferson*, I was ready to hit my TAC-Band with a hammer. Thirteen new messages. I skimmed some of them but didn't take the time to look at them all. Since I was less than two hundred feet from the bridge, I figured I'd save myself some time and headed off in that direction. I stopped and faced Hardy. "Head on up to the Symbio deck. Oh, and find Ensign Plorinne; you'll need his pass codes and help with reassigning those... Pleidian assets. And find out what Trent had on him. Kid's looking at some serious brig time if he doesn't have a good excuse."

Hardy offered back a casual two-fingered salute before striding off toward the GravLifts.

Entering the bridge, my eyes were drawn to the halo display, where a numerical timer was counting down by the second. At least half of the bridgecrew was on their feet, and there seemed to be a whole lot of discussion going on.

MATHR announced her typical "Captain on the deck," which caused a kind of universal spinning-around-in-unison of my bridge officers. Gail, also standing and slightly elevated upon the raised captain's mount, said, "Finally! Didn't you get my hails?"

"Hurried right over. What's up?"

Gail gestured toward the halo display. "That's what's up. That's not our clock; it's Thunderballs'."

"What's he counting down to?" I said.

I waited as Gail stepped down, then I stepped up and took the seat. I saw Derrota making his way out of the CIC and hurrying in my direction. He was now half walking, half running. Reaching us out of breath, he said, "They've detected that last transport of yours."

"Already? I knew it would be detected... but I was hoping we'd have enough time before that to make our offensive." I pointed to the display. "Is that what the timer is all about?"

Gail shook her head. "No, I've been trying to tell you. That's coming from Thunderballs. A feed from his ship."

I looked at the clock. "Thirty-five minutes? What's happening in thirty-five, now thirty-four, minutes?"

Gail looked hesitant to answer. Looking at Derrota, I saw he, too, was having a hard time telling me.

"Oh, for the love of Pete, just spit it out. How bad can it be?"

Gail stepped closer and placed a hand on my arm. "He has her, Galvin. He has the Empress."

I shook my head and smiled. "He's bluffing. I saw Shawlee's ship heading off toward—"

"And Thunderballs was right there, waiting to snatch her. We hadn't picked up on the pirates' cloaked presence in system," Derrota said, bringing his tablet up and tapping on it. A new feed on the halo display popped into view, and I took in an audible breath.

Empress Shawlee was seated within an armchair and looked pretty much the same as when I'd seen her last. She didn't look to have been mistreated. The thing was, she appeared to be within Thunderballs' private quarters. I could see home furnishings, a table next to her chair with a light, in the background a rock-clad fireplace with a portrait above the mantel. A portrait I recognized from Ironhold Station. It was an oddly seductive, bare-shouldered painting of his mother. I remembered his adoring reverence for the woman.

Suddenly jarred from my recollections, I realized Shawlee was now speaking.

"Galvin... I am so, so sorry. As you can see, I have been taken again. Cardinal has not harmed me in any way and promises not to do so... if you do as he asks."

I was scarcely conscious of the slow-burning volcano coming to life within me—the whitening of my knuckles, the difficulty I was having breathing. Because at the present moment, all I was capable of was picturing my fingers wrapped around Thunderballs' neck, squeezing and watching the life force drain from his eyes.

"I am aware of the situation... the plight of the 9th Fleet with the surrounding Varapin forces, that *Oblivion* vessel, and of course, the many Pylor pirates' warships. Galvin, this is a battle you cannot win. Do what the pirate leader asks... give him the transporter technology and save the lives of so many brave crewmembers." Shawlee looked away, perhaps into the eyes of Thunderballs himself, and then looked back. "As deplorable and horrible a person as Cardinal is, he is not a liar. He operates within some kind of code. Perhaps not a moral code, but maybe an honor code. Saving me should not be your prime objective, Galvin... but saving the good men and women of your 9th Fleet is essential."

Abruptly, Thunderballs' image replaced that of the Empress. He was standing upon the bridge of his ship. "I apologize, Captain Quintos... Galvin. I like you, so knowing what you just witnessed brings me no enjoyment. But business is business." The pirate made a somber face. "You now have twenty-three minutes to allow my cohorts entry onto your ship. We'll be taking the software, engineering plans, and now the hardware aspects of this technology as well. You do not want to try my patience, Galvin. You know what I am capable of."

The feed went black.

"Get him back," I said, now looking at the feed showing the 9th Fleet. The Pylor pirate might be willing to wait twenty-five minutes, but that didn't mean the Varapin would. How long before the *Goliath* received a similar fate to that of *Starlight*?

As if reading my thoughts, Stanley Handly announced, "Three fusion-tipped smart missiles just emerged from *Oblivion*!"

I mentally calculated how many of the *Goliath*'s crew could possibly be brought over in time. Zero. There was no time as the missiles were already closing in on the Fleet's command ship —*oh God, what have I done?* I looked away.

the bridge was as quiet as a tomb. No one spoke; no one breathed.

A chorus of audible gaps brought my attention back to the halo display. It took me a few beats to make sense of what I was seeing. The three missiles were gone. But the *Goliath* still remained where it had been.

"Incoming hail from *Oblivion*, Captain," Chen said with a shaky voice.

"On screen."

First Warrior Veesh Slat stared back at me with the cold eyes of a corpse. "A gift. A one-time gift, Captain Quintos. No more tricks, no more delays, no more trying to play the Pylor pirates against us. You will do as Thunderballs asks and allow his soon-to-be arriving shuttle access to your flight bay.

You have been the benefactor of my kindness; do not tempt fate. There is no need for further loss of life." The feed went black.

"Somebody tell me if there is a shuttle on its way here."

"Aye, Captain," Stanley Handly said. "Approximately eight minutes out."

Gail was at my side. "What do you want to do?"

I continued to stare at the back of Stanley Handly's head as if in a trance. "I want to give them exactly what they want." I felt everyone's eyes burning laser beams into my head. "Let me rephrase that. I want to give them exactly what they think they want. We have to move fast."

I looked at Derrota. "We have to acknowledge that Thunderballs has been spying on at least some of our communications. Can you do something... encrypt our internal comms or something?"

Derrota said, "Already did that. Altered all ship-wide encryption. Nobody's listening in on our comms now."

"Good." I looked to Gail. "XO Pristy, I'm guessing Thunderballs knows about the Quan-Tangler compartment from earlier comms. We need to hide what's in that compartment; section off that forward section. Talk to SWM Chief LaSalle and have a temporary bulkhead installed that will hide the Quan-Tangler and control console."

"So... he'll see what? An empty smaller compartment?"

I shook my head, "No, he'll see Sir Louis de Broglie's original prototype unit. Go make it happen. The unit is up on Deck 23, the LabTech area. Get some help and a hover cart."

Running out of the bridge, Gail was already barking off orders into the TAC-Band.

Next, I contacted Flight Bay Chief Frank Mintz and Captain Wallace Ryder, letting them know about the incoming Pylor pirates' shuttle and that any work being done to outfit

Arrows with the Lorg-Mav's RCHDs needed to be kept out of view. And finally, I contacted Hardy.

"Go for Hardy."

"I know you're busy, but we're about to have some guests."

"I know that... I've been listening."

I let go how creepy the ChronoBot's capabilities could be and said, "All the design plans for the Quan-Tangler and the Quan-Tangler compartment. Can you store them locally?"

"I already have those. And while we're speaking, I'm altering MATHR's files to indicate the existence of only Louis de Broglie's version of the tech."

"Excellent," I said. Still, I hated giving away even that older version of the technology.

"I'm also adding a bit of clandestine code to Broglie's device."

"You can do that?" I asked.

"Of course. The pirates will be able to operate the unit five times."

"And then?"

"And then it will self-transport back to *Jefferson*. If not close enough to do that, it will explode."

"Explode?"

"Kaboom."

"Nice." That gave me an idea, which I proposed to Hardy. He wasn't thrilled by the idea but said he'd work on it.

I said, "And let's keep this between ourselves."

"Sure. We'll call it Operation Dumb Fuck."

"Whatever..." I cut my TAC-Band connection to the robot.

Derrota, who had been standing at the tactical station talking to Handly, said, "Thunderballs will want full access to MATHR's files."

"Is that a problem?"

"It could be," he said, tapping on his tablet. "Fortunately, with *Jefferson's* upgrades, she has an ungodly amount of memory resources."

"What are you doing?"

"I'm making a mirror copy of her and putting the actual MATHR AI into slumber mode."

Stanley Handly spun around. "Pirate shuttle just set down within Flight Bay, Sir."

I contacted Gail. "Progress?"

"I need more time. The thing was plugged in, but much of it was in pieces. Coogong was—"

"Tinkering with the thing." The Thine scientist was like a child that constantly tore apart his toys to see how they worked.

"We're just now pushing the cart toward the GravLifts."

"I'll buy you more time. But hurry."

"Roger that."

I extricated myself from the captain's mount and said, "Stephan, you're with me. Mr. Handly, you have the conn."

By the time we reached the flight bay, a small army of twelve or thirteen Pylor pirates were gathered at the bottom of their shuttle's ramp. Chief Mintz was there, hands on hips and squaring off with one of the pirates. Mintz was not someone to give ground without a highly contested fight. He and I had had our own shouting matches over the years, and the man simply did not back down—which in this case was a good thing. Taking in the shuttle, I saw that it was an older BinJin Lore model. A kind of logo was stenciled onto the hull, a black skull and crossbones with the word PYLOR imprinted above.

As for our visitors, they certainly had embraced their pirate roots. Each wore brown trousers with a brightly colored knotted sash for a belt. Billowing white button-down shirts and wrapped bandanas worn around the crowns of their heads completed their fashion ensemble. Each was armed with a tagger-equivalent energy pistol, as well as a knife. The one Pylor pirate missing from the tribe of marauders was Thunderballs himself. Not a surprise. I would have killed him on sight.

As the back-and-forth shouting subsided, I saw that it was Mintz, of course, and a much, much smaller man with a large head making all the noise. Truth be told, the pirate wasn't just short; he was tiny. Like child-sized tiny—with the exception of his head. Four-foot-nothing tiny. Otherwise a perfectly proportioned man—hands, arms, and legs.

He wore a thin Errol Flynn–style mustache and had a hairline-thin scar that ran from his left ear over to his left nostril. It was then that I took notice of his ears. They were beyond small. Small to the point I fleetingly wondered if that physical anomaly would impact his hearing. Then again, didn't birds have small ears or no ears at all, and didn't they hear just fine? So, it wasn't that his head was all that out of proportion to the rest of his slight body; it was those doll-sized ears in comparison that made one come to that conclusion.

When his eyes leveled on me, I knew this little fucker was going to be trouble. Size be damned; he was a killer, and he was the leader of this little band of thugs.

"I am Captain Quintos. This is Science Chief Stephan Derrota, and I see you have already met Bay Chief Mintz."

The man eyed me. "My name is Vince. And I know who you are. Look, this can go easy, or this can go hard... real hard. But you need to understand right from the get-go, you're my bitch. You'll do as I say, and you'll do it fast." He snapped his little fingers to emphasize his point.

Not-so-subtle smirks on his men's lips didn't go unnoticed.

"Shall we get started then? I can show you—"

"Put a cork in it, Quintos. We're not here to take a tour. We go where we want, and we go without chaperones. Anyone gets in our way, I've given orders to cut their balls off."

I wanted to mention that not all of my crew had balls to cut off but let that go. I said, "Just so you know, you damage my ship in any way, things will get real uncivilized around here."

The pirates all laughed, with the exception of Vince. "What, so you're going to get uncivilized? Is that what you're saying? You a tough guy?"

"I'm tough enough. But if I'm not, he is." I looked beyond the band of pirates to the seven-foot-tall ChronoBot in full battle mode, with all of his polished metal cannons plainly visible. "And if he's not intimidating enough for you, your tour guides, or should I say, chaperones, might be."

They approached from behind Hardy. Sergeant Max, Wanda, Grip, Ham, and Hock were each heavily armed with shredders and fully helmeted combat suit attire.

"Now, I'm permitting you to take only the things agreed upon with Thunderballs. Nothing else."

Chapter 25

As we watched the not-so-merry band of pirates head off with Hardy and the five Marines, I stayed back with Derrota. All of his attention had been on his tablet.

"You checking on the Quan-Tangler compartment?"

He tilted the device so I could see a feed into that area of the ship. There was a lot of activity; thanks to several SWM crewmembers, the temporary bulkhead wall was nearly complete—sectioning off the part of the compartment with the four-pedestal Quan-Tangler and console. At the same time, a hover cart had just arrived, delivering the Sir Louis de Broglie transporter unit. Coogong was there as well.

"I should get up there," Derrota said.

"Go. I need to check on our Arrow modifications." I headed off toward the back of the bay.

I FOUND CAPTAIN RYDER HELPING ANOTHER PILOT install one of the duplicated Lorg-Mav RCHDs into the aft section of an Arrow Fighter. Looking around, I saw multiple rows of

Arrow Fighters. All of them, lined up in perfectly straight rows, had their cargo hatches open.

"What's the status, Wallace?" I asked.

Without looking up from what he was doing, he said, "We were doing fine until you jacked our copy machine."

It took me a second—the Sir Louis de Broglie unit. "Sorry about that; we're cutting things pretty close as it is. How many did we get?"

Ryder looked up at me. "One hundred and twenty, seventy-eight seemingly operational."

Ryder showed the pilot next to him how to connect the Arrow's multi-strand laser fiber braid conduits to the RCHD, then stood and wiped his hands on a rag. Looking at me now, he said, "You do know that old transporter is nothing but trouble, right?"

"We've had our share of issues with it," I gestured to the unit being installed next to us, "You check these out?"

"All were tested... as much as possible at least. Lorg-Mav technology is beyond what we are used to working with."

The pilot next to Ryder stood and took the rag from him to wipe his hands. He said, "Should be good to go."

"Let's see," Ryder said, climbing up an integrated hull-side ladder. He got himself situated into the cockpit and after several moments, he looked down and shot me a smile. The Arrow disappeared. Typical cloaking worked well enough, but more often than not, there was a good bit of visual artificing—small areas of a ship that produced visual distortions. Not in this case. I walked around the Arrow, keeping a discerning eye out for something, anything, that would give the craft's presence away.

Ryder's voice emanated from above me, "You won't find any anomalies, just as there won't be any short- or long-range sensor readings."

The Arrow popped back into view. Ryder climbed back

down and jutted his chin toward the conning tower. High above us, the large metal structure was the primary observation platform for a team of space-traffic controllers. It was also where Chief Mintz's office was located. Ryder said, "We have a full sensor array set up in there... can pick up all Allied ship signatures as well as, now that it's been updated, Varapin and Pylor ship signatures."

A uniformed woman stepped into view at one of the tall windows and gave us a thumbs-up.

"This Arrow is cleared for flight," Ryder said to the pilot.

I said, "And the ability to project faux warship signatures?"

"We messed around with that. It works... we think, but until we get our Arrows out into deep space where there's room, we won't fully know for sure."

"You said you had seventy-eight operational. How long before you've got them installed?"

"This was the last one... we're ready when you are. I need to talk to my pilots, but we won't be holding you back. We go at your command."

I LEFT RYDER AND THE FLIGHT BAY AND HEADED up to Deck 72/73. I had to ask MATHR where specifically the Symbio deck's admin control center was situated. It was there that I found Ensign Plorinne sitting at a terminal, looking to be hard at work. Considering the young Pleidian had assisted Trent with injuring my brother, and very easily could have been responsible for killing a crewmember, most likely me, I was irritated he was still allowed access to the Symbio deck's control system.

I cleared my throat.

Startled, Plorinne nearly jumped out of his seat. He stood so fast, his chair nearly toppled over. "Captain! Um... I didn't expect you—"

"Take a seat, Ensign."

I pulled over a chair and sat on it backward and rested my arms on the backrest in front of me. "You have some explaining to do."

"Yes, Sir. Sorry, Sir." He was glassy-eyed; tears had started to well up. He hesitated. "I want you to know, Sir, that being a part of this crew, your crew, has been the most important, the best thing that has ever happened to me."

"You sure have a strange way of showing your appreciation. Why'd you do it? Why did you alter the safety setting here on the Symbio deck? I want the truth, Ensign, no bullshit."

"I... did something I'm not proud of."

"We've already determined that."

"No, not that, Sir. You know I'm up here a lot. The Empress made me pretty much the go-to person for managing the Symbio-Poths. There are hundreds of them, far more than you would ever see playing the game. They're constantly having to be repaired, recycled, upgraded. There's a behind-the-scenes area, similar to what was here when it was the town of Clairmont. It's all AI-controlled, but there are still a lot of management-level decisions needed to be made."

"You're stalling. Get to the point."

"Well, like I said... I'm up here a lot."

"Got that."

"And I'm around the various Symbios like all the time."

"Got that too."

"There's this one, um, castle maiden... Elsa McDonald..."

I closed my eyes and rubbed at my temples. "Please tell me you're not... with that bot."

"In my own defense, she's different. She's more real to me than anyone I have ever met. I think I love—"

"Stop. I don't want to know about it."

I knew that the Symbio bots supposedly were anatomically

very close to human. How close, I really didn't want to conjecture. *Shit, kid, thank you for a mental image I'll never be able to disremember.* "Just tell me how Chaplain Trent got involved."

"Simply put, he caught us together. We'd been so careful. Only got together after hours, when the Symbio deck was closed for maintenance. But there he was, lurking around, spying on us in the blacksmith's shed."

"Blacksmith's shed? That's where you... never mind; I don't want to know. So, Trent was watching you. What then?"

"He waited till I was back at my admin post. He told me I was a sinner and a sick deviant. That he had no choice but to report me to Chief Mattis in Security. That I would assuredly be demoted, if not tossed out of Space-Navy completely. He then said he would make sure Elsa was destroyed... that he'd personally oversee her melt. That's what they call it when they recycle a nonrepairable Symbio, a melt. They're placed in a large canister and literally melted down to base elements with chemicals."

Plorinne swiped at his wet cheeks with a sleeve and swallowed hard.

"No one's going to melt anyone," I said, reassuring him. Hell, if the kid wanted to be with a willing Symbio-Poth on his own time, who was I to judge?

"So, Trent gave you an ultimatum, I take it?"

Plorinne nodded, "All I had to do was show him how to change the safety setting for the game's various action characters."

"He wanted you to show him?"

"I told him I wouldn't do it... He could blackmail all he wanted, but I wouldn't do it."

"Okay, Ensign." I stared at him for a few seconds. "What you did is wrong—"

"But I think I love her—"

"Let me finish! You keeping Trent's actions a secret. You should have come to me."

He lowered his head, clearly feeling ashamed. "I'm sorry. How much trouble am I in?"

"I'll think about it. Let's change the subject. You've been working up here with Hardy."

He nodded enthusiastically. "Oh yeah. We've been getting, um, creative with our army of medieval Symbios... they're ready when you are."

"Good." I got to my feet and put the chair back where I got it.

As I was turning to leave, Plorinne said, "Uh, Captain?"

"Yes?"

"Can I ask one favor? Even though I have no right to ask."

"What is it, Ensign?"

"Can I keep Elsa back? Not include her in whatever is planned?"

I almost chuckled. "That would be fine. But let's keep that between us, okay? Your... relationship should stay your business alone."

I was being hailed. "Go ahead, Stephan."

"Can you get over to the Quan-Tangler compartment? The pirates want to test that the device is operational."

"That's fine. You don't need me—"

"Actually, I do. The test Thunderballs wants to run is you transporting over to his command ship now."

Looking at the thing, I thought about the error percentage of Sir Louis de Broglie's transporter. What had Ryder said? Out of one hundred and twenty copied, transported RCHD units, only seventy-eight were seemingly operational. That was a mere 65 percent success rate.

Vince with the rodent-sized ears and four of his pirate mates were there in the modified Quan-Tangler compartment with me, along with Hardy and Coogong. Thus far, it looked as though the pirates were none the wiser about the modifications made here.

I looked to Coogong and then to Hardy for moral support. Coogong's typical smile was gone, replaced by a straight, thin line upon his helmeted worm face. Hardy, on the other hand, had come up with a new animation for his face display—a man, supposedly me, sitting within an old-fashioned wooden barrel, a barrel that was rapidly approaching a waterfall.

"Thanks for the vote of confidence," I said, now eyeing the fancy baroque detailing of a time where the use of too much ornate, some would say gaudy, French fleur de lis detailing wasn't only commonplace, but expected. I felt sick to my stomach. Once more I looked to Coogong—the one who had spent the most time under the proverbial hood of this device. I got nothing from him. I was going to have to take one for the Gipper. Again, those very-close-to-50-percent odds came to mind.

As I stepped onto the raised pedestal, Hardy said, "I insist that I go with you, Captain. You know I'm compelled to protect—"

"Yeah, I get it. Your inner LuMan is probably going crazy right now. But I have to do this myself, buddy. Keep your eye on our friends here."

Vince smiled, exposing tiny teeth the color of pond scum. "Bon voyage, Captain." He shook his head. "I'm betting that thing's more dangerous than chain-smoking."

I took in his discolored choppers again.

XO Pristy entered the compartment. I'd spoken to her briefly prior to coming here. She had scolded me appropriately but in the end saw no way around me doing this. Thunderballs needed a test of his newly acquired transporter technology. Couldn't really blame him for that. And I wouldn't chance anyone else going through with this roll of the dice. I saw the concern on her face and not for the first time, felt affection for my pretty XO.

I looked to Vince. "You have what you came for? The engineering and build schematics, the software?"

"Mostly. Elvish and Cornish are collecting the rest from Steven Demotta."

"Derrota; his name's Stephan Derrota."

"Whatever... seems they're getting what's needed from him."

"And you're sure you don't want to take the shortcut over to your vessel?" I gestured to the ornate device beneath my feet.

He flipped me the bird. His raised child-sized middle finger just didn't pack all that much of a punch. I clucked my tongue. "Quansport mc, Coogong."

Chapter 26

I materialized into Thunderballs' private quarters. I recognized the space from our earlier conversation. Here there were plush masculine furnishings, chocolate-colored overstuffed leather couches, wide-planked and roughly hewn timber flooring, a dining area with a table that looked to be made of polished concrete, and a stone fireplace large enough for a man to walk into without hunching over. Currently, there was a fire blazing; the sounds of actual burning logs crackled and popped. And there above the mantel was the portrait of Thunderballs' mother, Alexandria LeCorpus.

This was a different portrait than the one hanging on the fireplace within Ironhold Station. This one was somewhat more provocative. Here, her not insubstantial shoulders were exposed within a low-cut ruby-red dress—her deep cleavage led to the assumption she had larger than average breasts. As with the other portrait, the handsome dark-haired woman sported a kind of five o'clock shadow atop her upper lip. Her dark, humorless eyes conveyed tenacity and maybe something else—perhaps a lust for power.

"Ah, Captain Quintos... so kind of you to drop by."

I hadn't noticed the Pylor pirate sitting off to my right. Over his shoulder, a reading light illuminated a hardback novel situated on his lap. On the table next to him was a tumbler with, I guessed by its color, cognac.

Thunderballs stood and placed the open book upon the vacated chair cushions. He moved over to a liquor cart, reached for another tumbler, then poured two fingers of the same cognac-looking spirits from a crystal decanter. The man was showboating, going to great lengths to make an impression. *Yeah, I get it. You're more than just a ruthless, diabolical marauder. You have taste; you can be civilized.* I didn't buy it last time I was in his presence, and I didn't buy it now.

He handed me the tumbler; we clinked glasses and I took a sip. It wasn't bad. Spicy, fruity, sweet, as well as bitter, the alcohol burned just the right amount on the way down as I took another sip. I said, "Okay... you can see the technology works. My presence here proves as much. Right now, your little dwarf of a pirate is packing things up on *Jefferson*. You'll have everything promised to you. Now it's time for you to hand over the Empress."

"I assure you; Shawlee is safe and in no discomfort. The young Empress will be returned to you shortly. But right now, this is a time for two old adversaries to come together and, perhaps, make amends."

I put the glass down on the liquor cart. "I'm not looking to make amends here, Thunderballs; you and I are not friends. You're little more than a bandit and pillager. We are enemies. That's not going to change. So, where is she?"

"Yes, I am a bandit... the leader of other bandits. With that said, I am a man of my word. I would not last long in my position if I didn't live by a certain code."

I was tiring of this conversation. I wanted to retrieve Shawlee and get back to my ship.

"The problem is, the Empress..."

My heart sank.

"Is no longer on board my ship. She's on *Oblivion*."

He took in the measure of my stare, seeing that there was no longer any reason not to kill him.

"Hold on, Captain. Let me make you a proposition before you resort to hostility."

"You've already suggested that, remember? You lied to me. Chose to ally with the Varapin instead."

"You and I both know allying with those vile creatures would last only as long as it served the Varapin in their quest to rule the galaxy. But now I have, or soon will have, the transporter technology. That changes everything. With your help, the help of *Jefferson*, we can free your 9th Fleet... together we can defeat those Varapin ghouls."

"So, let me get this straight... you not only pilfered our US Space-Navy transporter technology, but you're now after a newly refurbished heavy dreadnought to add to your Pylor fleet?"

"A small price to pay for the lives of so many men and women of the 9th Fleet. We will rescue the Empress but do it together... of course. But such a selfless act would require due compensation."

"Like a multitrillion-dollar dreadnought?"

He bowed his head. "A fair exchange."

I just looked at him. The man had balls, that's for sure.

I said, "No." But what he was proposing got me thinking. Of course, there was no way I would simply hand over my ship to this pirate. But maybe there was a way I could do the reverse. Take command of his fleet of warships.

"Are you a wagering man?"

That had piqued his interest. "What pirate isn't?"

I shook my head, "Nah... it's a bad idea. Forget I brought it up."

He continued to look at me. "No...I would most appreciate you sharing your thoughts."

"It's too big of a wager... too big of a bet. A winner-takes-all-type thing."

He looked confused, but also intrigued. "What would be in the so-called pot of this wager?"

"You mentioned you wanted *Jefferson*, right?"

"Oh yes. It is a fine vessel, Captain. And what would you want in return? What do I have that you would be willing to risk so much for?"

"All of your warships."

The pirate laughed out loud.

"And all of your Pylor pirates as well."

He scoffed at that. "Come, come... you are out of your mind. Such a wager would not be possible."

"As I said, the stakes would be too high for you. You'd have much to lose."

"As would you, Captain Quintos... Galvin. I must say, you do have me intrigued."

I stayed quiet, walked over to the liquor cart, and retrieved my tumbler of cognac. I threw back what remained in the glass and smacked my lips, "That's some fine hooch, you've got there, Cardinal." I used his first name to show that our relationship had progressed some.

"And the actual mechanics of the bet? Perhaps a game of chance... cards maybe."

I shook my head and smiled. "No. Not for stakes as large as we're talking about."

"And what would be the equivalent for such stakes?" he asked.

"Life and death stakes."

Any bemusement he'd been harboring was gone in that instant. "You suggest we fight. Such as a hand-to-hand battle to the death."

"Winner takes all."

"Weapons? Knives perhaps... or swords?"

I made a face. "I prefer to keep to the basics. That is if you're open to that."

Thunderballs looked at me with uncertainty. He wasn't sure just how serious I was about all this. "No offense, Galvin, but I fight with my hands often... sort of comes with the territory as you might imagine. You, on the other hand, day after day, sit upon an elevated padded seat for hours on end. Sure, you look fit enough, but hand-to-hand combat is not for the, shall I say, meek?"

I slowly bobbled my head up and down, letting him know he'd made a good point. "Yeah, it was probably a bad idea anyway. No, if you want that ship of mine, you'll have to take her in battle. Then again, she won't come out of that fight in the best of shape. I'm sure you have the budget to do another ship-wide refurb... not cheap for a three-mile-long heavy dreadnought."

Thunderballs looked toward the fireplace and into the eyes of his ever-watching mother. "You would do this thing. Fight me for all the marbles... winner takes all?"

"What do I have to lose? It's not as if I can leave this system. Leave the 9th Fleet to slowly be annihilated by the Varapin, and maybe your warships along with them."

"And how would you suggest we guarantee the winner actually does take all? What is there to ensure there is compliance by the losing side?"

"I will order my crew to adhere to the rules of the match. I lose; you take possession of *Jefferson*. But not my crew... they are given safe passage out of system."

"And I will do the same. My Pylors would not like it, but they are honorable enough to do what has been stipulated. They are well accustomed to games of chance, perhaps not one with as hefty as stakes as this one, but well accustomed just the same. I lose, you take ownership of twenty-five fine warships—that and become the de facto leader of close to two thousand Pylor pirates." He scratched at his chin, contemplating our musings.

I saw him thinking about the imbalance of the wager. Twenty-five warships and their crews for one powerful dreadnought without her crew. He looked over to me, his eyes moving up and down my body, assessing my capabilities. He was cunning; he was a ruthless killer. Undoubtedly he had killed more men with his bare hands than anyone I had ever met. My guess was he was thinking there was no fuckin' way he could lose to me. And he just might be right.

He smiled, exposing his perfect white teeth. "Shall we make this match a public affair?"

"Oh, I insist we do. The outcome of this match affects everyone. My loss would be the loss of my crew."

"And mine, the loss of mine," he added, looking more and more excited by the moment.

"The Varapin are not a patient bunch. If this is going to happen, it has to happen today, within the next few hours," I said.

THE ARRANGEMENTS HAD BEEN LEFT TO OUR respective second-in-commands, XO Pristy and Pylor pirate Vince. The location of the match would be upon *Jefferson*, within her largest hold. SWM personnel were moving cargo out to adjoining holds now to free up space.

Once on the bridge, I contacted First Warrior Veesh Slat, letting him know I had indeed complied with his directives. I had transferred the transporter and associated software and build schematics over to Thunderballs' ship.

Veesh Slat took in the information without reaction other than a prolonged silence. But when he spoke, there was no doubt he was agitated. His grating voice seethed with measured animosity. "You were to deliver the device to me... to *Oblivion*."

I threw up my hands. "Now you tell me. Look, Veesh Slat... you didn't even tell me that you'd come to some sort of an accord with the pirates. Then I find out from them that you will be sharing the technology. I'm just trying to give you guys what you want." I overdramatically let out a frustrated breath. "This is the thanks I get for doing what I was instructed to do?"

"Our agreement with the Pylor Captain is most recent... and for that matter, terms of any agreement have not been totally defined."

"First Warrior, I will need the 9th Fleet released from your dampening field and Empress Shawlee delivered back to *Jefferson* immediately. I know she is now on board that ship of yours."

"That will not be possible. Not at this time, Captain."

"Can't you just ask Thunderballs to shlep the transporter over to *Oblivion*? He's your ally, not mine."

The Varapin commander and I both knew the Pylor pirate would never freely give up the technology now that he had it. Veesh Slat was probably in no better bargaining position than he had been with me. In the end, the Varapin tactical advantage would win out between their fleet of thirty-five warships and that mega-beast of a ship, *Oblivion*. But even though the Varapin were the dominant force here, they still had to play this latest hand dealt to them with some measure of finesse. Using brute force would only get the transporter technology destroyed.

The first warrior said, "You will retrieve the technology and deliver it to me... personally. For every two hours it takes, you will cost the US Space-Navy one warship and her crew. So, how about I start things off with a little incentive..."

"Four smart missiles just emerged from *Oblivion*, Captain," Stanley Handly said at Tactical. "They're fusion-tipped, high-yield."

First Warrior Veesh Slat's feed was still present on the halo display.

"You've made your point. I'll get you your damn technology... just call off your missiles."

The feed from the Varapin ship went black. the bridge went quiet as the four missiles moved in precise concert, dogging one 9th Fleet warship, then another, and then another.

"They're headed for *USS Maryland*," someone said. The resulting explosion flash from a direct port-side hit momentarily oversaturated the halo display. Then, as the horrific image came back into view, all that was left of the midsized destroyer were torn-apart segments, each venting debris and undoubtedly crewmembers.

I had never wanted to kill an individual like I did right then. First Warrior Veesh Slat was going to pay for this. The Varapin were going to pay for this.

Chapter 27

There was zero time to waste. Every second wasted was a second off the clock before another 9th Fleet vessel would be destroyed. As it turned out, under the current time restraints, the match would commence within twenty minutes. And although the cargo hold was immense, it still would be an audience that was by invitation only. Five shuttles were en route now from various Pylor warships. But Thunderballs would not be among those arriving that way. He would be using his latest technological toy to make his appearance; he would be transporting into the hold just minutes before the match was to begin. If only he knew the kind of risk he was taking... but I for one certainly wasn't going to tell him.

Gail had done an admirable job getting things organized. At my suggestion, she'd gone right to Wanda to help with setting up a kind of mixed martial arts ring. My only specific request was that it was enclosed somehow, where neither of us could escape when things got tense, and no one could interfere.

Now entering the makeshift hold arena, I saw the ring was more of an octagon cage. *Good job.* There had to be close to five hundred people jammed into the space; most were *Jefferson* crew, but at least two hundred were Pylor pirates. The air smelled acrid with sour body odor and cigarette smoke. Didn't these marauders know that habit was bad for their health? I mused with a crooked smile.

I made my way through the mass of bodies with Hardy before me, acting as my bouncer. Next to me was Wanda, yammering into my ear above the noise of the crowd.

"You don't want to get yourself on the mat... you're no wrestler, and you know shit about leg locks and using upper-body leverage."

"Got it; stay on my feet."

"And let's stick with jiu-jitsu and Krav-Maga; you're at least passable in those techniques. I know you like kung fu, but seriously... you'll have no time for all that fucking dancing-around shit."

We slowly made our way closer to the cage as I received backslaps and fist pumps from my crew while several of the pirates hawked loogies at me. We finally reached our destination, where XO Pristy, Doc Viv, Derrota, Ryder, my brother Eric, and LaSalle were standing, hopefully to cheer me on.

Doc Viv came right at me with a finger pointed like a gun. "Are you out of your damn mind, Quintos? For God's sake, this is the stupidest, most irresponsible insanity you've ever pulled!"

So much for cheering me on.

Ryder was less confrontational. "Any way you can back out of this shitshow, buddy?"

"No. This is happening."

Gail came close. "You have pirate spit in your hair."

"I already know that."

"Can you do this... can you beat him?"

"Maybe."

"A lot's riding on this... like for all of us."

"I know that too."

Her face was inches from mine. Her eyes were searching mine. A tiny line formed between her brows. "You're going to have to kill him, you know."

I nodded.

Then she did something I didn't expect. She kissed me. Not just a peck on the lips, but the kind of kiss that you see in the movies. The kind of kiss a man gets from his wife when returning from months away at war. The kind of kiss I hadn't imagined this pretty young woman could deliver. Pulling away, she placed a hand on my cheek. "Break his fucking neck, Galvin... I'm with you on this... you had no other choice."

I guess I had found my cheerleader.

Ham and Hock slapped my back while Max and I fist-bumped. Grip opened the gate to the cage. "Take care of business in there," he said in his low baritone.

Wanda was inside the fenced-in enclosure, waiting for me. For the first time, there were no streaks of color in her short brown hair, and she looked as serious as I'd ever seen her. "Are you sure he's not bringing any weapons to the fight?"

"We talked about that. No weapons."

"But you also said there were no rules; anything goes, right?"

I nodded.

"Well, expect him to bring in something... a hidden blade in his boot; a garrote, maybe, to wrap around your neck; or maybe something chemical to blind you."

"He is a pirate... guess that makes sense."

"Just know, if he pulls that shit and kills you... he won't walk out of here alive."

"Fair is fair. I have no problem with that."

That made her smile. "Even if he does play fair but kills you, Hardy will turn him into ground beef."

I let that go. I pulled off my sweatshirt and sweatpants and stood bare-chested in my gym shorts. I looked about the ring. Still no Thunderballs.

Derrota approached from the other side of the chain-link partition. He held up his ever-present tablet. "His transporter just went active. Stand by."

As if on cue, there he was, materializing in the middle of the cage. The older, slower Sir Louis de Broglie method of transporting. In block-by-block segments, starting with his feet and calves, then the rest of his legs, then his midsection, and then his upper torso and head.

Fully materialized, he stood tall and blinked his eyes in rapid succession. Perhaps he hadn't really expected the thing to work.

All the Pylor pirates within the compartment suddenly yelled out in tribute to their leader's arrival. Thunderballs, also bare-chested, but wearing snug white trousers and his long scarlet sash for a belt, raised his hands overhead as if already triumphant. "Welcome home to your new starship, my Pylor friends. Today we become a true threat within the quadrant!"

I looked out at those others in the hold that were far more hesitant—far more uncertain of their future here. I wasn't just risking my own life; I was risking theirs as well. It would be so easy to let second thoughts creep into my mind. But I owed it to my crew, not to mention the fate of what remained of the 9th Fleet, to stay zeroed in on just one objective. Kill the man standing in front of me.

Hardy was at the fence. He gestured me closer.

"I already know what you're going to say, that this is a really bad idea."

He said, "That is a true statement, but not what I was going to say. He's carrying a hidden knife in his left boot. He has a razor hidden in his hair at the back of his head. And his sash can be easily pulled free to use as a garrote."

"Anything else?"

"He's never lost a fight, according to several conversations I've picked up on while here. I'm sorry, but nobody is giving you very good odds of lasting more than a few minutes."

A humorous comeback to that would have been appropriate, but nothing came to mind.

Little Vince was with Thunderballs in his respective corner. Heads lowered, talking in low tones; they were obviously strategizing.

I checked my TAC-Band. I had less than an hour before *Oblivion* destroyed another 9th Fleet asset and her crew. We needed to get this show on the road.

I clapped my hands and yelled over the crowd, "Let's get things moving!"

On her way to the gate, Wanda said, "Don't just fight like your life depends on it. Fight like all our lives depend on it."

I watched as Wanda and Vince left the octagon. For the first time, Cardinal Thunderballs looked my way. We exchanged smiles that didn't reach our eyes.

There were actually not so many rules to this match as there were guidelines. 1) It was a fight to the death, no matter how long that took. 2) There was no conceding the match to the other. Either way, someone was going to die here today. That was pretty much it.

MATHR's voice suddenly emanated from above.

THE MATCH WILL COMMENCE IN TEN, NINE, EIGHT, SEVEN...

I cleared my mind and let out a breath.

THREE, TWO, ONE ...

The two of us circled one another twice as the crowd hooted and hollered. We came to a stop at the same time. I chose a simple taekwondo Dwi Kubi Seogi fighting stance. Primarily a defensive, wait-and-see-what-your-opponent's-going-to-do stance. Thunderballs stood hunched with his fists raised, boxer style.

He came at me fast, with a swiftness I hadn't anticipated. He lunged with his left boot at my head. There's a saying, "Pop it, don't stop it," in martial arts. A direct impact kick such as this one could break arms, wrists, fingers. I got under the kick, rotated my wrist while rising, and then pop-knuckle-punched the underside of his calf. It took little effort, while lessening the direct impact of the kick.

Thunderballs' grimace quickly evolved into a smile. "Somebody's been visiting the neighborhood dojo, eh?"

We circled, continuing to feel each other out. Taking the offensive once more, the pirate came at me with a combination of fist strikes—two consecutive right jabs, then an uppercut. The uppercut to my jaw got through, and now I was tasting blood. I offered him a smile—had to give credit where credit was due.

Thus far we had been playing nice. Sparring more than fighting. Even though I couldn't see the face of my TAC-Band, I was all too aware of the seconds ticking by. I stepped forward, feigning a front kick, but instead ratcheted around my upper torso fast, delivering a spinning back fist maneuver that, from the sound of snapping/crunching cartilage, had broken Thunderballs' nose. Then the blood came, along with the watering eyes.

He swung a wide haymaker and missed. He kicked out with

a sloppy side kick and missed again. As the kick floundered a tad too long in the air, I grabbed it. Using a Mawashi Geri defensive sweep, something Wanda had only taught me the previous week, I put Thunderballs down hard onto his back.

Without hesitation, I went for the face stomp. Thunderballs, anticipating that, rolled to his left and got to his feet. No longer was he smiling. No longer were we sparring. He reached back behind his head with both arms and came away with that razor Hardy had warned me about. It was no more than three inches long and, shaped like a triangle, it was designed so the hilt would fit within his fist while the blade protruded between his second and third fingers.

I said, "And our agreement of no weapons?"

That brought the smile. "This little thing can't really be considered a weapon. More like a toy." As the words left his lips, he attacked, punching forward with that little knife toward my face. I blocked it. And then the second knife, the one he had so deftly hidden in his other hand, pierced the side of my rib cage—I'd guess between the sixth and seventh ribs on the left side. With a gasp, I dropped to one knee. Blood oozed down my side.

Thunderballs circled, now brandishing the two blades openly. The pirate's smile was back. Looking cocky, he waited for me to get back to my feet. The loss of blood was already making me lightheaded. I needed to stanch the bleeding, or this fight would soon be over. I had an idea.

We circled each other, first moving left, then right. My bare feet slipped on something wet on the mat—my own blood. I used the infamous *come and get some* Bruce Lee finger gesture.

He came at me just the way I thought he would, with his bladed fists held high, poised for dual simultaneous strikes. I did the unexpected; I dove in between his wide stance. Spinning around while still making forward momentum, I grabbed the man's fancy red sash, aka his garrote, from around his hips.

As expected, it came away easily. As I was already below and behind him on the mat, Thunderballs thrust out his leg in an effective back kick. He nailed me in the cheek, which brought an assortment of floating stars into my vision. I rolled and then dove farther away. I needed space. Space and time.

Sitting up with the chain-link mesh behind my back, I managed to get Thunderballs' sash wrapped around my chest twice. Pulling the silk tight, I tied it off with a square knot. Not the best pressure wrap, but it would have to do.

I needed to change the dynamics of this fight. It didn't take a genius to see that I was losing. What I needed now was for the pirate to get careless. To deliver another one of those kicks. Don't get me wrong; I was in pain. Staggering and holding my side, I put on a bit of a performance. Unfortunately, *Jefferson* crewmembers also bought the act.

"Hang in there, Cap!"

"Don't let him get close to you!"

"You fight like a little bitch!"

I didn't know who made that last comment, but I intended to make him eat his words. I just needed this pirate prick to kick me again.

Thunderballs spun, attempting a spinning back fist, such as the one that I had used to turn his nose into a conversation piece, but the maneuver was slow and sloppy. I used a Hapkido double-hand knife-hand block, immediately followed up with a Budoshin Ju-Jitsu thumb driven into a soft under-jaw chin nerve strike. Thunderballs jolted upright, tensing as if he'd been struck by a stun gun. I stepped back and waited for my latest bout of dizziness to subside. It didn't.

Angered, teeth bared, and lips curled into a kind of feral snarl, Thunderballs kicked out with everything he had. Clearly aiming for my wounded side, he was just a tad too slow. I caught his foot and held onto his boot while he hopped and tried to pull his leg away from me. My fingers found his hidden sheathed knife. Pulling it free, I held it up between us. "Looks like mine's bigger than yours, cupcake," I said, letting go of his foot. He stumbled, and once again we began to circle one another.

I heard Hardy's voice in my internal auricular implants, "Uh... I may have missed something, Cap."

"A little busy here, Hardy... can this wait?"

"I don't think so."

Thunderballs lunged and swiped for my neck with one of his blades. Distracted, I'd allowed him to get closer than I should. "Hardy, I have to go."

"Wait... he may have another weapon."

"What kind of weapon? Another blade?"

"No."

"Dammit, Hardy!"

"I'm scanning his, um... groin topography."

"Groin topography... what the hell are you talking about?"

"I at first thought he was wearing a cup. You know, for protection against getting kicked in his grundle bundle."

"What is that? Speak English, for fuck's sake."

"His thigh slappers, his furry beanbag, his basket of fruit, his saggy daddies, his apple baggin', his Bojangles—"

"Shut up. Why didn't you just say his balls?"

"It's called taking creative license."

"So, you're saying he's got something hidden in his—"

Cutting myself off, I looked down to the seemingly ample mound at the pirate's crotch. Then the name hit me. *Thunderballs*. So, it wasn't that the man was endowed with moose-sized balls; it was that he had hidden—

Boom! I'd already been turning away from him when the gunshot erupted from Thunderballs' crotch. The bullet clipped my right shoulder. My arm went numb, causing me to drop my recently acquired knife. Wavering, I fell to one knee.

Not one to miss an opportunity, Thunderballs took two running strides and kicked upward, intending a field goal—the ball in this case being my head. His boot missed my noggin but grazed my ear. I fell onto my side, the world spinning around me.

Chapter 28

I was still losing. And something was jabbing into me on my right side. Something sharp. Something I somewhat remembered dropping a while back. But the damn spinning just wouldn't stop.

Thunderballs was now circling the cage, pumping his raised arms over his head. The Pylors were eating it up with hoots and hollers, egging him on to finish me off. The other voices in the hold, my supporters, were being far more subdued.

"Get up!"

"You can do it!"

"Don't give up!"

One particular voice said, "You have just a few minutes to find your balls, Quintos. That or another Space-Navy ship gets annihilated."

There was only one person that called me by my last name. Doc Viv.

What I needed was rest. To close my eyes for just a few moments... that would do the trick. A catnap... I drifted off.

When I woke up, Thunderballs had a fistful of my hair. He

was lifting me partially up off the mat like a safari hunter posing for a picture with his dead quarry. Maybe an African water buffalo, or perhaps a wildebeest. Nothing fast or courageous like a lion or a leopard. No, I'd lost this fight. I was a wildebeest... at best.

"Finish him off!"

"Take him out!"

And then I felt it. The object I'd been lying upon. My fingers brushed across the cold hard steel of Thunderballs' boot knife.

The Pylor pirate leader had now brought his fist back; his eyes were locked onto my exposed throat. It would be a death blow for certain.

Looking down at me with a crooked smile, he said, "Sorry, Galvin... I truly liked you. But business is business."

I mumbled something.

"What's that? You have some final words for me?" He leaned down closer, his face within a foot of my own.

I snatched up the knife and drove the blade into his left eye socket. I drove it in all the way to the knife's hilt. Thunderballs dropped on top of me like a sack of hammers.

Within seconds, I felt the weight of the dead pirate leader being lifted off of me. Indecipherable voices were yammering around me. Then something pinched my upper arm. An injection. Out of the fog, Doc Viv's face took shape before me.

"You should feel better in the next few seconds," she said.

Woozy, I said, "I'm no better than a wildebeest, or maybe a water buffalo..."

Rough hands were grabbing at me, lifting me up. I saw Derrota and Ryder's concerned faces. And I now saw that it was Hardy who had gotten me up to my feet. Two of his typically hidden articulating arm cannons were exposed, leaving little doubt the ChronoBot, my friend, would have intervened prior to Thunderballs' killing me.

Viv snapped her fingers in front of my face. "Hey, snap out of it, Quintos."

And I did. Whatever cocktail of chemicals the syringe contained, it was some good stuff. My mind was sharpening by the second. And the pain in my side, my shoulder, wasn't nearly so bad.

Ryder said. "Galvin, you need to talk to the Pylors... do you hear me? You have one shot at this."

I nodded. "Get me out of here. Get me out of this cage."

Hardy, propping me up, led me out of the fighting cage and into the now-all-too subdued crowd. *Damn, whatever Viv gave me was amazing.* I looked around me and saw the faces of both *Jefferson* crewmembers, as well as Pylor pirates. Strangely, their expressions weren't all that different from each other.

"Let me stand on my own, Hardy. I'm okay."

Reluctantly, Hardy took a step away from me.

I cleared my throat. "There was only going to be one victor here today. Only one of us to come out of that cage alive. We all knew the stakes. We all, Thunderballs, I, and all of you in this hold, had agreed to those stakes."

A low rumble of discordant murmurs erupted around me. I continued, "Pylors... Thunderballs told me a little about you. That you were indeed scoundrels...violent miscreants."

A few laughs.

"He also said that you live by a code. A Pylor code. So, let me ask you this: was he lying to me? Are you simply scoundrels and violent miscreants, or do Pylors have a sense of honor?"

A small man with bad teeth took up position in front of me. Shit, it was fucking Vince.

He said, "Sure, we have something like a code. But it's to each other. Not to outsiders."

The hold went quiet as the nasty little pirate continued to stare me down. He shook his head and scoffed. "You know... Thunderballs liked you. Even admired you. Said you were a pirate, a marauder at heart, but just hadn't come to realize it yet. He was hoping to redeem you."

I thought about that. There might have been some truth to that.

"We'd discussed this potential outcome, as unlikely as it was. That you'd best him in battle. And here we are... you not only bested him; you killed him with his favorite knife."

A few more laughs.

"So now, you all answer to me. I have taken Thunderballs' place as your leader."

Laughter from around the hold.

"No."

"No?"

"Sure, you'll have us for the rest of this conflict, but nothing more than that."

I took that in.

Vince continued, "Look, Thunderballs stipulated we needed to follow the Pylor code. But we're not going to make it easy for you. Who are you to be the leader of the greatest interstellar criminal syndicate in the quadrant? You got lucky in the ring today; that's all there is to it."

"And if you follow your own code..."

Vince made a face. "First, you'd have to be inducted into the Pylor syndicate. That would have to take place sometime within the next few days. Like after we deal with the Varapin. So, I guess until then, yeah... we'll call you our interim leader. How's that? And you can come to us when this is over, if you're still alive. We'll talk then."

"No, as of right now, I'm your interim leader. We can discuss this now."

Vince narrowed his eyes; his lips were moving—he looked as if he was chasing something around in his mouth with his tongue. Or perhaps a tooth had popped loose.

"I'll need to defer to my fellow officers," he said. He turned away and walked into a huddle of six or seven other pirates.

I was starting to sway on my feet. Viv's miraculous elixir was starting to wear off. Through my auricular implants, I heard Derrota's voice, "We're running out of time, Galvin. The Varapin will—"

"Understood," I said, cutting him off.

The huddle of miscreants had gotten unruly. Arguing was going on. Voices raised. It was clear Pylors made decisions more by consensus than line of command. A few more angry shouts, and suddenly, Vince was on his way back to me.

"What have you decided?" I asked. "What will it take to earn the right to lead your, what did you call it, your syndicate?"

"You'd have to return to the ring. Go up against the best of the best... another Pylor candidate that also wants to lead."

"And who would that be?"

Vince shrugged with a smile.

More chuckles from the other Pylors.

"I win...all of you will do my bidding?"

"Again...you'd have us for one full year. After that, to remain in charge, following the Pylor code... you'd have to defend your command in battle once more. But all this is ridiculous speculation... just look at you. Why talk about a year from now when you're barely able to stand on your feet? There's no way you'd be ready for any kind of combat in the ring in just a few days."

I couldn't argue with that. Then again, Doc Viv had done amazing things for me in the past.

"But hear this," Vince said, "We don't like you. We don't want to serve upon your ship. And we are who we are... we're not looking for any kind of redemption."

"Good. That's what I'm counting on," I said.

That got Vince's attention.

"I'm not going to ask you to do anything you're not used to. You can do your pirating and marauding as you see fit. Under two conditions."

"And what's that?"

"You never, ever attack an Allied ship or planet. Thine, Pleidians, and humans and their home worlds are off-limits."

"And the second condition?"

"That when I call... when I need your help, you drop what you're doing, and you come running."

Vince turned to look back at his fellow decision makers. Nods were exchanged, and he turned back to me.

"We agree. But we have a few conditions of our own."

I really needed another shot. "Go ahead."

Vince smiled, exposing his discolored teeth. *Huh, there was a tooth missing.* "That you don't ever attack a Pylor ship or one of our planets."

They have planets? As in more than one?

"And when we call for assistance... you drop everything and come running."

Now I was hearing multiple voices in my ears. I held up a finger, gesturing to Vince to hold on.

"You absolutely cannot agree to that!" Derrota barked.

"The US Space-Navy does not answer to a bunch of wild bandits," Ryder said.

Then I heard Bosun Johanna Polk, "You're treading on thin ice, Captain Quintos." "Just do it. Tell him we're with them," Gail Pristy said.

Interesting that Gail had been the only dissenting voice. I'd have to make her an honorary pirate. I pictured her with an eye patch and a parrot on her shoulder. God, I was getting loopy. I looked Vince in the eye. "You have a deal."

He smiled back. "Fine. But all this is moot if you do not best our champion, if and when you can defeat the Varapin."

"Fine." I turned toward Hardy, a hand holding my side and feeling like I was about to fall flat on my face.

"Oh, and Captain?"

"Yeah?" I said without looking back.

"Welcome to the dark side."

HARDY WAS BEHIND, PUSHING MY HOVERING MediCart along the Deck 10 corridor at what seemed like roller-coaster speed. Doc Viv and Gail were running along on opposite sides of me. Apparently, I'd toppled over. One second I was vertical, talking to Vince, the next, horizontal, laid out on the deck.

Gail, panting as she ran, leaned down close to me. "We have mere minutes before the Varapin will strike again. What do you want to do?"

"Commence phase one."

"What the hell is phase one?"

Had I not talked to her about that? It wasn't as if I had a lot of free time lately. "Derrota... he knows, as do Coogong, Ryder, and Sergeant Max. Ryder's operation is first and should fully distract the Varapin."

"When were you going to tell me all this?"

"I'm telling you now. Also, the Pylors. Once the Varapin start firing on the phantom ships, tell Vince it's time he starts firing on the Varapin fleet... we only need four or five of the ghouls' vessels to fall out of formation for that dampening field to start losing integrity."

The MediCart had passed into HealthBay. Doc Viv said, "That's it, Gail; he's lost too much blood. We're getting him into surgery."

I only now realized Gail had been holding my hand.

Hanging back now, she said, "So we're doing this? We're going into battle with our captain out of commission?"

I coughed up blood and sputtered, "You have my utmost confidence; you'll do just fine."

Chapter 29

XO Pristy was too nervous to sit down at the captain's mount. Instead, she paced back and forth behind the tactical station. Chen had set up open feeds to Captain Ryder within Flight Bay, Derrota and Coogong within the Quan-Tangler compartment, and Sergeant Max, who was with his team out in Whale's Alley.

There was also one more feed open to Decks 72/73. She looked up to the multi-segmented halo display—her eyes taking in what looked to be total anarchy, a crazy circus of activity going on up there within that Symbio deck. A hundred Symbio-Poths—hell, maybe twice that many—were gathering like stage actors taking their positions just prior to the curtain rising.

The Captain had come up with the multi-pronged plan but had not fine-tuned it yet enough to be viable. That, she had had to do on her own. She'd gained an extra thirty minutes from the Varapin, had hailed First Warrior Veesh Slat and explained about the Captain's injuries and subsequent last-minute surgery.

Obviously, she couldn't go into detail about the fighting

match between the Captain and Thunderballs; instead, she'd shared a live feed going on within HealthBay's surgery center, where two surgery bots, along with Doc Viv, were attending to Galvin's multiple life-threatening wounds. Veesh Slat was most curious as to how the Captain had been so badly injured, but Pristy again evaded that line of inquiry.

Before closing the channel, she said, "Captain Quintos' intentions were to shuttle over the transporter device. I assume you still want me to do that in his stead?"

"Do so immediately, and we can bring this confrontation to an end."

That had been fifteen minutes ago. She checked her TAC-Band. She had fifteen minutes before the Varapin would recommence attacks on the 9th Fleet.

She stopped pacing, stood, and tried to steady her breathing.

Awaale Samatar, the Ethiopian junior officer of the deck, spoke with a calming, accented voice. "You've got this, XO. Captain Quintos has put his trust in you for a reason. You are the very best at what you do."

"Thank you, Awaale... I hope your faith in me is warranted."

She knew the next words to come out of her mouth would change everything. They would either be the start of a battle campaign that would turn things around or be the beginning of the end for the 9th Fleet, *Jefferson*, and maybe even the Pylor pirates. The next words... so, so many lives at stake. She wished Hardy was here, as he usually was for the Captain. But of course, he wouldn't leave Quintos' side. She couldn't even rely on Derrota; he was up there on the halo display, waiting on her next command.

There were four phases to the Captain's ridiculous plan. Phase one, get Ryder and his cloaked Arrows out into space and into position nearby. Using the Lorg-Mav's RCHD's technology, they would start projecting close to a hundred faux US Space-Navy warships. Hopefully a convincing diversion.

Phase two, Derrota and Coogong would begin transporting Max and his team onto a forward deck within *Oblivion*—get them as close to the enemy's bridge as possible. Pristy had discussed sending the rest of *Jefferson's* Marines under the command of Colonel Bonell, but between the two of them had decided to hold the four hundred or so boots back, just in case of a Varapin invasion—something the enemy was sure to attempt.

Phase three had required quansporting back the Sir Louis de Broglie transporter from Thunderballs' starship. Coogong and Derrota would then start moving Symbio-Poths on over to *Oblivion*. Coogong had assured her that he would be able to remotely quansport multiples of twenty to thirty Symbios at a time, they not being human—there being less at stake. Pristy wondered how any one of the Symbio-Poths would feel about that.

Phase four was the one she was least confident about. Although, in reality, she wasn't all that confident about any of the other three phases either. Phase four was in the tiny hands of Pirate Vince. Would he, on Pristy's command, commence an all-out assault on the Varapin fleet? She didn't know.

As part of phase four, she would bring *Jefferson's* big guns into the battle. Where the pirates would be concentrating their attacks, along with *Jefferson's* cloaked Arrows, on the Varapin fleet, *Jefferson* would be going after *Oblivion*. With luck, at some point soon within the early stages of the battle, the 9th Fleet would become freed up enough to balance the odds. God, so much depended on her next words.

Gail swallowed. Looking at the live feed into the ship's flight bay, she said, "Captain Ryder, commence phase one. Godspeed, Wallace."

Cheers erupted in response to her directive. Pilots and bay

crews alike scrambled to get their modified Arrows up in the air and out into space.

She turned her attention to Sergeant Max's feed, which was out of Whale's Alley. "Sergeant Max... is your team ready?"

Before Max could answer, Wanda yelled over him, "We were born ready... come on! Pull the trigger!"

Max shrugged. "Yeah, we're ready."

Pristy watched as Arrows within the flight bay were now approaching the bay's shielding field at the access threshold. One by one, they disappeared, cloaking just prior to rocketing out into space.

"Mr. Handly?" she said without looking at him at the tactical station.

He shook his head, "Short-range sensors... negative on picking up any of the Arrows. They're invisible."

She waited for Ryder's squadron to separate and take up their predetermined positions. Ryder's voice came back, "We're as ready as we'll ever be."

Pristy felt an adrenaline rush. "Go ahead... let's show the Varapin that the US Space-Navy's 5th Fleet has just arrived in system, Captain."

All at once, dozens and dozens of Space-Navy warships began to materialize. Heavy battleships, destroyers, gunboats, two more heavy dreadnoughts, and too many other warships to count—each looking powerful and substantial.

"That should get the first warrior's attention for a while."

"We're ready when you are, XO," Max said, still standing by.

Pristy turned her attention to Coogong and Derrota, who were looking back at her with anticipation. "Quansport Max and his team, now!"

She looked over to Chen. "Send a communiqué via our

inboard RCHD to all 9th Fleet assets. Let the ship COs know what's happening and apologize for the lack of previous contact. Be ready to challenge the enemy once the Varapin dampening field is down."

"Aye, XO... I'm on it," Chen said.

Chapter 30

I awoke feeling like I'd been run over by a tank. Looking around, I saw that I was in the surgery center's recovery room. Taking a peek under my HealthBay gown, I saw liberal amounts of AugmentFlesh had been applied to both my shoulder and to the side of my ribs. I moved cautiously, twisting my upper body from side to side, and found the pain was minimal.

Doc Viv hurried into the room, checked my hovering overhead medical avatar, and said, "You're going to have to take it easy for a few days, Quintos." Her tone was cool and efficient. That, and she had yet to make eye contact with me.

"Thanks for patching me up, Doc. I hope I wasn't too much of a nuisance."

That got her to glance my way. "Are you being funny?"

"Obviously not, since you're not exactly laughing. What's up with you?"

"What do you mean what's up with me? Nothing's up with me... now get up and get out of here. The battle has started. Your four phases?"

I flung the covers aside and swung my legs over the side of

the bed. As I was attempting to stand, a bout of dizziness had me teetering. Viv was there to keep me upright, holding me around my waist. Our faces were mere inches apart. We looked into each other's eyes for a long moment.

"Viv..."

"Shut up and go do what you do... go save humanity."

"I have just one question for you..."

"What?"

"Where are my clothes?"

That brought the beginnings of a smile to her lips. "You have a fresh uniform in there," she gestured to an inset closet.

I FOUND HARDY WAITING RIGHT OUTSIDE HealthBay. "Give me a sit report while we walk, Hardy," I said, heading off toward the GravLifts.

"Hello to you too. You know some people were worried about you."

"No time for any of that. Sit report?"

By the time we'd reached Deck 13 and stepped out into Whale's Alley, I was sufficiently brought up to date on everything that had transpired over the last two and a half hours since I had gone under the knife. Ryder and his faux warships had surrounded the Varapin, as well as the joined-at-the-hip 9th Fleet. Max and crew were now on board *Oblivion*, staying out of sight and waiting for orders to proceed. They foresaw they'd have heavy resistance with onboard forces. What had apparently stopped XO Pristy from continuing on with the subsequent phases was an earlier comms transmission from First Warrior Veesh Slat.

I entered the bridge at a fast walk.

CAPTAIN ON BRIDGE

Pristy stepped down from the captain's mount. "Hardy bring you up to speed?" she asked.

"Pretty much." I looked up to the multiple feeds, but the one that had my full attention was that of Empress Shawlee. This was what had thrown a wrench in our operation. She was standing, her extended arms and legs strapped to a bulkhead. I tried to make sense of what I was seeing. The compartment the Empress was occupying was segmented; nearby were a number of knee-high enclosures, or maybe better described as pens. There was movement within the pens, but I couldn't make out what—

Pristy said, "According to Veesh Slat, what you're looking at are close to two hundred small rodent-sized creatures called Jippers."

"Jippers?"

"Uh-huh. They're delightful little things. Always ravenous and capable of eating flesh, bone, hair, you name it. I figure they're a land-based version of our South American piranhas."

"So, what's all this about... what am I looking at here?"

"It's somewhere within *Oblivion*."

"I could have figured that out."

Pristy rolled her eyes. "The compartment is configured with motion sensors, hundreds of them. If someone were to, say, transport into this compartment, the walls to those little pens would instantly collapse."

"Thus allowing the Joppers—"

"Jippers."

"Fine, Jippers, to head right for the Empress."

She nodded. "We are to cease all aggression, or they will release the little monsters while we watch the Empress being devoured alive."

"Any ideas?"

She shook her head.

I looked at the rest of the bridgecrew.

Shrugs. Blank faces.

"How about you, Hardy?"

"I have no idea."

"No, I mean how about you attempt a rescue? It's not as if you'd be at risk."

Pristy said, "We talked about that. The second Hardy materialized in there, hundreds of Jippers would flood the deck; he wouldn't be able to kill enough of them before they'd get to the Empress."

"How about if I went with him? Wearing a hardened combat suit."

"It's probably a trap," Hardy said, his face display now an animated snapping bear trap.

"Cute... but we have to do something. Have to try."

"Well, it certainly shouldn't be you. You just came out of surgery," Pristy said.

"No. It has to be me. I'm not putting anyone else in jeopardy."

"Including me?" said the ChronoBot.

"Sorry, Hardy. You and I are in this together."

Before turning to leave, I said, "As soon as we get the Empress out of there, resume where you left off with the plan."

Pristy pursed her lips, clearly wanting to say something.

"Just say it; I have to go."

She lowered her voice. "I don't see how you're going to pull this off... not this time, Galvin."

I didn't either. Shawlee and I had a special relationship. A special friendship. So, I wasn't going to allow her to be devoured by a bunch of hungry rodents. Not on my watch.

. . .

SUITED UP IN THE LATEST US SPACE-NAVY COMBAT suit gear, I was armed with a shredder rifle, a tagger holstered onto my upper thigh, and a battle blade sheathed onto my opposite thigh. We entered the Quan-Tangler compartment. Derrota and Coogong were there, ready to transport us directly into *Oblivion*, into that chamber of horrors where Empress Shawlee was being held.

Hardy and I took up our respective positions on the raised pedestal. Derrota looked as if he wanted to discuss things more.

"There's no time for talk. Just be ready to transport the three of us out of there on my command."

Coogong and Derrota exchanged a look.

"What?"

"It's just that there are the ever-present MTBFs with this thing," Derrota said, gesturing to the pedestal.

I made a face.

Hardy said, "The meantime between failures... the Quan-Tangler has been working perfectly for way too long. It's bound to have a hiccup soon; the meantime between failures is past due."

"Quansport us now... it'll be fine." I raised my weapon and released the safety. Hardy became fully armed by deploying all his hidden energy cannons—

SNAP! SNAP! SNAP! SNAP!

We were locked and loaded.

The two behind the console exchanged one more hesitant look before Coogong did as asked.

We materialized into *Oblivion's* holding cell. No sooner had we arrived than I heard an unlatching mechanism. *CLICK! CLACK!* And then came the squeals and the sounds of tiny feet scampering upon the deck. Hundreds of vicious-looking, hairy, oversized heads and sharp protruding teeth began their combined sprint toward Shawlee.

"Galvin!" She tried in vain to pull her arms free from their manacles.

Every one of Hardy's energy cannons was now active. His turreted shoulder-mount cannon was going nonstop, tracking, spinning, targeting, and firing rapid Phazon Pulsar blasts. I'm sure the compartment smelled like burnt hair and scorched flesh, but thankfully my helmet spared me those delightful aromas.

My tagger was out, and I was firing at anything that moved. Several of the little beasts had evaded Hardy's and my assault and had hopped up onto Shawlee. She screamed. And then she shrieked as one of the little fuckers got his canines buried deep into her left leg. Hardy shot the thing; amazing he hadn't hit the Empress in the process. I pulled my knife and went to work on the manacle straps securing her left arm.

"What the hell are these made of!" I yelled to nobody in particular. Clearly the Varapin had composite materials our side didn't. Another Jipper jumped onto Shawlee, and then another and then another. She was now whimpering; blood was streaming down her arms and legs in multiple places.

"Hold your arm out, Shawlee."

She did as asked, and I used my tagger to shoot the seemingly indestructible strap. That did the trick; she had one arm free.

"Give me your weapon!" she yelled. She tore it from my hand and proceeded to shoot the remaining three straps herself.

In the meantime, I was using my shredder—holding the trigger and releasing a deluge of weapons fire. The air was black with smoke, and it sounded like Shawlee was coughing up a lung.

I yelled, "Coogong! Get us the hell out of here!"

"Yes, Captain... attempting to... Oh no."

The barrage of bright, crisscrossing energy bolts continued

to fill the compartment. My shredder was getting hot; even wearing gloves—the thing was overheating. Shawlee was having trouble holding onto her tagger. Most of the Jippers had been reduced to smoldering hamburger patties on the deck, but not all of them. Twenty to thirty of them continued to circle around and in between our feet.

"Coogong!"

"I'm so, so, sorry, Captain... I did warn you about the MTBFs..."

"Shit! Hardy... can you blast our way out of here?"

He redirected one of his arm cannons toward the nearest bulkhead since there didn't seem to be an actual door or hatchway in sight. He changed from firing Phazon Pulsars to a steady stream of bright white energy that was making good progress cutting a narrow fissure in the metal. When Hardy had outlined a three-foot-by-seven-foot archway, I moved in and stomped my heel on the plate. It didn't budge—all I had accomplished was to send a painful shock wave jolt up into my leg.

Hardy moved me aside and gave the same area a magnificent kick. *Clang!* We now had a doorway out of there.

Chapter 31

Varapin Warship, *Oblivion*

Sergeant Max Dryer

Two hours earlier...

Sergeant Max and team, having quansported into an out-of-the-way power distribution junction, were trying to keep a low profile on their circuitous route to *Oblivion's* bridge. Because the plan was to inevitably take control of the vast ship, what would usually have been easy targets of destruction like the power junction, overhead conduit lines, or sub-deck network and comms lines—all those needed to remain in place. It had been determined, mostly by Science Chief Derrota and XO Pristy, that the power distribution junction would be the only viable, relatively secure and out-of-the-way quansport location. Unfortunately, it was close to a mile from the ship's command center.

"It would have been a lot easier if we'd just quansported right into the bridge," Grip said.

Wanda shushed the big man. "We went over this... there was too great a risk of transporting into valued equipment, like a command console... or even one of the Varapin crewmembers. Place is jam-packed. It's nothing like *Jefferson's* bridge."

Max, taking point down the corridor, noticed on his helmet's heads-up display, or HUD, that two virtual icons were lagging behind. "Ham and Hock, stay in formation."

"Sorry, Sarge," Ham said.

Max was still a little surprised *Oblivion's* onboard AI, MATHR's equivalent, hadn't yet detected their presence. Thanks to Coogong's ingenious tinkering, he'd come up with a way for their combat suits to emanate Varapin bio-readings. The only problem with this logic would be when the AI could not reconcile their five new bio-readings against crew rosters. Coogong was fairly certain that sort of function would not take place all that often—but inevitably, it would happen.

Thus far they had not encountered any enemy crewmembers—that was until now. Max held up a fist, bringing his team to a standstill. HUD readings had four Varapin beyond the next bend but making their way toward them within the same corridor. "We need to hide; look for an access panel or alcove... anything!"

"I got something here," Wanda said, working at getting a power door to slide open. "Hock, come put your weight into this," she said.

Between the two of them, the automatic door was, although way too slowly, being shoved open. Once there was enough space, Wanda ducked beneath Hock's arms and went inside. Moments later, Ham, Grip, and Max slid through as well. Once clear, Hock released the door as he, too, jumped inside. The door slid shut just as the sounds of Varapin voices filled the corridor outside.

Max listened at the door, making sure they hadn't been

noticed. As the scratchy, grating voices moved past, he felt confident they were safe. For now.

"Uh, Sarge?" Ham said.

He turned to face the others. They were all looking at the same thing Ham was looking at. Max had already noticed that the compartment was dimly lit, almost dark. And there was a fog-like mist rising up off the deck to about knee level. He joined the others and took in the spectacle. He said, "That's an Ebom-Pod," gesturing at the coffin-sized thing.

Wanda nodded. "It's where the ghouls sleep, or whatever it is they do in those things."

"Can we look inside?" Ham asked.

"Are you an idiot?" Hock said to his twin, "There might be someone in there. What then?"

"We shoot him?" Ham said.

Hock apparently didn't have an answer to that, so he said nothing.

"Let's go... leave it be," Max said. "Wanda, Hock, how about you pry that door open once more?"

Once the five of them were back within the corridor, they moved at a fast jog. the bridge was actually two levels up. This corridor had been determined to be the least occupied. The problem would be ascending upward. Since the Varapin had the innate ability to hover, they didn't need stairs or elevators; they simply slipped into any one of the vertical service access tubes placed all around the ship. There were also horizontal tubes for high-speed passage forward and aft within the ship.

They passed by an access port to one of the vertical service tubes. Ham said, "I wish I could float... ya know, like the ghouls."

"Your fat ass, float? Yeah, I don't think so," Grip said.

"Screw you, Grip... you know I've been trying to lose weight."

"Suggestion: one slice of pumpkin pie after dinner... instead of the whole damn pie."

Max was used to the back-and-forth ribbing within the team. It typically didn't bother him. A good stress reliever. But this wasn't the time for it. "Stay present, people; we're coming up to our transition point."

In unison, they slowed to a fast walk, then a quiet shuffle as they approached the next vertical access tube. Checking his HUD, Max confirmed this one rose two levels up and came out within fifteen feet to the entrance to the bridge. He moved closer to the access port and snuck a peek upward. All clear. Sensing movement, he looked downward. Five feet below him, and rising fast, was a Varapin crewmember.

He took in the ugly, skeletal face with its two beady black eyes. As the Varapin's jaw opened to yell out, Max did the only thing he could think of—he reached down and grabbed the quickly rising alien.

Having caught him around his bony neck, Max tightened his grip and simultaneously stepped backward while pulling the now frantic and flailing Varapin along with him. Having to hold him with two hands now, Max managed to bring *Oblivion's* crewmember onto the deck, where he continued to squirm about like a fish out of water. Grip got a boot on the Varapin's neck just as Max pulled his hands free. As Grip put his full weight down, there was an audible *CRACK!*

Movement.

Max noticed more ascending dark shapes moving up the tube just feet away. This obviously was a busy thruway to the upper levels. He'd noticed there were plenty of hand- and footholds within the tube, so climbing up would not be a problem for them. But going unnoticed; that wasn't going to happen.

"Ideas?" Max said.

Wanda took a peek into the tube. "They're fairly wide. Guess it's so those going up and those going down don't bang heads."

"Interesting, but not a big help," Max said.

Grip said, "Why don't we just chuck this guy's body down the tube? I'm sure there are accidents all the time. Fucker's not paying attention, does a header into someone else. Lights out."

"I like it," Max said, smiling. "But we'd have to weigh him down. Better yet, let's try to get him tangled up below. Block anyone from ascending."

Wanda was already reaching for her utility belt, one compartment having a twenty-foot coiled length of high-tension cable. The team worked quietly and efficiently. Once the dead crewmember had the cable tied around his middle, Wanda secured the other end around a horizontal support strut.

Grip lifted the dead Varapin with one hand. "Guy's light." Carrying the corpse more or less like luggage, he tossed the body down the tube. It made a variety of thumping and clunking sounds before the cable went taut. Max took a look. The dead Varapin was completely blocking the access tube from below.

"Okay, we need to hurry. They'll eventually discover that cable and know something's amiss. Ham, start climbing."

"Nah. I'll go last."

"Why?"

"I don't want everyone looking at my fat ass—"

"I'll go," Wanda said, already scurrying up into the tube.

By the time the five of them had reached two levels up, there was a commotion down below. Screechy yells were making their way up the access tube.

Grip said, laughing, "Hey, Hock, you clog the pipes again with one of your monster-sized craps?"

"Bite me."

The team came out fast, weapons raised and ready to

confront the enemy. But the anteroom area, a convergence point between multiple corridors and other service access tubes, was empty. While climbing the tube, Max had been contacted by XO Pristy and told to hold back on attacking the bridge until further notice. She wanted to coordinate the timing with Ryder's faux warships arrival in local space. That and there were complications with Empress Shawlee.

Wanda tapped Max's shoulder with a gloved hand, pointing to an open accessway with an upward-rising ramp. Written in alien hieroglyphic–like characters, his HUD produced a meta-tag translation: OBSERVATION DECK.

Without another word, and with Max in the lead, they all hurried through the entrance and hustled up the incline. Entering the circular domed area—an area that was all glass, allowing spectacular views out to space beyond—Max came to an abrupt stop. There before him, looking out to the heavens beyond, was none other than First Warrior Veesh Slat.

Suddenly, a loud Klaxon began to wail—the sound seemingly coming from all directions. Veesh Slat slowly tore his attention away from his view of the confined 9th Fleet beyond and looked at Max. Reading the Varapin commander's expression would have been impossible, but one thing was for sure—Max being there with his team was of no surprise to him.

The Varapin leader's harsh voice sounded like death itself. "Enjoy your last few minutes of life, humans... take some time and enjoy the view. It will be the last thing you ever see."

Max raised his shredder and fired. The others behind him did the same. Targeted energy bolts flew into and out of the first warrior without his long robes so much as fluttering.

"It's a damn hologram; hold your fire!" Max said.

Hock said, "This was a trap." He gestured, hitching a thumb over his shoulder, "Hatch closed when the alarms started."

Max moved over to the entrance. Sure enough, a closed hatch was now present at the top of the ramp.

Wanda said, "If we're going to be stuck here, at least the view is awesome."

"These windows... a form of diamond glass, maybe?" Max said, his face showing concern behind his helmet's faceplate. "We need to find a way out of here. Let's get to work."

Then they heard it. The clicking and clanking sounds of automated clamps being disengaged.

Wanda said, "Mother of God... we're being..."

"Set adrift," Max said, completing her words.

All at once, the five of them reached out for something, anything to grab onto. As the glass dome began to drift away from *Oblivion*, the big vessel's gravity generators no longer had influence over the now-tumbling-away compartment.

Chapter 32

Perseus Arm of the Milky Way
Open Space

Captain Wallace Ryder

Present time . . .

Ryder looked out through his Arrow's canopy, seeing a spectacular view of US Space-Navy warships that he would have sworn were actually there, were the solid and substantial might of the US Space-Navy's 5th Fleet. None of it was real. What was real were those Arrows that were not assigned as faux behemoth warship decoys, such as his own, moving in triangular formations of twelve fighters each. There were six such squadrons moving within the illusionary fleet. Ballbuster, aka Akari James, was among the other squad leaders out here.

He decided to hail the XO again. "J-Dog to Command. Over."

Chen answered the hail. "Go ahead, J-Dog. Over."

"Waiting on status... we can't fly around out here indefinitely. Over."

"Hold... XO wants to talk to you, J-Dog. Over."

"Dammit, Ryder," Pristy said just below a shout. "I told you I'd give the command as soon as the time was right."

He offered up a crooked smile. She'd ignored proper fighter craft comms protocols for one thing. The young XO was obviously stressed. Even though she was surrounded by a full bridgecrew, he knew she was basically all alone. The Captain and Hardy were off the ship, and Derrota was still in the Quan-Tangler compartment, so a lot was riding on her small shoulders. "Talk to me, Gail... what's going on? Over."

He heard her let out a breath. "Captain wants to hold on moving to the next phase or phases, at least until Max can take the bridge. But communications to the five Marines have been terminated. It may be they're in a part of the ship that's hindering communications."

Ryder debated whether to say what he wanted to say. *Screw it.* "Look, XO Pristy... you have the con; you're sitting at the captain's mount. You are at the center hub of this operation, not Quintos. Make the call as you see fit. I go by the philosophy that sometimes it's better to ask for forgiveness later than get permission first. And I know the Captain has practically made that his personal motto."

She laughed. "You're right, J-Dog... have your squadrons commence their attacks on *Oblivion* now. Over."

XO Pristy turned to Stanley Handly. "You're still on with the pirate... um, what's his name, Vince?"

"Yes, Ma'am. Surprisingly enough, the Pylor fleet, albeit cloaked, has stuck around."

"Tell them to commence their attack on the Varapin fleet. And wish them good luck."

"Chen, hail the Captain again."

She'd been nervous that the Captain's comms, just like Max's, might have gone dark.

The feeds from the Captain flickered up on the halo display. There were two feed viewpoints, one that showed a slightly distorted perspective of his face, taken from his inside helmet cam, and the outside helmet cam view of what the Captain was seeing. Pristy got a quick glance at Hardy and then the Empress—she was ashen-faced and limping. Pristy grimaced at seeing the multiple, bloodied bite marks on her arms and legs.

"Go for Quintos... we have the Empr... tell Coogong to trans... her now."

Pristy said, "You're breaking up. But I got the gist of your transmission. Look, Captain... Max and crew are no longer in contact."

"I already know th... we'll investi... Will keep yo... informed."

"It may be a trap, Captain."

"Agreed. You sho... procee... all phas... now."

She held back on telling him she was already doing just that. The Captain's feed flickered out.

Stanley Handly said, "I contacted Coogong; he has a lock on the Empress... quansporting her back to *Jefferson* now."

Pristy watched as J-Dog, Ballbuster, and the other squadron leaders were now initiating their attacks on *Oblivion* like minuscule fruit flies attacking a Bengal tiger. Although their Arrows had cloaked, the halo display continued to show the small craft as icons.

"Pylors are engaging the Varapin fleet," Handly said. Again, the pirate vessels were cloaked, so only their respective icons were visible on the display.

USS Jefferson

She let out a breath. This next phase was the most screwball of all. She found Coogong's helmeted face there up on the display, looking back at her.

He said, "Gail, the Empress is now on board. Stephan is escorting her to HealthBay."

"We need to get moving on the next phase. Can you proceed without Derrota? We'll need every available Symbio-Poth quansported over to *Oblivion* like ten minutes ago."

"I will get started immediately. The Sir Broglie device has been moved up to the Symbio deck, and Stephan will be manning that one. We will get this done, I assure you. And you have no preference as to which Symbio-Poth goes where on *Oblivion*?"

"Random... we're looking for unbridled havoc and mayhem."

"Yes, Gail, I believe we will achieve just that."

"And again, make sure our own people are not attacked."

"Yes, yes... Ensign Plorinne assures me he has programmed those safeguards into each and every Symbio... and might I add, he is very sorry for his previous actions. He hopes you and the Captain can forgive him."

"We'll just have to see. Redemption rides on how today evolves. You have a lot of work to do; best you get started, Coogong."

"We've got incoming!" Stanley Handly said far louder than he needed to. "Forty-two smart missiles from *Oblivion*."

"Battle stations, everyone," she said, taking her seat. She wasn't quite sure if she should curse the Captain or thank him for this opportunity.

Handly turned in his seat to look at her. "Orders, Sir?"

Pristy hesitated and looked at the halo display. She said, "I want as many of those missiles taken out as possible before they get anywhere near us. Helm, bring *Jefferson* about. I want us portside to portside with that ship. Fire all Phazon Pulsars... target those missiles, full barrage."

Handly said, "Varapin fleet is now firing on the Pylors or trying to at least. Huh, their cloaking is excellent."

Pristy looked back at her JOOD. "Mr. Samatar, you're trained on the tactical board, yes?"

"Yes, Ma'am... fully certified on each—"

"Cut the chitchat. Get up here and help out Handly. Tactical's about to get real busy."

A bright flash on the halo display broke her concentration. Everyone knew the tell-tale sign—another ship had been destroyed. The question was, whose was it?

Samatar said, "*USS Bravo*. That was a smaller gunship. All six hundred lives lost. Nothing is left of the vessel, XO."

"It's not all bad news though," Handly broke in. "There's a disruption, more like an unbalancing of the Varapin dampening field."

Chen said, "I'm getting hailed by two, three, hell, all of the remaining 9th Fleet vessels now! Comms back online."

"Keep your cool, Crewman Chen... tell them to confront the enemy and do so with everything they have. There won't be any second chances here."

Grimes at the helm said, "In position, Sir... portside to portside... we're at two hundred and fifty clicks."

"Tactical, fire off sixty smart missiles. Make it a combo of nukes and fusion-tipped. Target the stern. Let's concentrate on *Oblivion's* propulsion, and just maybe we can avoid killing our own people in the process."

"Thirty of the incoming birds taken out," Samatar said. "The last twelve getting through undeterred."

"I guess we now get to see how well these new shields of ours can take a punch," Pristy said.

The first of the missiles struck *Jefferson* portside near the bow, and not so far from the bridge. Pristy heard the impact prior to the ship rumbling and vibrations coming up through the deck plates. Then the rest of the missiles hit in rapid succession.

"Talk to me, somebody... damage report!"

Bosun Polk spoke up, "Preliminary damage reports coming in now... Deck 5, we have atmosphere venting into space. Minimal breach though. Deck 38, we have another missile breach, but it didn't detonate. Looks like our shields stopped the other ten."

"Okay, get SWM crews dispatched. And find somebody that knows how to deactivate a live Varapin missile."

Stanley Handly said, "Four of our birds cleared *Oblivion's* shields. Waiting on CIC's damage assessment."

More bright flashes on the halo display.

"One Pylor ship, not sure what it was... and a Varapin battle cruiser...one of their heavies!"

Cheers and hoots broke out from the bridgecrew.

Finally, some good news.

"More incoming from *Oblivion*... thirty-three fusion tips."

"Match them bird for bird, Tactical. And someone give me that damage report on *Oblivion's* propulsion system."

Handly leaned down closer to his board as if studying the readings. "All I can say, XO, is she'd have a hard time making FTL. But I suspect sub-light maneuvering is still intact."

"Keep at it. I want to pound the hell out of her stern."

"XO, we have—"

"I see them, Mr. Samatar," Pristy said. They were like angry bees spewing from a kicked hive; hundreds of Varapin Cyclone Death Fighters were emerging from *Oblivion*. She hadn't realized the vast ship had more than one flight bay—in fact, the enemy ship had three.

"Phazon Pulsars engaging," Handly said, "and letting J-Dog know now they'll soon be getting some unwanted company."

"XO... we're picking up an object."

"Think maybe you can be a tad more specific, Mr. Samatar?"

"Yes, Ma'am. Sorry, Ma'am. I'm putting it up on the halo display now."

The new feed came alive. Pristy leaned in, squinting her eyes. "What the hell is that?" To her, it looked like an oversized, slowly tumbling, melted ice cube. Then she saw movement within it.

"MATHR's picked up bio-readings... It's Max and his team," Handly said.

"Chen?" Pristy said. "Can you—"

He shook his head, "Must be something to do with the glass surroundings. Working on it."

She said, "Coogong? Can you get a lock on them?"

The Thine scientist did not look up from his console. She knew he was more than a little busy remote-transporting groups of Symbios from Decks 72/73 onto *Oblivion*. It took nearly a minute before Coogong looked up. "Sorry, Gail... let me see if I can... yes, I have a lock. I see five individuals. Shall I bring them back onto *Jefferson?*"

She thought on that. "No... put them in close proximity to the Captain. Obviously, taking the bridge with such a small assault team was not the best of ideas. Can you do that?"

"Of course. Quansporting them now."

Chapter 33

I was happy to hear the Empress had successfully made it back onto *Jefferson*—although the comms transmission was barely decipherable. Within a kind of narrow service corridor, Hardy and I were approximately midship and moving forward at a slow jog. We knew it was only a matter of time before we would be coming up against serious enemy forces. An alarm Klaxon was blaring overhead, and there'd been a number of rumbling vibrations—incoming missile strikes, no doubt.

Hardy said, "My sensors tell me this vessel has a crew size of approximately twelve thousand hands, or should I say bony claws, more specifically. Huh, that's weird... I'm not picking up on any human bio-readings other than yours."

We were headed forward toward the bridge, specifically to assist Max, who, last I'd heard, was holed up, unable to break out of a domed compartment.

Hardy said, "This accessway is coming to a dead end twenty yards forward, Cap."

"Any other surreptitious routes we can take?"

"Uh... that would be a big fat no."

"So, you're saying we'll have to fight our way forward up on a crew deck?"

He attempted one of his odd shrugs that just looked ridiculous on a robot. "We can request Coogong to quansport us..."

"No, he and Derrota are more than a little busy right about now." I pointed to one of the service tube ports coming up on the left. Great for Varapin that could float or hover; not so great for bipedal beings that had to climb. I came to a stop and looked up and then down into the tube. "All clear. You first, Hardy. And try not to make as much noise as last time. You clanging around like an old church bell is sure to attract a drove of unwanted ghouls."

"You know... I have feelings too. The latest issue of *22nd Century Psychology* has an issue on just that subject. 'Your Body-Image—Improving One's Self-Esteem Through Positive Reinforcement.'"

I rolled my eyes. Considering Hardy had the brain of a human, he'd never had any issues having a mechanical body. In fact, he was quite conceited when it came to his ChronoBot exterior. Any damage to his perfectly polished chrome, say dings or charred energy bolt craters incurred during a battle, always required a full exterior restoration of his plating later on. With that said, there were times Hardy liked wearing human clothes. I suspected he was caught somewhere in the middle, being part human, part ChronoBot and not fully assimilating to one or the other.

He pulled his large noggin out from the tube. "There are a whole lot of Varapin up there. We'll be the proverbial turds in the punchbowl, showing up unexpectedly."

I waited for an appropriate face-display animation, but he maintained his nostalgic once-human-looking face likeness. Why he preferred a black and white effigy, I didn't know.

"I got this," he said. He craned his teardrop-shaped head

downward, as if looking at his own belly button, that is, if he had a belly button, and started murmuring something undecipherable. There was a soft glow now emanating from his vest's breast pocket. I saw a little pixie head peer out and then the tips of tiny, fluttering translucent wings. Iris. The little fairy sprite looked up at Hardy, smiled, and pushed herself off into the air, leaving a sparkling wake of what could best be described as fairy dust. *How does she do that?*

She circled us twice, giggled, then shot up into the access tube.

I said, "She's a Disney character come to life, I'll give you that... but I don't see her taking on any of those Varapin warriors up there."

"O ye of little faith. Just wait... and watch."

Suddenly, Hardy's face display erupted in a wild rush of darting and weaving movement. I realized Hardy was displaying Iris' visual perspective on the corridor up above. Up and down, then circling a particular ghoul's hooded head, then another, and then another. I saw glittering fairy dust and heard lots of giggling. No less than thirty or forty Varapin warriors were stopped in their hovering tracks, transfixed.

She was too fast to be caught in their bony clutches, although most of the ghouls were trying to do just that. The total disruption was comical, and I couldn't help laughing out loud. And then the little sprite was heading off down the corridor, a tiny rocket, leaving a trail behind her. It was like a dinner bell had been rung; with no exception, all of the Varapin took up fast pursuit.

Hardy said, "We should probably get a move on up there... the coast is clear."

Hardy went first, and halfway up the tube, I saw a flash of golden light as Iris disappeared back into the ChronoBot's leather vest pocket.

As I was extricating myself from the access tube, several ghouls rounded a corner in front of us at an intersecting passageway. Hardy shot them, vaporizing their heads. Interesting; their lifeless robed bodies remained suspended, still hovering there in the air.

I tried to contact *Jefferson* with no luck. We continued moving forward, ready and expecting enemy confrontations. What I didn't expect to see, not ten feet in front of us, were five forms rapidly, block by block, being quansported.

Wanda, fully formed and looking slightly discombobulated, turned and saw us. Her smile evaporated. She yelled, "Get down!" Her shredder was up and firing before I hit the deck. Looking behind us, all I saw was black. The robes of hundreds of Varapin warriors—and they were armed. The bright blue plasma bolts of the five crisscrossed above me, followed by the bright red return bolts from the Varapin. *Why didn't Hardy's sensors pick up on this attack?* No doubt, like the disruption of our comms, his sensors were being affected or jammed in some way.

Still lying prone on the deck, I got my own shredder raised and began firing. I was only partially aware that Hardy was striding off in the opposite direction, away from the oncoming attack. "Where the hell are you going?" I yelled over the mayhem.

He yelled back, "There's more coming! A lot more coming from the other direction... just going to say hi."

I heard his big ChronoBot cannons coming alive—the sound of so much weaponry in such a confined space was both frightening and exhilarating at the same time.

What was becoming all too apparent, though, was that the seven of us, even with Hardy's amazing combat capabilities, were ridiculously outmatched here. I had yet to release the trigger on my shredder, and the weapon was starting to overheat. Even through my gloves, soon I would find the thing too hot to hold.

I tried to hail *Jefferson* for the fifth time. Nothing. I looked back toward the access tube port. There was no way to get to it; the Varapin had almost reached it. *There has to be something we can do here! This can't be how my life ends.*

There was a hard thunk next to me. With a quick glance, I saw that it was Grip. His combat suit was riddled with blackened scorch marks. The dim glow of his helmet light illuminated his face. I saw his staring eyes. And then he blinked. He said, his voice muffled, "I think we're screwed here, Cap."

My own combat suit was on the verge of shutting down. I wondered, *How many plasma bolts can one of these new suits take before it just gives up?* I glanced at my HUD display and the multiple flashing warnings.

WARNING!
Suit Integrity Has Been Compromised
WARNING!
Temperature Compensators Off-Line
WARNING!
Power-Assist Servos Overheating

I felt several more plasma strikes pound my arms and torso. The scalding heat from each was like a hot poker being jabbed into me. For the first time, I had to struggle to stay conscious. Turning my head, I saw Grip and then Hock go down. Wanda was starting to waver on her feet.

I closed my eyes. Hardy was out of my sight line, but I was fairly certain he was close. His inner LuMan would not allow him to venture far from protecting me. I thought about the people I'd grown the closest to over the years. The people that mattered. Ryder and Derrota, even Coogong, were my friends. Brothers in arms. And then there was Doc Viv, of course. I knew she was not back on board *Jefferson* by sheer chance. She would never admit it; she was far too proud for that. We had a connection that was, well, complicated.

I thought of Gail Pristy. She was an amazing young woman. A woman just now coming to terms with her own capabilities—her own strengths as a starship officer. My feelings for her were growing—that, I could no longer deny. But would my feelings for her serve her over the long run? Because what had become an unmistakable truth over these last few years was that I was not long for being a US Space-Navy Captain. I not only defied command directives; hell, I actively looked for ways to do so.

Growing numb to the melee around me, it was getting hard to keep my eyes open. Sleep was what I needed. There's nothing I can do here... there's nothing any of us can do here. Losing isn't so bad. We tried... we all tried. Gave it our best. Shouldn't that be good enough?

Dammit! What was that sound? A voice. *Fuck... calm down. Stop with the yelling already. Oh yeah... it's Derrota.* That Mumbai-accented voice. It just sounds funny when he yells like that. I smiled. I'll miss that voice. Or will I? Does one smile when they're dead? Why would I... I'd be dead. I allowed myself to tune into that funny, clearly frantic voice.

"Stand by for incoming! Get clear!"

Incoming what? I tried to raise my head. Oh yeah. I remembered one of the HUD warnings...something about power-assist servos crapping out.

Something from behind me got ahold of my shoulders. Something strong. Suddenly, I was being yanked upward—a rag doll incapable of resisting. Hardy's voice was muffled since my suit was basically inoperable. Then, like Derrota, his voice was loud within my ocular implants.

"Get your ass moving, Cap; you can sleep when you're dead!"

That was enough to get some well-needed adrenaline coursing through my veins. I said, my voice barely a whisper, "Get me out of this suit... it's totally fucktipated."

I felt Hardy's metal fingers working the torso fasteners, the leg and arm battens, and finally, my helmet being turned and lifted over my head. I gasped in putrid, disgusting, smoke-filled air. Hardy had hauled me into an alcove. Looking around, I saw Max, Ham, and Wanda lying on the deck, each of their combat suits looking as if they'd been used for live-fire target practice—which wasn't that far from the truth.

Having stripped me out of my suit, Hardy shoved a shredder into my hands. "Nap time's over, princess. We've still got work to do." He looked like hell. Every inch of his highly polished chrome was now blackened with cratered scorch marks. His face display was just as bad. The ChronoBot looked around the corner and began firing from his left forearm cannon. I noticed the turret-mounted plasma cannon on his shoulder was broken, flopping around like a ball on a string.

I took a knee, took a look around the corner, and began firing. There were hundreds of Varapin warriors making slow but steady progress forward within the corridor. Although the deck was certainly covered with dead ghouls, there were also just as many floating around aimlessly, bumping into one another.

What happened next, well, let's just say, was most unexpected. And it coincided with what Derrota was so desperately trying to tell me.

The corridor was easily as wide and tall as Whale's Alley back on *Jefferson*, and also as long. My guess, a mile at least.

And it was about a quarter-mile down the corridor that I saw them quansporting into view. First three, then five, then three, then seven... they kept coming and coming. Big horses. And, to add to the craziness, knights wearing full metal armor were atop those horses. No less than forty horses and riders had materialized. For a brief moment, I wondered if I was dreaming this. If I was still out there lying on the deck, drifting in and out of unconscious dreamland.

Wanda, her helmet off, was up on her knees and at my side. Together we watched in dazed wonderment.

"Ready for battle!" a knight bellowed off in the distance, his seven-foot-long lance coming around, extending out before him. The other horses and riders spun and jockeyed around to face forward. The excited animals whinnied, and nostrils flared and snorted.

"Charge!" came the voice of that same knight. And they were off. A small army of Symbio horses and Symbio riders, each horse and rider having a combined weight of two thousand pounds, was advancing. Now, as they reached full gallop, the sounds of so many hooves clanging on the metal decking were, well... nothing short of exhilarating.

I wasn't sure if it was confusion or fear that kept the Varapin warriors from raising their weapons and firing, but not one did. The best word to describe the enemy ghouls was dumbfounded. With lances extended far out over his mount's head, the lead rider pierced—more like skewered—a hovering warrior. Still alive and screeching, he flailed and writhed in pain until his arms and legs drooped, his body going lifeless. Continuing on, that same knight skewered a second Varapin and then a third.

Hardy said, "Ah, nothing like shish kabobs to kick-start a party."

Both Wanda and Max seemed to have recovered at least

enough to sit up. Max said, "This isn't a spectator sport... engage the enemy!"

We began taking out the now-fighting-back-as-best-they-could enemy. Being the lone combatant without the protection of a combat suit, I pretty much stayed behind Hardy's large frame while taking shots at the robed ghouls. As large as the corridor was, it was still a confined space when you had some forty horses and riders circling this way and that. With longswords unsheathed, the Symbio knights were now cutting down any and all Varapin within striking distance. By the time the skirmish was over, ten Symbio horses lay still on the deck and just as many knights.

Dismounting, the knights retrieved their absconded lances and began dislodging any accumulated dead bodies. The lead knight, seemingly no worse for wear, approached me. He removed his medieval helmet, which I'd learned was called a Sallet helm, and with sweat-plastered-down hair, made a fist with his right gauntlet and banged it against his breastplate. He lowered to one knee and bowed his head. "We serve thee with honor, your majesty Quintos."

Hardy shook his head. "As if you don't have a high enough opinion of yourself already... ugh, you're now a king?"

I didn't know how to respond. The knight had yet to rise again, and I got the distinct feeling I was supposed to do something.

I placed my hands upon his broad shoulders, "Rise, brave knight. You, all of you, have honored us today with unmatched skill with sword and lance. The bravery you have exhibited will be recorded in the annals of time."

"Annals of time?" Wanda murmured from somewhere behind me. "What does that even mean?"

The knight rose to his feet and hammered his breastplate again with a fist before hurrying back to his awaiting mount.

I said, "Continue on, good knights; do not stop until all enemies of the kingdom have been vanquished. Now, ride!"

And they did just that as several horses reared up onto their back legs while others leaped ahead—and back was the thunderous sound of galloping hooves upon metal decking.

Wanda came up beside me to watch them disappear around the curve of the corridor. She said, "And these guys are a part of that game?"

"It's called Convoke Wyvern."

"Okay, Convoke Wyvern... you know I was born to play that game, right?"

I nodded, but a part of me wondered if there would be any of the Symbio-Poths left to return to *Jefferson*. Now connecting those dots herself, Wanda closed her eyes and shook her head.

Movement. From within the black carpet of ghoul robes came the fast, block-by-block materialization of an unarmed combatant. A combatant who immediately toppled over.

"What the hell?" I said, cautiously approaching. I leaned over and tried to see inside the helmet's visor. There was no face, no head inside. It was an empty combat suit.

Hardy said, "Yeah, I managed to get a message through to Derrota. Figured you were getting tired of hiding behind me."

Grip laughed. "Yeah, looked like a toddler hiding behind his mother's skirt."

That garnered laughs from everyone.

"Ha ha... how about we knock off the jokes and finish what we came here for?"

I looked at the dismal condition of Max and his team. Talk about a ragtag squad. "Hardy, see if you can get five more combat suits delivered here."

Chapter 34

Five minutes later I was suited up and helping the others with their newly arrived suits. I positioned Ham's helmet over his not-insubstantial head and twisted it down into place. I patted his shoulder. "You're all set."

Comms were still intermittent, so when I finally got through to *Jefferson's* bridge, I was surprised.

"Good to hear from you, Captain," Chen said. "Putting you through now."

I saw XO Pristy sitting upon the captain's mount. She looked tired but fully in charge.

"Captain, that was quite a spectacle... the knights and horses and all that."

"You saw that?"

She smiled. "Seems we're able to pick up your feeds better than you can receive ours."

"Sit-rep, XO?"

Her smile dissolved. "Things are not going well, Captain. Ryder's taking heavy losses and is down a full squadron of Arrows. The Pylors are holding their own, having lost three warships, but are still attacking the Varapin fleet. As for Space-

Navy assets, we've lost the *Victorious* and the *Plymouth*... all crew lost. No more Varapin warships have been destroyed."

I took that in and let out a measured breath. "And *Jefferson?*"

"Well, we're getting pounded. As mighty as this old ship is, she's no match for *Oblivion*. We're still concentrating fire on her aft propulsion area, but the Varapin shields are thwarting most of our missile strikes."

There was a long silence before either of us spoke. At the current rate of fleet-loss attrition, there was no doubt that we were going to lose this battle.

"We need to take this ship," I said. "It's the only scenario where we come out of this—"

"Alive," Pristy interjected, completing my words. "Coogong and Derrota are still sending over more Symbios. Let's just hope they can make a difference."

I nodded. "And what about you, Gail?"

"What about me?"

I knew the entire bridgecrew was watching our exchange. It was a dumb question.

"I'm good." She gestured to those around her. "We're all doing our part, and we're doing damn well. So, Captain, if you don't mind my boldness, it's time for you to do your part and take that damn ship."

I saw smiles and heard chuckles from those around her. "I'll do my best."

She said, "Hold on..."

I watched as Stanley Handly stood and raked fingers through his thinning hair. Clearly upset, he said, "Here they come... I knew this was going to happen." He threw up his hands—a ten-year-old having a tantrum.

"XO?" I said.

She shook her head and began chewing on the inside of her

lip. I'd seen that many times, a sure sign she was nervous. "The Varapin have dispatched their hull landers, ten of them... Captain, they're coming to invade the ship."

"Calm down and tell Handly to act his age, not his shoe size." *Did I really just say that?* "This is what they do... it's what they always do," I said. "It's the MO for this kind of battle situation. That's why we left Colonel Drake Bonell there on *Jefferson* and his four-hundred-plus Marines. We still have Arrows that can deal with those vessels, not to mention *Jefferson's* Phazon Pulsars. They won't all get through." But she and I both knew the truth; those particular Varapin craft were remarkably robust. They had six independent shield layers and spewed shadow decoys that could outsmart the smartest of smart missiles.

I followed her on my HUD display; she was moving toward the back of the bridge, and she'd taken me off the open channel. Talking now in an angry, hushed voice, she said, "Thanks for the pep talk, Galvin, but come on; no less than ten Varapin hull landers? Where each carries a hundred MF-ing ghouls? I'm not the best at math, but even I can make the determination that that's an invasion force of a thousand, minimum!"

I didn't have a ready response for her, so I said nothing.

She continued, "They don't just invade a ship; they bend you back and suck the very life force out of you!"

"I know that."

"I want Hardy back here on *Jefferson*. That will give us at least a fighting chance."

"I don't know if he'll agree to that. LuMan—"

"Screw LuMan! You make that ChronoBot understand, and you get him over here!"

I was watching her; her back was turned away from the rest of the bridgecrew. But I had no doubt everyone could hear her. I had to smile; no more was she that timid waif junior officer of the past. She was a force to contend with, and it was about time.

"I'll try to convince him. You talk to Coogong; have him quansported over the second any of those hull landers sets down."

"Thank you, Captain. I need to get back to the captain's mount."

"Good luck, XO." I cut the connection.

I had zero doubt Hardy had been eavesdropping on our conversation. Hardy had no qualms about invading anyone's personal space, including mine. I looked up to his wrecked face display. "I don't want any arguments about this from you. You understand?"

The ChronoBot stomped off. "They're moving slowly, very slowly. We have twenty-eight minutes before the first hull lander touches down," he said. "Let's go kill some ghouls."

I looked up and down the corridor. It was odd that another wave of warriors hadn't attacked us these last few minutes. Obviously, they were being kept busy somewhere else on the ship.

Chapter 35

Perseus Arm of the Milky Way
Oblivion

First Warrior Veesh Slat

Veesh Slat paced the lower bridge, inwardly cursing the humans, those double-crossing Pylors, and whatever the hell those things were that were currently transporting onto his ship. Some kind of bioengineered artificial life form. He didn't quite get their archaic forms of weaponry though. Edged weapons... spears and the like, not to mention those four-legged beasts. Quite odd, this attack philosophy.

He turned to appraise his bridgecrew. Configured like a small encircling stadium, with the central holographic display below from where he now stood at the compartment's center, he saw the furtive glances toward him, the not well-hidden apprehension on their faces. This was supposed to be a simple operation. *Oblivion* was the Varapin flagship—perhaps the most powerful vessel in the quadrant, dare he say, the galaxy?

His orders had been clear. Apprehend the transporter technology at all costs. If not possible, destroy it—even if that meant self-destructing *Oblivion* in the process. The humans, and subsequently the Alliance, could not be allowed to wield this technological advantage any further.

Jefferson, having come alongside *Oblivion*, albeit at hundreds of miles' distance, was matching his warship's own firing of missiles and plasma weaponry. The upgraded shielding on both vessels was well matched. This battle would not be won by brute force alone.

He took in the multiple internal ship feeds. More and more of those bio-creatures were transporting onto his ship. Self-destructing *Oblivion* was becoming more and more likely. Of course, in doing so, he would be taking out *Jefferson* in the process.

Veesh Slat made a mental note to have the first warrior's escape pod readied for emergency departure. Sacrificing the ship was one thing; his life was another.

"First Warrior, an update on the hull landers..." came from his second.

He took in the primary display and saw the comparatively tiny vessels making their approach, having slipped through *Jefferson's* shielding without incident. Ah, finally, some good news.

"The invasion squads are waiting on your orders, First Warrior."

Veesh Slat knew what his second was really asking. Would this be an attack merely to exterminate the humans, or would the invading force be allowed to feed in the process? He himself had already started to salivate at the prospect. The *Ghan-Tshot*. A process of life-force extraction. The bending over backward of the prey, the subsequent involuntary opening, overextension, of the jaws, and only then, the rapture. The recantation of all life force from a living being.

"Ghan-Tshot will be permitted."

"Hmmmm..."

Veesh Slat both heard and felt the bridgecrew's combined unanimity. Ghan-Tshot was a shared experience. All of those here, including himself, would reap the rewards of the invasion squad's impending feeding.

"First Warrior, our Cyclone Death Fighters are taking the upper hand with the enemy's Arrow Fighter squads."

More good news. Perhaps there would be no need for his escape pod after all.

The display suddenly flashed bright white. Veesh Slat looked to his second.

"Two fleet vessels eviscerated. An enemy destroyer, as well as one of our own, also a destroyer... seems they destroyed each other almost simultaneously."

That is not good news. Those remaining of the 9th Fleet will take encouragement from that. Even with the loss of one of their own vessels, they now have hope. He shook his head in disgust.

"Let my ship captains know this... Any further losses to a human warship come with a high price. The death of their respective extended families. They die, and so will everyone important to them."

Distant noises were filtering in through the bridge entrance. There were now over two hundred warriors stationed close by outside. That squad of Marines had nearly penetrated the bridge. It demonstrated just how vulnerable this ship, any ship, was against that damn transporter technology. Even now, what was to stop the humans from trying that again?

Veesh Slat now thought he knew the answer. A firefight here within this bridge could, at least temporarily, bring *Oblivion* to its knees. But Captain Quintos needed a fully functioning *Oblivion* bridge as he tried to commandeer her. Only then would he have any chance of winning this battle.

"The first of the invasion teams has penetrated *Jefferson's* hull, First Warrior."

Veesh Slat allowed himself a semblance of a smile. It won't be long before the crew of that vessel experiences true, unmitigated terror. No, this battle has just begun.

Chapter 36

Perseus Arm of the Milky Way
USS Jefferson **Bridge**

XO Gail Pristy

Pristy was having to spin far too many plates in the air, and it wasn't the first time she wondered if she was in over her head.

Chen said, "XO, J-Dog's ready to pull the plug on any further Arrow space defenses. Says they're currently outnumbered five to one, and he doesn't want to lose any more pilots for what is becoming a lost cause."

MATHR's announcement interrupted Pristy's reply.

**HULL BREACH! HULL BREACH!
ENEMY FORCES HAVE INFILTRATED
DECKS ELEVEN, TWENTY-FIVE,
AND FORTY-ONE...**

Awaale Samatar said, "Colonel Bonell is already on it. Same with Chief Mattis... both deploying defensive teams to those areas."

Pristy looked at the Somalian JOOD officer, both undoubtedly thinking the same thing—would those poor souls be the first to have their life forces, their very spirits, extracted from their bodies?

She took in a long breath, her eyes now leveling on the halo display. There was movement within the Quan-Tangler compartment. Coogong was standing at the console, and, blocky segment by segment, Hardy was materializing. His beautiful, lustrous chrome finish was now a charred and blackened mess. Pristy had to smile; the ChronoBot hated getting even an errant scratch. She used her TAC-Band to contact the now fully formed robot.

"Go for Hardy," he said.

"You're aware of the infiltration points on the ship?"

"Perfectly... I'm on my way to the one closest to the bridge, then the one closest to Engineering and Propulsion."

"Good luck, Hardy."

He said, "Just so you know, as soon as I deal with the ghoul issue, I'm heading back to *Oblivion*... I have a score to settle. Look at me. Just look at me."

"Copy that." Pristy cut the connection.

In a stifled but still raised voice, Stanley Handly was arguing with someone via his personal comms.

"Petty Officer Handly, who are you speaking with?"

He spun around with an "I've been caught doing something I shouldn't be doing" expression. He swiped at his thinning hair and sniffed. "No one... well, not no one. It's of no concern..."

"And you don't think we have enough going on right now? You felt you have to be quarreling with someone?" Pristy said with narrowed eyes.

"No, well, yes; I mean, this isn't... I'm not quarreling with someone, XO."

"Well, who the hell is it?"

"It's the chaplain."

"Trent?"

Handly nodded.

"What does he want... isn't he still in the brig?"

"Yes, he got ahold of a TAC-Band though. Somehow."

Pristy had no shortage of things to juggle as it was, but she had to know. "What? Spit it out. What does he want?"

"He wants to be transported over to *Oblivion*. Right away. He's certain if he can get in front of First Warrior Veesh Slat, he can negotiate a ceasefire. He says that God has spoken to him, and he must be allowed to follow His directive."

"No. Get off the line with that ass-hat and start concentrating on your job."

"Aye... yes, Sir, I mean, Ma'am."

She caught both Grimes and Chen eyeing the overly nervous petty officer.

Chen said, "Captain Ryder and the rest of the Arrow pilots are safely back on board *Jefferson*. He's accompanying Lieutenant Akari James up to HealthBay... she's in pretty bad shape."

Chapter 37

Perseus Arm of the Milky Way
USS Jefferson
GravLift Deck 11

ChronoBot / Hardy

Hardy arrived on Deck 11, hearing nonstop weapons fire. He saw both a team of Marines and some of Chief Mattis' security forces actively engaging the Varapin warriors. He didn't want to be here, but now, seeing the numbers of the black-cloaked ghouls off in the distance, he acknowledged the need for his intervention. He saw Colonel Drake Bonell barking off orders as Hardy approached what looked to be a temporary line of defense made up of portable battling constructs, or PBCs, basically four-foot-tall crates on wheels, slathered with multiple layers of Smart-Coat. The colonel did a double take at seeing Hardy.

"What the hell happened to you?"

Hardy ignored the question. "Situation, Colonel?"

"We were fortunate. We caught them as they were just coming in. That's one of the ship's waste recycling depots. Call them WRDs. Not a lot of crew activity. All automated. But we've already lost two of Mattis' people from security... a man and a woman. They're little more than dried-up husks now."

"So, adding insult to injury, ghouls are implementing Ghan-Tshot as part of their infiltration," Hardy said.

Bonell just looked at him, "Isn't that basically what I just said? So, are you going to jump into action or what? We have a number of other breaches, and we have limited resources. They don't seem to be coming out of there... which is a little strange."

Enemy energy fire had increased since Hardy's arrival, and several more Marines were down. Hardy said, "All of your Marines should be wearing combat suits."

Bonell was now clearly getting irritated. "Gee, thanks for that bit of wisdom. Nobody had time to suit up. Unlike you, we don't sleep in our armor."

Hardy deployed his energy weapons, noticing his left forearm cannon hadn't actually fully emerged from its internal compartment. The little access door was hung up by a burnt chunk of charred metal. He scraped at the spot with a metal digit, and the door sprang open and the cannon clicked into place.

"Tell your people to hold fire; I'm not in the mood to get shot in the ass."

Snorting, the colonel found that funny.

Without further conversation, Hardy took off toward the waste recycling compartment. Being a ChronoBot, he didn't so much feel the first energy bolt to hit him in the ass as he sensed it. Hardy was fairly certain it was a parting shot directed by Bonell. *Ha ha. Very funny.*

He'd wondered why the Varapin had yet to make their full attack and now knew. They had chosen the absolute worst place to enter *Jefferson*. The WRD was basically a big pumphouse with countless incoming and outgoing pipes, centrifugal filtration units, turbine motors, treatment caldrons, ionization caldrons, and more pipes. Apparently, upon making their hull breach, the Varapin warriors had opened a section that was interspersed with a mass of supply channels. Basically, conduits from Deck 11's forward section's toilet lines. Three large pipes had been fractured, and geysers of brown muck were dousing everything, including the two hundred and eight, according to Hardy's sensors, Varapin warriors, who, surprisingly, were mostly not hovering, but standing on the deck. Hardy fired upon the few dozen warriors that were firing. The others were bent over and choking—no, not choking, more like gagging and throwing up.

He advanced forward. Now standing knee high within the unthinkable liquid, he began firing with all of his weapons. Agonized screeches filled the WRD. Even when all of the enemy invaders were clearly dead, Hardy continued to fire for a full minute.

Upon exiting the WRD, Hardy passed by Marines and security forces. There was no shortage of jeers and snickers.

Smiling, Colonel Bonell took a step back as Hardy approached. "Oh boy, you stink something awful." He waved a hand in front of his face. "Hey, I know it was a shitty job, but someone had to do it."

All the Marines within earshot laughed at that.

"Terrific. Everyone's a comedian today," Hardy said. "By the way, I've just put in an interdepartmental request for your Marines to assist with that WRD's cleanup job. Have fun."

Hardy contemplated how he'd gotten here. Not as Hardy the omnipotent ChronoBot, but John Hardy the man. More and more of late, memories of his proper life had been returning to him, some good. Some not so good.

~

The year was 2031. Hardy was twenty-three; his brother, Aiden, had just turned eighteen.

"Mr. John Hardy," the detective said, swiping at his tablet like it had offended him in some way.

Hardy feigned a yawn.

"The car you were driving is registered to your brother. What were you doing driving it?" Detective Hoff leaned across a heavily worn table in the sixth precinct's interrogation room. A miasma of stale coffee and something else, something foul, drifted over to Hardy.

Hardy leaned away in the molded plastic chair, scrunching his nose. "Aiden's car's got a better sound system."

Another angry swipe at the worn-looking tablet. "I did a background check on you and your brother; looks like a pretty tough road you boys have traveled. Abusive alcoholic father left the family when you were twelve; his body was found floating in the river near the space docks." Hoff looked up.

Hardy shrugged with indifference.

"Your mother found another man, then died of stomach cancer a year and a half later."

Shrug.

"You and Aiden have been on your own since... what? You were fifteen?"

"We do all right." Hardy laced his fingers together; the cuffs on his wrists clanked against his belt buckle.

"You work on the docks, operate a hover-fork. Is that how

you support your family?" Hoff's thick index finger swept through the pages of his tablet.

"That and my modeling career," Hardy grinned, flashing a broken tooth.

Hoff snorted. "You must be doing quite well. Your brother drives a one-year-old Pearston 775 hovercar. That costs about an entire year's salary for me."

"Clearly you're underpaid." Hardy sniffed.

"Look, sure, I'm underpaid. But do me a favor. My patience is running thin... it's the middle of the fucking night here. And I'm sick and tired of dealing with two-bit hooligans like you. So why don't you knock off the smart comebacks."

Hardy made a sympathetic woe is me expression. "I was pulled over for speeding. What's the big deal? Is all this really necessary? And I don't appreciate you calling me a hoodlum." Hardy attempted to cross his arms, but the manacles prevented it.

"Yeah, speeding; it's almost as if you wanted to get caught. The officer who pulled you over noticed blood on the door handle and steering yoke. Coincidentally, four miles away, we discovered a trio of freshly murdered bodies and a truck loaded with stolen Plaszzer 9s."

Plaszzer 9s were this year's energy weapon of choice for those of independent means. *Damn you, Aiden.* Hardy knew that was coming. He did his best to keep his face void of expression. "I don't know what you're talking about. I just went out for a Marie's bacon burger."

"Uh-huh... at two in the morning? With blood all over your brother's car?"

"I like my burger rare, still mooing... gets kinda messy sometimes. By the way, can you open a window?" He looked about the small, enclosed space. "Or maybe that door? It reeks in here. And by the look of those fresh stains on your tie and the smell in here, you're more of a late-night Tex-Mex than a burger-and-fries kind of guy." Hardy suppressed a mocking smirk.

Hoff ignored the comment. "That truck had phony plates. Did you know that the, um, recently deceased found at the scene were a part of the Gomez gang? Basically, your average, run-of-the-mill gunrunners?" The detective burped into his fist.

Feeling queasy, Hardy turned his head away. *I'd be better off being waterboarded.* The detective peered up from his tablet with heavy-lidded, bloodshot eyes.

Hardy shrugged. "I don't know why you're telling me all this. I've got to get home to my wife and get some rest. My shift at the docks begins at eight."

Hoff looked at the clock on the wall. "You're not going to make it. You're under arrest for suspicion of murder. The blood samples are being processed now...you'll be our guest until we get those results, sometime before noon."

"Where's my brother?"

"Waiting room down the corridor."

"Since you've impounded the car, can I at least tell him to head on home? Let him know I won't need a ride?"

"Sure, you can have five minutes once you're back in the holding pen. Then we'll get you booked and processed."

Hardy nodded. He wondered if when he had the chance, he should strangle his brother or simply beat him to death with his bare knuckles.

Hoff stood and opened the door and looked out around the corner. The momentary waft of fresh air was heaven-sent. Hoff gestured, undoubtedly to the armed guard stationed outside. The heavyset uniformed officer came into view, sidestepped around Hoff, oversized belly to oversized belly, leaned down, and rechecked Hardy's cuffs.

Six minutes later, Hardy glared at his kid brother. "You told me you traded currency online."

"You're not taking the fall for me," Aiden hunched over and whispered. They were in a clear polycarbonate cubicle, supposedly soundproof. "I'll do the time."

"No way. You've got high cheekbones and an ass like an altar boy. Prison would be hell for you," Hardy hissed.

"That's not funny."

"I've been taking care of you since you were ten; I'm not stopping now. How the hell did you get mixed up in this?" Hardy snapped, clearly furious at the eighteen-year-old fool in front of him.

Aiden looked down at his fists. Faint traces of blood still stained his calloused hands. "I just kept getting sucked in deeper and deeper. Once you run guns for those guys, there's no way to quit."

"You killed three men?" Hardy snarled. "What happened to you? I knew you should have moved in with Alicia and me."

"They were going to off me. I delivered my crates and two of the guys turned on me. I was never supposed to walk away from that meet. Truth is... I don't know how I did it. I jammed my thumb into one guy's eye. I think I gouged it out. Then I grabbed his gun. The rest is a total blur. I didn't know what else to do. So I called you." Aiden looked into his big brother's eyes. "You didn't have to swap cars with me, John. I didn't mean for you to take the fall for me on this shit."

A heavy knock pounded the door. The same big-bellied guard stuck his head into the small room. "Time's up!"

Hardy stood. His hands were still manacled in front of him. "Go to my house. Tell Alicia everything. Take care of her until I get back. And maybe now you'll stay out of trouble."

Aiden's eyes welled up with tears. "I will. I'm sorry..."

Once inside his new cell, Hardy stuck his hands through the small opening in the bars so his guard could remove the cuffs. He rubbed at his wrists and turned to take in his new surroundings. He had three cellmates. Two were sound asleep on the two top bunks. Their loud snoring crescendoed in a weird kind of harmony. The third cellmate lay sideways on one of the lower bunks. He looked at Hardy through strands of long greasy hair. His features were angular. High cheekbones above sunken cheeks, a long slender nose, and lips as thin as knife blades. He was now studying Hardy.

"Both of these bunks are mine," the skinny, overly tattooed inmate said. "You're free to sit on the shitter... at least until one of us needs it."

Hardy smiled. "You're a funny guy. Bet you keep the other inmates in here in stitches."

"I don't think I much like your attitude, young sprout," he said, rising up on one elbow.

Hardy took in the scabbed needle marks on his now exposed arm.

"Don't mind me," Hardy said and sat down on the open bunk. At the ripe old age of twenty-three, Hardy had spent the last six years loading freight at the space docks. He was stout and muscular. His forearms, not unlike those of the old Popeye cartoon, were ridiculously overbuilt. Hardy smiled. If he'd learned one lesson over the years at the docks, it was that you never ever showed fear. Not to anyone.

The tweaker inmate stood and dramatically craned his neck —first left and then right. The sounds of craniovertebral junction bones crunching were audible. Hardy had always been fascinated by anatomy; it was actually somewhat impressive.

"I knew you were trouble the minute you stepped in here. That you'd need to be taught a lesson in manners," Tweaker said, smiling and exposing too many missing teeth to count at a glance.

The conversation was over. Hardy said, "Have a seat over there, buddy... on the throne. I'll be needing your bunk as well as this one." Hardy's face was once again expressionless. His eyes went cold and sharp as two coffin nails.

After a brief bout of indecision, Tweaker stood up and loomed over Hardy—trying to look like a badass. And perhaps he was a badass. Clearly he was the master of his domain here in this cell. Hell, he'd probably had to fight and brawl his whole pathetic life. And he probably won most of those fights. He was probably a killer several times over. He was wiry. He would be fast.

There was another lesson Hardy had learned early on in life. The one that struck first was usually the one that stayed standing. There was no such thing as a fair fight in the streets. It was about survival. This here, now, was about survival.

Hardy looked up into Tweaker's eyes and then turned his eyes to right over his shoulder. As if someone else was now standing there. Tweaker stole a glance, and that was all it took. Probably less than two seconds of diverted attention.

Hardy reared back and kicked his fellow inmate in the groin. And because he was lying down, Hardy had been able to use his heel. Using the heel was far more preferable than the balls of the toes, far more kinetic force being unleashed. Hardy knew he'd made a direct impact to the man's testicles by the cross-eyed, open-mouthed expression on his face. Seeing him bent over and unable to make a sound, Hardy almost felt bad for the guy. Almost. Without haste, Hardy got to his feet and assessed the now squealing inmate. The two other inmates were both awake—their attention on Tweaker. Neither made any attempt to assist.

Hardy assisted, almost gently now, putting Tweaker on the shitter. The open space beneath his wounded ball sack would be preferable to the overly thin, hard mattresses provided here.

Hardy said, "You never know who you're fucking with, my friend. Lesson learned, right?" He gave the now openly weeping man a pat on his shoulder. Before returning to his bunk, he looked out through the bars and shook his head.

∼

Eight hours later, Hardy was standing at the front of the district courtroom, hands cuffed and doing his best to look respectful. He turned and scanned the benches behind him.

He scowled at the few nearby locals sitting within the gallery section. One guy was eating a sandwich. A glob of mustard clung to one corner of his mouth. Then Hardy noticed Aiden and Alicia. They were seated against the back wall. They both waved while trying to look supportive. Hardy glared at his little brother. His gaze shifted to a tall, stooped man with a beak of a nose, sitting in the middle of the gallery. He wasn't dressed like any of the locals.

His public defender had been worthless. Sure, there'd been no time to prepare a proper defense, but some semblance of effort would have been nice. The blood on Hardy's car matched the samples taken from the three corpses at the murder scene. Hardy had been caught speeding away from the crime scene. Broken bits of wood in the trunk of the Pearston 775 hovercar were identical to those of the crates of weapons found at the scene. *Shit!*

"I've reviewed your case and personal history," the judge was saying. "Despite your challenging childhood, you have a fairly clean record. Seem to have worked nearly full-time at the docks... going on several years now. A reasonably stable life, other than a few drunk and disorderlies. That and getting mixed up with the Gomez gang."

"That was my brother."

The young defender shrugged, disinterested at Hardy's clarification.

Hardy inwardly cringed. *Will Alicia believe I was mixed up with the Gomez gang? That I was the one that killed those three runners?* He glanced back at them. No, Aiden would come clean to her. The real concern was the gang taking revenge on Alicia.

The public defender—Hardy couldn't remember what his name was—droned on about circumstantial evidence and possible alibis. Hardy slowly turned, peering over his shoulder. The man with the beaked nose sat with arms folded, his hard features facing Hardy. There were gold stripes on his sleeves and multicolored ribbons on his chest.

Ten minutes later, Hardy was on his feet, facing the bench. The judge, looking as ancient as Methuselah, said, "Although the evidence in this case is quite incriminating, it is also circumstantial. The question for you, young man, is... do you really want to take this to trial? Face what could amount to a thirty-year stint at Hapsburg Supermax?" the judge continued without allowing Hardy to respond. "I'm feeling generous today. I'm giving you the opportunity to serve your country, Mr. Hardy. But you have to decide. Decide right now."

Hardy stole a glance back at Alicia. She looked devastated. Her makeup had smeared, and her nose was red. She wiped at her tears, then offered back a resigned nod.

The judge continued, "You'll enlist as a junior spacer in the EUNF United States Space-Navy; they're always looking for young recruits. That... or go to trial and most likely begin a prison term that will eclipse the bulk of your life. It is up to you, young man."

Hardy blinked and straightened. "Thank you for this opportunity, your honor. I'd prefer to serve. Join the Space-Navy."

The gavel struck with finality.

USS Jefferson

Ten weeks later, Junior Spacer John Hardy was wearing his recently issued SWM overalls that neither fit well nor were very comfortable. Coming out of basic spacer training, he'd been given a new appreciation for the military. He'd done okay for himself. Even caught the eye of his NCO. Was given more responsibility than the other recruits.

Hardy, oddly enough, actually liked the military. He would make the best of this. Sure, he missed Alicia—missed her something awful. But he'd see her during his periodic leaves. And hell, he'd be sending her the lion's share of his wages. Things could be worse. He could be in prison.

He and his fellow still-wet-behind-the-ears spacers had been given a tour of USS *Underwood*, a frigate that was long overdue to be retired. In addition to having the name of the fifty-third president, Hardy recollected it was also the name of a kind of antique typewriter.

Hardy would be assigned his regular deck duties first thing in the morning. As for now, he was being shown the ship's barracks. The last stop on the tour. It smelled remarkably like a hamper full of sweaty jock straps and gym socks. It didn't take him long to find an open lower bunk. The barracks were anything but full. He'd discovered during the tour that this frigate was one step above a ghost ship.

He flopped down onto the bunk and felt the weight of the preceding ten weeks dissipate into the surprisingly comfortable mattress beneath him.

"Hey, pussy recruit. You're lying on Nathan B's bunk. Head out of here... try the barracks up on G6."

Hardy opened his eyes to find a spacer twice his size looming over him. He'd seen the over-muscled recruit lying upon a bunk just one row over.

"Who's Nathan B?"

"Me. I'm Nathan B."

"Whatever." Hardy closed his eyes.

A quick slap to the face, and Hardy was brought back fully awake. "Get up, and get out of these barracks, shit for brains."

Hardy let out a weary breath. "Let me introduce you to Mr. Foot Heel."

"Foot Heel? Who the fuck is Mr. Foot Heel?"

Two hours later, Hardy was lying down upon a rigid plastic bench within the old frigate's unoccupied brig—a brig that smelled only somewhat better than that of the barracks. Now, already drifting off to sleep, Hardy reminisced on his most recent, highly strategic strike to Nathan B's ball sack. He chuckled... *Mr. Foot Heel? Did I really say that?*

Hardy snapped back to the present as he exited *Jefferson's* GravLift on Deck 25. MATHR was making another announcement.

HULL BREACH! HULL BREACH! ENEMY FORCES HAVE INFILTRATED DECKS 2 AND 3...

Striding forward, heading off in the direction of loud rapid weapons fire, an errant thought occurred to him... *I really need to clone myself.* He stopped. It would be possible. *First, I'd need the Captain's permission. Then I'd need to contact Derrota up on the Symbio deck.* His internal LuMan spoke up, something that was uncommon for him to do.

What you are considering, using the Sir Louis de Broglie transporter device to make physical copies of... us, although possible, violates Sheentah law.

Hardy knew that ChronoBots were originally developed by an advanced society called the Sheentah several centuries past. And there were a limited number of the battle bots manufactured. Today, there were less than three hundred still in existence—scattered around the galaxy.

Just how ironclad is that law? And is there anyone, namely the Sheentah, even around to enforce that law? Hardy asked.

It seemed a long while before LuMan responded, but in actuality it was mere nanoseconds. The Sheentah, as a society, have moved on to a nonphysical existence within MACS0647-JD, which is the farthest known galaxy from the earth... approximately four billion parsecs distance.

Hardy was well aware of LuMan's preprogrammed moral compass. It was one of the things he liked most about the original factory-installed AI, one who had the personality of a cardboard box—but just the same, an AI with whom he intimately shared organic biomatter space.

So, tell me, LuMan... is there room for compromise here? How many duplications could you live with?

LuMan again hesitated. I am not alive, so that is a nonsensical question.

You're stalling, LuMan. How about ten... would the Sheentah be okay with ten of us?

No.

How about eight? That seems to be a good number... not too many, not too few...

No.

Hardy hadn't actually expected the inflexible AI to budge. But what the hell; he had to at least try.

Perhaps three.

Had he heard him correctly? Had the somber, characterless personality just capitulated? Maybe if he was willing to go to three, he'd go to four, or even five? No. Why look a gift horse in the mouth?

Okay, LuMan... three it is.

Chapter 38

Perseus Arm of the Milky Way
Oblivion

Captain Galvin Quintos

Coming out of the access port one deck up, we found total and complete mayhem. Sure, there were plenty of Varapin warriors whisking around in the air like so many witches on broomsticks, but there were at least fifty Symbio-Poths here as well.

The medieval attire consisted of men wearing stockings on their legs, tunics and leather boots, while the equal number of women wore long gowns with sleeveless tunics and cloth to cover their hair.

Wanda said, "These peasants are outnumbered three to one, and yet, they're holding their own."

"And doing so without modern weaponry," Max added.

The Symbio-Poths here wielded little more than ancient farm utensils, long iron axes, and pitchforks.

"What's that thing?" Grip asked, eyeing two pieces of wood, one with a longer handle and one shorter and thicker.

Wanda said, "It's a grain flail. That floppy length of wood attached at the end with rope is called the striker."

I wondered how the young Marine knew that. She was not only a badass; she was smart too.

As if on cue, an elderly looking Symbio-Poth woman suddenly swung her flail handle up into the air, using the separated end like a whip. *Whack!* An unfortunate ghoul took the brunt of the hit at the back of his skull. It was as if a switch had been turned off—the Varapin warrior dropped to the deck, either unconscious or dead.

Each of the ghouls was armed with a plasma weapon. Yes, seemingly, they had little effect on the Symbio-Poth anatomy. Sure, there were a number of Symbios lying motionless on the deck, but there were even more ghouls down, crumpled heaps within their oversized black robes.

The six of us, nestled within the access port's quasi-sheltered alcove, had yet to jump into the fray.

"Seems to me," I said, "the Symbios are holding their own here."

Max said, "We'd just be getting in the way."

Ham said, "Maybe we head to the next deck?"

So up we went, one after the other, climbing our way up to the next level within *Oblivion*. As with the previous deck, there was more mayhem here. But here it wasn't so much peasants fighting ghouls, but bandits fighting ghouls. And instead of axes, pitchforks, and flails, they were fighting with swords, knives, and spears.

"They look like pirates," Ham said.

Unfortunately, here there were far fewer bandits than there were peasants on the previous deck.

A Symbio-Poth took a plasma bolt to the forehead and dropped with a thump at our feet.

I said, "These Symbios won't hold out long with such limited numbers. What do you say we even the playing field?" I rushed from the alcove with my shredder already raised and firing. The others followed suit, and soon we were standing shoulder to shoulder, unleashing a hell-storm of weapons fire upon the enemy.

Ignoring the Symbio bandits, the Varapin warriors now came at us like a hoard of angry black bats. Bats with plasma guns.

The problem with this Varapin ship was the lack of anything to take cover behind. Sure, it worked well for the ghouls, who needed clear, unobstructed thruways to fly through, but it left us mere bipedal beings pretty much always standing out in the open—and easy targets.

The front of my combat suit was soon peppered with blackened burn craters, and I thought of Hardy and how he must feel. My HUD was already spewing out warnings concerning suit integrity, and major systems were red-lining.

Ham, to my left, toppled over like a giant redwood. Max stumbled backward and was forced down to one knee.

The temperature in my suit was high enough to boil an egg—I thought of my own huevos and had to stave off panic. This was not working. About to give the order to retreat, I saw something was suddenly happening at the enemy's rear flank. My HUD sensors, albeit reacting slower than usual, provided a visual interpretation of what was happening. The Symbio bandits had fallen back, seemingly unwilling to further confront the ghouls. But that hadn't been the case at all. They had simply regrouped and were now attacking as a more unified fighting force. Although it was difficult to see the onrush of Symbio-Poths, I could see the tell-tale reflection of light on metal as swords slashed and stabbed upward.

Once again, the Varapin warriors' attention was diverted as they became drawn into a frenzied battle with the faux bandits.

Not letting the Symbios' sacrifice go to waste, we collected our injured off the deck and made our way into the access port alcove, where we reassessed our fighting capabilities. Hock was alive but in no shape to continue on. Max was back on his feet and insisted he was fine to fight on. It took several tries, but I got ahold of Coogong. "Lock onto Hock and bring him home... in fact, send him right into HealthBay if possible."

Coogong said, "Please stand back from Ham. Too close a proximity to him and someone could lose a hand."

We all watched as Ham, his once sterile white combat suit now looking more like a piece of burnt kindling, quansported away.

Up the access tube we went. I thought of those poor Symbios we were leaving behind. They would not survive the enemy's overpowering numbers. Yes, they were programmed to sacrifice themselves, as it was. But inside, I felt heavy misgivings. Humans had free will. Human combatants had made the conscious choice to be here. But we, no, I had sent these beings here—beings which were far more than simple robots— into harm's way. It wasn't right, but at the moment, I couldn't think of any alternative. War truly was hell.

I wondered how many more decks would be just like the previous one. Valiant fighting that, in the end, would prove fruitless for my forces. Was this all a waste of time? Inevitably, would the superior Varapin combatant numbers, as well as superior fleet warship assets, rule the day? Was all this just a fool's errand? But what was the alternative? For us to transport back onto my ship and quickly jump away. To save the good men and women on board *Jefferson*. Accept that we had done all we could, but in the end, we were outmatched? But could I do that? Leave what remained of the 9th Fleet to fend for itself? Go back on my word to the Pylors here, fighting alongside the US Space-Navy, even though I had personally killed their leader? Of course not.

Well... if this was truly going to be the end, we should make it a spectacular end. I continued to climb, finding it difficult to mount enough energy to reach for even one more handhold.

What we needed to do was take that damn bridge. Undoubtedly, it would be the most protected, well-fortified area on the ship. And since Max's attempt at a surprise assault by a small team had failed so miserably, there had to be an alternative. What I needed was Hardy back here on board *Oblivion*.

I tried to reach *Jefferson's* bridge, but comms were back to acting flaky. I tried to reach Hardy directly and got an annoying message.

"Hi, you've reached Hardy. I'm unable to take your call right now, but if you leave a short message at the tone, I'll try not to ignore it."

"Hardy, if you want to ever have that metal carcass of yours replated and buffed out again, get back to me pronto!"

Chapter 39

The next deck up, you guessed it, there was fighting—a lot more fighting. Here, the largest, widest passageways we'd encountered thus far, there were hundreds of combatants in the midst of battle. The ghouls were screeching, and the Symbios were yelling.

Grip used his shredder to take down a Varapin warrior that had circled around overhead while coming in too close to the entrance of the access port.

As for the Symbio-Poths, there were the peasant variety and the bandit variety, as well as the knights upon their powerful steeds.

Max yelled above the noise, "Captain... we enter that fray, and not all of us, or any of us, will survive the day! Are you sure you don't want to return to *Jefferson's* bridge?"

I looked over to Max, finding his eyes behind his helmet's darkened faceplate. The others were also looking at me with similar concern. After several beats, I said, "If this was simply about destroying *Oblivion*, obliterating her... yes, *Jefferson's* bridge would be the right place for me. I'd find a way to win, to turn things around. But that's not my objective. For all the chess pieces on this gameboard, this match, this contest, to result in a win for our side, we need to take this ship. And I can't do that from anywhere else but right here."

"So, I guess it'll be us Marines who'll have to make sure you don't get yourself killed in the process," Wanda said. "Now, can we stop playing spectators here and get into the fight?" With raised brows, she gestured to the ensuing battle going on before us.

I said, "Yeah, let's go kill some ghouls..."

We fought side by side with the Symbio-Poths. I found myself using the butt end of my shredder as a club almost as much as using it for its intended purpose.

The Symbio horses were amazing during the fight. Brave, stalwart. I suspected they were more intelligent than their earthly biological brethren. I even saw a Symbio stallion rear up on its hind legs while using its forward hooves to strike down an approaching enemy warrior. I also saw that some of the fallen Symbios were periodically being quansported off the deck. *Thank you, Derrota.* Hopefully there would be sufficient operational technology left for them to be repaired—maybe to experience a kind of Symbio-reincarnation, then come back just as they had been, or perhaps in another form completely.

The fighting continued. With the swarm of ghouls continuously attacking from above, exhaustion was getting the better of me. Like an embattled heavyweight boxer in the twelfth round, I felt as if my arms were laden with heavy bags of sand.

I'd lost visuals on the Marines. Only by referencing my HUD screen did I see their respective moving icons and know they were still in the fight. To my right, I saw one of the knights was down, his horse nowhere in sight. His armor was cratered, and his helmet was gone. A Varapin warrior hovered over him—attempting that Ghan-Tshot bullshit. I was more than angry. Rage boiled. There were too many combatants between them and me to do anything about what I was witnessing. I watched as the ghoul's black, skull-like face moved to within inches above the Symbio's now open, slackened jaws.

I yelled, "They're not even human! They're not alive! Get away from him!"

Distracted, I was attacked from above. I took three consecutive energy bolts to the chest—propelling me off my feet and onto my back. Disoriented, I waited for the searing pain in my sternum to retreat. For the ability to catch my breath again.

Staring up, I saw a peasant woman standing there. She was holding the shaft of a pitchfork in one hand. She knelt down next to me. And then my heart missed a beat.

"Oh my... Mom?" Realization set in. No. It couldn't be... my parents were long gone. Her hair was different, what I could see of it. Matted strands had escaped from beneath her handwoven linen cap. There were strategically placed smudges of soot on her cheeks and chin, but my mother's eyes—they were the same sky blue as I remembered.

The peasant woman continued to look down at me... first with confusion, and then with something akin to bemusement. The corners of her lips turned up.

"Hello, Galvin... oh my; it seems you've gotten yourself into quite a pickle here, no?"

I so wanted her to be real right now. To be the actual person I knew and loved as a small child. Then again, didn't I have a connection to this form of her as well? This identical-looking Symbio-Poth replica of my mother? I'd often wondered what had happened to my faux family once the small, reenacted town of Clairmont had been dismantled. Had my young mother and father, along with my twelve-year-old brother, been simply dismantled—thrown onto a Symbio-Poth heap somewhere, perhaps to be used for spare parts?

So, now I knew. But what do I call her?

"Mom, what are you doing here?"

"Galvin, you need to get up. You need to get yourself back into this fight." She placed a motherly hand upon the side of my helmet and leaned down. "Do you understand what I'm saying?"

I nodded. "I know. But I'm so tired. I don't know if I'm the one to—"

"Oh, knock it off. Save the excuses for someone who'll buy it. This is what you were born to do... this is what you live for, Galvin."

I stared up into her eyes. Saw what could only be described as the spark of life there. It was a stare that was fully present—that and self-aware. And all too human. My mind flashed back to the ghoul leaning into the downed knight. *Oh my God...* that Varapin warrior hadn't been mistaken; he had detected a living life-form energy from within that Symbio. *This changes everything.*

I said, "I'm sorry, Mom. I'm sorry I sent you here. I'm sorry I sent all of you here. It was wrong. It was cruel."

It was as if someone had changed the channel on an old-fashioned TV or radio. What glimmer of life I'd witnessed just moments before had now receded back into her unconsciousness, or whatever that region was called within a Symbio-Poth's complex artificial intelligence. But I'd seen it. I'd experienced it. What those highly advanced Pleidian Weonan engineers had not anticipated when building these amazing beings was that they would someday, inevitably, evolve.

I got to my feet. *Where is she? Where is my mother?* I desperately started looking for her. *She shouldn't be here.*

Suddenly, Wanda was in front of me. Helmet to helmet, her hands were on my shoulders. "Are you here?"

"What?"

"Are you here!"

I blinked my eyes in rapid succession. "Uh... yeah... I'm here."

"Then stop acting like a lunatic and get into this damn fight!" She slapped the side of my helmet hard enough for me to see stars. And then, like my Symbio-Poth mother, she, too, was gone.

I raised my shredder, and I began firing. Even when the weapon became hot enough to sear the inside material of my gloves, I kept firing. With each overhead ghoul, I replayed the downed knight having his burgeoning life force being sucked out from his gaping jaws. White-hot rage fueled my forward charge. With each pull of the trigger, I unconsciously repeated a mantra of *kill them... kill them all.*

Chapter 40

Perseus Arm of the Milky Way
US Space-Navy
USS Jefferson

Captain Gail Pristy

All of Pristy's concentration was on the halo display. Split between the ENUF US Space-Navy's 9th Fleet along with the mismatched assemblage of Pylor warships—they were still trading blows with the Varapin fleet. It had been hours since a vessel had been destroyed on either side. That, and she was absorbed in the ongoing battle with *Oblivion*.

Both warships were in effect hog-tied—not giving this fight anything close to their all. The Varapin, desperate to get hold of functional transporter tech, were being careful not to destroy *Jefferson*. It was the same for Pristy. Capturing a still-operational *Oblivion* would be essential for *Jefferson* and the 9th Fleet to survive this battle. But at some point, one side would have to pull the plug on being careful and cut its losses. Go for the proverbial jugular and bring home a win.

She leaned back in her seat and contemplated what her next move would be. It was at that moment she realized she was smiling. Certainly not because she was happy or giddy. No, she was in her element. She got off being in this high-adrenaline state of mind. *I must be crazy.* She flashed back to the first time she realized she was destined to do something worthwhile. Realized working under high-pressure stakes was something she was good at.

Adrenaline pulsed with every pounding heartbeat; determined, Gail was going to do this. Like the bitches in the pool, where she'd leave them in her wake. She followed after her father, swam in behind him, grabbed his shirt in two tight fists, and kicked her legs. Up, up, up, she struggled to rise—to ascend. *Oh God... don't let me give up... don't let me die.*

Her face broke through the surface, and she gasped in a breath of beautiful, wonderful air. It was dark out. Overhead, the stars glistened and sparkled. And it was the most beautiful sight she had ever seen.

"Gail! Gail! Over here..."

She followed the sound of her mother's desperate pleas. Gail's father's lifeless body was submerged beneath the surface. She repositioned him onto his back, doing her best to raise his head. Her legs kicked nonstop; treading water was something she was used to, although not while suspending the weight of an unconscious or dead two-hundred-pound man.

"Bring him to the shore, Gail! Hurry!" her mother screamed.

"What do you think I'm doing? I'm trying! Help me!"

Her mother, pacing the bank of the river, waded back into

the water. The pathetic-looking, shivering, half-drowned woman looked beyond distraught—she looked borderline hysterical.

Reaching hands grabbed for Gail's father, and together, they maneuvered him onto the rocky riverbank. Too heavy to be hefted all the way out of the water, his lower legs remained submerged.

"Oh my God... he's dead... Oh, Mitchel..."

"Stop it! Just stop it, Mom!" Gail snapped back. "Help me turn him on his stomach. Move, Mom! Help me!"

Together they flipped him over. Immediately, Gail jumped onto his legs and pushed on his back. Tried to get some of the water out of his lungs. She had no idea if it had made any difference. She had learned CPR; it was a requirement of swim team. "Flip him back over, hurry!"

Together they got him onto his back. She didn't hesitate; she got on top of him, placed a hand beneath his neck to raise his chin, and then forced two deep breaths into his mouth. It came automatically. Just as she'd learned in school—she placed the palms of her hands on her father's chest and began compressions. *How many? Twenty? No... thirty.* She stopped to listen for breaths. Her father's face was blue; his eyes were open and glassy. She started again with mouth-to-mouth. Then, again, she began compressions.

"He's dead, Gail... he's gone," her mother murmured into her open palms.

But Gail continued for another five long minutes. And then he coughed and sputtered. Water fountained out from his gasping mouth.

"XO! We're being hailed," Chen said from Comms. "First Warrior Veesh Slat."

"Put him up on the display."

the bridge went quiet as the Varapin ghoul's feed went live.

"First Warrior... what can I do for you?" she said.

First off, Pristy noticed he wasn't on *Oblivion's* bridge. Handly was busy tapping away at the tactical board; she was certain he was trying to inquire as to the Varapin's specific location.

"Please, Executive Officer Pristy... it is I that would like to assist you." His jutting bone-white jaws shifted, which she took as an attempted smile.

"I'm listening."

"This conflict serves no one. We have warriors battling on your vessel; you have warriors, and I use that term loosely, on mine. I propose we put an end to this. Here and now. Shall we chalk it up to a stalemate?"

"You would do that? Give up. Not leave here today with what you came here for. Our transporter technology?"

Veesh Slat hesitated. "Well... there will be other opportunities, other battles."

"I would, of course, have to run this by the Captain—"

Slat interjected. "Yes, yes... who is here upon my ship... we have zeroed in on his specific location. Sure, your attempts to camouflage his bio-readings were impressive, but they were no match for our differential, down-to-the-molecular-level biometric sensors."

Before she could reply, Veesh Slat raised one of his bony claws. "I know that your communications with those on board *Oblivion* are intermittent at best. Again, more advanced Varapin technology at work. Have you not been left in charge of *USS Jefferson* in the Captain's absence? Do you not have faith in your own abilities to command such a grand vessel?"

She almost laughed at the ghoul's transparent attempt to undermine her confidence. But with that said, the Varapin commander had brought up a valid point. Did she have the confidence necessary to command? Wasn't that the exact question she'd been asking herself for months, maybe even years? Would she be willing to take Veesh Slat's offer if it was up to her?

She thought back to when she was fifteen. How she had fought against the odds to persevere and save the lives of her mother and father. She hated the idea of giving up. She wouldn't do it then, and she wouldn't now. "Okay, you want an answer? I'll give you one… you can shove that chalk-it-up-to-a-stalemate offer right up your bony ghoul ass. We're going to win this battle, Slat. And we're going to take that ugly ship from you in the process." Pristy looked to Chen. "Close the channel. I'm done with him."

The feed on the halo display went black. Letting out a breath, she glanced about the bridge. All eyes were upon her. Were they condemning her for her knee-jerk, undoubtedly irresponsible actions? Then she saw it. A smile on Awaale Samatar's lips. The same on Stanley Handly's. Even the always-critical bosun, Johanna Polk, looked to be pleased. But it was Grimes at the helm station who said, "Well done, XO. That was epic."

She certainly hoped so. Because there would be no turning back now. She put all her concentration back onto the multiple ensuing battlefronts. Almost imperceptibly, she shook her head. Taking it all in, things were close, but they were still losing this battle.

Chapter 41

Perseus Arm of the Milky Way
Oblivion

Captain Galvin Quintos

Currently, I was taking cover behind the flank of a fallen Symbio horse, periodically rising up to take a shot. Then I laughed out loud.

"What's so funny?" Wanda asked. Presently she was wielding a fallen knight's lance, using it to skewer any airborne ghouls that came within reach of the weapon's pointy end. There were two of them already impaled, one still moving.

I said, "Pristy. Picked up part of a hail coming in from Veesh Slat. The gist of it is he wanted to make a deal for both sides to cut their losses and go their own ways. She told him to go pound sand."

"Good. Personally, I have a vested interest in seeing this to the end." She looked over to me, her expression more serious now. "And I know you do too."

Only a handful of Symbio-Poths were still operational. Most

were lying still upon the deck. Max, Wanda, and I were the only ones of our team still engaging the enemy. Ham, of course, was back on *Jefferson*, and Grip and Hock were down and not responding—although there were bio-readings coming back from both, albeit weak ones. At present, I was picking up some comms chatter, but unable to make an outgoing hail.

On the other hand, there was no shortage of Varapin warriors flooding into the passageway. It was as if they were toying with us now. Certainly, they could finish us off with their superior numbers. Hell, there were far worse ways to go out than this. I thought of the infamous historical line spoken while in the midst of battle. And without realizing it, I said it aloud, "Today is a good day to die…"

Max, from somewhere behind me, said, "Oglala Lakota chief Low Dog."

Sounding out of breath, Max joined me behind the horse. "Figured you might want some company, Cap. You sounding so despondent and all."

I rose up, fired off three shots, then ducked back down as a flurry of return-fire energy bolts thudded into the horse's carcass. "I'm not despondent," I said. "Just being… well, pragmatic."

"Uh-huh… you need a tissue to dry your eyes."

"Bite me."

"That's better. Now, you have any ideas how we're going to get out of this mess?" Max asked in between taking shots over the Symbio horse.

I'd been trying to come up with something, *anything*, for the last hour.

Wanda yelled, "Finally!"

Max and I stole a peek in her direction. While she was still on her feet with her ridiculous lance, there was something far more interesting going on farther down the passageway.

Three quansporting figures were in the process of taking shape.

"What the..." Max said.

It was the unmistakable shape of a ChronoBot. Times three. Each of them was battle damaged, cratered, and charred almost beyond recognition. I said, "Hardy?"

There was a crackling over my comms.

"Cap... those Chrono... ts...are not... only LuMan AI... may ha... issues..."

The transmission had come in from *Jefferson*. It was good hearing Hardy's voice again. And I'd gotten the gist of what he was saying. These robots were not Hardy. And they had issues. What kinds of issues, I wasn't sure.

Wanda said, "Battle-bot reinforcements. Now we're talking!"

I was less enthusiastic as I watched the three big bots having yet to take any action.

"What the hell are they waiting for? Christmas?" Max exclaimed.

One of the ChronoBots, now having perked up, strode toward a far bulkhead. *Where's he going?* Taking weapons fire from no less than two dozen high-circling ghouls, the bot walked headfirst into a low-hanging girder. It teetered, clearly exhibiting balance issues. A moment later, it toppled over—never having fired a shot.

"Terrific. Idiot battle bots." Wanda said. "As if things for us weren't already pathetic enough." She crouched down as several low-flying ghouls swooped by her—one of which peppered her combat suit with plasma fire. "And no, today is NOT a good day to die, Cap. In fact, it would be a really shitty day to die. I have plans. I have ambitions!"

But I was only half-listening to her. The other two idiot ChronoBots were on the move. But it was as if they shared the same mind, the same central AI. The bot on the left raised its articulating arm and fired its forearm canon—as did the one on the right. But only the one on the left had taken down a ghoul. The two spun around in unison; the one on the right fired from its shoulder-mounted turret, making a kill shot, while the one on the left fired into empty air.

"I'm almost embarrassed for them," Wanda said, reading my mind.

I said, "Forget the ChronoBots. At the very least they're good diversions." I took down three more of the flying Varapin, while taking two more shots to my chest. *Shit, that hurt.* My suit, like Max and Wanda's, was operating on borrowed time.

"What's... what's happening?"

"Stay down, Grip. You've taken substantial enemy fire."

The big man suddenly sat up. His suit's faceplate was cracked, but I could still make out the features of his face. I checked his bio-readings on my HUD. He was by no means healthy, but who among us was?

"Where's my shredder?" Grip said.

"I think you're lying on it, big guy," Wanda said.

With some difficulty, he retrieved his weapon and began firing at the enemy. By now, all of the Symbios were down. Once again, the guilt of using them in this way weighed heavy on me.

"What's with the Hardy twins?" Grip said, finally noticing the two active bots. "Something's not right with them."

"You think?" Wanda said.

Previously, I'd made it clear to both Coogong and Derrota that they were not to quansport us back to *Jefferson* unless our bio-readings went critical. I knew the others in the team here felt the same; we were either going to die here on this massive ship or take it as a trophy of war—which at the present moment seemed an almost comical proposition.

"Maybe we should start moving toward the bridge again, Cap," Max said. "The clown bots won't stay standing much longer."

"Let me check on Hock. Cover me," I said, staying low as I dashed over to his prone form on the deck. He was mostly hidden below several lifeless Symbios and one ghoul. There was a gooey green slime covering most of his suit. I wasn't sure if it was from the Symbios or the ghoul—either way, it was disgusting. I shoved their bodies off of him and peered into Ham's helmet. His eyes were closed. I used my knuckles to knock on his faceplate. "Ham! Ham, wake up!"

The big man's eyes opened, but I could tell he wasn't focusing.

"Ham... you need to get up. Marines don't nap on the job."

"Where's my brother?"

"Back on *Jefferson*."

"Is he... dead?"

"No, he's not dead. He's in HealthBay getting patched up."

"You wouldn't lie to me, would you, Cap? Tell me he's alive so I wouldn't fall apart?"

"No, I wouldn't lie to you. Hock'll be just fine; at least I think he will be. But he'd want you to get back in the fight. Can you sit up?"

"Think so."

I helped him as best I could, first to sit up and then to stand. But it was like hefting a snot-covered two-hundred-and-fifty-pound boulder—every part of him was slimy and slippery. Once on his feet, off balance, he thrust his arms out sideways and wavered.

"Incoming!" Wanda announced.

I'd already noticed the six or seven Varapin warriors breaking away from their attack on the two bots. Ham, a mammoth-sized man, wouldn't have gone unnoticed for long.

I handed him his shredder and began firing. "Let's get moving!"

Wanda was the last to join us. She'd dislodged her victims from her lance, throwing it high like an oversized javelin. She nailed two in-flight ghouls. "Now that's killing two birds with one stone," she said, catching up to us. Both Ham and Grip were moving slowly, but at least we were all now moving.

Strange; the Symbios and the bots had been attacked with a vengeance while, again, the five of us had been pretty much left unaccosted, at least for the most part. It should have been obvious to me—they wanted us as prisoners. That or used for Ghan-Tshot. The Varapin had unquestionably held off our siege, but they had taken many losses in the process. As few of us left as there were, perhaps our life forces would help replenish them. Strange. I realized I was already thinking in terms of losing this battle.

I tried hailing *Jefferson* again, something I'd been repeating on a regular basis. Frustrated, I was desperate for a sit-rep concerning each of the ongoing battlefronts: the situation with 9th Fleet, and were the Pylor pirates still in the fight? Were Colonel Bonell and his Marines staving off the insurgent Varapin warriors? I already knew, from the looks of those three quansported-in ChronoBot copies, how Hardy must look at this point. How close was he now to a total shutdown?

But most of all, I wanted to know how Gail was doing. Currently, she was the ringmaster of this crazy circus. She would either fail miserably or show everyone that she was one hell of a starship captain. My bet was on the latter.

According to my HUD, we were still over two miles from *Oblivion's* bridge. It might as well be one hundred miles, I thought, but kept that to myself. Hoofing it at a faster jog now, we moved as a tight unit. Coming around one more gradual bend in the passageway, our sight-line forward was coming all the way into view. The five of us came to a sudden stop.

Ham said, "Now that's just not fair."

Max said, "We could turn around..."

Wanda said, "Nah... today's a good day to die, right, boys?"

I didn't answer. Instead, I just took in the spectacle. There had to be over a thousand Varapin warriors waiting for us. Between us was one hundred yards of open passageway.

"I don't like the looks of that," Grip said, pointing.

I didn't either. It was a metal cage of sorts being moved into position before the hordes of ghouls. A cage that could easily facilitate five humans.

"Oh look; they've left the door open for us," Wanda said.

I said, "I'll die before anyone puts me in that thing..."

Chapter 42

I honestly don't know what suddenly triggered me to feel giddy and then start smiling like an imbecile. Which, of course, then turned to laughter. The others looked at me—first concerned by my ill-timed outburst—then, as if it was contagious, they, too, attempted to hold back their own hesitant smiles. Soon, in unison, we were all laughing uncontrollably. We must have been an odd sight—five war-torn combatants stumbling around, several with hands on knees, all cackling like lunatics.

Catching my breath, I looked down the passageway once more and assessed those too-many-to-count robed reapers of misery and death. No longer laughing, I stood up straighter and prepared for what was, undoubtedly, going to be my—our—last stand.

"What do you say we make a final charge? Right here. Right now," I said.

Wanda nodded. "We go out in glory."

"With fire in our eyes and guns blazing," Max added.

"I wish Hock was here," Ham murmured.

Grips said, "So, we're really going to do this?"

We all nodded and readied ourselves—physically and mentally.

"What the fuck is that?" Grip said, annoyance in his voice.

I knew exactly what it was. Someone was quansporting into the open space before us.

A ChronoBot. A ChronoBot wearing a leather vest. Now fully materialized, he looked off toward the mass of Varapin warriors, then turned back toward us. He said, "You weren't just planning on attacking that, were you?"

"We were contemplating something like that," I said defensively.

"I may have a better idea," Hardy said.

And with that, something else, something big—very big—was now quansporting into view.

No one spoke for several seconds. Understandable. What does one say when a full-sized, fire-breathing dragon suddenly arrives upon a battlefield?

The dragon had made its appearance facing the enemy. *A good thing.* But even from behind, the mythical winged creature was truly awe-inspiring. Black, undulating scales glistened as if slick with oil. As it raised its head, it was evident this monster was far larger than any of those I'd seen upon the Symbio deck back on *Jefferson*.

Hardy strode forward, catching a sideways glance from the dragon. It let loose with a quick burst of fire while watching Hardy with interest.

Hardy looked back at me. "Upon your command, Captain."

I wasn't sure what he meant.

"Give the order, Cap," Max said. "That attack dog is chafing at the bit to make a move."

I looked to the others. "I like this. Instead of just bringing a knife to a gunfight, we brought a dragon..." I gave Hardy the signal by raising a fist in the air and saying, "Let him loose."

USS Jefferson

Reptilian muscles began to coil and bulge beneath scales—wings began to beat. And then the creature was airborne, picking up speed as it flapped forward within the open passageway.

Only now did the throng of robed ghouls start to break ranks and edge backward. But it was too late. The dragon was already upon them. The first spewing, fountaining burst of flames came up short. But the second burst incinerated no less than a third of the Varapin warriors where they hovered. Hundreds of bright, blazing balls of fire all ignited simultaneously. It was a beautiful sight.

"I don't know about you, but I want a piece of this!" Wanda shouted over her shoulder as she stormed forward toward the mayhem. We fell in behind her with shredders raised and began firing.

Several of the high-flying Varapin broke away from the dragon's onslaught. Grip, firing up at them, yelled, "Here's a lesson to you, motherfuckers! Payback's a real bitch."

I caught up to Hardy, and together, side by side, we confronted the dwindling enemy with weapons fire. Glancing over at my ChronoBot friend, I noticed Iris. Circling around the two of us, there were sparkling, glittering trails of Symbio fairy dust lingering in the air.

I said, "And the other five dragons?"

"Let's just say there's a similar rampage taking place on other decks as we speak."

Twenty minutes later, comms were fully operational again. I hailed Gail and got a full download on what had transpired over the last few hours. It was a lot.

So, what had I learned? First, prior to arriving here, Hardy had implemented a dry-run scenario. With Derrota and

Coogong's help, the colossal-sized dragon had been quansported into those areas of *Jefferson* that were under siege by Varapin warriors. To say the results had been nothing short of spectacular would be an understatement. Second, once the 9th Fleet had been released from the dampening field, the US Space-Navy warships rallied.

Working side by side with the Pylor warships, most of the Varapin ships were destroyed—most but not all. Ten of the enemy ships jumped away.

And third, XO Pristy had been contacted by EUNF US Space-Navy Executive Five Star Fleet Admiral Cyprian Block. Apparently, we should expect the 13th Fleet here in system within two days' time. A little too little, a little too late, if you asked me. Apparently, there was much newly acquired intel concerning the Varapin. According to Gail, who had relayed what she'd learned from the Admiral back to me, the enemy was mounting new offensives throughout the quadrant. The Varapin home world of Devastin was actually but one of five exoplanets they occupied. The combined population of all the ghouls was estimated to be in the low Trillions. That's Trillions with a capital T.

After signing off with Gail, I got the six of us, seven, if you count the dragon, whose name I discovered was Sadon, all headed off toward *Oblivion's* bridge. En route, I further formulated my future plans. After that, I reached out to a number of individuals. I had multiple subsequent, often heated, private conversations with XO Pristy. Then I spoke with Marine Colonel Drake Bonell, Stephan Derrota, Coogong, and Doc Viv. I also contacted a number of other people. What I needed was to get information and to provide certain information.

What Gail had passed on from the Admiral, concerning the unimaginable Varapin numbers, was a lot to digest. Discouraging? Sure. But it only reinforced what I knew needed to happen next. I would be leaving the US Space-Navy—leaving for good.

Still a quarter-mile out from *Oblivion's* bridge, I looked over at Hardy.

"You're the only one I'm going to outright ask to come with me." I knew he'd been listening in on my private conversations. Hardy was anything but dull-witted. I don't know if he'd already anticipated the questions or had connected the dots here and now.

"Do you really need to ask?" he said.

"Guess I need to hear the actual words, so yeah."

"I'm with you, Captain. But, with one condition..."

"Let's hear it."

"I'll need my chrome plating fully restored. I'm talking spit and polished like a mirror."

"I think I can manage that," I said with a chuckle.

Hardy stopped and looked down at me. I could barely make out the retro John Hardy's facial features on his encrusted face display. "If you go ahead with this, we'll be on the run. Hunted... there will be no turning back. There'll be a price on your head."

"So be it. Look, I've known for a long time now this war would be hard to win. With what I've learned today, well... it's unwinnable. The enemy is far too powerful, far too ruthless."

"And leaving will accomplish what?" a voice said with raised indignation.

It was Wanda, and I hadn't been aware she'd been listening in. Apparently, I'd been speaking via our open comms channel. *Shit!*

I turned to face the team. I saw mixed emotions in their eyes —anger, confusion, and hurt.

Max said, "AWOL is no small thing for a US Space-Navy officer... the consequences—"

"I know full well what the consequences are, Sergeant."

"Let me finish, Captain." He hesitated. "You're not leaving to shirk responsibility or to hide from battle."

"No, I'm not."

"You have an idea... a plan?"

"I do."

Grip crossed his tree-trunk-sized arms over his chest. "Go on..."

I collected my thoughts. "I've never been a rule follower. I'm a terrible CO... I don't lead anything like other officers, like other captains."

"What you do, though, works," Wanda said.

"Perhaps. But the point I'm making is that I can be far more effective by not being a part of the EUNF, the US Space-Navy, or any formal military complex. What I do know, especially in light of what the Admiral has told us about the Varapin numbers, is that winning this war won't happen through conventional means. A whole lot of rules will need to be broken. Something that I cannot do while still taking orders from high command."

Ham was nodding, a contemplative expression on his face. "Wait, I still don't understand." He looked to the others of his team.

Wanda, a bemused smile on her lips, said, "You're joining them... the Pylors."

"No... actually, I'm leading them." I gestured to our surroundings. "And this is my first of hopefully many spoils of war."

Max chuckled, "You're taking *Oblivion*. Just like that. Perhaps the most powerful warship in the quadrant? You do know you are one crazy dude, right?"

"There's one minor problem with your, um, plan," Grip

said. "A vessel like this, larger than any dreadnought within the Space-Navy, requires a substantial crew."

"I'll make do. I'll bring in some of the Pylors—"

"Get real, Cap... you need a real crew," Wanda said with conviction.

"I don't know what you want me to say, Wanda. I've talked to several, um, individuals on board *Jefferson*... letting them know my plans. I owed them that much... people I care deeply about. Better to hear it from me than later from high command."

"You asked them to join you?" Wanda asked.

"No. Other than Hardy here, I've not directly asked anyone to join me. This is far too serious a situation. People's careers are at stake. I'll be an outlaw; those who join me... will also be outlaws."

"Anyone volunteer?" she asked.

I nodded. "Uh-huh. Yeah... several."

"Can I ask who?"

"Coogong, for one. He was always going to be key. Especially since I'll be taking all of the remaining Symbios with me." I gestured to the dragon looming above us. "Ensign Plorinne has also—quite willingly, by the way—volunteered to jump ship. Apparently, his work with the Symbios has been the most rewarding aspect of his young life. He'll continue doing that, but do it upon *Oblivion* instead. With luck, many of the fallen Symbios here can be repaired... reanimated."

The five Marines exchanged glances.

I continued. "Also, the original Sir Louis de Broglie Quansporter unit, as we speak, is being quansported over to *Oblivion*."

They nodded, but still nobody spoke.

"SWM Chief LaSalle and eight of his department are coming over. Captain Wallace Ryder, Lieutenant Akari James, and twelve other top Arrow pilots. Chief Craig Porter, which was a surprise.

He's already here. I wasn't aware that the constant bombardment of *Oblivion's* propulsion system had taken down her drives. Craig's working on the ship's propulsion system as we speak. Once we take *Oblivion's* bridge, I'll need those big engines online, pronto."

"And you didn't ask any of these people directly... to join you?" Wanda asked, looking unconvinced.

"No. Not a one. All were volunteers."

"How about from the bridge?" Max asked.

"Grimes and Chen both are coming over to *Oblivion*."

Wanda gave me a sideways glance. "And not Pristy?"

"No. And I would not have allowed her to anyway. She's an amazing officer... an amazing captain, and the US Space-Navy needs her far more than I do. And before you ask, I informed both Stephan Derrota and Major Vivian Leigh of my impending plans and emphatically made it clear they would not be welcome here. Like Gail, they will be needed upon *Jefferson*."

Max nodded. "Still... that's not much of a crew."

"Meager," Wanda said.

"Scanty," Grip said.

Ham looked quizzical, but not able to come up with a word.

Hardy, who was twenty paces away next to the dragon, said, "Insufficient."

I let out a breath. "I know. But we'll make do with what we have."

"I'm with you, Cap," Wanda said. She looked over to Max, the team's leader, and shrugged. "Sorry, boss, but..."

"No need to apologize," Max said. "I'm with the Captain as well."

Grip simply nodded. "I'm in."

All eyes went to Ham.

"I don't know... Hock's back on *Jefferson*."

Max interjected, "You can talk to your brother later."

I said, "Thank you. Truly. I understand the decision is a big one. And I don't take it lightly."

Max placed a hand on my shoulder. "Come on, Cap... did you really have any doubts? Who's better suited than the five of us to go the pirate route, huh?"

Approaching, Hardy interjected, "Hate to break up this little lovefest, but we still have a bridge to take. And don't forget, we need to be long gone before that 13th Fleet arrives in system. And according to Craig, getting this ship's drives reengaged will take a full day, maybe two. It'll be close."

"There's one more thing you may not have factored into the equation," Wanda said.

I looked at her with raised brows.

"Those ships out there... what remains of the 9th Fleet. I'll guarantee word of your secret plans to defect, to abscond with this ship has already leaked."

That, I had not considered. If it came down to it, would I fire upon my brethren? Go up against my fellow Space-Navy captains? No, of course not.

"Let's head forward. We have a bridge to take."

Chapter 43

The closer we got to the bridge, which was at the most forward section of *Oblivion's* bow, the more all the central passageways began to narrow. Two hundred yards from our objective, we were forced to leave Sadon behind.

My HUD indicators foretold of a significant cluster of Varapin warriors up ahead.

Max said, "We've been here before, Cap. I suggest we separate, put the ghouls into a crossfire situation. We know which access tubes lead where... how about we Marines hustle in from below, get forward, and then we hit them at the same time?"

"I like it. We'll wait till you're in position."

We watched as Max, Wanda, Grip, and Ham disappeared down the closest access tube. Alone now with Hardy, I said, "How you holding up?"

The plasma cannon on his thigh, as well as his shoulder turret weapon, was obviously damaged. That, and I wondered how he could even see through that mess of a face display.

"Right as rain... nothing some time with Coogong, and

maybe a little R&R, won't fix. I'm more worried about you, Cap."

I looked down at my combat suit, which looked as if I'd walked through a lava flow. "I'm fine. Looks worse than it is."

"I'm not talking about your suit, and you know it."

It wasn't like Hardy to get all philosophical. I made a "no big deal" expression and shrugged.

"Your decision to go AWOL... to leave behind people you care for more than you'd like to admit. It has to be hard."

"Sure, it's hard. But knowing our home, Earth, won't be around much longer is harder. The Alliance, the Thine, humans, and Pleidians are nowhere near up to the challenges that they'll soon be facing. The Varapin are a threat to more than the quadrant; they're a threat to the entire galaxy. Like a fast-spreading cancer, they need to be decimated, completely excised from this realm of existence."

"Tall order."

"It is, so you better not get yourself killed today. We'll have a lot of work to do in the weeks and months ahead."

My comms crackled. "We're in place, Cap," Max said.

I said, "You have any idea what we're up against? They're so bunched together my HUD's not differentiating life forms all that well."

"I'd guess no more than two hundred. Most likely, these ghouls here are the last of them on board. The holdouts."

"Six against two hundred..."

A nearby sound caught my attention. Behind us, the tell-tale materialization of quansporting figures took shape. I said, "Hold on, Max... looks like we're getting some assistance."

Captain Wallace Ryder and Akari James were the first armed personnel to arrive. Within seconds, Colonel Bonell himself had taken form—along with five, then ten, and eventually thirty Marine combatants. A good number of them had brought along weaponry far more serious than a simple shredder.

Bonell strode up to me; the old colonel had a wet nub of a cigar wedged into the corner of his mouth.

"Colonel... if you're here on behalf of the US Space-Navy to lay claim to this vessel—"

"You can just stop right there, Captain. I'm not here to piss on your Wheaties."

Ryder stepped closer. "Galvin, these fine men and women are not here to take this ship for the US Space-Navy any more than Akari and I are. They're here to join you."

I looked at the colonel, who was still gnawing on what was left of his cigar. I now looked at the older man with appreciation.

He scowled, "Ah, Christ, don't make this into a fucking chick-flick moment. Some of us understand what you're doing. Realize that without serious intervention, we're all destined to be tits up."

I looked to the others behind them. All were smiling. I wondered if they had any clue as to what they were signing up for.

The colonel continued, "There are more. A lot more."

I shook my head, not getting his meaning.

"Word has spread on board *Jefferson* and out the 9th Fleet. You certainly won't fill this big boat, but you'll have a crew. If you want them."

Hardy interjected, "As long as everyone knows one simple truth. We won't be playing by the rules anymore. We'll be doing what it takes to win, and that won't always be pretty."

"No shit, Sherlock," the colonel said. "But know this: there'll be a price to pay for the kind of person that joins this kind of going-native... operation. Some will have issues with authority;

some will have anger management issues. Others just like hurting people."

"The real cream of the crop," I said.

"These aren't the kinds of recruits that are afraid to run with scissors."

I was seeing a new side of the colonel.

Ryder said, "So, you want them or not?"

Akari said, "Yeah. They're crazier than a fish with tits, but isn't that what you need?"

I held Bonell's stare for several beats longer. "I won't stand for a pissing contest with you, Colonel. And you'll need to keep some kind of order within the ranks."

"I can agree to that."

I held out a hand and he shook it.

I gestured with a thumb over my shoulder toward the bow of the ship. "One more thing. Max and his team report directly to me."

"I can live with that," he said. "We done? I'm getting conversational blue balls... all this jabber-jawing. How about we help you take that bridge?"

"the bridgecrew, and most importantly, First Warrior Veesh Slat. I need them alive. Find out if there's a brig or the equivalent on this ship."

"You got it, Captain." The colonel signaled his Marines, now pirates, forward. A minute later, I heard distant weapons fire.

Both Wallace Ryder and Akari James stayed back with Hardy and me.

"What now?" Ryder said.

"Now? We make this official."

"Make what official?" James asked.

Chapter 44

Outlaw Misfits.

More specifically, Quinto's Outlaw Misfits was the ridiculous moniker that someone came up with over the ensuing eight hours. I had to admit, though, it did have a certain ring to it.

Everything moved fast after *Oblivion's* bridge was taken. As directed, Max and crew, along with Colonel Bonell's thirty-plus Marines, managed to take First Warrior Veesh Slat into custody. Only half of the Varapin bridgecrew had survived, but half was better than none.

At first, I didn't like the layout of the ghouls' bridge. On *Jefferson*, I sat upon a slightly raised captain's mount, and for the most part was even with the rest of the crew. But here the ship's CO was seated down low on a kind of ornate throne, close to a stage-like platform that was about twenty feet long by fifteen feet wide. It was a stage where the CO could supposedly pace while assessing the goings-on of the bridge around him or her. At its center was a projection and quite a large 3D display. I subsequently learned the Varapin called it, once translated, the watchtower. Which was kind of clever.

But it was the layout of the bridge as a whole that was most disconcerting. The high overhead compartment was built like a theater. Rising up, there were seven concentric, increasingly large levels. The various bridge consoles were situated around each level. Seemingly, there was a rhyme and reason for the placement of the various stations. Tactical, like on *Jefferson*, was close to the CO's throne, as were the helm and comms stations. But unlike the bridge on *Jefferson*, there was no separate combat information center. Those functions and personnel were situated on the higher levels.

New crewmembers had been arriving pretty much nonstop since the word had gotten out that the Outlaw Misfits were taking on members. I use the word *members* because this was anything but a formal or rigid military construct.

With that said, there still needed to be rules. There needed to be basic operating instructions. And who better to develop those than the stickler for guidelines and regulations, Bosun Johanna Polk? I was still finding it difficult to believe she wanted to be a part of this chaos.

There was so much, too much, I hadn't accounted for here on day one. Like getting the environmental systems spewing out the proper levels of breathable atmosphere for the human crew, or a better way to navigate within a five-mile-long star craft, or how to feed the rapidly growing crew without human-compatible food replicators on board. But none of those things were as important, at least at the moment, as getting the ship's advanced propulsion system operational. By the time the 13th Fleet was to arrive in system, we needed to be long gone.

One of the latest arrivals was SWM Chief LaSalle. Currently, we were en route to the farthest aft section of the ship, the equivalent of the engineering and propulsion department. Maintaining a fast jog, I noticed the older man—I'd guess he was in his mid-fifties—was in impressive shape and barely breathing hard.

"First of all, welcome aboard, Chief. And thank you."

"Your gratitude isn't necessary. I'm good with my decision."

LaSalle was a man of few words. Probably didn't have an education much past high school, but he was the most learned, well-read individual I knew.

"Talk to me about installing a lift system for this ship. Doesn't have to be as involved as *Jefferson's* GravLift system, but—"

LaSalle raised a gentle hand. "Sir, may I interrupt?"

"Go ahead."

"Do you think the Varapin crew on board this ship moved cargo, heavy equipment, system consoles, all manually?"

"I... well, I guess I hadn't thought about it all that much."

"There is a fully functional lift system already present on this vessel. Just because the ghouls preferred to fly about like witches on broomsticks doesn't mean they weren't ingenious." He tapped my shoulder with the back of his hand. "Can we walk for a second?"

"Of course."

Slowing, LaSalle veered off to the right, heading to an adjacent bulkhead. He waited for me to join him there. He used his knuckles to tap on a wide span of metal plating. "This is just one of the many access gateways to the ship's StreamLines."

"StreamLines?"

"I gave it that name." He placed a palm on the plating and made a circular motion. The seemingly solid panel opened into dozens of small vertical louvers, which then both ascended and descended out of view within a split second. Beyond was a lift about the same size as a GravLift car.

LaSalle stepped inside. "I think I can get this thing moving in the right direction."

Before stepping inside, I said, "You know, if you can't, we could be stuck in here for a while. It's not like anyone would know where to look for us."

"Have a little faith, Captain." He motioned me forward.

I joined him while he brought up a projected kiosk menu. "Everything, all system controls on this ship, is gesture-activated. Yes, you can use touch, such as what I did to open the access panel, but hand gestures are the primary input and control medium."

"How do you know all this?"

"Remember Haite Caheil?"

"Of course." The Varapin pilot had been dangerous, and in the end, a treacherous adversary. He had spent months on board *Hamilton* while pretending to be a collaborator.

"Yes, I know he was a distasteful being. But I had the opportunity to learn much about Varapin technology. He was quite the chatty Cathy when it came to divulging the secrets of Varapin tech."

"Good to know."

"Ah! Best you hold on. I'm not sure if these StreamLines have functioning acceleration dampeners."

With a combination of sign language–style hand gestures, the lift was on the move. And, thus far, it was a smooth ride.

"Is there any way you can adapt the various ship interfaces to something akin to what we're used to?"

"Already on it, Captain. From bridge stations to StreamLines to toilets—"

I slapped my forehead. "I hadn't even considered the onboard heads!"

LaSalle gave me a patient, albeit somewhat tired expression.

"Fortunately, the ghouls had to piss and crap just like humans. Their facilities are configured for different anatomies, but nothing that can't be worked out. You'll have to piss standing on your head though."

I looked at him with a serious glower. "You are kidding... tell me you are kidding."

"Yeah, Captain, I'm kidding."

We arrived at the aft section of *Oblivion* within seconds. The same louver-style panels opened and disappeared above and below.

Stepping out of the lift, I realized we had arrived at a location high up. It was a metal scaffolding with a bird's-eye view of the entire department. Four tall, looming reactors, the size of buildings, encircled us. Catwalks spanned everywhere. Strange, since the Varapin crew didn't have the necessity of walking.

LaSalle headed aft. "We'll have to hoof it to get the drive engines area."

We hurried along the various catwalks, our footfalls clanging upon the metal runways. What was missing were handrails—something the floating Varapin had little use for. I said, "One false step..."

He finished my sentence, "And it's ass over tea kettle for a long, long way down."

I'd always thought *Jefferson's* drives were about as big as they came. But *Oblivion's* drives were on a whole other scale. There were four of the things; each glowed and throbbed a bright azure blue within its glass-like structure. Perfect spherical orbs. Each was as large as its reactor counterpart and seemingly hovered without any kind of support structure or mounting mechanisms keeping it in position.

"You can pick your jaw up from the deck now, Galvin," came Craig Porter's voice. I looked down to see him on the lower level, three stories below us. He gave us a casual wave. "Come on down here... got something I want to show you."

Two minutes later we were standing beneath one of the immense drive orbs. All three of us were illuminated in the wash of that azure glow.

"Is it safe to be this close to the thing?" I yelled above the constant hum of the drive.

Craig looked up and scratched at his chin, making the universal "I'm thinking" expression.

"Ha ha... is it? Is it dangerous?"

"No. Well, I don't think it is."

"So, what is it you wanted to show me?" I said, not in the mood for antics.

He looked up. "It's this particular orb."

"Yeah?"

"It was the reason the whole kit and caboodle went haywire. In some ways, this kind of propulsion system is decades, maybe centuries, more advanced than what we're used to with conventional HyperDrive systems. And if you look around, you won't see any jump spring coils like on *Jefferson*." He gestured to the orb again. "These magnificent drives do all that and more. These are what you call quantum transposers. And you need all four of them for the system to work. One goes down or out of alignment, and you're fucktipated. That's why they're floating; nothing physical to ground them in this realm of physicality."

I nodded but was not entirely tracking.

"You see," Craig continued, "Each of these four quantum transposer drive orbs, QTDOs, actually reaches out to alternate spatial realities. They work together, securing a foothold on another quantum plane of existence." Craig slapped his palms together with a whack! "And then the ship and her crew are transported away from this point within the current time/space continuum into a pure energy quantum state. And then," Again he slapped his palms together, *whack*, "Kazooie, you're up to twenty-five light-years away. No need for old-fashioned wormhole manufacturing or any of that rubbish. This system is much faster and safer."

"And you understand how it all works?"

"Fuck, no. It'll take me weeks, months to figure this out. But I did know enough to get this one orb back into phase alignment with the other three."

"You're telling me we have propulsion capabilities?"

"Darn tootin'... I just have to figure out how the navigation aspects work. Hardy's working on it." Craig turned to look at the seven-foot-tall ChronoBot nearby. He so blended in with his surroundings that he hadn't been noticed.

I scratched my chin. "You know, a lot of what you described sounds a hell of a lot like the theory used for our quansport devices."

Another voice, just as recognizable, said, "Very astute, Captain Quintos."

He stepped out from behind Hardy. Coogong had a tablet in his hand. "I believe this drive technology is well beyond anything the Varapin would have had the ability to develop on their own. In fact, much of this ship is of a technology well beyond their capabilities."

"You're saying they had help?"

"No. I'm saying they probably absconded with this ship and modified it to their own needs."

I thought about that. It was actually good news. The prospect of going up against an entire fleet of these all too capable warships was daunting. "That would explain why they still so wanted our Quansporter technology. Hell, it may even have helped them understand their own ship's propulsion system."

"Perhaps," Coogong said, then disappeared behind Hardy once more.

I turned to LaSalle. "Anything you can volunteer here? This seems to be one more system that needs a human interface."

LaSalle shrugged. "I can certainly try."

Chapter 45

I awoke, not having a clue as to where I was. I tried to sit up and quickly regretted it. My side, specifically the location where I'd been stabbed by the late Thunderballs, was on fire. Gritting my teeth, I took in the dark and gloomy surroundings. I started to remember. Leaving Engineering, I'd faltered. Battle-worn, my body had simply given out. It had been Ryder who had practically carried me here. *But where is here?*

Scanning the compartment, I saw it seemed to be someone's no-frills sleeping quarters. Then I took in the bed I was on. *Not a bed.* More like a coffin. *I'm lying in a damn Ebom-Pod.* This was where a ghoul went nighty night after a hard day wreaking evil havoc within the galaxy. One thing I had to admit, though, taking in the surrounding contoured and well-padded Ebom-Pod walls, was that this thing was damn comfortable. I was glad Ryder hadn't actually secured the top lid on top of me—that would have been more than a little creepy.

It occurred to me I wasn't wearing a helmet. I took in a deep breath. *Good.* Reconfigured environmental systems were operational.

USS Jefferson

My TAC-Band started to vibrate. It was Bosun Polk. Before answering her hail, I saw that there were multiple blinking icons. I had no less than ten messages waiting for me. I quickly reviewed the log. Two of them were from Gail. I felt a tight pang in my chest. I hated the fact she wouldn't be coming along with us. I mentally chastised myself. *Knock it off, Galvin—don't go down that road.*

"Go for Captain," I said.

"Yes, Captain," the prim-sounding bosun said. "Two things."

"Go on."

"As instructed, *Oblivion*... accompanied by the Pylor fleet, has departed the system. The Perseus Arm of the Milky Way is now 6.5 light-years behind us. What remains of the 9th Fleet, along with *USS Jefferson*, is now in our rear-view mirror, so to speak."

When did I give that order? Oh yeah. I'd mentioned that to Ryder as he carried me here.

The bosun continued, "There are a number of recorded video logs... well-wishers from *Jefferson* who have left you messages. You can read them at your leisure, Sir."

Again, there was a tightening noose around my heart. I thought of Derrota and Viv and, of course, Gail. It might be months, even years, before I saw any of them again.

"And someone named Vince from the Pylor fleet has been relentlessly hailing *Oblivion*."

"What does he want?"

"He says it's time. Whatever that means. He also said... and let me get this right, that you better be ready to rumble."

I cut the connection and leaned back. *Shit! Shit! Shit!* My epic battle for the leadership of the Pylor syndicate had come due. Feeling the way I did, there was simply no way I was in any shape to take on a musclebound toothless pirate.

Again, my TAC-Band began to vibrate. I answered without looking at it.

"Go for Captain."

"You better get down here. We're burning daylight. And those wounds of yours aren't going to repair themselves."

I now looked at my TAC-Band and saw Doc Viv's annoyed, albeit beautiful face staring back at me.

"Where exactly is down here?"

"HealthBay, you moron. Where else?"

"So, you're..."

"Uh-huh. I'm here. And don't ask me why... let's just chalk it up to my impulsive nature."

"Okay... so, *Oblivion* has a HealthBay?"

"Oh yeah. And Momma has a whole lot of new toys to play with."

Thank you for reading **USS Jefferson - Charge of the Symbios**, *Book 4 of the* **USS Hamilton Series**. *GOOD NEWS! Several more of the USS Hamilton Series are available NOW on Amazon.com*

Join my mailing list here: **http://eepurl.com/bs7M9r** *to be notified the moment the next and all future books are released. I hate spam and will never, ever share your information. And if you enjoyed this book, PLEASE leave a review on Amazon.com—it really helps!*

Acknowledgments

First and foremost, I am grateful to the fans of my writing and their ongoing support for all my books. I'd like to thank my wife, Kim—she's my rock and is a crucial, loving component of my publishing business. I'd like to thank my mother, Lura Genz, for being a tireless cheerleader of my writing. Others who provided fantastic support include Lura & James Fischer, Sue Parr, Charles Duell, and Stuart Church.

Check out my other available titles on the page that follows About the Author.

About the Author

Mark grew up on both coasts, first in Westchester County, New York, and then in Westlake Village, California. Mark and his wife, Kim, now live in Castle Rock, Colorado, with their two dogs, Sammi, and Lilly.

Mark started as a corporate marketing manager and then fell into indie-filmmaking—Producing/Directing the popular Gaia docudrama, 'Openings — The Search For Harry'.

For the last nine years, he's been writing full-time, and with over 40 top-selling novels under his belt, he has no plans on slowing down. Thanks for being part of his community!

Also by
Mark Wayne McGinnis

Scrapyard Ship Series

Scrapyard Ship (Book 1)

HAB 12 (Book 2)

Space Vengeance (Book 3)

Realms of Time (Book 4)

Craing Dominion (Book 5)

The Great Space (Book 6)

Call To Battle (Book 7)

Scrapyard Ship – Uprising

Mad Powers Series

Mad Powers (Book 1)

Deadly Powers (Book 2)

Lone Star Renegades Series

Star Watch Series

Star Watch (Book 1)

Ricket (Book 2)

Boomer (Book 3)

Glory for Space Sea and Space (Book 4)

Space Chase (Book 5)

Scrapyard LEGACY (Book 6)

The Simpleton Series

The Simpleton (Book 1)

The Simpleton Quest (Book 2)

Galaxy Man

Ship Wrecked Series

Ship Wrecked (Book 1)

Ship Wrecked II (Book 2)

Ship Wrecked III (Book 3)

Boy Gone

Expanded Anniversary Edition

Cloudwalkers

The Hidden Ship

Guardian Ship

Gun Ship

HOVER

Heroes and Zombies

The Test Pilot's Wife

TheFallen Ship

The Fallen Ship: Rise of the Gia Rebellion (Book 1)

The Fallen Ship II (Book 2)

USS Hamilton Series

USS Hamilton: Ironhold Station (Book 1)

USS Hamilton: Miasma Burn (Book 2)

USS Hamilton: Broadsides (Book 3)

USS Hamilton: USS Jefferson –
Charge of the Symbios (Book 4)

USS Hamilton: Starship Oblivion –
Sanctuary Outpost (Book 5)

USS Hamilton: USS Adams – No Escape (Book 6)

USS Hamilton: USS Lincoln – Mercy Kill (Book 7)

USS Hamilton: USS Franklin - When Worlds Collide (Book 8)

USS Hamilton: USS Washington - The Black Ship (Book 9)

USS Hamilton: USS IKE - Quansport Ops (Book 10)

ChronoBot Chronicles